The
TRICKING
of FREYA

The
TRICKING
of FREYA

Christina Sunley

St. Martin's Press

New York

THE TRICKING OF FREYA. Copyright © 2009 by Christina Sunley. All rights reserved. Printed in the United States of America. For information, address St. Martin's Press, 175 Fifth Avenue, New York, N.Y. 10010.

Portions of this novel appeared, in different form, in *The Icelandic Canadian*.

Grateful acknowledgment is given for permission to reprint the following:
"I dreamt a dream" from *Icelandic-Canadian Memory Lore*, Magnús Einarsson, Gatineau, Canadian Museum of Civilization 1992 pp: 39–40 © Canadian Museum of Civilization.

"I have seen the cat sing" from *Icelandic-Canadian Memory Lore*, Magnús Einarsson, Gatineau, Canadian Museum of Civilization, 1992 p: 95 © Canadian Museum of Civilization.

www.stmartins.com

Library of Congress Cataloging in Publication Data

Sunley, Christina.
The tricking of Freya / Christina Sunley.—1st ed.
p. cm.
ISBN-13: 978-0-312-37877-6
ISBN-10: 0-312-37877-7
1. Family secrets—Fiction. 2. Icelanders—Manitoba—Fiction. 3. Grandparent and child—Fiction. 4. Immigrants—Canada—Fiction. 5. Iceland—Social life and customs—Fiction.
I. Title.
PS3619.U5636T75 2009
813'.6—dc22   2008035455

First Edition: March 2009

10 9 8 7 6 5 4 3 2 1

In memory of

my mother, Edith Bjornson, who told me about Our People,

and my father, Robert Sunley, who always believed

The
TRICKING
of FREYA

1

You want a bit of Birdie?

Try this, a June afternoon, early 1970s, on the beach at Gimli: Birdie in a skirted turquoise swimsuit and cat-eye sunglasses, lounging legs crossed at the ankles on her aluminum chaise. Just past forty and still glamorous, on her good days. Not a movie star but a kind of star you don't have a name for. You're just past eight and far from glamorous. Birdie compares you, kindly, to an egret as you stride the beach, your legs long and skinny as stilts, your wispy white-blond hair tufting in the wind, your eyes a blue so light they startle.

"See?" Birdie is dangling something in her hand, something small and glistening, jewel-like. You've played this game before. She's going to throw it and you're going to catch it. By mouth. You stand a few feet from the edge of the blanket, bare toes clenching sand, arms swinging restlessly at your sides. Your eyes fix on the prize.

"One . . ." Birdie teases. "Two . . ."

"Come on!" you shriek.

"Three!" Birdie tosses the thing in the air. It's a single mandarin orange segment, straight from the tin. You're a dog, no, a seal, a trained dolphin leaping up, snapping your jaw, swallowing the slippery minnow whole. Orange syrup dribbles down your chin. You smack your lips in citrus triumph.

Birdie claps and laughs, claps and laughs. "Bravo, *elskan*! Bravo!" *Elskan* means love in Icelandic. Like honey or dear. Birdie always calls you *elskan*. Then tosses you another mandarin fish.

Gimli is Icelandic for heaven. Except this Gimli isn't in heaven or even Iceland, but on Lake Winnipeg. Manitoba, Canada. Birdie lives in Gimli with your *amma* Sigga. *Amma* means grandmother, *afi* means grandfather. Your *afi* was a hundred and one years old when you were born except he was already dead. Some words are Icelandic and some are English. *Mama* is the same in both. Your mama and Birdie share a mother so they're sisters. You don't have a sister or a brother or a father you remember.

Every year from your eighth on, you and your mother take the train from Windsor, Connecticut, to Grand Central to Winnipeg to spend the summer on the lake at Gimli. With Your People. In an old white farmhouse with song-yellow trim and book-lined walls. The house is called *Oddi*—in Iceland even houses have names, and some in Gimli do too—after a place where famous writers lived, like Saemundur the Learned, a wizard who rode the back of the devil disguised as a seal. And Snorri Sturluson, esteemed historian and saga scribe, was raised at Oddi too. He's one of your ancestors.

Birdie says writers run in the family, all the way back to Iceland, to the greatest Viking poet, Egil Skallagrimsson. You descend from him.

And your grandfather's uncle, the famous farmer-poet Pall.

And of course your grandfather Olafur.

"And you?"

"And me," Birdie admits.

Me too? you want to ask but don't. The ancestor-poets race through your mind in a line, crossing frozen ocean, one after the other, words flying off their heels in a spray of ice, skating all the way back to Iceland, Egil and Snorri and Pall, your grandfather Olafur, who died before you were born, your Auntie Birdie.

"Why not Mama too?"

"It's something you're born with. Your mother can sing and play the piano, embroider and knit, a very talented woman in her way. But she's no poet."

"Does she want to be?"

"Hardly."

You can't imagine not wanting it. Words live inside you, rearranging themselves in your mind like building blocks. *A shy fly. A pig's wig.* This before you can spell or even write. When words are pure sound. *Plants at a dance. A lonely bonely.* Strings of words to make your mother laugh. But it is Birdie who says, *You have an ear. A tongue.*

Doesn't everyone?

If it's hot at night and the mosquitoes keep buzzing you awake you can knock on Birdie's door and sometimes she'll let you in and you can lie in your white cotton nightie on Birdie's four-poster bed watching her fingers dance along the typewriter keys like your mother playing piano. Except it's a different kind of music, typing. Like a rainstorm. Or hail. Birdie's been working on the same poem forever. One poem, years long.

"What's it called?"

"It changes. At the moment I'm calling it *Word Meadow.*"

You smother a giggle with your hand. Birdie could get mad if you laugh but she doesn't. "*Word-meadow* is a kenning for *tongue,*" she explains. "And I suppose now you'll want to know what a kenning is." She sits beside you on the bed and rubs your head like a pup's. "A kenning is a different name for a thing. Instead of calling the sun *the sun,* you can call it a *day-star.*"

"Why not use its real name?"

"It's boring, that's why! The old poets were never content with just one or two words for a thing. Masters of periphrastic trickery, magicians of poetic circumlocution, tossing kennings right and left." Birdie's speeding up, the pupils of her eyes widening black saucers, shiny as record vinyl. You're older now, nearly eleven, but even if you live to be a hundred you'd never keep up with Birdie, not when she's revving buzzing humming words.

"Kennings were a way for poets to show off, verbal razzmatazz of the Vikings. A fierce warrior-poet like our infamous forebear Egil Skallagrimsson could choose from over a hundred kennings for the word *sword* alone!" Birdie shakes her curlered head in wonderment. "A marvel, how those Vikings loved their swords. Problem is, a thousand years later the poems don't make sense, because most of the kennings reference Norse mythology, and who remembers the old myths anymore? A common kenning for *poetry* was *Odin's mead,* but if you don't know the story of how Odin tricked the giants out of their mead so he could imbibe the gift of verse, you'd be utterly lost anytime a poem made reference to the *All-Father's malt-surf*, or the *raven-god's holy drink*. That's why our ancestor Snorri Sturluson wrote down all the Norse myths in the twelfth century, so that Iceland's new Christian poets would understand what the kennings meant. Without Snorri, those myths would be lost to us for eternity."

Birdie pauses for the barest fraction of a second. She is pacing now, back and forth in front of the window in nothing but her pink teddy. It doesn't matter, there is no one to peer in and see her. At two a.m. all Gimli sleeps save you and Birdie. Her words swirl your mind, a vast Milky Way of glittery word-stars, most of it far beyond your grasp, but you're used to that, to being drawn into word-spells that riff like the jazz music she plays on her phonograph late at night. But sped up, 78 rpm, talking faster than the speed of light. *Getting talky* your mother calls it. *Birdie's getting talky.* Sometimes Birdie gets so talky she stops making sense. That's when your mother says *Birdie's going over.* Over what? But not tonight. You hear logic in Birdie's voice, even if you can't follow it.

"Today no one but a scholar can wade those kenning-thick verses," Birdie continues, curlers bouncing off her shoulders. "Kennings wrapped within kennings. And translators beware—as your *afi* Olafur well understood it's nearly impossible to translate skaldic verse into English. Please, promise me, baby"—she comes and sits on the edge of the bed, turns on you her vast mental enthusiasm—"promise me you'll never read those poems in translation. Some of the greatest pagan verses, the most magnificent poetry ever written, reduced to drivel!" She looks as if she is about to weep.

You nod, happy to promise her this, or anything. "What's a scholar?"

"Someone who studies things."

A school-er. "Are you a scholar?"

"Me?" Birdie snorts. "I'm no scholar, baby. I'm a pretender. A dabbler, a dilettante, heir to the air, a quack of the worst kind, a—"

"Tell me one of the ones for *sword*."

"One of the what?"

"The kennings. For *sword*. You said there were a hundred."

"Let's see. There's *striker*. And *lying-striker*. And *life-quencher*. And *wind-bright*. And some really gory ones, you wouldn't want to hear those."

You would.

"Okay then! *Leg-biter. Pain-wader. Corpse-pain. Skull-crusher. Terrifier. Pale-maker. Night-bringer.* And then there are the bloody ones. Too bloody for you!"

"No they're not!"

"Don't tell your mother."

"I won't."

Birdie whispers: *"Blood-band. Blood-warp. Blood-eddy. Blood-waker. Blood-grip.* And here's a kenning for *tongue: sword of speech.*"

"And *word-meadow,*" you add. "That's the other one for *tongue.* Like the name of your poem. Is it a meadow because words sprout on your tongue like flowers?"

"On a good day," Birdie says. "On the good days they do."

A bad day: your mother sends you upstairs to knock on Birdie's door because it's past noon and Birdie isn't out of bed yet.

"Go away!" Her voice is scratchy, thick.

You bite your lip. "But the day-star came out from behind the clouds. Mama says you'll take me to the beach."

A hard silence.

"I want you to."

More silence.

"Please?"

"You know what you are?" The voice has changed now. It's low, a spider creeping over gravel. "Do you know what you are?"

You hold your breath on the other side of the door.

"You're a pest. No wonder I can't get any work done."

"But you're not even working!" You haven't heard a single drop of raining-type for days.

"How do you know what I'm doing, you little sneak? You think I don't know how you lie with your ear to the wall every night? Mama's little spy, her tattler. So go tell your mother this"—she is speaking slowly now, mean-slow—"*Leave. Me. The hell. Alone.*"

You try not to cry on the way down the stairs. You can't tell your mother what Birdie said to say or it'll start a wild fight. And besides, Birdie doesn't mean it. That's what she says afterward. After a week of living in her night-gown, hair lank and snarled, voice rusty and eyes dull. All the beauty saps out of her and the faults of her face rise to the surface. Her eyes drift too close together, her mouth slackens, her plump cheeks sink into saddlebags. She stares at the floor, the wall, nothing. And then one day she emerges from her room again, blond hair curled and shining, mood sunnier than sun.

"Come here, *elskan,* and kiss your rotten aunt." Her cheeks high and apple-bright. "You know I don't mean it, baby, when I say mean things. You know that, don't you?"

You nod, though you're never sure. Your mother says Birdie's moods turn on a dime. Whatever that means. You think of Birdie like lake weather—she shifts fast. You learn to keep alert, read the signs: a dark flash of the eyes, a mean twitch of her lip. You learn when to take cover, when it's safe to emerge into Birdie's light again.

But this is farce. A masquerade of pronouns. You were not that girl. That girl was me.

And Birdie? Meet your mother. My aunt. Our mothers were sisters. The difference being, my mother got to raise me and *your mother had to give you away.* Get it?

Sorry. I was hoping that if I recorded for you my Birdie-memories I could make you me. I'd become a cousin in the shape of an umbilical cord, reattaching you to a mother you've never known. But I knew Birdie only as an aunt. An aunt is not a mother. Though Birdie doted on me with a feroc-ity I suspect was surrogate for you.

So, yes. *Meet your mother:* Ingibjorg Petursson. Birdie nicknamed herself early on: she couldn't wrap her tongue around *Ingibjorg. Birdie* stuck. Be-cause a bird can be so many things. A sadglad bird. A madmad bird. A mock-ingbird chattering at hummingbird speed. A snarky gull, a brooding raven. A finch smashing itself against windows. Or a woman who mistakes glass for air, words for wings.

Our mothers have passed.

Trying to be gentle here, genteel even. But what's the point? Birdie's manner of death precludes gentle mention: your mother committed suicide.

On my fourteenth birthday, no less. The gift that keeps on giving. My own mother went next, linked like dominoes those sister-deaths, despite seven years wedged between. Aneurysm was the official cause of my mother's death; I call it giving up.

Your father? I have no idea. Then again, I have little idea of my own, either. He died before I formed a single memory of him.

It's a lot of death, I know. Believe me, I know. But we'll try not to focus on that. The point here is resurrection, wordly reanimation. Infuse the dead with words and they'll spring to life on the page, just for you.

And your name is?

Sorry, can't hear you!

Feeble, I agree. But you see the problem, don't you? I'm writing a letter addressee unknown. So let's do like the skalds; when a name can't be spoken a kenning will do. Take your pick: Nameless Child, Lost One, Birdie's Secret, Ingibjorg's Loss, the Unknown Cousin . . .

Plain *Cousin,* you say?

Cousin it is.

And who am I? you'd like to know. Freya Ingibjorg Morris, a.k.a. Frey, the only child of your aunt Anna Petursson and your uncle, an American accountant named Ed Morris. Prepare for my measly particulars. Despite (to spite?) Birdie's best efforts, I have not joined the long line of family poets skating back to Iceland. *You have an ear. A tongue.* So Birdie gaveth and so Birdie tooketh away. I've turned my back on words, consort with images instead. Give up? I'm a darkroom hack, a black-and-white printer of archival photographs, ungainfully employed at Klaus Steinman's Photographic Ltd., near the Hudson River piers. Not that I see much river view—the lab is two floors down, sub-basement. My fellow printer, Frank, calls it the Sub because it reminds him of the three months he spent on a submarine during a brief stint in the navy. To me it seems more like a mid-Manhattan Hades, dark and dank, the sound of water running, sloshing, dripping constantly. To enter my darkroom each morning I pass through a revolving door called a light trap.

No, it's not the life my mother envisioned for me, hands immersed in harsh chemicals, daylight spent in blackness. Well, if Mama wanted a different life for me, she should have hung around! It was after she died that

I dropped out of college and began spending most of my time underground. At twenty-one I was too old to call myself an orphan but I certainly felt like one. Lose your balance for a moment and there you go, the world flings you off its spinning surface and it's not so easy to scramble back on.

Time gets reduced by a darkroom. It's not only the lack of daylight, it's the way time itself is constantly slivered: ten seconds here, three minutes there . . . eight years. Eight years. And still I made no move toward the earth's humming surface. And so life—which as we all know stands still for no one—made a move toward me.

Last month an invitation arrived for my grandmother Sigga's one hundredth birthday celebration. *Our* grandmother, I should say. Having out-lived her husband and both daughters, she resides at Betel, a retirement home in Gimli on the shore of Lake Winnipeg. I did not intend to attend. I hadn't returned to Gimli since Birdie's suicide. Sixteen years Gimli-gone and Gimli-free. Sixteen years without visiting my own grandmother. Each the other's only living relative. (The unknown you withstanding.) How could I do such a thing? You'll understand later. Maybe. The point is that I succumbed to pressure from Uncle Stefan (no relation to either of us). I flew to Canada, I attended Sigga's birthday party in Gimli. And that's when I learned about you.

You think someone told me straight out? Ha! I pieced you together from scraps. A dream Sigga had about an eagle-swiped lamb. Fragments of con-versation floating out the window of the old folks' home in Gimli. I began investigating. At first no one admitted your existence. I searched for evi-dence, found none. I hung around Gimli sniffing up false trees and hound-ing everyone who would speak to me and some who wouldn't. It was a most unlikely somebody who told me, finally, skimpily—if only to get me out of town—*Yes, Birdie had a child.* Taken at birth. Given up for adoption: closed, blind, and secret.

According to my source, you were born in 1962. That makes you three years older than me. I don't know if you are a boy or a girl. Or rather, a man or a woman. You're thirty-three years old, whatever and wherever you are.

Why didn't my own mother adopt you? She and my father were childless at the time. It's not uncommon for aunts and uncles to adopt a niece or nephew when circumstances warrant. We could have been siblings, you and I.

It's a good question, but I doubt we'll ever learn the answer: everyone involved in making that decision is either dead or senile. My theory is that Birdie wouldn't have stood for it. Your mother did not approve of mine. Then again, Birdie may not have had any choice in the matter. The hospital where you were born was no maternity ward but an insane asylum. Birdie was resident there throughout the pregnancy and birth.

Whatever the reason, you were *given away to a good home*. That's all I've been told. And suddenly and more than anything else in my life I want to find you. You raison d'être, you! In the month since I've returned from visiting Sigga in Gimli I've been busy busy busy. First, I hired a private detective in Winnipeg to look into the matter of your adoption. A limited search to match my limited funds. We'll see what if anything he unearths for the fee.

And I've been writing to you, evenings when I get home from the Sub. I can't seem to stop. It's all I can do for you, Cousin, until I locate you. Just write.

2

Just write.

Ha! Here you have it, the all and sum of this past month's work: zero zippity zilch. Those first weeks back from Gimli I was on a roll, hiring the detective, starting this letter. Now nothing but glacial stall.

Judge me not, Cuz. I'm no talky Birdie, no teeming word-meadow. Not these days, anyway. And it's not for lack of effort. I take my scribal responsibilities seriously. Look around my apartment. No, not at the unmade futon on bare floor, the stacks of books leaning Pisa-like against the wall, the burial mound of unwashed clothes, the great dirty-dish shrine on the kitchen counter. Kindly avert your eyes from my slovenliness. I meant only to point out the crumpled balls of paper littering my desk (over there, that unpainted door straddling two file cabinets). A month's worth of false starts. Ho hum, the storyteller's perennial conundrum.

Just start at the beginning, you say? And what beginning might that be? I've come to the conclusion all starts are false ones. Tap the fragile shell of any beginning and you'll find another nested inside.

You want beginnings, I'll give you beginnings:

Ginnungagap. This universe when it was nothing but a grinning gap, this earth when it was the big nowhere. No sand no sea no ground I tell you no sky. Grew nothing but nothing upon nothing. The Sun knew not when or where or how to shine, bewildering to her brother Moon the arts of waxing and of waning, and the planets those lost souls wandered the heavens dazed and orbitless. Then convened the Aesir—the High Gods, the rulers—and began to name. To Dawn and Dusk they gave names, and Morning and Night, and so learned Day to start and finish and start again. And so things originated, according to *Voluspa,* the ancient Norse poem that tells us how the world begins—and how it will end: *Ragnarok,* the End-Time, the doom of the gods, when the earth will sink into the sea, the sun turn black, stars plunge from the sky, everything afire.

Not to worry. As foretold in *Voluspa,* life then begins all over again, the earth emerging from its scorched state fair and green, the gods cavorting in the golden heaven called Gimli.

Cut the cosmic rigmarole? Sorry. Norse myths, Icelandic sagas, skaldic verses: your mother lived and breathed the stuff, ate it for breakfast, imbibed it at night. Dunked me in it too. And heady it was, for a suburban kid from Connecticut.

Sure, I could attempt a proper biography of Ingibjorg Petursson. Start with your mother's birth in quaint little New Iceland and build a grand portrait of her talented and tragic mad-poet life. It would make a good story— but nothing more. When it comes down to it, what do I know, really, of Birdie's life? My childhood perceptions. Or to be more exact, memories of perceptions. Paltry, to be sure. You are welcome to try elsewhere, Cousin. Our grandmother Sigga for one. If she's still alive by the time I locate you, and if senility has not left her with cheese for brains, you can propose an interview about her star-crossed dead daughter. Or try Birdie's loyal suitor, our "uncle" Stefan of the Stiff Upper Lip. He lives in Gimli still. I haven't had much luck with either of them myself. But maybe to you, Birdie's prodigal child, they'll reveal all. In the meantime, you're stuck with me. If I were old and a man you could call me a curmudgeon: *an ill-tempered person full of resentment and stubborn notions.* Or in another era I'd be known as a spinster, nearly thirty, childless and unwed. Luckily, no one calls me anything. I keep to myself; attempts at intimacy only lead to disaster. Yes, I'm bitter. I won't deny it. I like to say—to myself of course, who else would listen?—that Birdie wrecked my life. That if it weren't for Birdie I might have achieved some semblance of normalcy by now. But bitterness is a long time brewing. When I first knew your mother I was a mere child, and bitter-free. I'll do my best not to infect this account with anachronistic cur-mudgeonry.

Okay, I'll quit stalling. We'll start with my beginning, which is as good as any. Or rather, my birth. I do not suffer from that most American of delusions, that our lives begin at birth. Our People taught me well in that regard.

I may have been named after the goddess Freya but mostly I got called Frey. Which made me sound less like a deity and more like a drunken brawl. Or some badly wrecked nerves. Or a thing that is always unraveling at the edges.

A late-in-life child, I arrived long after my parents had given up the possibility of children. Barren, fruitless, sterile: these were the terms against which they'd had to contend. Eventually they accommodated themselves to their destiny and moved out of the baby-booming subdivision where they'd planned to raise a family—with its station wagons, baby carriages, tricycles, two-wheelers with training wheels, sleds, wagons, slides, and swings—to an older neighborhood inhabited mostly by retirees. Not a tricycle in sight. The only commotion the occasional wailing of a she-cat in heat. My father worked as an accountant, my mother a part-time copy editor for the local paper. He tamed numbers, she tamed words: orderly work, orderly lives.

I've seen a photograph from this pre-Freya era. My mother smiles gently into her wineglass, no trace of the scowl lines that my childhood would etch between her brows in the years to come. My father wears a starched white shirt and skinny black tie, looking thoughtful in his black-framed glasses. The living room has a museum-like air, and the dining table, which I would soon mar with Kool-Aid stains and crayon scribblings, gleams like an ice rink of pure mahogany. If my parents were unhappy with their child-less life, the photo does not show it.

And then along I came, a startling splash into the calm waters of my parents' middle age. *Out of God's clear blue heaven,* my mother would say.

Our grandmother, Sigga, took the train down from Canada, arriving shortly before my birth, remaining three months after. I have a photograph of Sigga cradling the infant me, her hair coiled in a precise bun, eyes keen behind wire-rimmed librarian's glasses. So competent Sigga was, so in command, one arm cradling baby, the other expertly tilting the bottle to my lips. My mother stands to the side, peering over at me. Her expression looks tentative, perplexed. It was a look I would come to know well.

I don't claim to remember Sigga from this postnatal visit, and it would be seven years until I would see her again, seven years before I would meet my Aunt Birdie, seven years before I would step onto the wide sandy beach of Gimli. Before I was born, my mother and father had visited Gimli every summer; once I arrived, my mother kept putting it off. Seven years my mother remained absent from her people. I don't think your mother ever forgave my mother those seven years.

The first thing I remember is teaching myself to spin. Red-sneakered feet planted in the center of our green square lawn in Windsor, Connecticut. "Mama, look me!" My mother on the front porch, wicker mending basket in her lap. "I'm looking, Frey."

I twisted at the knees, flung my arms wide as propeller blades, then spun myself once around, nearly tipping then spinning again without stopping, one spin spinning into the next—

"Not so fast, Frey!"

Brain whirling quicker than feet, quicker than the twirling trees and the blur of our brick house, I crashed to the ground and lay on my back clinging to handfuls of grass. The sky swirled around me like a blue tornado. Then I lurched to my feet and began stagger-spinning diagonally across the yard, twirling again again again until to my amazement I crashed to my knees vomiting a creamy mound of vanilla wafers onto the grass.

"See," I heard my mother say. With a hankie she wiped a splotch of vomit off the tip of my red sneaker. I examined the crisscross marks etched by the grass on my green-stained knees. "See what happens, Frey?"

I saw. I stood up, I lifted my propeller arms, twisted at the knees. Look me again: inventor of spin.

Every morning I woke with the urge to climb. My limbs ached for it. A quick slurp of milk and Cheerios, then I was scaling the maple that shadowed the house. My legs and arms were nimble monkeys fluent in the language of branches, my shins bled from scraping bark, but at the top of the tree I felt no pain. I gazed down at the roof of the house, at my tricycle tipped on its side in the yard, without fear.

"Frey, come down!"

Frey come down, Frey slow down, Frey stop Frey now—even when spoken from two feet away I heard such commands only dimly. From my treetop perch my mother's words floated lighter than birdsong, and she appeared to me doll-like as the toys scattered in the yard.

My middle-aged mother could not keep up. I frayed her ragged, pun intended.

Where was my father in all this? Dead of a heart attack before I turned two. I have no memories of him, except the ones my mother tried to give me. She recounted these so often it seemed I almost remembered him myself. How I would beg my father to carry me on his shoulders, crying *Up Up Up!* How he taught me peekaboo and tickled me until I squealed. When I learned to add and subtract, Mama told me, "Your father would be so proud to see you now. He was a genius with numbers."

It made me sad not to have a father, but I felt my mother's grief more than my own. I often came upon her holding the photograph of him that took center place on our mantel. "He's still with us," she would say, reassuring herself. It was to marry my father that she'd left Canada in the first place—they met while he was at an accountants' convention in Winnipeg— and without him she found herself stranded with a frenzied toddler in a bland Connecticut suburb. My mother wasn't good at suburbia. The women of Windsor played tennis in the afternoons, or bridge; my mother was embarrassingly poor at both. And although she'd been born in Canada, not Iceland, my mother radiated foreignness, as if she'd come not only from another country but from another era altogether. Modern America frightened her; her decision not to own a television was as much to protect herself from the world—the Vietnam War, with its body bags and massacres, the hippies with their LSD and free love—as to protect me.

It was an isolated life during those years before I began school. There were no children in the neighborhood for me to play with, no relatives to join us on holidays. My father had been an only child whose parents died before I was born, and my mother's family all lived in a place called Canada. Their photographs were arranged shrine-like on the mantel in the living room. Keeping an eye on things. Mama's father, my grandfather Olafur the poet, holding a pipe. I wasn't sure what a poet was but I liked the sound of it, the long *oh,* the clip of the *t.* Amma Sigga in her *Fjallkona* costume: a tall white headdress with a floor-length veil and a green velvet cape trimmed in white fur. Each year in Gimli, my mother explained, one woman was chosen to represent the motherland, and there was a big celebration, *Islendingadagurinn.* I understood perfectly: Sigga was some kind of queen.

There was also a black-and-white photo of my mother as a child leading your mother, a toddling Birdie, through the shallows of Lake Winnipeg. Both in funny one-piece black swimsuits that fell halfway to their knees. Another photo of Birdie grown up, her hair in layers of soft blond curls down to her shoulders, her cheeks high and round as apples.

"Birdie is the beauty," my mother would say matter-of-factly.

"No, Mama, you're the beauty," I insisted. But secretly, shamefully, I agreed. It was hard to say why Birdie seemed more beautiful than Mama when they looked so much alike. Both were tall, both were blond, and yet Birdie's face was somehow radiant and Mama's somehow plain. It made my love for Mama even more fierce.

There were other photos too: Mama's dear friend Vera and Vera's father, the Great Dr. Gudmundsson, and other names that giggled my ears, like the Finnbogason Boys and Old Gisli. Collectively, these friends and relatives were known as Our People. Mama spoke of Our People as if they lived around the corner, as if she'd seen them just yesterday.

"You and Old Gisli, always joking." As if Old Gisli and I had been swapping jokes that very afternoon.

"You're as devilish as those Finnbogason Boys." Who were by then grown men in their fifties.

Birdie and Sigga ruled our home in absentia. Sigga was our household's moral guardian, invoked by my mother to bolster her authority. *What would Amma Sigga think?* Amma Sigga does not tolerate lies. Amma Sigga does not allow girls to play outside with their shirts off. Amma Sigga expects children to color only in coloring books and never on walls. Amma Sigga, Queen

Sigga, expected so much of me. I tried not to look at Sigga's photo on the mantel when I raced bare-chested through the living room and out the back door.

Birdie taught by negation. According to my mother, Birdie forgot to look both ways and almost got hit by a car on Victor Street. Punched Tommi Finnbogason and gave him a black eye, which brought shame upon the family. Got locked in a trunk in the attic and nearly suffocated to death. Threw her shoes down the sewer because she wanted a new pair and this was during the Great Depression.

When I learned to read, shortly after my fourth birthday, my mother said, "You're going to be as clever as Birdie. God help me."

And of course the photo of my father, in the center of it all, gazing out from behind his black-framed rectangular glasses. "He's still with us," my mother had said, and so I would often stop in front of his portrait. "Two plus two is four," I would whisper, hoping to impress him.

My tiny family of two supplemented by a cast of invisible relatives looming from the mantel place: it was all I knew. Yet Mama was the only one who was *real*. If I got overexcited she would pull me onto her lap and stroke my hair while I squirmed to get away. And then, magically, I too would become calm. When I looked up into her soft green eyes it was like entering a pine forest. If I put my ear to her chest I could feel the gentle steady pulse of her heart.

Night was when I loved my mother best. It was a lengthy process, unwinding my brain for sleep, requiring a continuous stream of story and song. After pulling the crisp sheet up to my chin, Mama would take her seat in the rocking chair at the side of the bed. Sometimes she sang, dreary songs she called Lutheran hymns, but I always begged for a story and she usually gave in. Reading aloud required holding the book and turning its pages, and Mama preferred to keep her hands free for knitting, crocheting, and embroidering. So mostly she talked story from memory as she stitched tiny flowers to border our pillowcases and nighties. While Mama talked and sewed I listened and stroked Foxy. Foxy was a stole sent as a gift by our distant cousin Helgi, a mink farmer in British Columbia. Mama refused to wear the stole, with its head, feet, and tail intact. Who on earth would want such a disgusting animal around her neck?

I would. Thumb in mouth I'd lay my cheek against Foxy's auburn fur, waking in the morning to find his pelt stiff with drool.

"A long time ago, when your grandfather Olafur the poet was a little boy, he lived on an island near the top of the world, below the North Pole, in a house with a sod roof."

"A sad roof?"

"Sod is grass."

"His roof was made out of grass? It was green?"

"It was green in the summer, but in the winter the house was so buried in snow the only way out was a set of stairs cut into the snowdrifts. Above where Olafur slept was a window as small as my hand. One morning when Olafur woke up, he looked out the window as small as my hand and saw that the sky was dark instead of light. It was so dark it looked like night. He lit a candle and climbed down from the sleeping loft. He could hear the sheep in the next room."

"Sheep in the house?"

"So they wouldn't freeze. And the sheep were crying, baaaaa, baaaaa, as if they knew something bad had happened. Olafur scrambled up the icy steps leading out of the house. And you know what he saw? Black snow falling from the sky."

"There's no such thing as black snow!"

"It turned out to be ashes, a blizzard of ashes blocking out the sun. For three days Olafur's family lived in darkness. Mount Askja had erupted, and its lava spread in a thousand rivers of hot burning mud. But worse than the lava was the ash. It killed cows and horses and sheep and buried people's houses."

"Was Olafur's house buried?"

"Not completely. But nothing would grow on their land anymore, and all their sheep died because there was no grass for them to eat. Olafur's father and mother decided to leave Iceland and find a new place to live. Just think of it: their people had lived on that island for a thousand years! But they had no choice. On a summer evening, Olafur and his brothers and mother and father packed up their things and climbed onto their shaggy horses. They rode away from their farm, which was called Brekka, and they never saw it again. Olafur kept falling asleep in the saddle. They rode into midnight but it was bright as day, because in summer the sun shines at night in Iceland."

"The sun can't shine at night!"

"It can in Iceland. And in the winter, the sun never shines. But this was summer, and they rode all night until they reached Seydisfjordur, where they boarded a boat crowded with hundreds of other Icelanders who were starting a new life in a place called Canada. The waters were rough, and Olafur was seasick the whole way to Scotland. From Scotland they got on another boat, and this boat took them all the way to Canada. In Canada they boarded a train. Olafur had never seen a train before, none of them had. He thought little men were pushing it from behind. Finally they traveled by boat to a big lake, Lake Winnipeg. This was going to be their new home. And do you know what they named their new town?"

"What?"

"Gimli. Now listen closely: I'm going to tell you why they named the town Gimli. A long time ago, the Icelanders believed that in heaven was a beautiful palace with a gold roof. And the most beautiful room in the palace, where the very best people went after they died, was called Gimli. Gimli shone brighter than the sun. And so that was the name Our People chose when they arrived in their new land. And someday, I'll take you to Gimli. Would you like that?"

I wasn't sure. Which Gimli did my mother mean: the town in Canada or the palace for dead people? I fell asleep dreaming of black snow falling onto gold-roofed houses.

3

One Sunday afternoon each month Mama and I sat side by side on the orange plaid couch to telephone Our People in Canada. My job was to dial. As Mama called out the numbers I'd drag the dial with my index finger over to the small lick of metal that curled around the number one. Then I'd release it, savoring the *clickety-clickety-click*.

Mama let me speak to Amma Sigga first. The receiver felt big and black and heavy in my hand. I was always afraid Amma Sigga would ask if I'd run outside without my shirt or colored on the walls, but she never did.

"Hiya-amma-sigga!"

"Well hello, Freya *min*."

Freya mine. "Does that mean I'm your Freya?"

"It certainly does."

If Amma Sigga had sent me a present, for Christmas or Easter or my birthday, Mama would remind me to thank her. Usually Sigga sent things she'd knitted from Icelandic wool, slipper-socks and sweaters and scarves in white, gray, black, and brown.

"How did you like the mittens?" Sigga would ask.

"They're pretty," I'd answer politely, running my tongue over the small holes of the mouthpiece. "But they're too scratchy so I never wear them."

Mama frowned at such comments, but Sigga took them in stride. The conversations usually ended on a literary note. Sigga always wanted to know if I was reading yet, and once I'd started, what. "Icelanders love to read," she'd say. "It's in our blood."

I thought Sigga's *r*'s sounded funny.

"That's because she rolls them," my mother explained. "Icelanders like to roll their *r*'s."

Whenever Amma Sigga said a word with an *r* in it, I imagined a pack of *r*'s somersaulting on her tongue.

While my mother spoke with Sigga I wandered the living room, sticking Lego pieces onto my fingertips, half-listening. It was a lot of talk about Our People with the funny names, all easy and pleasant, up until the moment when Mama asked Sigga to put Birdie on the line. No matter how happily the conversation with Birdie started out, it nearly always took a bad turn at the end. Mama would grow silent, and as she listened to Birdie she'd wrap the long coils of phone cord around and around her wrist into a massive black bracelet, then unwind it, then coil it up again. Usually, it was talk about why Mama hadn't brought me to Canada yet to meet my *amma* and my aunt.

"I know you're looking forward to us coming."

. . .

"Of course I want to come!"

. . .

"But you know I'm afraid to fly—"

. . .

"I can't manage her on a train for three days—"

. . .

"Birdie, believe me, she doesn't know how to behave!"

"I can so behave!" I'd shout in the background. "I'll sit still on the train. Watch." I'd sit stiffly on my chair, knees pushed together, hands folded on my lap. "See?"

Then I got to speak to Birdie. It always surprised me when Birdie got on the line—even if Birdie and Mama had just been arguing, Birdie's voice would sound happy and excited. "Well, kiddo," she'd say. "How's life in America?"

I told her about the midget inside the traffic light at the end of the block who switched the light green-yellow-red.

"Clever little fellow!" Birdie laughed. She didn't ask if I had actually seen the midget or not. Another time I told her about a leaf I'd found that was exactly half green and half orange.

"Sounds like a case of split personality to me," Birdie pronounced. "Doesn't know if it's spring or fall!"

Once I confessed to Birdie that I wanted to learn to fly.

"You come to Gimli this summer, baby, I'll teach you how to fly!"

"You know how to fly?"

"Why do you think they call me Birdie?"

After the phone call was over Mama and I would sit at the kitchen table for an afternoon snack. If the call had taken a particularly bad turn, Mama wouldn't eat anything. I'd dip vanilla wafers one by one into my glass of milk.

"Well, Birdie's sick again."

"She didn't sound sick." I swirled the cookie crumbs into the milk with my finger. "She didn't cough or sneeze or blow her nose."

"Well," Mama insisted. "She *is* sick."

"Will she be better by summertime?"

"I don't know, honey. Why?"

"She wants us to come visit her and Amma Sigga this summer." I often imagined it, me and Birdie soaring over the lake, swooping and twirling like trapeze artists, then diving off the edges of clouds into the sparkling water below. Mama and Amma Sigga watching from the beach, mouths open in awe.

"When you can behave, then we can go to Gimli for the summer."

But I did not behave, not well enough, not often enough. More summers passed, and as each approached I'd hear my mother arguing with Birdie on the phone. "I did not abandon you! I married an American. Really, Birdie. Everything doesn't have to do with you."

But it did. In the end it did.

In addition to the phone calls there was a steady stream of letters back and forth between Mama and her best friend, Vera. Vera had flown from Winnipeg to help my mother after my father died, but I was too young to remember her. The letters came in blue airmail envelopes, the kind where the letter and the envelope are one and the same piece of paper. Vera's neat slanting script would fill the page. Mama would read Vera's letters at least twice, and she always seemed sad after. "Homesick," she would say. "Vera makes me homesick." I decided I didn't like Vera very much, not if she made my mother sick.

It was not until I was seven and safely out of first grade that my mother announced we would spend the summer in Gimli. She bought me a suitcase for the trip, and each morning the week before departure I squirmed under the bed to slide it out for a look. The suitcase was a red so bright it made my cheeks tingle sour cherry, with brass hinges and irresistible brass locks: nudge the button with your thumb and *snappity-snap*—the latch popped open with a crisp metal *ping* like a popcorn kernel exploding itself against the lid of a pot. *Snappity-snap! Snappity-snap! Snappity-snap! Snappity-snap! Snappity-snap! Snappity—*

"You'll break it, Frey."

"I won't." But quit for fear of it. "Could a person travel *inside* a suitcase?"

"I don't suppose."

I imagined a shrunken version of myself settling onto a bed of dungarees, my mother latching me snugly in, my head resting on a pillow of socks while Foxy whispered me to sleep. In the morning my mother would carry Frey-in-the-suitcase to the train station, swinging me lightly in white-gloved hands until the train screeched its arrival and everyone climbed all aboard, all aboard.

The night before we left, Mama called Canada one last time. I was not allowed to talk. "You'll see them soon enough." The call was mostly arrangements: what time the train would arrive, who would meet us at the station. Then: "Is Birdie all right?"

. . .

"If she's not, we could always postpone."

. . .

"Of course we're coming. I never said we weren't. We'll wait for them at the station then."

"Not go?" I asked as soon as my mother hung up.

"We're going, we're going!" Mama untangled the black phone cord coiled tightly around her wrist. "Why does everyone think we're not going?"

Aside from an alarming episode when I got stuck between cars and had to be rescued by a conductor, I behaved on the train. While Mama stared out the window or knitted, I played endless games of solitaire. As we came within a few hours of Winnipeg she began dropping stitches left and right, sighing and ripping out whole sections of scarf. Every once in a while she would sound a warning. "Your *amma* Sigga is a proper lady, Frey. You're going to have to be very well behaved."

"I will." Red seven on black eight. Black queen on red king. Red two on black three.

"Amma Sigga won't put up with any nonsense."

I imagined Sigga in her velvet *Fjallkona* cape, regal and strict as a queen. "What about Auntie Birdie? Will she put up with nonsense?" As far as I could tell from our phone conversations, Auntie Birdie seemed fond of nonsense.

"Auntie Birdie . . ." Mama began, then stopped herself.

"Auntie Birdie what?"

"You'll see soon enough."

Out the window things became very flat. There were no trees. Just miles and miles of fields. Barley and wheat and alfalfa, Mama explained. Once when the train stopped she took me onto the platform for my first glimpse of prairie. All I could see was sky, blue in all directions. Except far to the west. In that one corner of the sky, dark black clouds. From their underside a gray streak connected sky to ground.

"Storm clouds," Mama said. "It's raining there."

How could it be raining in one part of the sky and blue in another? The dark clouds brightened for a second. Lightning. The storm raced our train to Winnipeg and won; when I stepped onto the platform raindrops fell so hard they pinpricked the skin of my arms and the back of my neck. Mama didn't seem to notice. Her gaze was fixed on the large group of people waiting under a tin awning. Suddenly a pair of arms shot up above the crowd. The arms were long and pale and slender, crisscrossing dramatically through the air like those of a person stranded on a desert island signaling to rescuers. The arms moved through the crowd until they reached the front edge of it, then connected to a person, a woman in a lilac dress, who began running toward us in the rain. Still waving grandly.

"That's Birdie," Mama said, raising her own hand in a modest gesture of acknowledgment.

"I know that!" I started running to meet Birdie but my mother gripped my hand and we walked instead.

First Birdie threw her arms around Mama, then she stepped back and took Mama's two hands in hers. "Anna," she said. "Anna Anna Anna!" Her voice was like a song. Then she knelt onto the platform and looked me in the eye. "Little Freya."

"I'm not little. I'm the tallest girl in first grade."

"Frey," my mother admonished. "It's not nice to boast."

Birdie didn't seem to mind. "Of course you are," she said apologetically. "We'll call you Freya the Tall." Then she pulled me to her.

"Birdie," Mama said, after a few moments. "That's enough. You'll ruin your stockings on the pavement."

Birdie did not let go. My chin rested on Birdie's shoulder, my nose against Birdie's long soft neck. "You smell purple."

"Good nose, kiddo." Birdie sounded pleased. "That's Lavender Dawn. I'll dab some on you when we get home."

I took my mother's hand, then reached up for Birdie's. Every few steps I swung in the air between them, a feat I'd often watched other kids—ones with two parents—perform with envy. By the time we reached the parking lot, a very tall man in a dark suit was putting my red suitcase into the back of his car.

"Stop, thief!" I shrieked. Foxy was in that suitcase.

Birdie laughed. And laughed and laughed. There seemed no end to her laughing. "That's no thief," she managed to get out, gasping for breath. "That's your uncle Stefan."

"It can't be. I have one aunt no uncles."

Stefan stood awkwardly at the side of the car.

"Stefan's not a blood uncle," Birdie explained. "He's the kind that chooses you. Even better."

"Does that mean he's like your brother?"

"Exactly!" Birdie seemed pleased. Stefan blushed.

Stefan's car was old-fashioned and shiny. A Rambler, he called it. I sat up front between Stefan and Birdie. Mama sat in the back. "I can't see anything," I complained. So Birdie pulled me onto her lap.

"Take us through Winnipeg, Stefan," Birdie commanded. As if Stefan was a chauffeur. "Let's give Freya a tour of the old West End."

"Oh no," Mama protested. "That's out of the way. No need for that. Stefan's nice enough to come all the way from Gimli to fetch us."

"It's no trouble," Stefan said.

"I won't hear of it," Mama insisted. "Anyway, Frey and I have had a long trip. We're exhausted."

"I'm not exhausted!" I protested.

"Just a quick tour," Birdie pleaded. "Freya's never seen where we grew up."

"I thought you grew up on a farm."

"We did at first," Mama explained. "In Arborg. And then after our father died we moved to Winnipeg. The Gudmundssons were kind enough to take us in until your *amma* Sigga found work in Gimli. I don't know what we would have done without the Gudmundssons."

"The Grand Gudmundssons," Birdie said mockingly. "The Great Doctor Gudmundsson."

"Why was he great?" I wanted to know.

"He was the first Icelandic doctor in Canada," Mama began. "And his daughter Vera was my age, and treated us like her very own sisters."

"Are you kidding, Anna? She treated us like country bumpkins fresh off the farm. She made fun of our accents. You were her special charity project, she only wanted to My-Fair-Lady-ize you."

"Vera was good to us," my mother insisted. "Dear Vera!"

"Dear Vera," Birdie echoed. But she didn't say it fondly, the way Mama did. Her voice had what Mama called *that tone.* Don't use *that tone* with me, Birdie. That tone had a name, *sarcasm,* that made me think of an unhealed scar. But all that would come later.

"Stefan," Birdie commanded. "Pull over!" Stefan parked the Rambler in front of a two-story brick building with bright blue shutters and a pair of white columns out front.

"Jonsson Funeral Home," I read the sign out loud. "Is someone dead?"

"Plenty of people are dead," Birdie said. "People die all the time. But that's not why we're here. Tell her, Stefan."

"My family runs this business," Stefan said. "I grew up here."

"In a dead people's house?"

"Indeed. All the old Icelanders came here, some young ones too. My father sent them on their way."

I studied Stefan closely. His glasses looked like the kind my own father had worn, black and rectangular. "Do dead people wear glasses?" It was something I had wondered about for a long time, and Stefan seemed like a good person to ask, given that his family were experts in the ways of the dead. He thought it over for a moment.

"I doubt there's a need for eyeglasses in heaven," he replied. "But probably no rule against it, either." He pulled away from the curb and a few blocks later said, "We're in the old neighborhood now. The West End."

"Home of the Goolies!" Birdie said it like a radio announcer.

"Who are the Goolies?" I asked.

"Who are the Goolies?" Birdie repeated. "Who are the Goolies?" As if it were impossible for anybody not to know. Then she laughed. "I'm a Goolie, Stefan's a Goolie, Anna's a Goolie. You're a Goolie too."

"I'm not a ghost!"

"A Goolie's not a ghost. A Goolie's an Icelander. It's what the Anglos used to call us, when we first came to Canada. It comes from the word *gull*, which means yellow. For our blond hair." She ruffled mine. "And right there"—she pointed to a beige cement building on a corner, plain and square, with a sign that read GOOD TEMPLARS—"that's the Goolie Hall. Center of it all. And now we're turning onto . . . Victor Street! Home of the First Lutheran Church, where all good Goolies go on Sundays."

"And home of the Gudmundssons," Mama added from the backseat.

"Oh yes, the grand home of the Gudmundssons—pull over, Stefan."

Most of the houses on Victor Street were small and wood-framed, but the Gudmundsson house was brick and imposing, surrounded by a wrought-iron fence and framed by rosebushes. "Can we go inside?" I asked.

"Yes, let's," Mama said. "Maybe Vera's home."

"No time for visits now," Birdie decided. "Sigga's making dinner for us back in Gimli. The tour must go on! Besides, you'll see Vera tomorrow. We're having a little coffee party in honor of your homecoming."

I turned around and looked at my mother over the backseat. To my surprise, Mama was wiping tears from her face with one of her embroidered hankies.

"Why are you crying?"

Mama didn't answer.

"Seven years is a long time, Anna," Birdie said. She didn't sound worried about Mama, just . . . satisfied.

"It couldn't be helped, Birdie. You know that."

"All I know is we missed her first seven years." Birdie locked her arms around my middle. "We missed you." Birdie was starting to sound mad. Suddenly I didn't like her anymore—she'd made my mother cry!—and I tried to squirm out of her grasp, but she held tight.

"Well we're here now," Mama said cheerily. "Isn't that what matters?"

"That's right," Birdie answered, cheery-mean. "Sweep everything under the rug like you always do! Sweep sweep sweep—"

Stefan put a hand on Birdie's arm. "That's enough, Ingibjorg."

"How come you call Birdie *Ingibjorg*?" I asked Stefan.

"Because that's her name," he answered.

"Because Stefan is ever so proper," added Birdie.

"Next stop, Gimli!" Stefan called it out like a conductor. Ever so proper.

By the time we were out of Winnipeg and heading north to Gimli the rain had stopped and Birdie rolled down her window. It was still very flat outside but there were trees and shrubs the new light green of early summer. I stuck my head out like a dog.

"Frey!" Mama called from the backseat. "You know you're not allowed. Something could get in your eye."

I pulled my head back in, but later I stuck it out again because Mama was sleeping in the backseat. Except she was only pretending. Normally she slept with her mouth a bit open. Now her lips were closed tight, hands folded in her lap. I wondered if Birdie would make me stick my head back inside, but she didn't.

"Good dog." Birdie laughed, patting my head. I liked her again.

"Woof!" I barked, but quietly, so my mother wouldn't hear. Then hung out my tongue and panted all the way to Gimli, imagining the gold-roofed houses I would find there—Gimli the town and Gimli the heaven having become one in my mind—dreaming of flying. Surely tomorrow Birdie would take me flying.

4

Forgive me, dear Cousin, for having confused that most splendid dwelling of the gods with a rinky-dink resort town on the mosquito-laden shore of Lake Winnipeg. I was simply a seven-year-old girl with my own ideas of majesty. And Gimli itself had harbored grand ambitions once: to serve as the capital of a New Iceland, est. 1876. It was a lofty dream almost instantly punctured by grim reality. In its first year, the New Iceland settlement was ravished by smallpox, a few years later by devastating floods. The lands the settlers usurped from the Indians and so painstakingly cleared quickly reverted to bog. Only the foolish and die-hard remained, our grandfather, Olafur, among them.

Granted, Gimli revealed itself no home of the gods, but let's give the settlers due credit for optimism. Remember, it doesn't take much to look heavenly when the land you've left behind is covered in a foot of volcanic ash, your farm littered with the rotting corpses of your entire flock of sheep, the air itself burnt and stinking of rotten eggs. And the Ash Districts accounted for only a portion of the Icelandic diaspora. A spell of particularly wretched climate, lives of grim servitude in a near-feudal social structure, the seemingly unending suffering bestowed by foreign rule: reasons aplenty to get up and go. Life in Iceland was harsh; life in New Iceland only differently so.

By the time I arrived in Gimli, nearly a century later, all that remained of the capital of New Iceland was a floundering fishing village masquerading as a beach resort. *Welcome to Gimli—Your Place in the Sun!*

So I suppose it won't surprise you, Cousin, when I tell you that Oddi, our grandmother's house, was no palace capped in gold but an old dingy-white farmhouse with yellow trim, roofed with utterly ordinary red shingles. But you are, by now—assuming you've made it this far—an adult. I was a child fully expecting gold when Stefan pulled his old Rambler station wagon onto Second Street. I ran ahead of my mother and arrived at the door first, eager to meet my grandmother the queen. But Sigga too was a startling disappointment, in her plain brown apron and sensible lace-up shoes.

"*Elskan!*" She held out her arms to hug me, but I shrank back.

"Where's your crown?" I demanded.

"My—?"

"And your green velvet cape!"

Sigga began to laugh. Then she stepped past me and folded my mother in her long arms. *Mama,* my mother said. *Mama. Mama.*

That too shocked me. To hear Mama call someone *Mama.* Wasn't Sigga a grandmother, an *amma*? But she was also the mother of my mother. That idea cramped my brain. I turned to Birdie. "Mama and Amma," I said.

"Indeed," Birdie replied. "The big mother-daughter reunion. Quite a moment to behold."

I had no idea what she was talking about. I tried again. "Mama and Amma," I explained. "They . . . have the same letters in their names. But scrambled."

"Indeed, *elskan*. How clever you are!"

While Mama and Amma stood in the kitchen chatting and Uncle Stefan brought our suitcases from the car, Birdie led me on a tour of the house, beginning with the living room, which she called a *parlor,* a small room nearly overpowered by the dark wood of the wainscoting and a gleaming black piano. Lace curtains hung in the window, lace cloth covered the coffee table, lace doilies rested on the arms of a plush green couch. I tested the couch, bouncing on it lightly, then stood by the fireplace examining the photographs on the mantel. Some were identical to the ones on our mantel in Connecticut—Olafur with his pipe, Mama and Birdie wading, even a photo of me with two front teeth missing—but there were many unknown to me as well. "Are these Our People?"

"Indeed," Birdie said.

"You like that word, *indeed*."

"Indeed I do."

"Indeedy-do!"

Birdie didn't miss a beat. "Righty-o!"

"Okeydokey!"

"Hokeypokey!"

"Hocus-pocus!"

We stared at each other, grinning.

"Come see your grandfather Olafur's study." She took me to a door at the far end of the living room. "You open it."

I turned the beveled glass knob, so shiny it made me think of diamonds. Inside was a small room brimming with books. Books on every inch of wall, piled on the chairs, stacked on the floor, covering the surface of a long bench. Birdie led me to a wooden desk. She ran her hand over its surface, like she was petting a very beautiful cat. "This is the desk where Olafur wrote his poems. Of course, not here in this exact room. He died before we moved here. But Sigga and I have reconstructed his study exactly as the great poet liked it. *Skald Nyja Islands.*"

"*Scowled* what?"

"*Skald Nyja Islands.*"

"Oh."

"You say it, Freya." Her brow was furrowed and she sounded cross.

"Skowld. Knee-ya. Eece-lands."

"Good. What does it mean?"

"Mean?"

"In English."

I bit my lip.

"It means Poet of New Iceland. Hasn't your mother taught you a single word of Icelandic?"

"*Alltaf baetist raun a raun,*" I said. "Mama says that to me a lot."

Birdie laughed. "Do you know what it means?"

"No," I admitted.

"It means trouble always follows trouble."

"Mama says trouble is my middle name," I offered.

Her smile disappeared again. "Trouble is not your middle name! Ingibjorg is your middle name. You were named after me and I was named after my father's grandmother and she was named after her mother's sister. Ingibjorg has been in our family for as long as anyone has kept track."

I nodded obediently. Birdie made my head spin: in the space of one conversation she'd gone from happy to cross to laughing to mad again. I sat down in my grandfather's chair and picked up an empty ink bottle from the desk.

"It smells like moss in here," I observed. "Everything is old."

"Except you," Birdie said. "You're new." To my surprise she kissed me on the top of the head. Her lips stayed there for a long time, and I thought I could feel them moving, as if she were talking without making any sound.

Upstairs were two bedrooms next to each other. One was Birdie's. It had a four-poster bed with a canopy, a view of the lake, and a desk with a typewriter. The other room, Birdie explained, would be mine. My red suitcase was sitting on the bed, and I felt happy to see it. I opened the suitcase *snappity-snap*. "This is Foxy. He comes from Cousin Helgi the mink farmer."

"Handsome beast," Birdie said.

While the grown-ups drank coffee, I sat on the couch between Birdie and Amma Sigga. Mama and Stefan sat in stiff wooden chairs across from us. I closed my eyes and stroked Foxy, from snout to tail, tail to snout, listening to the conversation without understanding. It was all in Icelandic. Every once in a while I'd hear a word I knew, usually a name, like Freya, or Anna, or Birdie, and then I'd open my ears wide for a moment. I wondered if they could really understand each other, or if they were just making sounds like gurgling water. Soon I fell asleep with my head on Birdie's lap, dreaming Mama singing hymns.

The entire next day was spent preparing for Mama's homecoming party, an event Birdie and I were to ruin—the first of our many conjoined disasters—though looking back, I can't find any trace of impending calamity in that bright June morning. I remember waking with one thought only: This was the day I would learn to fly. But where was Birdie?

"She's sleeping in," Sigga said. We were sitting at the breakfast table, Mama, Sigga, and me, eating soft-boiled eggs on toast.

"And don't you even think about waking her," my mother warned. "Or there'll be a scene."

"What's a scene?"

"Birdie has trouble waking up, is all."

"It's her dreams," Sigga added. "All that dreaming she does, all night long. If she sleeps at all."

"Everyone dreams," my mother said. "But not everyone bares their fangs at the breakfast table."

"Birdie has fangs?"

Sigga's kitchen was old but immaculate. It had none of the suburban colors I was used to, the burnt orange and avocado appliances, the flower-power wallpapers of my classmates' homes. Everything here was white and silver. A shiny toaster that reminded me of Stefan's Rambler. Tin canisters labeled SUGAR, FLOUR, SALT. A Scotch plaid thermos. A wall of glassed cabinets with bronze latches that went *clickity-click, clickity-click*. And a large table with a lemon yellow Formica top and bowed chrome legs. My job for the morning was to help Sigga in the kitchen while my mother went out for groceries. It was the first time I was alone with my grandmother. *Amma Sigga won't put up with any nonsense.* Even lacking her white headdress and green velvet cape, I still viewed her as queenly.

"Now, *elskan*," she said in her thick accent. "Let's get started, shall we?"

I nodded, afraid to speak. Around my waist she tied an apron that hung almost to my ankles, then dragged a chair over to the counter and told me to stand on it.

I thought maybe she was testing me. "Mama never lets me stand on furniture."

"Well, I suppose it'll be all right this one time." When Sigga smiled her face crinkled like a paper fan.

"How old are you?"

"Oh, fairly old I'd say. Older than many but not as old as some. Now, *elskan*, climb up on this chair and help your old *amma* with the *ponnukokur*."

"What's *ponnukokur*?"

"What's *ponnukokur*?" a voice repeated. But it wasn't Sigga's. I turned to see Birdie standing in the doorway, hair mashed onto one side of her head, wearing a long pink bathrobe. "What's *ponnukokur*?" she said again. I was glad she didn't know either.

But instead of answering, Sigga said, "Let her be, Ingibjorg. She's just a child."

"How can she not know what *ponnukokur* are? Doesn't Anna teach her anything? Are you aware that this child doesn't know one single word of Icelandic?"

Alltaf baetist raun a raun, I said silently. Trouble always follows trouble.

"It may not have occurred to you, Birdie, but they don't teach Icelandic in American elementary schools." It was my mother, coming through the back screen door with an armload of groceries.

"Of course they don't," Birdie said. She was nearly shouting. "That's why it's your duty to teach her!"

"That's easy for you to say." Mama spoke quietly but firmly. "I can barely teach that child to hold still long enough to tie her shoes."

"She seems perfectly well behaved to me," Birdie insisted. "And if you don't start her soon it'll be too late. Look at Vera's children. They're nearly out of high school and they can't speak a word of Icelandic."

"And why should they?"

"Fine. Maybe Vera's children don't need to. Let them turn their backs on the most expressive language this earth has ever known. But not Freya. Freya is the granddaughter of one of our greatest poets. He's probably turning in his grave. You have a responsibility, Anna. Doesn't she, Mama?"

Sigga sighed wearily. "Oh, Olafur's turning in his grave all right. Listening to his two girls fighting."

At least that's what I imagine she said, because most of the argument in the kitchen that morning took place in Icelandic. It was an argument that was repeated over many summers, in many variations. An argument I came to know by heart.

"This language is who we are."

"What good could it possibly do her?"

"Good? What good? I'll tell you what good. 'Language is a solemn thing. It grows out of life, out of its agonies and ecstasies, its wants and its weariness.

Every language is a temple, in which the soul of those who speak it is enshrined.' Oliver Wendell Holmes. That's what good it does. Sacred good."

And on and on. Even then, I sensed these arguments were about something more than whether I could speak Icelandic. Birdie was never satisfied. I was the living symbol of my mother's betrayal, of my mother's turning into an American.

"Why do you stay there?" I heard Birdie demand once. "Now that you're a widow? What keeps you there? You belong here with your people."

I wondered that too. My mother had no real life to speak of in Connecticut. Sometimes I thought staying in Connecticut might simply be my mother's way of avoiding fighting with Birdie all year round.

Sigga let me crack three eggs into the *ponnukokur* batter, and this I managed with only one small speck of shell. I tried to dig it out with my fingers, but it was impossible to retrieve from the slippery whites. Sigga said, "Leave it, *elskan,* it's too small to matter." I was allowed to stir the batter and also to lick the spoon. I watched while Sigga poured the batter into a small black frying pan, making the thin pancakes one by one until there was a pile on the plate. Then we rolled them up and sprinkled them with cinnamon sugar. Next, I helped spread purple-black prune filling with a special knife, wide and dull, on seven round yellow cakes Sigga had taken from the oven. She gingerly placed one layer on top of the other to make the *vinarterta*. On the very top layer we spread white frosting, in little wavelets. "Whitecaps," Sigga called them.

"What are whitecaps?"

"You'll see soon enough. When we get a storm on the lake."

I licked the cake batter off the knife, and it tasted like almond. Then Sigga led me into the living room. "This china cabinet," she said, "was a wedding present for me and Olafur."

The cabinet was dark wood and hand-carved, with rounded glass doors. Each of its four shelves was filled with teacups and matching saucers, each cup different from the rest, and each, Sigga explained, with a story behind it.

"What are the stories?"

"Not now. Another day, I'll tell you the stories of the cups. There are nearly sixty of them. For now we just need to pick some for the party. And I'd like you to select them. Since you're a guest of honor today."

I liked the sound of that.

"Use both hands, *elskan*. One at a time. We need twelve in all. Set them on the table by the window."

Oh, the careful, excruciating selection. Each cup with its own charms. Some had lips rimmed with gold. One had a dark red rose at the bottom. Another was green as a lime with pale pink buds on the saucer. A black one with gold stars and rim. And then ever so steadily reaching in, lifting them out one by one and carrying each to the table as if it were full of something hot and precious. It kept me busy a long time. Which was, I suppose, our grandmother's intention.

In the early afternoon I noticed Birdie's bedroom door was open. Birdie was sitting at a small table, still in the pink bathrobe she'd worn while arguing with Mama that morning. The table looked like a desk, but it wasn't for writing. It had a big mirror attached, and its surface was covered with little bottles and jars, curlers, hairbrushes, combs. Birdie was outlining her lips in red when she noticed me in the mirror.

"You've caught me at my vanity!"

I didn't know what that meant.

"It's a pun," Birdie explained.

I didn't know what that meant either. Birdie pulled a chair from a corner of the room and sat me beside her. I could smell roses and lemons and something like cinnamon—or was that a smell from the kitchen drifting up the stairs?

"A vanity is a table where women do themselves up. But *vanity* also means being conceited."

"Oh."

"Do you know what *conceited* means?"

"No."

"If you don't know a word, just ask me. *Conceited* means being overly proud of your own looks."

"Are you conceited?"

"Some people say that. Some people have called me vain. Not to name any names. But really, I'm not so beautiful, if you look closely. See how small my eyes are, how they're too close together, and I have hardly any lashes and my eyebrows are skimpy and my ears refuse to lie flat against my head, which makes it hard for me to put my hair up. Without all this"—Birdie swept her hand over the vanity—"I'd be downright homely."

And before I could ask: "It's a nicer way of saying ugly."

"Mama says you're the beautiful one."

"She does? She says that? Nonsense!" But I could see Birdie was pleased.

"Mama doesn't have a vanity table."

"That's because she's not vain. Sensible Anna!"

"Are you sensible?"

"Hardly."

I didn't see how anyone could think Birdie was homely or ugly or anything but beautiful. Later I would. Birdie's face nearly purple with rage, or bleached of life, or her eyes truly small and scowling. But not today. Today Birdie was glamorous. Like a swan. But she had yet to mention our flying lesson.

"My wings itch," I hinted.

"Wings," Birdie repeated, buffing her chin with powder.

I couldn't stand it any longer. "When are we going flying?"

Birdie laughed like she had when I'd yelled "Stop, thief" to Stefan at the train station. A loud, raucous laughter that filled the room, that made my ears burn. I didn't see what was so funny. "You said you'd give me lessons if I came to Gimli."

Birdie caught her breath. "And I will, *elskan*. Not today though. The wind isn't right. No breeze. Impossible to lift off."

"Tomorrow?"

"Sure, baby. Tomorrow we'll go. If the conditions are right, tomorrow we'll fly."

"Fly in the sky."

"Glide in the sky."

"Gliding sky high."

"Oh, you are the clever one, aren't you?" She pulled me onto her lap, kissed me, then showed me in the mirror where she'd left the glossy red imprint of her lips on my cheek.

Later, Birdie came down the stairs in a splendid dress, white with red flowers nearly black in their centers. Fancy as the teacup roses.

"What do you think?"

"It's beautiful," I said. Then my mother came in the room, brushing flour off her hands and onto her apron.

"That's really something," she said evenly. "I didn't bring anything that dressy." She bent down and wiped the lipstick off my cheek with the corner of her apron.

"Of course you didn't." Sigga leaned her head in from the kitchen doorway. "No need. This is a simple Saturday afternoon coffee party with relatives, not some fancy dress ball. Really, Ingibjorg."

"Are you saying I shouldn't wear it? Just because Anna is going to wear some plain old Jane dress?"

"It has nothing to do with Anna. It's too much, that's all."

To my surprise, Birdie went upstairs without a word. You could be a grown-up and still have your mother tell you what to wear. When Birdie came back down, she was wearing a beige skirt and a short-sleeved top. Sigga and Anna were in the kitchen, but Birdie modeled it for me, spinning once around.

"Dour enough, don't you think?"

Even in a simple outfit, Birdie shone. *Dour,* I decided, was simply another word for pretty. "Very dour," I agreed. "Dour indeed."

My mother took me upstairs to dress. I ran to open my red suitcase, *snappity-snap,* but it was empty. Mama pointed to the closet, where my two dresses were hanging, then opened the bureau drawers one by one. The top one for my panties and socks, the next for shirts, the bottom one for shorts and pants. Mama had unpacked it all for me, without my knowing, without saying a word. I hugged her around the waist, burying my face in her flour-damp apron.

"What's that for?" Mama asked, stroking my hair. She didn't smell like roses or lemon or anything but pure mother.

Mama and I greeted all the guests who came to the door, each enveloping Mama in a Viking-size hug. "And this is your . . . ?"

That was my cue to cross one shiny black shoe over the other, lift the lacy edges of my dress, and curtsy. Say "Pleased to meet you. My name is Freya."

Except everyone seemed to know my name already. They wanted to talk about who I looked like (my grandmother, my grandfather, my mother; no mention of my ghostly father), and they wanted to pat my head and pinch my cheeks. Especially Mama's best friend, Vera. Vera was tall, nearly as tall as Birdie and Mama, and had a long skinny neck. Vera fussed over me for a long time, and then her husband, Joey, lifted me high in the air. But where was Birdie? Vera wanted to know.

"Oh, she'll be down soon enough," Sigga said.

"Probably in her room," my mother added. "Waiting until everyone gets here so she can make a grand entrance."

I peered up the stairs. There was Birdie, standing in her bedroom doorway, listening. She wasn't wearing the beige skirt anymore. She was back in the white dress with red flowers. When she saw me, she turned away and shut herself inside her room.

Some people stayed all afternoon: Uncle Stefan and his grandfather Old Gisli, Vera and Joey and their two boys. Others came and went. Friends of Sigga's, friends of my mother's—and who could have imagined my mother with all these friends? She seemed not to have a single friend at home in Connecticut, none that I could think of. None who hugged her fiercely, none who wept at the long-lost sight of her.

Sure enough, once the room was crowded Birdie came down the stairs, oddly glamorous. All attention went to her, for a moment, then back to my mother and me. The guests of honor.

Stefan's grandfather Old Gisli kept me occupied for a time. True to his name, he was by far the oldest person I had ever seen. He wore a brown suit shiny at the knees and frayed at the cuffs, and his shirt collar was yellowed around the neck where it met the white of his scraggly hair. He walked with two canes, each topped with an elaborately carved knob. Cane-step by cane-step he made his way across the room, then leaned the canes up against the arm of the green couch before lowering himself down. While Stefan went to get Old Gisli coffee and cake, I snuck over for a closer look at the canes. Each handle was carved into a different but equally ugly gnarled face, with huge eyes and wide leering mouths.

"Trolls."

I turned to find Old Gisli leaning over the arm of the couch, watching me with his watery eyes.

"Huh?" *Huh* was not a word I was allowed to use, but Old Gisli didn't seem to mind.

"Trolls," he said again, and this time I understood him, despite his thick accent. "Whittled 'em myself."

I ran my finger over one of the troll's roiling eyebrows. Then Old Gisli began speaking in Icelandic, as if he were singing a song but without a tune. When he was done he leaned back into the couch with a toothy grin. "That," he said, "was a little verse of your *afi* Olafur's."

"Skowld Knee-ya Eece-lands?"

"That's right. He was a good friend of mine, your *afi* was. And did you understand the poem?"

I shook my head. I was afraid he might be displeased with me for not knowing Icelandic, but he didn't seem to mind. The poem, he explained, told about when the Icelanders came to America, but their trolls and elves stayed behind in Iceland.

"Why?"

"Nowhere to hide. Elves prefer twisted bits of rock and cave. Manitoba's too flat for an elf's taste. But Gryla came over. That she did." He began reciting again, and then took me through the poem line by line in rough English. *Here comes Gryla . . .* Gryla has six ears that swing down to her thighs, and three heads, each the size of a cow, and a nose like a goat's but with eighteen bumps, swollen and blue. Two long teeth descend below each of her chins. She is very picky about food and eats only children; she is so picky that she eats only the lazy children, the ones who make noise and trouble!

For a moment I was too stunned by this gruesome vision to speak. Had my grandfather written that poem too?

"Hardly!" Old Gisli's laugh was hoarse and grizzled. "Gryla's been around since long before your *afi* was even born."

"Is she still around?"

Old Gisli nodded. Then he might have winked. Or he might have caught a speck of dust in his eye. A moment after finishing his *vinarterta* he was dozing chin on chest.

Vera's boys were teenagers. Back home my mother had warned me away from teenagers, especially hippie teenagers. Hippies, my mother advised, wore flared pants called bell-bottoms, and the boys had long sideburns and, worse, long hair. While I was being introduced to Vera's teenagers, I studied their pants: flared! Not only that, but one of them, Andrew, had hair nearly to his shoulders. The boys ate two plates of *ponnukokur* each, then announced they were going for a walk on the beach.

Maybe they would like to take little Freya with them? Vera suggested.

"Sure," Andrew agreed, reaching for my hand. I quickly hid both hands behind my back and shook my head no.

Many times since I've wished I'd gone with those boys. We would have run on the beach chasing gulls, and by the time we returned to the party I'd have been tired out, my flying energy expelled. Instead I endured hour after hour of curtsying to new arrivals, carrying plates of *ponnukokur* around the room, and eating far more than my fair share of *vinarterta*. Mama and her dear Vera were sunk deep in conversation on the couch, Sigga kept pouring more rounds of coffee. And Birdie? She seemed truly like a bird to me, flitting from guest to guest, telling coy little jokes, pecking at *vinarterta* crumbs. Once she drew me up on her lap.

"Looks just like her mother, don't you think?" Vera's husband, Joey, asked.

"You think?" Birdie sounded dubious. She studied my face, traced my nose with her finger. "Yes, I suppose she does, just a little," she conceded.

But mostly Birdie ignored me, and Mama too. I began to get antsy. My new shoes hurt, the lace collar of my dress itched, my legs had that twitchy run-starved feeling. I began taking little hops as I walked, I went up and down the stairs three times for no reason. "Settle down, Frey," I heard my mother say. "That's enough, Frey."

I was bored with grown-up talk. Although mostly in English, it still seemed like a different language. Long discussions about people with funny names and how they were related to other people with funny names. Uncle Stefan gave me a pat on the head whenever he saw me, but mostly he was occupied with keeping an eye on Old Gisli, or hovering several feet from wherever Birdie happened to alight. Keeping an eye on her too. I tried to get Birdie's attention, to see if maybe she would change her mind about taking me flying, but she was too busy talking to an old woman named Thora. It seemed Birdie didn't even see me. So I put my hands around her eyes from behind and shouted "Guess who?"

Birdie's coffee spilled on her lap and she screamed, *"Goddamnit!"*

The room fell silent.

"Frey!" My mother was across the room in an instant. "Frey, I told you to settle down. Oh, Birdie, I'm so sorry. Your fancy dress."

A large stain bloomed in the lap of Birdie's dress, a brown rose among the red.

"It doesn't matter," Birdie said.

"Oh, that's good of you to—"

"What matters, Anna, is that you insist on calling the child Frey."

My mother stared, mouth open.

"When her name is Freya! Not Frey. *Frey*—and you should know this, you *would* know this, if you remembered anything our father told us—*Frey* is one of the names for Freyr, who was a male god, a fertility god—"

"Ingibjorg," Sigga interrupted. "It's just a nickname."

Birdie stared at Sigga impatiently, then tossed her head. "Frey was a male fertility god," she repeated. "And you know what that means?" She paused and looked around the room, daring someone to answer. Everyone stared at the floor or into their coffee cups. Except Old Gisli. He was leaning forward on one of his troll-headed canes, studying Birdie intently through his rheumy eyes.

"You know what that means, Anna?" Birdie continued. "That means he had a giant phallus. So when you call her Frey instead of Freya, you're calling that darling child *a giant phallus!*"

"That's enough, Ingibjorg." It was Stefan, putting a firm hand on her shoulder. "Come in the kitchen and we'll get you cleaned up."

Birdie shrugged him off. "Oh, yes, you'll clean me up all right!" Then to my surprise—for she seemed hardly to have registered my presence—she suddenly pulled me onto her lap with one arm. I could feel the coffee stain from her dress spreading warm and wet onto my back, but I didn't move, sat stiff and silent while the guests began to leave, thanking my mother and Sigga in hushed voices at the door. Then Mama came and tried to lift me off Birdie's lap.

"That's right," Birdie said. "Poison her against me."

"I don't need to," Mama answered. "You'll do that yourself."

Birdie let go of me, but I held on to the arms of the chair, resisting

Mama's attempt to pry me off. My mother caught my eye. "Frey," she said. Then hesitated. *"Freya."* She turned and went into the bedroom she shared with Sigga, shutting the door behind her loudly. The closest my mother could come to a slam. The house was silent except for the muffled whooshing and clinking sounds of Sigga washing dishes in the kitchen. Around us in the empty parlor were cups still filled with coffee, half-eaten pieces of *vinarterta* abandoned on plates. The coffee spill on Birdie's dress was beginning to turn clammy against my back. Abruptly Birdie shoved me off her lap. "Go on," she said.

"I want to stay here with you."

She laughed, not her loud and raucous laugh but a defeated imitation of a laugh. "And why, little Freya, would you want to do that?"

What I wanted was to cheer her up, to change her back into the smiling, flitting Birdie of an hour ago. "I'm sorry I made you spill your coffee."

She rubbed my head but didn't speak. I noticed for the first time long creases on the sides of her mouth. The scent of gloom rose off her perfumed skin.

"Birdie?"

She didn't answer.

"Birdie?"

Nothing. If only I could fly already—that would distract her! Then it came to me: I would do a cartwheel, one of those feats of acrobatic magic performed by fourth-grade girls on the playground at recess. I loved to watch their legs sail through the air, skirts flying up, one leg following the other, making a perfect sideways-spinning wheel of flashing flesh and white ankle socks. That I had never actually done a cartwheel did not hinder my confidence for a second.

"Birdie, I can do a cartwheel!"

She nodded vacantly. No matter.

"Birdie, *look me!*"

Sugar-charged I sprang from my feet, the flats of my hands slapping the wooden floor, my legs flying upward, not in a neat arc but wobbling and flailing in a graceless handstand, then plummeting uncontrollably backwards over my head. *Splick-splack:* first one then the other of my sharp-heeled Mary Janes split the glass doors of Sigga's precious china cabinet. Side by side we crashed to the floor, me and the cabinet that had been Sigga's fancy wedding present—

I lay stunned in a pile of splintered wood and china fragments, the broken handle of a teacup curled around my pinkie. All Sigga's stories, smashed to bits. I closed my eyes.

"Oh my God," Birdie screamed. I kept my eyes closed. I heard the kitchen door burst open and then Sigga was leaning over me. "What hurts, child? Tell me what hurts."

Everything, nothing. I couldn't talk. Sigga was wiping a bloody cut on my forearm with a hankie when I heard my mother cry out "Lord, Frey!" I turned my head just in time to see Mama fall in a dead faint, twisting at the ankles, crumpling down. Then a loud *smack* as the back of her head hit the edge of the telephone table. *Thud* as she hit the floor.

Birdie reached her first. "Anna," she cried, gently shaking my mother's arm. *"Anna!"* But my mother didn't answer. She was dead.

Or so I believed. My mother was dead, and I was the one who had killed her. I began to sob. *Here comes Gryla,* I heard Old Gisli say. I closed my eyes, but it was too late, she'd appeared in my mind, her three heads bobbing hungrily, her six ears swaying, her dangling chin-teeth sharp and glistening.

5

The next thing I knew it was me and Birdie, alone in Gimli. Mama in the hospital in Winnipeg. Sigga staying at Vera's on Victor Street, spending her days at Mama's bedside even though Mama couldn't see or hear her. Or anyone. Or anything. It turned out Mama wasn't dead. But she was lying in a coma.

"You understand what a coma is?" Uncle Stefan asked. He'd come by to check on me and Birdie.

I nodded. I figured *coma* was just the Canadian way of saying *comma,* long *o* instead of short. I imagined my mother in a hospital bed curled on her side in the shape of a comma. What would happen if she curled all the way into a ball? Would she become a period? A period would be the full stop . . . but a comma was only a pause.

"Birdie said it's like sleeping. Except Mama might not ever wake up again."

"She said that to you?" He tapped the bowl of his pipe sharply against the ashtray and hot ash tumbled out. "That's crazy, to tell you a thing like that."

I wasn't sure what he meant. Was it a crazy thing to say—or just crazy to tell me?

The house with me and Birdie alone in it was very quiet, except when the phone rang out like an alarm, trilling its *r*'s just like an Icelander.

Brrrrrrrrrinnnnng! Brrrrrrrrrrinnnnng! Which sounded like *Bring! Bring! Bring Mama home.* When it rang Birdie and I would both jump up, anxious for and dreading news. Usually it was Sigga or Vera, providing Birdie with an update, or trying to convince her to bring me down to Winnipeg. Birdie would have none of it.

"We're fine here, Vera."

. . .

"I know you have plenty of room. But it's better for Freya here. She can play at the beach all day, take her mind off things. Water soothes the soul."

. . .

"Believe me, Vera, everything is under control. I can take perfectly good care of this child."

On the phone with Vera and Sigga, Birdie sounded cheery; as soon as she hung up she sank back into her gloom. We never went to the beach. In fact, we never left the house. Mostly I was on my own. At night I'd change into my nightie by myself and brush my teeth, but I was afraid to fall asleep. If I fell asleep I too might never wake up. Instead I kept myself awake listening to Birdie's word-rain. Birdie typed all night, then slept half the day. In the mornings I'd go downstairs and cut myself a slice of leftover *vinarterta* for breakfast. When Birdie finally woke up, she had little patience for me.

"I miss Mama."

"You should have thought of that before turning that cartwheel."

Other times, Birdie insisted it wasn't my fault. "It was that pesky *fylgja,* to be sure."

"What's a *fylgja?*"

"A *fylgja,*" Birdie explained, "is a follower. An attendant fetch. A spirit that's followed our family all the way from Iceland. Our *fylgja*'s responsible for a lot of mischief. If dishes break, you can be sure our *fylgja* is at hand. And an entire china cabinet?" Birdie shook her head in disbelief. "That is surely the *fylgja*'s work!"

I didn't believe her. I didn't doubt the *fylgja*'s existence, but I took all the blame for Mama's accident upon myself. I stopped asking Birdie for flying lessons; my wings no longer itched. I was the girl who put her mother in a coma: I no longer deserved to fly. If my mother died because of my cartwheel, would that make me a murderer? Would I get sent to jail?

"Don't be so hard on yourself, *elskan*." Birdie found me one afternoon crying on the landing.

I tried to speak between gasping sobs. "Is . . . Gryla . . . going to . . . eat me?"

Birdie let out one of her raucous laughs. "Child," she said, sitting down next to me on the stair, pulling my head onto her lap and stroking my hair. "It was an accident. It wasn't your fault. You're not a bad kid. There are much worse kids for Gryla to munch on. You want to hear about a bad kid? A really really bad kid?"

I felt a glimmer of hope. Children worse than me? I wiped my nose on the back of my hand and caught my breath.

"A long time ago," Birdie began, "there was a little boy named Egil Skallagrimsson."

"It's a fairy tale?" I felt disappointed.

"Not a fairy tale. Egil was real. His story is written in a book called *Egil's Saga,* which someday you will read for yourself. Egil is one of our ancestors, and he grew up to be a very famous poet in Iceland. But he lived a long long time ago. A thousand years ago! And he was the ugliest little boy you ever set eyes on. When he was only six years old, he murdered another boy. Split the child's head open with an ax. Then he bragged about it in a poem."

"Did he go to jail?"

"They didn't have jails in those days. If you committed a crime, you paid your victim or his family money for it. And if it was a really bad crime, you got exiled to the interior of the island, to wander the lava fields and glaciers, and battle trolls and ghosts. But Egil was too young to be exiled."

"So what happened to him?"

"Absolutely nothing. His mother was proud of him, in fact. She said he had the makings of a real Viking."

I thought about Egil a lot in the days that followed. Especially at night while I was trying to stay awake so I wouldn't fall into a coma. Why did Egil brag about killing someone? Why was his mother proud? My own mother, I was certain, would not be proud of me. If she lived. And if she died? Maybe

I wouldn't get sent to jail after all. Maybe instead I would be banished to the lava fields of Iceland, left to the mercy of gruesome trolls and raging ghosts.

On the third night Uncle Stefan came over with a whole whitefish, harbor-fresh, mashed potatoes, and green beans. It was the first real food I'd eaten since Mama's accident.

Birdie looked awful. She wasn't wearing any makeup. Her skin was pale, her eyes were red. "Haggard," she said, as she sat down at the dinner table. "I look haggard. An old hag."

"Nonsense," Uncle Stefan protested.

But Birdie ignored him. "I had one of my dreams," she said. "The night before it happened."

"Before what happened?"

Birdie looked at Stefan as if he were an idiot. "Before Anna fell. I dreamt that I was back on our old farm, and I was standing outside in the sheep pen—"

"But you didn't have sheep on the farm, Ingibjorg. Only cows."

"I know that! It's a *dream,* Stefan. So then who drives up but Anna. She opens the door to the car and steps out, and at the same moment, I open the door to the sheep pen. Then all the sheep come rushing out and trample her."

"Why?" I asked.

"There's no why in dreams, Freya." She turned back to Stefan. "So?"

"So what?"

"So, you have to admit, even a skeptic like yourself. That was a prophetic dream."

"You know what your father would have said about it, Ingibjorg? *Draum-skrok!*"

"What's *draumskrok*?" I asked. It was a hard word to pronounce with a mouthful of mashed potatoes.

"Dream nonsense," Stefan explained.

Birdie left the table in a huff.

Stefan and I cleared the dishes, then I sat with him in the parlor while he smoked his pipe. I thought maybe he was waiting for Birdie to come back downstairs, but he seemed content enough to sit there with me, side by side on the moss green couch. He asked if I would like to light his pipe, and then if I would blow out the match.

"You must be worried, *elskan,* about your mother."

I nodded, too choked to speak.

"I think she'll come out of this just fine." He draped his long arm around my shoulders and gave a squeeze. Even though he was skinny, his body felt solid, something I could lean against. I wondered if that's what a father might feel like.

That night I woke screaming in my sleep. A sheep was biting at my ankles with its rubbery black lips. Birdie heard me cry out and came to me from the next room. "A sheep dream?" she asked. I must have spoken in my sleep. I nodded.

"Oh, those sheep dreams can be awful. I know. But think about it, baby. Those sheep never hurt a soul."

During the week my mother was in the hospital, I woke at least once a night with bad dreams. I dreamt Amma Sigga fell out of my maple tree. I dreamt the ambulance men were piling broken cups onto stretchers and racing them out the door. If I woke screaming, Birdie would soon appear at my bedside. "I'm gonna wash that dream right out of your head," she'd sing, and scrub my scalp with her fingers like she was giving me a shampoo.

One night I dreamt that my mother was curled in a ball floating on the lake. I didn't call out. I woke up silent. I went across the hall to Birdie's room. She wasn't typing, for once. She was sitting on her bed, looking out the window. I stood next to her. We could see the full moon above the lake, its reflection floating on the surface. Birdie was crying. I knew why without asking.

"It's not your fault," I said, stroking her lank blond hair. "It was that *fylgja.*"

As each day passed that Mama didn't wake up, Birdie sank further into gloom. The house smelled close, days of dishes heaped in the sink. I'd been wearing the same clothes every day. I had no clean underwear. Who needs underwear? Gloom-Birdie said. I hadn't had a bath. I'd eaten no vegetables. Mama would not be happy. But Mama didn't know. Mama was sleeping.

Time passed slowly. I wandered the house, into the bedroom Mama had shared with Sigga. I opened her dresser drawers and took out each item—the simple cotton blouses, the knee-high stockings—and refolded them clumsily. I climbed into her bed and discovered underneath the pillow her nightgown with the embroidery across the chest. If her nightgown was here, then what was she wearing in the hospital? I wrapped the gown around Foxy so I could sleep with it at night. Tracing the embroidery with my fingers, I wondered if the doctors were trying hard enough to wake Mama up. Couldn't someone let loose a super scream into Mama's ear? Or jump up and down on her bed? Mama's best friend, Vera, told me on the phone that God would be the one to wake Mama up. I imagined him with his great white beard and a megaphone: *TIME TO WAKE UP! TIME TO WAKE UP!*

How could Mama eat and drink if she was sleeping all the time? Was she dreaming? Was she lonely? Did she miss me in her sleep?

"Mama tucks me in every night," I instructed Birdie. "Mama sings me the church songs. Mama tells me to brush my teeth."

"Mama does this," Birdie mimicked. "Mama does that."

Through the gaps in the lace curtains I caught sparkling glimpses of day. Sometimes Birdie got sick of my moping and ordered me to play in the yard. I'd stand on the lawn remembering like a dream teaching myself to spin back home in Connecticut. I couldn't imagine it anymore, whirling myself around, or even climbing a tree. My legs and arms felt heavy, my feet dragged when I walked. I lay down on my stomach and pressed my face into the grass. If Mama woke up again, would she still love me?

On the sixth day after my cartwheel, at 7:38 p.m., Mama woke up.

"Why did she wake up at night," I wanted to know, "instead of in the morning?"

Birdie stared at me in disbelief. "It doesn't matter *when,* silly. She woke up! She woke up!"

Birdie grabbed me by the hand and pulled me through the house. *"Anna's awake!"* she chanted. *"Anna's awake!"* I sang it too, but I couldn't bring myself to call my mother Anna. So Birdie sang "Anna's awake" and I sang "Mama's awake" at the same time. We ended up on the green couch, gasping for air. Then I ran to the front door. No sign. I sat down on the stoop. It was nearly nine o'clock, and the sunset still glowed behind the trees. I turned my head back and forth, up the street then down. Not a single car in motion, or person. Gimli was tucked in for the night.

"What are you doing?"

"Waiting for Mama."

It turned out Mama wasn't coming home that night, or the next night either. She would check out of the hospital tomorrow, then stay at Vera's for a few days while she regained her strength. But Sigga—Sigga would be home tomorrow night.

"And look at you. Pale as a ghost." For the first time since Mama's accident Birdie opened all the curtains in the house, and the windows. "Air," she proclaimed. "Air, and light, and water. Tomorrow we're going to the beach."

The lake was blue as the glass ink bottle Birdie kept on her windowsill, sheening with light, and so big you couldn't see the other side of it. It seemed more ocean than lake. The beach ran as far as I could see in either direction, wide and flat and filled with people. Family after family packed together on the sand. I could hear the high-pitched shrieks of kids and gulls.

"The mob has descended," Birdie proclaimed. "Summer's here, and all the city folk swarm to the lake at Gimli like lemmings to the sea. *Welcome to Gimli, home of the gods, your place in the sun!* You don't see them up here in winter, when the lake is covered with ice and the wind'll bite your nose right off." But she didn't seem to mind. In fact, she seemed happy again, fluttering down the beach in her floral jacket like a wild pink kite. We took off our shoes and the sand felt warm and rough on the skin of my virgin soles. I carried my sneakers with the laces tied together, twirling them in my hand. Birdie wove in and out among the people on their blankets, kids racing back and forth, women in swimsuits lying on beach chairs. I followed in her wake, struggling to keep up. Sometimes she waved a hand here or there, but she never stopped to chat. Finally she picked out a spot at the far end of the beach.

"Far from the madding crowds," she said. The crowds didn't seem mad to me, but I said nothing. I didn't want to wreck her mood; I'd seen by then what Birdie's moods could do. Birdie spread a plaid blanket on the sand, then held a towel around me while I changed into my blue checkered swimsuit. I thought of it then, for just an instant: my sailor cap. Birdie forgot my sailor cap.

Birdie lay down on the blanket and pulled a book out of her bag. "Go play, sweetie," she said. Instead I sat on the sand. Playing, like spinning, didn't feel right somehow. As if I wasn't a kid anymore.

"All right then," Birdie said. "How about a swim?"

I shook my head.

"Okay, scowly face, I'll go by myself." She stood up and slipped out of her jacket. Underneath she wore a two-piece bathing suit. I'd wanted a two-piece suit, but Mama said it wasn't proper attire. Then Birdie was off, kicking sand in a spray behind her, and without even stopping to test the temperature with her toe like my mother always did, she rushed straight in and dove her whole body under, headfirst. She disappeared for a long time. I got worried and ran down to the water's edge. Finally she popped up, far far out, and waved at me. I felt silly standing by myself on the shore, so I waded in a bit. The water felt like a slippery new skin covering my feet and legs. I gasped when it reached my crotch, then waded deeper until it licked my armpits. I held my arms in the air and shivered. Large white clouds hung in the sky and I thought of Birdie's dream, of Mama being trampled under the puff of sheep. I looked for Birdie, but she was gone, under.

"Birdie!" I screamed. A few seconds later she shot up behind me, shaking the water off her shoulders like a dog. "Do you like to float?"

"I'm not good at floating. I sink."

"Well if a giant like me can float I'm sure a little elf like you can too." She placed her hands on my back and told me to lean backwards. The beach dropped away, then blue sky, clouds, and sun tilted into view. The sun burned a yellow hole in my eyes, so I squinted them shut. Birdie held me with one hand at the base of my spine and one between my shoulders. I let myself rest solidly in her hands, the water lapping over my midriff. "Think air," Birdie said, and it worked, I started floating on my own, off her hands, for just a few seconds. The sun felt hot on my body and I seemed to be drifting, like it wasn't Birdie's hands anymore but the water itself bearing me up. Brightly colored shapes floated into my mind: fragments of broken cups. Mama curled into a comma on the water's surface. I snapped open my eyes and tried to stand, my legs churned frantically for the lake bottom, but I couldn't find it. Was I over my head? Then Birdie caught me by the waist and set me upright.

"You said you'd hold me!"

"I was right here," Birdie insisted. "I'm right here."

For lunch we ate peanut butter and jelly sandwiches cut into triangles and slurped orange juice from a red thermos. "Soon," Birdie predicted, "you'll be floating like a boat and swimming like a fish. Did you know Freyja was the daughter of a sea god?"

The Freyja comment caught me off guard. My father had been an accountant, not a sea god, so I knew she wasn't talking about me. "Freyja who?"

"Freyja *who*? Freyja *who*?" Birdie spat a mouthful of orange juice onto the sand. She put her sandwich down and turned her full attention to me. "The *goddess* Freyja, that's who! The goddess Freyja has no last name. Hasn't Anna told you anything about your namesake?"

I felt the same as when I'd admitted that I'd never eaten *ponnukokur,* as if I'd gotten my mother in a kind of trouble I couldn't quite fathom. "I know about Freyja. I just got confused is all."

"What, exactly, do you know about Freyja?"

It felt like a test and I couldn't think of anything. What had my mother told me? Freyja is a goddess. Gods and goddesses are powerful and people pray to them. I'd always imagined Freyja like Supergirl, flying over Iceland in a red-and-blue cape, tiny people far below on their knees gazing up at her, hands clasped in prayer. "She was super," I said.

"She was super all right!" Birdie seemed pleased. "Let me tell you a few things about Freyja. Would you like that?"

I would. I lay on my stomach, my pale skinny legs parallel to Birdie's long tan ones. When it got too hot we drifted down to the water and Birdie held me while I floated, but I never stopped listening, not for a moment. In those hours I forgot all about my crime.

"Freyja's father," Birdie began, "was none other than the sea god Njord, master of wind and waves. Her mother was the earth goddess Nerthus, and her brother was the fertility god Freyr."

"But what was Freyja the goddess of?" I asked. I was sitting up now, legs crossed Indian style on the edge of the blanket, sun hot on my shoulders while I funneled sand from one hand to another like an hourglass.

"Freyja," Birdie proclaimed, "was the goddess of many things. First of all, she was the goddess of love, it was Freyja people turned to for matters of the heart, and she was the goddess too of birth, often invoked when women went into labor. Freyja was also the goddess of magic, able to see into the future. It was Freyja who taught Odin himself the art of prophecy. Although gods and goddesses were not the only ones who had this power. A few humans did too, mostly women, and such a women was called a *volva*. The *volva* sat on a high platform, dressed in cat-skin clothing, because it was believed that cats would escort her to other worlds. The *volva* would close her eyes, her head would sway, sometimes she would wave her hands, or her magical staff—the word *volva* means wand-bearer—and then she was on her way, traveling to other worlds, to consult with the spirits and then return to her audience with news of the future. And who do you think it was that a *volva* would turn to for inspiration and guidance?"

"Freyja?"

"Indeed. And not only was Freyja a seer extraordinaire, she was a shape-shifter as well. She could turn herself into a bird and travel great distances, into other worlds, wearing a cloak of falcon feathers. She rode around heaven in a chariot pulled by wild cats, and on her neck she wore the Brising necklace, which everyone was always trying to steal from her because of its great power. Oh, some giant or other was always trying to carry her off, but Freyja called the shots when it came to men."

Birdie paused for a breath. I knew that behind her cat-eye sunglasses her eyes were large and spinning. "The trickster god Loki accused Freyja of sleeping with various elves and gods, including her brother, Freyr. And on the cusp of the conversion to Christianity a rogue Christian poet in Iceland referred to Freyja as a wild pig in heat, a she-goat bitch roaming the countryside. A blatant attempt to denigrate the fertility cults, which had a lot of staying power, let me tell you! Long after the so-called loyal followers of Thor and Odin traded them in for the one God almighty, pockets of Freyja worshipers continued on in sacred groves, until the Christians started calling them witches and their cats familiars, claiming they used their magic not only to predict harm but to cause it. Oh, blasphemy! But so it goes, when one religion gets taken over by the next, one god substituted for another. Fickle we are, fickle fickle fickle!"

By this time I was completely lost. *Fickle denigrate blasphemy rogue bitch.* It seemed Birdie had forgotten I was only seven, forgotten I was even there. Had Birdie said that Freyja was a witch? Witches were bad and I didn't want to be named after one. I lay down again, pressing my face into the sandy beach blanket, but out of the corner of my eye I watched Birdie talking, her hands gesturing in the air, her voice high-pitched and excited, the words so fast and strange I couldn't understand them at all anymore and soon they were swallowed up into a strange seashell roar deep in my eardrums. A cloud eased itself over the sun and I felt a shiver travel up between my shoulder blades. I sat up and my teeth began chattering, slamming jackhammers so loud it broke Birdie out of her trance.

"Baby, are you cold? How can you be cold?"

"I'm hot."

Birdie took off her sunglasses and stared at me. Her eyes were all pupil, holes of black with only a tiny perimeter of blue. "Oh my God," she said. "You're a lobster."

Hardly anyone was left on the beach. The last families were packing up, trudging back to their cottages. I couldn't walk; sand rubbing against the burned soles of my feet made me scream. So Birdie carried me piggyback, trading the beach bag back and forth between hands. "We forgot my sailor cap," I whispered in her ear. "Mama makes me wear my cap. Mama doesn't let me stay in the sun long. Mama puts lotion on me so I don't burn. Mama—"

"Enough *Mama*," Birdie snapped. "Mama isn't here. You're stuck with Birdie now, okay? And next time maybe you could think of telling me these things first? Because I don't know you, Freya. I've only known you a week. So help me out here. Don't keep secrets." Her words had sharp edges, like broken pieces of china and glass. I wanted to plug my ears but I couldn't because I had to hold on. I gripped the silver chain around Birdie's neck. Freyja had worn a necklace too. The *Brising* necklace.

"Let go," Birdie demanded as we climbed up the stairs to the front door of the house. "You're choking me!" Sigga's car was back in the driveway. Even though Birdie admitted nothing, I knew she was scared of what Sigga would do when she saw me. Where my chest pressed against Birdie's back I could feel her body trembling against mine.

Sigga dunked me in a tub full of water so cold I shrieked. I tried to squirm out, but she held me down, one broad wrinkled hand covering half my skinny chest. My chest and stomach were the only white parts. The rest of my skin was as red as a brand-new pair of Keds. "We have to break the fever, *elskan,*" Sigga said calmly. I stopped resisting then and lay my head back in an icy float. *Think air.* Then I was standing on the bath mat while she blotted me gently dry. She took Noxzema from the top shelf of the medicine cabinet. The jar was blue like the glass of the lake and the cream inside was white as cloud. She slathered it onto my body with long strokes until the fumes of menthol seared my nostrils.

Once during the night I woke to the sound of Birdie and Sigga arguing in hushed Icelandic whispers outside my door. The only word I understood was my name, repeated over and over. Then I heard a clatter of footsteps on the stairs, a slam of the front door, a few revs of the engine on her old VW Beetle, and Birdie was gone. When Sigga opened the door to my room I pretended to be asleep, but all night long I lay awake waiting for the sound of Birdie's footsteps on the stairs. Instead she arrived at dawn outside my window trailing a cloak of feathers. She gathered me up in her arms, still naked and covered in white cream, and flew me out the window and over the lake, holding me in front of her like an offering. Yet she seemed not even to be touching me, her palms barely making contact with my back, and then we were floating, up and away into the lightening sky, the feathers of her cloak soothing the burned surface of my skin.

6

The next morning Birdie was gone still. The sun shone onto her empty bed, unmade from the day before. Birdie didn't believe in the daily making of beds. But her desk she had cleared before she left. All the piles of paper— her *Word Meadow*—gone. Maybe she'd packed it into her suitcase. I stood in front of her full-length mirror in my nightie. Red face, neck, arms, legs against white cotton, a burning hot, striped candy cane. I heard a noise downstairs and my heart leapt—maybe Birdie had never left? Maybe she'd spent the night on the couch. But it was only Sigga alone in the kitchen making breakfast. The stove glistened silver, the sink gleamed white again, the cups and dishes that Birdie had piled up were now returned to their proper places.

"Good morning, *elskan*." The morning seemed anything but good. Behind her round glasses, Sigga's gray-blue eyes seemed like snowballs, hard-packed and icy. She set a bowl of oatmeal onto the table for me, thick with raisins and topped in brown sugar and cream. I leaned over to take a bite and yelped: the rising steam stung my sunburned cheeks. I began to cry.

"Whatever is the matter?" Sigga asked.

"Where did Birdie go?"

Sigga was silent a moment, lips taut. "Birdie took a little vacation."

Wasn't Gimli already a vacation? Why would Birdie need to go any-where else? I suspected Sigga of not telling me the truth. Was that the same as lying? Or maybe it was more like a game of pretend, a game I could play along with. "When is she coming back from her vacation?"

"Any day now." For an instant Sigga's eyes softened and I could see the blue of them again. But I wasn't hungry. Birdie had taken my appetite on vacation. I swirled my oatmeal with a spoon while Sigga stood at the sink scrubbing the pot.

"Do you believe in Freyja?"

"You mean the goddess?" Sigga turned from the sink, her yellow rubber gloves laced in suds. *"Elskan,"* she said. "Nobody believes in Freyja anymore. That was a long, long time ago. Now people only believe in one God. Or none at all."

If no one believed in Freyja anymore, could she still wear her bird cloak and fly to other worlds? Could she still frolic in the waves with her brother, Freyr, and their father, Njord? How many people needed to believe in her before she could fly again?

I believe in Freyja, I said. Only I said it to myself. Sigga turned back to the sink and I revisited my cereal, lifting large spoonfuls in the air, then tipping the spoon and watching the oatmeal slide glop by glop into the bowl.

The Sigga-days had a rhythm the Birdie-days had lacked. I was not allowed out in the midday sun until my burn healed. Afternoons Sigga and I walked down Second Street to the library, where she worked part-time. The Gimli library was called Evergreen, a small one-story brick building under a group of pines. If I got tired of being quiet in the library, I was allowed to sit outside but only under the shade of the trees, where the sun couldn't reach me. Sometimes I lay on my back staring up into branches the green of Mama's eyes. Or I made piles of fallen brown needles, then dashed them with sticks. Mostly I stayed inside, sitting at one of the long tables reading silently, or following Sigga as she returned books to the shelves. It seemed everyone who came in the library asked after Mama. Some of them Sigga introduced to me, but instead of curtsying I stared at the floor in sunburned shame.

In the evenings we walked down to Gimli harbor and watched the boats returning with tubs of fish still flipping and flopping, squirming and slimy, startle-eyed. "If fish can't shut their eyes, then how do they sleep?"

Now that Birdie was gone it was Sigga who put me to bed.

"Nightie time," she'd say. I liked it when she said that, because it could mean two things: *time to put on your nightie* and *time to say good night.*

"Would you like a story," Sigga asked, "or a rhyme, or a song?"

"A rhyme."

Tunglid, tunglid taktu mig . . . she began reciting.

When she was done I asked, "What does it mean?"

Moon, moon, take me up. Carry me up to the clouds. Because there sits my mother and cards raw wool . . .

My sunburn began to peel in large flakes off my skin and still Mama had not come back to Gimli. Every day it was *maybe tomorrow*. That's what Mama would tell me on the phone. She called each night after dinner from Vera's in Winnipeg. Sigga wouldn't let me talk long. Talking could wear Mama out. Every day it was *maybe tomorrow*, but when tomorrow came to its end Mama only called instead of coming. *I wasn't up to it today, Frey. I'm so sorry. Maybe tomorrow.*

So it was *maybe tomorrow* for Mama and *any day now* for Birdie.

The rule was not to mention Birdie's name while she was gone. But I knew Sigga was thinking about her. When Stefan came by, they talked about Birdie in whispered Icelandic—double secrecy—but I managed to figure out that Stefan was receiving phone calls from her. I decided that Birdie was not on vacation, she had run away from home. One night I dreamt she'd joined a circus. She stood on a platform in the middle of the ring, splendid in her cat-fur robe, glowing in the spotlight. People from the audience shouted out questions about the future. But there was only one question I wanted her to answer, and I was too afraid to ask. *When are you coming home?*

It was six long days after my mother uncurled from her comma that she finally returned to Gimli. I wore a dress but not the one I'd worn to the fateful coffee party. And I refused to put on the patent leather shoes that had cracked the china cabinet glass. I never wanted to wear them again. Instead I sat barefoot, peeling strips of dead skin off the soles of my feet. The rest of my body had turned from red to tan. My mother didn't know about the sunburn. Sigga said it would only worry her so I never mentioned it on the phone. I wanted to get all the dead skin off before she arrived. But some pieces would not come unstuck.

As soon as Mama stepped out of Vera's car I could see she was not the same Mama. Her face was pale and her wave was slow motion, fluttery and vague. I ran to hug her, but Vera held up her hand like a stop sign.

"Gentle, Freya. You have to be gentle with your mother now."

I stood in front of Mama and let her put her arms around me. "So golden," she said, stroking my face. "My little toasted marshmallow."

It turned out Mama's balance was off and she tipped over easily. Light gave her headaches so she wore sunglasses all the time, even inside the house. Like a movie star but pale and sad instead of tan and happy. A few times she got dizzy and grabbed on to my shoulder or a chair for support. She said it felt like a stirring inside her head. I imagined an eggbeater whipping her brains into froth. Most of that first day she sat in a brown armchair in the parlor staring out the window. I tried to get her to play Crazy Eights but she kept losing track of the game. I could keep her playing War if I turned over her cards for her. But that made it feel like solitaire.

Vera stayed for dinner and Stefan came too. It was a welcome-home meal for Mama of roast lamb with mint jelly, boiled potatoes, green beans slick with butter, doughy rolls hot from the oven. Vera and Sigga did most of the talking. Mama took small nibbling bites. I jiggled the mint jelly on my plate with a fork. I wanted to feel happy Mama was back, but it was hard to feel happy with this not-quite-Mama. I longed to see her spruce green eyes behind the sunglasses.

Sigga was serving saskatoon berry pie for dessert when we heard the front door open then slam shut. A moment later Birdie was standing in the doorway to the dining room.

"Greetings all!" she sang out. Then she saw Mama and stopped cold, taking in her wan face and dark glasses. "Anna?"

Mama cringed and gave a little wave.

Birdie was dressed in a brand-new outfit. It was the shortest skirt I'd ever seen, its magenta color nearly as shocking as its length. We all stared.

"It's the latest," Birdie announced. Her tights were pale lavender, her top a fringed tunic.

"Where on earth?" Sigga said finally.

"Not Gimli, you can be sure!" From the doorway Birdie lifted up a large shopping bag that said *Eaton's* in fancy letters on its sides. "You didn't think Crazy Aunt Birdie would return empty-handed?"

Like a miniskirted Santa, she made her way around the table, present-ing each of us with a gift. "Unwrapped," she apologized. "No time, no time!" She took a small white box out of the bag first. "For she who rules the roost!" Before Sigga could react, Birdie had pinned something to her dress: a silver and black brooch shaped like a crowing rooster. I thought Sigga might rip it off but she left it on, sitting stiffly with her hands folded in her lap.

Next to Stefan's plate Birdie placed a small statue of a dog. "For our ever-loyal Stefan. And for the sweetest sister a girl could have . . ." She pulled a box of chocolates from the bag and presented it to Mama, who reached for it with two trembling hands. "And our dear Vera." Birdie shook her head. "If only I'd known you'd be here! Nothing for you, I'm afraid."

Then it was my turn. Birdie stood behind my chair. I couldn't see her but I could hear her excited breathing. "Little Freya," she murmured. "Dar-ling girl." The next thing I knew she'd wrapped a scarf around my neck. It was light blue with a pattern of trapeze artists hanging from swings and clowns turning somersaults. I couldn't help but lift it in front of my eyes and marvel.

"Thank you, Auntie."

"Nothing but the best for our little gymnast," she crooned. And then, to my horror, she cried out in a high shrieking voice: *I can do a cartwheel! Birdie, look me!*

In that moment I felt my first hate.

It was Sigga who put me to bed that night because Mama didn't trust her-self on stairs. "Nightie time," she said wearily.

"Why did Birdie bring us presents if she's mad at us?"

"Birdie does things that are hard to understand."

"I thought when Mama woke up that meant she was fine."

"Give her time, *elskan*. She had a bad fall."

Then I was alone in the room. No story, no song, no rhyme. I reached under my pillow and found Mama's nightgown. Would she be looking for it? I couldn't bring myself to give it up. Tracing the embroidery with my fingers, I stared out the window into dark night. *Moon, moon, take me up . . . carry me up to the clouds . . . because there sits my mother . . .*

7

In the days that followed Mama's homecoming, Birdie was eager to make amends. It was a pattern I would soon learn to recognize: rages and denunciations, followed by disappearances, concluding with a chastened period of trying to unburn bridges. Respectful to Sigga, solicitous to my frail mother, and toward me—perhaps fearing she'd lost my affection for good—an excess of auntly attention. Since my mother felt unsteady on the stairs, Birdie took it upon herself to put me to bed each night, plying me with bedtime stories the way other aunts might dole out candy. I was a greedy audience. Tales from Birdie's childhood, Norse myths, ghost stories, and sagas—I devoured them all, then begged for more.

But there was one story I requested again and again. Birdie called it "The End of the World as Olafur Knew It," and she told it like this:

"The infant who would one day become the grandfather you'd never meet was born in a turf-roofed farmhouse in the East of Iceland with two teeth cutting through his gums.

"'Skaldagemlur!' cried his grandmother Ingibjorg, who was also the midwife."

"What's a midwife?" I interrupted.

"A woman who delivers babies. In Icelandic a midwife is called a *ljos-modir*, which means light-mother."

"Were you named after Ingibjorg the light-mother?"

"Indeed I was."

"Are you a light-mother too?"

"Me? No, I'm a word-mother. Now listen." She paused, then switched back into her story voice:

And so Ingibjorg lifted the newborn in the air and bared his upper lip so his exhausted mother could witness the tiny nubs: a baby skald. Infants born with teeth were called *skaldagemlur* and destined to become poets. Or so it was said, and so some believed.

The child Olafur was raised on a farm called Brekka, which sat at the bottom of a cliff so tall and sheer and gigantic it made Brekka look like a tiny dollhouse. In summer, tall grasses and wildflowers topped the turf roof; in winter, lids of snow. Brekka belonged to Olafur's uncle Pall, a farmer-poet, and Olafur's family lived there with him because they couldn't afford a farm of their own. Times were lean in Iceland, people scrambled just to stay alive, and in the summer the farmers worked so hard there was little time for poetry. Winter was another story.

Winter in Iceland, Freya *min,* was much longer and darker than here. Little work could be done outdoors—light was scant, the weather forbidding. Dark day after long dark day the Icelanders were trapped inside. How did they stand it? They read. Members of the household took turns reading out loud by the smoky glow of a lamp lit by whale oil: sagas and poetry and the Bible and newspapers and any books they could get their hands on. Books were passed farm to farm. The name for these evening readings was *kvoldvaka,* meaning evening-wake. In Iceland in winter, words took the place of light.

One night, after the evening reading, Pall took Olafur aside. He had taken a special interest in his nephew, who early on showed signs of the fate his grandmother had predicted for him. There was nothing Olafur loved more than the feel of a good rhyme, the words bouncing off each other like a pair of lambs butting heads in a bright green field. Like the Viking skald Egil Skallagrimsson, Olafur had composed his first poem at the age of three, and there was no stopping him after that. Nor did his uncle try, though he was careful to correct the boy's meter. Now, Pall had something else in mind.

"Do you know the poem *Voluspa?*"

"Of course I know it!" answered Olafur.

"Recite it."

Olafur could not.

"My boy, you can't say you know a poem until you learn it by heart. A true poet brands the words of the best poems into his mind. He breathes them in and out. He speaks them from memory, he can recite them in his sleep. *Voluspa* is our most ancient poem: it tells how the world began and how it will end. It was composed in the oral tradition, in pagan times before Icelanders knew how to write. I want you to learn it by heart."

"Isn't it very long?"

"Sixty-some verses. If you memorize one each day, you'll know the whole by Easter. Then you can surprise everyone with a recital during the evening reading."

The book was small enough to fit in one hand, to slip into a pocket, and Olafur decided to carry it with him everywhere. The spine was frayed at the top and bottom, exposing the yellowed binding, and the leather cover was worn soft as the underbelly of a newborn lamb.

"How could the pagans know how the world would end if it hadn't ended yet?"

"You know what *Voluspa* means?"

Olafur shook his head.

"It means Prophecy of the Volva. A *volva* was a woman who could see the future. It was she who looked back in time and told how the world began, then looked forward to foretell its end. But enough questions for now. Once you can recite for me the first verse without any mistakes, then you can ask more questions."

Over the next week Olafur memorized the first verses. He learned about the beginning of time, when there was no sand or sea or surging waves, no earth, no heaven, nothing but the vast chasm called *Ginnungagap*. When Olafur lay awake at night, the nothingness of *Ginnungagap* terrified him, impossible to envision. But standing outside on a day when the entire sky was the same shade of white-gray as the snow-covered valley, it was easier to conjure such nothingness, the earth forming itself from the body of a frost-giant.

The memorizing of *Voluspa* became Olafur's secret pleasure. He whispered whole verses to indifferent sheep and into the ears of the winter-furred horses. In bed at night he started from the beginning and went through the poem entire up to that day's verse. To keep himself awake he moved his lips, a light whisper he hoped the others would mistake for prayer.

Of course his favorite parts were the verses about *Ragnarok*, when the *volva* shifts into a deep trance and recounts for the god Odin the menacing events that would one day bring about the end of the world:

Arm-rings and necklaces, Odin, you gave me
To learn my lore, to learn my magic:
Wider and wider through all the worlds I see.

The *volva* goes on to predict that the ferocious Fenris Wolf will break its fetters and devour the sun, the fire giant Surtr will consume the wondrous world tree Yggdrasil, and the Midgard Serpent that has lain undersea tail in mouth, encircling the entire earth, will rise from the water, spewing poison and whipping up tidal waves of terror. All day long Olafur hears the haunting words as he goes about his chores, and at night as he tries to fall asleep.

Earth sinks in the sea, the Sun turns black,
Cast down from Heaven are the hot stars,
Fumes reek, into flames burst,
The sky itself is scorched with fire.

Is that the end, then, of everything? No, it is not, the *volva* says.

And Olafur now feels as if he himself were in a trance. It is Easter, and he is reciting, just as his uncle Pall promised he would, the *Voluspa* entire for his family during the evening reading. He is beginning the final section, reciting with great passion the *volva*'s vision of the world's rebirth:

I see Earth rising a second time
Out of the foam, fair and green:
Down from the fells, fish to capture
Wings the eagle; waters flow.

And finally little Olafur—he was just eleven at the time—comes to the end of the poem. He stands in the murky whale-light, in front of his entire family, and recites from memory (astonishingly, he has made no mistakes so far) the *volva's* last line, the end of the great poem:

"I sink now."

"But the *volva* was wrong, wasn't she?" Olafur asked his uncle Pall that night before bed.

"Wrong how?"

"The world never came to an end as she predicted."

"Not yet, my boy," Pall said with a wink. "Not yet."

It was the very next morning, the day after Easter 1875, that Olafur woke to the rain of ash, the obliterated sun and blackened sky. *"Ragnarok!"* he screamed, convinced the wolf had swallowed the sun. And who could blame him? What else was he to think? True, it was not the end of the world as the *volva* foresaw it so many centuries ago. But it was certainly the end of the world as Olafur knew it. The volcano Askja's ashfall poisoned the entire East of Iceland in a wide swath all the way to the coast. A year later, Olafur and his mother and father and brothers were on a ship bound for a New Iceland in Canada.

"Did Uncle Pall go too?" I asked Birdie.

"He stayed behind," Birdie said sadly. "Olafur never saw his uncle Pall again. But he wrote him many letters over the years, and mailed him the poems he began composing in New Iceland. But that's another story altogether."

Wider and wider through all the worlds I see . . . That first summer in Gimli I began to think of Birdie as a kind of *volva* when she told me bedtime stories, an enchantress folding me into her wings with words, soaring us far from the scene of my cartwheel crime. I loved her for that.

8

Pardon me, Cousin. The Olafur story was a diversion, then and now, distracting me from my mother's fall. The truth is I've been dreading this next part. About how Mama never got much better again, never uncurled completely from the comma. The doctors said the symptoms might go away in time, or not. In Mama's case it was not.

Vertigo was one symptom. *Ver-ti-go.* I couldn't help loving saying that word. What it was and what it did I hated. It was that eggbeater inside Mama's head making her feel like she was a lawn-spinning two-year-old—when she was standing still. She had to walk with a cane to keep her balance. For the rest of her life, she walked with a cane. Different canes. She was always losing them. She'd prop one up in the soup aisle at the supermarket deciding between Campbell's Chicken Noodle and Campbell's Chicken with Rice, and then she'd walk out of the store without the cane. By the time she discovered it was gone, she couldn't remember where she'd left it.

And her blond hair turned white, in just two months. She didn't seem to notice, but I did. Back in Connecticut, kids at school thought she was my grandmother. And I let them.

Plus she stopped reading. She could still understand the words, but the movement of her eyes on the page, scanning back and forth and back and forth, brought on the vertigo. When we returned to Connecticut, she had to give up her job as a copy editor. For a while she didn't work at all. She just sat home handcrafting. Then she started selling her pieces at a couple of boutiques in town. Hand-knitted Icelandic sweaters and scarves and caps and slipper-socks that go halfway to your knees, made from real Icelandic wool she ordered from Iceland. Scratchy, yes, but warm enough to keep a sheep through a long Icelandic winter. People bought it up. That's what we lived on: sweater money, and my father's life insurance and pension.

It meant Mama couldn't read to me at night anymore. It meant I read to her instead.

Light became a bad thing. Migraines. In Connecticut we pulled the venetian blinds down to the sills and tilted the slats so no light could get in, and at Oddi in Gimli, Mama sewed heavy curtains for the parlor windows that matched the moss green couch. And whenever she went out in Gimli or Connecticut or anywhere else she had to wear sunglasses, even if it was cloudy, even if it was raining.

Even snow. Especially snow.

Worst was how she stayed curled in on herself. I'd have to call her name three times—*Mama. Mama. Mama!*—before she'd answer. She had a distracted look, like a person always on the verge of remembering a dream that keeps slipping away. She'd forget stuff a lot. Her keys, where she parked the car in the supermarket parking lot, what day it was. I had to remember things for her. I kept track of her for her. When we left the house, I checked her purse: sunglasses keys wallet Kleenex brush. Sunglasses keys wallet Kleenex brush.

About the accident itself Mama remembered zero. Sigga said that was best. Let her think she slipped and fell. (And not that I turned a cartwheel in the parlor at her welcome-home-to-Gimli party and smashed the china cabinet and she found me lying in a pile of broken glass and shards of china and fainted and cracked her head on the way down.) *Slipped and fell,* Mama would say if she had to explain the accident to someone.

I hated to hear Mama lie like that, even though she didn't know it was a lie.

Sigga said it was best for Mama not to know, but I believed Sigga thought I was the one it was best for. Because if Mama knew it was my fault she broke her head, she might decide to never talk to me again. She might not want me for a daughter anymore. In the back of my mind lurked the worry that Mama might remember, that one morning she might wake up with her pillow-mussed hair and sleep-sanded eyes and that dream-remembering look on her face. *Cartwheel . . .* she'd say, rubbing her eyes with the heels of her hands. *Crash . . . ?* And then her eyes would sharpen to hard points and she'd say, *It was you, Frey. You did this to me.*

I had to prepare for that day by being good. Gooder than good. So even if she did remember, she might decide to keep me anyway. That's why I took such good care of her, acting like a mother even though I was the child. Draping cold washcloths over her eyes during migraines. Running all over town looking for lost canes. I told myself it was because I loved her, but inside I knew it was because I wanted her to keep me.

Sometimes all the not-telling-Mama piled up inside me. Sometimes I thought I might burst the truth. Say *It was me.* And have her pull me on her lap and stroke my hair and gaze at me with her spruce green eyes and say, *It doesn't matter, elskan, I'll always love you anyway.* But what if she didn't? So I kept it secret. And blamed myself double, to make up for Mama not knowing.

No, she never found out. And so I never got punished for my crime. That's why I had to get busy and punish myself, so I would never do anything that bad ever again. In those first few weeks after Mama got back from the hospital, I would sit quietly with her in the parlor in the daytime with the drapes pulled and figure out my punishment. I considered my options. Like *Never speak again,* which only lasted halfway through breakfast until Sigga said, *Enough of that nonsense, child.* Another one I tried was *Never smile again,* but Mama kept wanting to know if I was sad over and over until I got so sad I almost started crying. Then she tickled me and I rolled off the couch giggling. It wasn't until I was at the beach one day with Birdie that I figured out the perfect punishment. Birdie was trying to read and I kept asking her to tell me a story about Freyja the goddess or Egil the poet or anyone but me. Finally she looked up from her book to a group of kids playing catch with a blue-and-yellow beach ball, and three girls racing in the sand, and a girl and a boy doing handstands, and she said, "Go play. Go play, damn it, like a regular kid."

Never play again!

It made perfect sense: Only children played. And I'd done something so bad I didn't deserve to be a child anymore. So I would be a not-kid and not-play with other kids. At school back in Connecticut during recess, I would stand on the edge of the playground and not-play jump rope and not-play tetherball and not-play hand-slapping rhyming games like Miss Mary Mack Mack Mack. In Gimli summers it meant that I didn't race girls or even boys on the beach even though I was a long-legged egret and could have beat most of them. Or build rafts out of driftwood and pretend to be Indians canoeing. I could watch other kids doing those things, but I couldn't do them myself. Even if they asked me. Which they stopped doing pretty quickly.

No thanks. I don't like to play.

You don't like to *play*?

You'd think someone would have noticed that I wasn't being myself, but the thing is no one in Gimli really knew me. I'd only been there one day before the accident. Only Mama knew the old me, but she wasn't herself anymore either. There was the Before-Mama and the After-Mama. The Before-Freya and the After-Freya. There was Before and there was After.

Even Mama's eyes seemed to change, from crisp spruce green to the fuzzy color of an algae-choked pond.

After Birdie ran away and came back bearing meanie-gifts, she shaped up for the rest of the summer. That's what Sigga told her to do, and Sigga was the only one with any influence over Birdie. It was the day after Mama got home from Winnipeg, and Sigga was sitting at the kitchen table packaging all the meanie-gifts to send back to Eaton's department store. The silver-and-black rooster pin *for she who rules the roost*. The miniature dog statue *for our ever-loyal Stefan*. And the beautiful silk acrobat scarf *for our little gymnast*. (The chocolates *for the sweetest sister a girl could have* Birdie devoured herself. I found the wrappers under her bed.) I was standing behind the kitchen door peeking through a crack. Birdie was sitting across from Sigga with her elbows on the table and her forehead pressed into her hands. After she was done repackaging, Sigga put all the gifts into a cardboard box and taped it up. That's when she said it. "You either shape up, Ingibjorg. Or you ship out."

Birdie said nothing, didn't even lift her head out of her hands, but I guess she was listening because she hardly fought with anyone again for the rest of that summer, not even Mama, not even once. Which was nice except it turned out she was saving it all up for our last day. Somehow Birdie got it into her head that Mama and I would leave at the end of the summer and never return to Gimli again. All summer long Birdie would ask Mama if we were definitely coming back the next summer. Mama would just nod her head vaguely yes or shake it vaguely no or say *We'll cross that bridge when we come to it*. Which I didn't understand because I hadn't seen any bridges on the way to Gimli.

On the last day of my first Gimli summer, Stefan drove up early in the morning in his Rambler station wagon to drive us to the Winnipeg train station. Just as he was loading my cherry red suitcase, Birdie came running out of the house in her negligee wailing. Sigga tried to hold her back, but she wasn't strong enough. Birdie ran after us as the car rolled down the driveway, sobbing and banging her hands on Mama's window until Mama said, "Stefan, stop the car." I was sitting in the backseat. Mama rolled her window down and said in an unusually definite voice, "We'll come back to you next summer, Birdie. I promise."

And we did. We went back every summer until the year when there wasn't a Birdie to come back to anymore.

By now all those summers have blended in my mind. What took place when I couldn't tell you. It's just one long Gimli summer. Until the last one. Which strictly speaking doesn't even count as a Gimli summer.

I'm getting ahead of myself.

A typical Gimli summer day? Okay. That's a good idea. I'll take you through a typical day if you promise to remember that nothing was ever typical. Not where Birdie is concerned.

9

Sometime after the accident Mama began spending the bright mornings of our Gimli summers at Betel, the old folks' home for Icelanders (founded by the Great Dr. Gudmundsson, father of Mama's best friend and Birdie's archenemy, Vera). Keeping company with the old folks. Every morning before the sun got too high I would walk Mama over to Betel. Sand is uneven and not good for canes, so instead of taking the beach we went straight across on Second Avenue, past the cottages brimming over with families and visiting relatives. Mama knew most of the cottagers and stopped to talk to anyone we ran into. Betty Vigfusson, who made the best *ponnukokur* my mother had ever tasted but don't tell your *amma* Sigga that. The elderly Brandson sisters, who shook their heads sadly from their front porch at the sight of my poor tragic mother, a widow, and then that terrible accident and now look at her, old before her time and raising that child all by herself in the States—then waved at us with their tremulous hands. And the Arnasons, who had a little girl exactly my age and didn't I want to come over and play with her? Just once?

Five blocks with my mother on a Gimli morning walking cane-paced and stopping to chat with every single person we encountered could easily suck an hour from a summer's day. While Mama chatted I would hopscotch in place and count leaves in Betty Vigfusson's elm or stare into the sky shaping clouds into palaces. By the time we got to Betel, I felt like I might explode from impatience. But inside Betel, inside Betel made our walk down Second Avenue seem like a speed-of-light sprint to Mars. Inside Betel everything took place in the slowest motion possible. First I'd open the front door for Mama and we'd stand in the entranceway while her eyes adjusted. Betel was redbrick exterior, dark wood interior, and in the summer the shades were drawn to keep it cool because, as Mama said, old people can't abide heat. Which meant Betel was dark inside the way Mama liked for and needed it to be. Still her eyes behind the sunglasses required a moment to adjust. As we passed the portrait of Vera's father, the Great Dr. Gudmundsson, Founder of Betel, Mama would say, "Bless that man for his good works." Every morning Mama said *Bless that man for his good works.*

Then we would stop by Mrs. Thompson's office. Mrs. Thompson was the Matron of Betel, and she held a special place in her heart for Mama. "The good your mother does cannot be underestimated," she would say to me, often and reprovingly. Mrs. Thompson did not hold a special place in her heart for me. I was convinced she knew about my crime and held it against me. If I was running an errand for Mama or one of the old people, fetching a book or a knitting bag, and I saw Mrs. Thompson coming, I'd slink back against the wall, but she always saw me. She'd sink a bony claw into my shoulder and say, "Your mother has suffered a tragic accident that will likely debilitate her for the rest of her life. Do you understand that?"

I did.

Mostly everyone at Betel was nice to me. Mostly they doted on me and said what a well-behaved and grown-up little girl I was. Which made Mama happy because no one had ever said anything like that about me before. Which made me happy because it meant my punishment was working.

Mama and I would settle into the downstairs common room and pretty soon the old ladies would come sit with us. Runa and Thora, Gudbjorg with the three chins, and sometimes Margret hobbling along on her walker. And others, depending on who was feeling well that morning or who was alive that summer and hadn't died during the winter when we were back in Connecticut. All morning long Mama and the old women knitted things to sell through the Lutheran Ladies Aid to raise money for Betel, and while they knitted they talked, sometimes in Icelandic, sometimes English, depending on who was in the room and what was being said. Runa and Gudbjorg liked to talk about dreams. Not just their own dreams but dreams people they knew had dreamt and even stories about dreams people had dreamt back in Iceland. Dreams that came true. Like a woman named Agusta dreamt that three moons fell into Lake Winnipeg and that summer three men died in fishing accidents. Once while Mama was in the bathroom I told the old women about the dream Birdie had the night before Mama's accident, where Birdie was back at their old farm in Arborg and they had sheep instead of cows and Mama pulled up in a car and got out and the sheep trampled her. Runa nodded seriously and said Birdie had the dreaming gift. Thora shook her head and said, *En er petta ekki skritid? But is this not strange?* Which meant yes, things are strange. (Mama agreed with Stefan that dream-talk was *draumskrok*—dream nonsense—but I believed in it. I had lots of dreams myself. And nightmares. My good dreams I told to Mama and Sigga at the breakfast table, but the nightmares I saved for Birdie when she heard me cry out in the middle of the night. Birdie knew all my nightmares.)

Mama tried to teach me to knit, but all I produced were tangled messes.

There were old men at Betel too, squinting seriously at the chess board from behind their thick glasses. It was a slow-motion game where maybe you moved one piece an hour.

Every once in a while one of the old people would try to send me out to play. *Betel is no place for a little girl on a summer morning.* I knew they were right. Sometimes it felt like I couldn't breathe inside Betel, but I figured it was part of my punishment. What better way to be a not-kid than to spend my time with people in their eighties and nineties? Some lived to be over a hundred. Every July we celebrated Runa's birthday and every July she said it would be her last but it never was. She turned 100 my first summer and then 101, 102, 103, 104, 105, 106. Maybe 107, but I can't say because after Birdie died we stopped going to Gimli. An old man named Siggi said Icelanders lived a long time because they ate so much cod. Some of the men chewed on *hardfiskur* while they played chess. I tried it once and spat it out. It was stringy and salty. But I guess it was worth it if you wanted to live to be 100.

Birdie didn't like Mama taking me to Betel with her. "How dreary, Anna."

"Someone needs to visit Our Old People," Mama insisted. "It makes them so happy, to see a child. And Freya likes to go, don't you?"

I said yes even though I hated it. What I hated most was not how slowly everyone moved or how boring it was just sitting and knitting and moving one chess piece an hour. It was seeing Mama there with all those old people. Mama was in her early fifties then, but she could have passed for nearly seventy with her white hair and her cane. I'd almost lost Mama once. I didn't want to see her growing old before her time.

All this, while Birdie was sleeping. If she wasn't up by the time Mama and I came home from Betel for lunch, it was my job to wake her. Carefully. Once Birdie was up, who knew how the day would go?

After lunch Mama napped, which Sigga explained was another side effect of her head injury. Sometimes she'd even fall asleep sitting up at the kitchen table with her sandwich half-eaten, and Sigga and Birdie would have to move her. Each afternoon she slept for hours and hours, so deeply that you had to shake her shoulders to wake her. It scared me when she slept like that. I was afraid she might curl back into her comma.

While Mama napped Sigga went to her part-time job at the library. And me, I was all Birdie's from then on. If she would have me.

A horse is *hestur*. Unless you're riding it or hitting it or even just looking at it, in which case it's no longer *hestur* but simply *hest*. Take something *from* a horse and suddenly it spells itself *hesti*. Walk over *to* it, presto change-o you're looking at *hests*. Same horse, many spellings. A horse is a horse of course of course . . . unless it's an Icelandic horse. Icelandic words are tricksters. Acrobats. Masters of disguise. Shape-shifters.

And don't go thinking that if one horse is *hestur* more than one would be *hesturs*. Ha! Icelandic is too tricky for that. Horses in plural are *hestar,* unless you're talking *about* them, in which case they're *hesta*. Sit *near* them and you've got to start calling them *hestum*. Bring some hay *to* them, they turn back into *hesta*.

And that's just if they're horses in general. *The* horse in particular is *hesturinn*. (You attach the *the* to the back of the horse like a tail.) But try to pet the horse, it's *hestinn*. Take something from the horse, it's *hestinum*. Bring water to the horse, it's *hestsins*. Once there's more than one particular horse, you've got *hestarnir*. But watch out: touch them, brush them, look at them, say anything about them, even one word, they turn into *hestana*. Stand opposite the horses and you've got yourself *hestunum*. Bring 'em some water and abracadabra they're *hestanna*.

"Do you see?" Birdie demanded. We were working our way through *The Primer of Modern Icelandic* by Snaebjorn Jonsson, Sometime Translator to the Icelandic Government, published Reykjavik 1927.

I could see why most people spoke English. Icelandic was clearly a lot of trouble. I'd never even been on a horse. And that's just one way to decline a noun. Nouns in Icelandic can decline in nearly 200 different patterns. And then there are adjectives. One single adjective can have 144 variations, depending. Numbers shape-shift too, and even personal names decline. You can say Guttormur Guttormsson was a great poet. But if you said a poem was written *by* him, you'd have to call him Guttormi Guttormssyni.

Only Icelandic adverbs are spared these gymnastics. As Snaebjorn stated in his primer, "Adverbs are indeclinable and do not suffer any change." I had a fondness for Icelandic adverbs. I too preferred not to suffer change.

An hour a day after lunch Birdie and I had our lessons. Sigga approved. Mama didn't disapprove, exactly. She said, "Don't you think it's a bit much for a little girl?"

"The older she gets the harder it'll be for her to learn," Birdie insisted. "A child's brain at this age is a sponge for language."

"If you say so." Despite the fact that Mama questioned everything Birdie did, especially where I was concerned, in the end she usually let Birdie have her way. At the time I figured Mama felt sorry for Birdie because Birdie was childless. Now I wonder if Mama knew about you, the child Birdie gave away. She must have.

I wanted to learn Icelandic, I truly did. Icelandic was the language of secrets. Icelandic was a code I'd been unable to crack, no matter how much or how hard I listened. I believed that if I could learn Icelandic I would understand all the things about the world that I didn't understand yet. I worked hard—Sigga and Mama and Birdie all agreed I was very *dugleg*—but I guess my brain wasn't spongy enough because I could hardly manage to construct a single correct sentence in Icelandic. Even a simple sentence like *I caught one big fish*. Because by the time you figure out whether if you catch a fish it's *fiskur* or *fisk* or *fiski* and whether *fish* is male or female or neuter-neither (in order to know whether *one* should be *einn* or *ein* or *eitt*, or maybe *einum* or *einni* or *einu*), there were still all the different versions of *big* to choose from (*stor* or *stort* or *storan* or *storum* or *storri* or *storu* or *storrar* or *stors*), and by that time, the one big fish got away.

That was *malfraedi* (mowl-fry-thee). Like *vertigo,* it was a word I loved to pronounce while hating what it meant. *Mal* is language and *fraedi* is study of, so *mal* plus *fraedi* equals *grammar. Malfraedi* made me bite my lip until it was bloody, so pretty quickly Birdie would move me on to *aefingar* (eye-vin-gar). Exercises. Some *aefingar* were English that you had to make Icelandic, and some were Icelandic you turned into English, but no matter which way I translated them, they never made sense. Looking back on it now (and I've got my copy of Snaebjorn's *Primer* right here on my lap), I can see why. The individual sentences may have been correct, but Snaebjorn's paragraphs defied all sense. Take *Aefingar* 25:

> *After all this time we are still here. I am going to walk round the lake; I wanted to walk up the mountain slope, but it was too steep for me. The maids saw it through the key-hole. I put the flowers in the windows and the plates on the table. The beautiful poem "Locksley Hall" is by Tennyson. You have never been kind to me. Now come with me across the river. Bring the knives and forks, please. I pay nothing beyond what was agreed to. It is raining on the new white tents. Let us see you run round the table.*

What was Snaebjorn thinking?
So much for *malfraedi.* So much for *aefingar.*
All this, while Mama was napping.

Once in a burst of frustration I blurted out the unthinkable. "But *why* do I have to learn Icelandic?"

"*Why?*" Birdie paused, stunned. "Because our language connects us as surely to our ancestors as our blood. Once you learn Icelandic you'll be able to read the Sagas and the ancient poems in the original, even though they were written nearly a thousand years ago. Our language is pure, Freya *min.* Can the English read their *Beowulf* untranslated? They cannot!"

I must have looked less than eager to delve into centuries-old Icelandic manuscripts, because Birdie added, "Plus, you'll need to know Icelandic when I take you to Iceland."

"You're taking me to Iceland?"

"Indeed I am. Someday we'll go to Iceland, *elskan,* just you and me."

I was not inclined to believe her. Hadn't she once promised to take me flying?

Sometimes instead of Icelandic lessons in the afternoon Birdie took me to the beach. Once we even went in the morning. It was the day Birdie and I were the very first people on the lake. First to make our marks on the sand slated clean by night rain, tempting as a fresh sheet of manila paper awaiting crayon. My small footprints premiered, the half-moons of my heels, the five astonished dots of my toes. The lake flat and sleepy, the sky a blue so soft I wanted to lay my cheek on it like felt. I'd never seen the lake so early. I wasn't allowed there by myself because I could drown, and by the time Birdie woke each day and we packed a lunch and changed into our suits, it was the other side of noon, no patch of sand unchurned by running kid-steps and mother-size footprints dragging beach chairs and umbrellas, the whole thing a sprawl of towels, shovels, beach balls, buckets.

This day was different. Birdie had been up all night—I'd heard the sound of typewriter keys splattering deep in the night like rain. She'd typed straight into dawn and then tiptoed across the hall into my bedroom and whispered, *Come, elskan, we're going to watch the sunrise.* I said *No,* I didn't want to, cranky with broken sleep, shivering in my nightie, hating Birdie for dragging me down the stairs, shooshing me past the bedroom where my grandmother and mother lay sleeping, through the kitchen, and out the back door along the two blocks to the beach and no sun to be seen. Just a cool darkness fringed pink. Birdie led me to the edge of the shore and took my hand. I jerked it away, scuffed my feet in the hard cold sand.

And then it began, not my first sunrise, but the first I had witnessed with my own bare eyes: a small lump of ember on the far eastern rim of the lake spilling its sly orange grin over pale water. I grabbed back Birdie's hand, the squeeze between us a pulse of light. Then Birdie spread a plaid blanket onto the sand and the next thing I knew she was sleeping, her head a blond mess nested in the crook of her elbows. And I was alone with the ember-risen sun, the sand flat and perfect as a just-made bed.

Unattended, my mother would have said, if she'd known.

On afternoons when Birdie wanted nothing to do with me, when she locked herself in Olafur's study to work on her *Word Meadow* poem, or took off on one of her shopping sprees, or during those days or even weeks when who knew where she was or when she was coming back to Gimli, if ever, I helped Sigga at the Evergreen library. Sigga was the Head Librarian, elderly but vigorous. When I was with Sigga in the library, the world became, briefly, orderly and safe.

"Is it true Icelanders cared more about their books than their babies and that's why they brought so many books with them from Iceland but left so many of their babies behind?"

"Of course it's not true." Sigga pushed her glasses up the bridge of her nose indignantly. "Infants couldn't survive the journey to America, and in those cases the parents left them behind to be raised by relatives."

"What happened to them?"

"Nothing happened to them. They grew up in Iceland is all."

"But the Icelanders did bring a lot of books with them?"

"They surely did. What else did they own worth bringing? Nothing. Most of them were destitute. But you know the saying, *Blindur er boklaus madur*—Blind is the bookless man. Who told you that nonsense anyway?"

"I don't remember." It was Birdie, of course. I hadn't known if she was joking or not about the babies. About the books the evidence was clear: the Gimli library was full of books that had come over in immigrant trunks. When the old people died, their children would donate the books to the library, since most couldn't read Icelandic themselves.

"When you came to Canada, did you bring your books in trunks?"

"No, I shipped mine later. But that was different. I came in 1920. I had a place to come to. When the first Icelanders arrived in the 1870s, they didn't have anyone to ship anything ahead to. They hardly knew where they'd end up. Besides, I thought I was only visiting for a summer."

"Where did you stay when you came?"

"With your *afi* Olafur. In Arborg."

"Even though he wasn't your husband yet?"

"No, he wasn't. But he took in all sorts of visitors from Iceland. He welcomed anyone. As long as they were willing to work his farm!"

"And then your books arrived?"

"A year later they did. They came by the slow boat. By that time Olafur and I were engaged to be married. Imagine the scandal—he was thirty years older than me! Eight sets of shelves he had to build, to hold all our books."

Gimli's library had new books as well, in English and even some in French, but the old Icelandic ones were my favorites. Sometimes I couldn't help wondering as I ran my fingers along their crinkled leather spines if maybe a particularly heavy book had taken the place on the ship of a baby who grew up in Iceland never knowing its parents.

In the late afternoon came Coffee. Except coffee was for grown-ups, so I drank milk. In Gimli milk still came in bottles from cows that lived in places like Arborg and Geysir and Hnausa. Sigga baked the sweets we ate for Coffee, using the cookbook published by the Ladies Aid of the First Lutheran Church, Victor Street, Winnipeg, 1937 edition. There was a new volume every couple of years, but Sigga swore by the 1937 edition. The cookbook had a soft green cover that was worn and torn and creased and stained, but Sigga said it had held up pretty well considering. It had four different recipes for *ponnukokur*, but Mrs. B. B. Jonsson's was the best. There were two recipes for *vinarterta;* Mrs. B. J. Brandson's was best. Especially if you added an extra egg. Mostly Sigga baked cookies, like gingersnaps (two recipes, Mrs. Peterson's best), or Pearl Palmason's Thimble Cookies, which meant I got to roll the dough into balls and press the centers in with a thimble and fill them with jam. For visitors Sigga wanted to impress, like Mama's dear friend Vera, who ran the Ladies Aid of the First Lutheran Church singlehandedly, we made layer cakes, sometimes with frosting and sometimes icing. My favorite recipes were Frosting for Featherweight Cake and Celestial Icing. The Ladies Aid cookbook even had recipes from people who weren't Icelandic, like Scotch Crumpets from Mrs. J. Campbell. Sigga said there were lots of Scots in Winnipeg. At the back of the book was a page of Household Hints. *Heat clothespins in oven in cold weather and they will retain sufficient warmth to keep the fingers comfortable while hanging out the clothes on a cold day.*

For coffee cups we used what Birdie called the Lucky Dozen: the ones I'd picked out on the day of Mama's welcome-home-to-Gimli party. Those twelve were the sole survivors, the only ones not inside the cabinet when I kicked it over. The first time we had Coffee after Mama came back from the hospital she noticed that the china cabinet was nearly empty. Stefan had replaced the glass, but three of the four shelves were bare.

"What happened to your beautiful cups?" she asked Sigga.

I froze. I didn't know yet that Mama couldn't remember anything about her accident. I felt my cheeks burn and I stared at my sneakers. For a long time no one said anything. Then Sigga explained that she was getting klutzy in her old age, what with her arthritic fingers and all, and if she kept it up there would be no cups left.

I adored the Lucky Dozen, with their dainty feet and gold-lipped rims. I wanted to be the one to set them out for Coffee, but Sigga said no. She never let me near that china cabinet again.

Coffee was served in the parlor. "It's like a morgue in here," Birdie complained after Mama put up her special heavy drapes.

"I'm sorry," Mama said. "It's my eyes."

"You have nothing to be sorry about, *elskan*." Sigga touched Mama's head.

Sometimes it was just us for Coffee, but often we had visitors, like the Arnasons with their little girl exactly my age. Her name was Nancy and she always had a doll or two tucked under her arm. Did I want to play dolls? I did not. Or the elderly Brandson sisters with trembling coffee-spilling fingers. On weekends Vera came; Birdie never came to Coffee on the Vera days. Best was when Stefan appeared with his grandfather Old Gisli, who walked with the two troll-headed canes. He was the one who had entertained me with Gryla poems at Mama's welcome-home-to-Gimli party.

"Here comes Gryla . . ." he would tease me when he walked in the door. I sat on his lap while he taught me funny verses line by line, first in Icelandic, then in a rough English translation. His knee was bony, but I didn't mind. I

was especially thrilled by the *lygirimur*—lying rhymes—nonsense poems brought over from Iceland.

> *I have seen the cat sing from a book,*
> *The seal spin flax on a spinning wheel,*
> *The skate curry a hide for a pair of breeches,*
> *And the skua knit a sock of yarn.*

I soon surprised everyone by reciting entire lying rhymes from memory, in Icelandic. Despite my failures at grammar, it turned out I had a good ear for pronunciation and a talent for what Gisli called *leggja a minnid*—laying things in my memory. Gisli taught me other verses too, verses he'd composed himself and others that had been circulating through the community for years, verses about topics lofty and mundane: scathing caricatures of locals, satires of ministers, brawls, family feuds, rumors, desires, regrets. Each verse had a story that went with it, an occasion or circumstance that prompted the versifier to compose the verse, and as told by Gisli these stories were often as entertaining as the verses themselves. The verses composed by Gisli and others like him were considered not high art but a form of common sport. Gisli called himself a *hagyrdingur,* a versifier, which was not the same as a true poet like my grandfather Olafur, *Skald Nyja Islands.* A great poet like Olafur was in a different class altogether, Gisli insisted. His own verses he referred to as *arnaleir*: eagle muck. Sigga said *Nonsense,* Gisli had a true talent.

One thing Gisli was very strict about was that any verse measure up to the standard of the form: four lines, with complicated requirements for alliteration, rhyme, and meter. "None of that free verse for me," he'd insist. "*Apamensskubragur.*"

"*Baboonish nonsense* indeed!" Birdie huffed. "Some of the greatest poetry today is written in free verse. Do you think poetry should stand still exactly as it was invented on a faraway island a thousand years ago?"

"That I do." Gisli grinned. "That I do."

Birdie's own epic poem, *Word Meadow,* was in free verse, but I myself became a traditionalist, endeared to the form Gisli taught me, with the first and third lines alliterative, echoed by the first letters of the second and fourth lines. Soon I was composing verses of my own, in English, which Gisli would attempt to translate into Icelandic, often with hilarious results.

Once Birdie realized I had a knack for recital, she tried to get me to memorize poems by Olafur, *Skald Nyja Islands,* but they were over my head and I much preferred lying rhymes and scary Gryla verses. Each time Gisli came for Coffee, he would teach me a new verse, nodding his grizzled head approvingly while he sucked coffee through the sugar cube clenched between his yellowed teeth.

I liked to memorize things because that way you could make the words stand still. You didn't have to know whether a horse should be *hestur* or *hesti* or *hestum* or *hests;* that was already done for you. Once an Icelandic word got stuck in a poem, its shape-shifting days were over.

Each person in an Icelandic family can have a different last name. Here's how: Say the wife is named Thora Palsdottir because her father was named Pall; her last name means daughter of Pall. Women don't take their husbands' names when they get married but keep their fathers' their whole lives. And say her husband's name is Thorgeir Arnason because his father's name was Arni, so he's son of Arni, except it's spelled Arn*a*son with an *a* because even proper names decline. Now if Thora Palsdottir and Thorgeir Arnason have a son, his last name will be Thorgeirs*son.* And if they have a daughter, her last name will be Thorgeirs*dottir.* That's how in one family you can have four different last names. But people in Iceland don't go by last names much, even to this day. Your real name is your first name, and everything is done on a first-name basis. All the names in the Icelandic phone book are alphabetized by first name; you might have to search through five hundred Bjorns to find the one Bjorn you're looking for. Even if you're the president, they call you by your first name: a headline in an Icelandic paper might read PETUR WINS ELECTION. That's why everyone refers to our grandfather as Olafur, even when he's written about in books and articles, which is like writing a scholarly essay on how William wrote *Hamlet.*

In North America the immigrants abandoned the naming system they'd used for over a thousand years. The first crop of children born in Winnipeg or Gimli or North Dakota or Wisconsin took the last names of their fathers instead of the first. And just like that, there were no more Jonsdottirs, only

Jonssons, which soon became Anglicized to Johnson. First names changed
too: Bjarni turned to Barney, Olafur to Oliver, Vilhjalmur to William, Ses-
selja to Cecilia, Kristin to Christina. Generation by generation, names that
couldn't be assimilated began to disappear entirely, names that had been in
use since the Saga times and before, men's names like Ingimundur, Sigtryg-
gur, and Steingrimur; women's names like Adalbjorg, Siggurros, and Pet-
rina. Vanished to the land of lost immigrant names.

All this I learned from Sigga, our very own *aettfraedingur. Aett* (rhymes
with *light*) means family as in family line, so an *aettfraedingur* is someone
who studies family lines: a genealogist. Sigga wasn't a professional, but Stefan said she could have been. She was often called upon to help Canadians
and Americans track down their long-lost relatives back in Iceland, or help
Icelanders locate distant cousins in North America. Even strangers who
weren't related to us Sigga helped. Although by the time Sigga got done
with them it usually turned out they were. Related, I mean. In Olafur's
study, Sigga stored four tall wooden file cabinets of family papers. All sorts
of people's families', not just ours. That's what Sigga did in the evenings
mostly, work on her *aettfraedi.* She had a special project she was doing on
Olafur's *aett* (which was also my mother's *aett* and your mother's *aett,* and of
course yours and mine as well). It was called the Blue Book because she
was binding all the pages between two blue leather covers. By the time I
came to Gimli my first summer, she was already in the sixteenth century.
She said one day she'd trace Olafur all the way back to the Viking poet Egil
Skallagrimsson.

I couldn't imagine anything more boring than *aettfraedi.* Just looking at
Sigga's endless charts made me dizzy. How could I possibly care if Jon
Petursson was the son of Petur Jonsson, who was the son of another Jon
Petursson, if I'd never met any of them and they all lived nearly two hundred
years ago in a country I'd never even visited?

"When you get older," Sigga said. "You'll care."

"Or not." Birdie declared genealogy to be tedious. "Thank God for the
Siggas of the world," she'd say. "Someone's got to do the dirty work."

So there you have it, a typical day in one of my Gimli summers: old folks at
Betel in the morning, midday grappling with Icelandic grammar or stalking

the beach like an egret, Coffee with visitors in the late afternoons. In the evenings, each of us had our work: Mama knitting or embroidering, Sigga researching the Blue Book, Birdie composing her *Word Meadow*. Me, I wrote verses of my own, and at the end of the summer Birdie would help me bind them into little books.

No, I can't show you one. They're gone now. I burned them, after Birdie died. It doesn't matter. They were childish *arnaleir,* eagle muck. Baboonish nonsense.

10

The way I saw it, Mama and Birdie divided me in two: Mama had me in the mornings, and Birdie had me in the afternoons. Birdie and Mama tried to stay out of each other's way; when their paths crossed, quarrels ignited between them. I thought badly of Birdie for picking fights with Mama, and I thought badly of Mama for not standing up to her younger sister. I liked to imagine that she used to, before her accident. But now she backed down quickly, growing silent and far away while she absently rubbed at the spot on the back of her head where she had fallen.

Sigga pleaded for peace between sisters. "What would your father think? Two middle-aged women squabbling like children." And if that didn't work, she'd just shake her head sadly and sigh. *"Fraendur eru fraendum verstir."* *Kin are worst to kin.* I knew all about that. Hadn't I nearly killed my own mother? Every time I saw Mama wearing sunglasses inside, every time I saw her gripping her cane during a spell of vertigo, every time I saw her run her fingers through her coarse gray hair, I felt shame. Each time I was introduced to new people in Gimli I'd stare at my shoes, glancing up quickly without moving my head, searching their faces to figure out if they *knew.* I tried to stay as invisible as possible. I figured with my pale skin and white-blond hair I could easily blend into walls or even air.

People mistook my shame for shyness, and I let them. *She never used to be shy,* Mama would say. *At least* (and here she would rub the back of her head, as if she could draw lost memory to the surface) *I don't remember her being that way.*

Only Birdie saw through my act. "You can't fool me, Freya *min*. With that Goody Two-shoes business."

I pretended not to know what she meant, but I knew that she knew that I wasn't myself anymore. And I was glad she knew. Because someday, when my punishment was over, I could go back to being my old self again. And if I had trouble remembering exactly who I really was, then maybe Birdie could help put me back together again. Except of course it didn't work out that way. When Birdie died, she took the old me along with her.

Sometimes even Mama wouldn't put up with Birdie anymore. If Birdie said something Mama deemed *absolutely unforgivable,* Mama would announce she needed to go to Winnipeg for supplies. She would pack up my cherry red suitcase and her overnight bag, and we'd catch a ride with a cottager heading to Winnipeg, where we would stay with Mama's best friend, Vera, on Victor Street, at the house where the Gudmundssons had taken in Sigga and Birdie and Mama after Olafur died. That's when Mama and Vera had become friends—and when Vera and Birdie had developed a resoundingly mutual dislike. Vera considered Birdie disgraceful, Birdie thought Vera a horrid snob. But Mama wouldn't put up with Birdie talking badly about Vera. All of Mama's vagueness would vanish, her eyes would sharpen, and she'd say in a strangely crisp tone: "Not one more word, Birdie. Not one."

Vera was Mama's haven from Birdie. The supplies Mama needed were yarn and embroidery thread and fabric, all things she could have bought in Gimli at Tergesen's General Store. But then we wouldn't have been able to escape from Birdie. Once we arrived in Winnipeg, Vera would drive us over to Eaton's Department Store. It was the same store Birdie frequented for her spending sprees. Vera's husband, Joey, was the general manager of Eaton's, which is how Vera secretly arranged that Sigga could return the things Birdie bought—or stole—during her sprees. "You're never to tell your aunt Ingibjorg," Vera warned me. "Or there could be a lot of trouble."

What kind of trouble I couldn't imagine. Except maybe out of spite for Vera, Birdie would choose a different store for her sprees. Then again, maybe it was out of spite for Vera that Birdie chose Eaton's in the first place.

At Eaton's, Vera would convince Mama to buy something bright and flowery. "Honestly, Anna, you're letting yourself get a bit dowdy, if you don't mind my saying." Mama didn't seem to mind, though I never saw her wear the outfits Vera made her buy.

I too became a target of Vera's improvement efforts. "Honestly, Anna, you mustn't let that child act so shy. It's becoming odd, is what it is." Once I recited one of Gisli's verses to Vera in my loudest voice, to prove I wasn't so shy, but all she said was "Honestly, Anna, I don't know why you allow her to learn that kind of doggerel." Vera didn't approve of my Icelandic lessons either. Once when she was visiting us in Gimli, she arrived in the middle of one of my sessions with Birdie. "Honestly, Ingibjorg, why on earth are you torturing that child with a language she will never use?"

Vera didn't speak with an accent the way Mama and Birdie did because she'd been raised not in the rural Interlake area but in urban Winnipeg. "Daddy," Vera would boast about the Great Dr. Gudmundsson, "never let us speak Icelandic. He didn't want us to have accents. As far as Daddy was concerned, we were born Canadians and should sound that way." And then she would look around her living room, with all its fancy objects from Eaton's, as proof of how well they'd done for themselves. Vera lived in the biggest house on Victor Street, but she and Joey were thinking of moving because the neighborhood was starting to crumble, and other areas of town were beginning to seem more desirable than Winnipeg's old Icelandic ghetto, the West End.

Vera always watched me very closely, as if she was afraid I would turn a cartwheel and bring all her precious knickknacks from Eaton's tumbling to the floor. If Mama got a dizzy spell and had to lean on her cane, Vera would look directly at me and shake her head slowly. Pity, or disapproval? I was never sure.

There was nothing Birdie loved more than to imitate Vera. "Honestly, Anna," Birdie would say, mimicking Vera's faux British accent, "I don't know what you see in Vera. Is it that her father, the Great Dr. Gudmundsson, was the first Icelandic doctor in Canada? Or her husband is the manager of Eaton's? Maybe it's just that she doesn't have a crazy sister. Or that her boys don't speak a word of Icelandic. Do tell."

"At least," Mama replied, "I have people I can call my friends."

"I have friends."

As were many things Birdie said, this claim was an exaggeration. Your mother had exactly one true friend in the world: Stefan. Stefan in his old-fashioned cardigans and old man's pipe, though he was the same age as Birdie. "Like one of those elderly bachelor farmers in Arborg," Birdie would tease.

"Why don't you marry him?" I asked once. It was clear even to me that Stefan would marry Birdie in a moment, if she would have him.

"Marry Stefan?" When Birdie stopped laughing she explained, "Stefan's a square, that's why."

"Then what are you?"

"I'm a . . . trapezoid."

"And me?"

"You're a little ovoid."

"What's that?"

"Like an egg. Ready to hatch."

Into what? I didn't want to know.

Square or not, I adored Uncle Stefan and his kind, steady presence in my Gimli life. He taught history and English at the Riverton High School during the school year, but summers he was free to pursue his life's work: a history of the New Iceland colony. Sometimes Birdie and I would tag along with Stefan on his research expeditions. Once he took us to the plot of land, on the lake north of Gimli, where my grandfather Olafur's family had first settled. There was nothing left, just empty scrubland and an old grave site. Inside a wobbling wooden fence, several headstones leaned in the high grasses. The graves, Stefan explained, belonged to an Indian family, the Ramseys. The Ramseys had been living on the land the Canadian government had given to the Icelanders.

"You mean land the Icelanders stole from the Indians," Birdie interrupted.

"The Indians ceded the land. It was a legal transaction." Stefan sounded irritated.

"And then the Icelanders killed them off with smallpox," Birdie continued. "Entire Indian families, like the Ramseys, wiped out."

"On purpose?" I asked.

"Of course not," Stefan answered. "Many Icelanders died too. Your grandfather was lucky, his family was vaccinated. Otherwise you wouldn't be here today."

"I'm sorry," I whispered to the Ramsey gravestones before we left that day. "I'm so sorry."

Our summers in Gimli always came to an end in the same way, with what Mama referred to as *Birdie's god-awful scenes*. Other families marked their end-of-summer leave-takings with hugs and kisses and best wishes; our departures were marred by tears and accusations, silences, even threats. No matter how well a particular summer had gone, Birdie always seemed to think the worst of us when we were on the verge of leaving. My mother, Birdie raged, exploited her as an unpaid babysitter. Mama's symptoms were all an act to prevent her from facing the meaninglessness of her life. Me, I was a pest whose presence rendered Birdie completely unable to work. If it weren't for me, she would have finished her *Word Meadow* long ago. Sigga's crime was treating Anna as her favorite, when she, Birdie, was a poetic genius and the true heir to Olafur's legacy. Anna was nothing but an American housewife. Zip-zap: Birdie's tongue could lash you like a stroke of lightning.

Once I woke on the morning of departure to find my cherry red suitcase lying open and empty on the bedroom floor. During the night Birdie had snuck in, removed all my clothes, and replaced them in the dresser drawers. All this, while I was sleeping.

Other times Birdie ruined our last days in Gimli by refusing to speak to us. Birdie could emit the loudest silence ever heard. If we passed on the stairs, she looked right past me, like I was less than a ghost. At the time I figured she was preparing herself for what it would be like at Oddi once Mama and I were gone. Looking back, I wonder if it wasn't me she was preparing, for the huge silence I would face once she was dead.

Several times she threatened to kill herself if we left. Sigga said it was because Birdie never got over her father dying when she was just a girl. Mama said Birdie was trying to grab the limelight as usual. I didn't say anything. I was too scared to speak. What if I said the wrong thing and she killed herself? What if I said nothing and she killed herself anyway?

One time Mama arranged for Stefan to secretly fetch us a day early, at six o'clock in the morning, just so we could avoid Birdie's god-awful scene. I tip-toed past Birdie's bedroom with my cherry red suitcase. The plan was for Stefan to meet us around the corner so the rumble of his aging Rambler wouldn't wake Birdie up. But somehow she knew. Mama and Sigga and I were almost to the corner when Birdie came flying down the driveway screaming, "Plotters! Schemers! *Traitors!*"

"Please," Mama begged. "You'll wake the neighbors."

The last day of my last Gimli summer was different. It was quiet. No screaming, no god-awful scene. That's because Birdie wasn't there. She'd been committed. To Selkirk Asylum. For kidnapping me.

No, it wasn't really a kidnapping. It was just a vacation. Except no one believed us.

11

Your mother would be very proud.

Of me, that is. Of the way I've been writing: on the subway in my head, in the darkroom illegibly on the backs of discarded test strips, in my apartment through the night on Birdie's old Underwood. Now I keep myself awake with the same raining type that percussed my Gimli summer nights.

If I don't write to you, I dream. Silly dreams: Birdie rising up out of Lake Winnipeg, strands of wet hair knotted around her neck like blond seaweed. The truth is that things haven't been going well for me since I found out about you. Screwups at the Sub. I stay up late writing you, then oversleep in the morning. It's no easy feat, waking up in a basement apartment. Each morning, I have to trick my brain awake, make it believe *day* when all my senses register night. I show up to work late and bleary-eyed, and my prints keep turning out flat. *Flat trash!* my boss, Klaus, calls them. *Flat* means lack of distinction between shades of gray. In other words, mud. Klaus is a hot-tempered old man, ex-officer in the Prussian army. He is rarely kind, but lately he has been especially harsh. Today he went so far as to rip up one of my prints. Says I'm losing my eye. I've already lost my ear, my tongue. What's next?

The summer Birdie kidnapped me was the same summer Mama's friend Vera was chosen to be *Fjallkona*. What's a *Fjallkona*, you ask? In a minute.

The more important question is what's a kidnapping. Know this: your mother did not steal me from my bed in the night. I was not bound and blindfolded. There was no ransom note collaged with letters cut from newspapers. I vanished voluntarily, if unwittingly. Birdie called it *a surprise vacation,* just the two of us, and I believed her. I chose to believe her. I could claim in my defense that I was only a child, simply being a good girl, doing what I was told. That I didn't know any better.

The truth is I'd turned thirteen. My wings itched. It was my first chance to fly and I took it.

Birdie and I set off for Iceland in the middle of Vera's speech at *Islendingadagurinn.* That's *eece-len-ding-a-dagur-inn.* Quite a word, I agree. Except it's not one word but three: Icelandic words are sticky. *Islendingadagurinn = Icelanders-Day-The.* A kind of St. Patrick's Day for Icelanders. Each year, a different *Fjallkona* reigned over the festival. The *Fjallkona* was supposed to represent an upstanding matron of Canadian Icelandichood and was selected by committee each spring. The costume remained the same over the years: the white peaked headdress for Iceland's snowcapped mountains; the green cape for her verdant slopes. It was the same costume Sigga wore in her own *Fjallkona* portrait, which adorned our mantel back in Connecticut. Back then, in the years before I made my first visit to Gimli, I'd believed Sigga to be a queen. I was not so far off. The title of *Fjallkona* in our little Gimli world imbued only slightly less than regal status. So when Mama's dear friend Vera was chosen to be *Fjallkona* for *Islendingadagurinn* 1978, Mama was thrilled. "Our very own Vera," she kept repeating. I was thrilled too—even if I didn't exactly like Vera, even though I sensed she disapproved of me, I couldn't help getting drawn into the preparations, watching Vera try on her green cape and white headdress, listening to her practice her speech. Sigga too seemed pleased and passed along various practical tips to Vera for her coming reign.

And then there was Birdie.

Sometimes I wonder if the whole kidnapping escapade would have occurred if it hadn't been for Vera being chosen *Fjallkona.* It irked Birdie so terribly. (Other times I'm convinced she'd been planning our *surprise vacation* for years.) Vera, Birdie insisted, had about as much right to be *Fjallkona* as a seagull. It demeaned the position, to choose someone like Vera. Now your *amma* Sigga, Birdie went on, she deserved to be *Fjallkona*. But Vera? Vera, who never taught her boys a single word of Icelandic? Who can barely speak the language herself, and proud of it? What does Vera represent? Eaton's, that's what. The Ladies Aid. A do-gooder. Why they might as well have picked Anna!

"What's wrong with Mama?"

"Nothing's wrong with her. It's just that she's not exactly qualified to be *Fjallkona*."

"Why not?"

"She's an American housewife, that's why not!"

"What about you? Could you be *Fjallkona*?"

"Never in a million years, baby. Never in a million years would they pick someone like me to be *Fjallkona*. Someone who spends *every single day of her life perpetuating our ancestors' literary heritage*. Someone who actually *speaks the language*. Someone who actually *studies our history*! Oh no, baby. Not me."

"Why not?"

"Because I'm not a pillar of the community. Because I'm not married to the manager of Eaton's, with two boys on the Winnipeg High School hockey team."

"But Amma Sigga was chosen, and she wasn't married to the manager of Eaton's."

"You don't understand, do you? They'll never choose a crazy spinster."

"What's a spinster?"

"A woman who never marries."

"Are you really crazy?"

"So they say, *elskan*. So they say."

Usually Birdie thrived at *Islendingadagurinn*, the yearly infusion of visitors enlivening our insular Gimli existence. By the hundreds they came, maybe thousands, pouring into Gimli from Winnipeg and all the little towns throughout the Interlake region (some of which had their own Icelandic festivals, though none as big as Gimli's): Lundar, Hnausa, Hecla, Selkirk, Riverton, Arborg, even little Reykjavik on the next lake over. And from beyond Manitoba, from anywhere Icelanders had settled and their descendants still lived, towns in Saskatchewan, Alberta, and British Columbia. Small towns just over the border in North Dakota: Cavalier and Akra, Gardar and Mountain. Wisconsin, Minnesota, Washington State. Even Iceland.

If only you had been there, Cousin! I imagine you almost as an older brother or sister, sitting by my side at the harbor forking up syrup-soaked pancakes, the great days of the festival unfurling before us like a colorful Viking sail. Together we'd have watched the kite-flying contests and raft races, horse shows and fireworks, performances by the Icelandic National Theatre Troupe flown in from Reykjavik, not to mention the New Iceland Music and Poetry Society. The *glima* wrestling, the sailing displays in the harbor, the poetry contest (I won three years in a row, children twelve and under). Kinsmen barbecues and beer gardens. We'd eat sausages called *rullupylsa* and brown bread (to think you've never tasted our *amma*'s brown bread!), even sneak out of the house to spy on the grown-ups at their drunken midnight dances. Maybe tie two of our legs into one and enter the three-legged race.

But you weren't there.

Mostly I tagged along with Birdie. It was one big family reunion of the Icelandic diaspora, such as it was. The kind of occasion where Birdie shone: the daughter of the great Olafur, *Skald Nyja Islands*. (Yes, my mother too was the poet's daughter, but she hated attention and kept a low profile, especially after the accident.) Birdie milked the occasion for all its worth, leading tours of the poet's study, showing off his library, consorting with visiting dignitaries from Iceland, even the president himself. But Birdie was no snob; she talked to everyone, and listened too. Of course, what Birdie said *to* people's faces and *about* them behind their backs varied considerably. Like Icelandic grammar, it was all in the prepositions.

Islendingadagurinn was the one time of year when Birdie could reliably obtain all the attention she craved—that's why it was so shocking on that Saturday morning in 1978, the first day of the festival, when Birdie announced she was staying home. If she'd been depressed, her absence would have seemed plausible. When she was depressed she wanted nothing to do with anything human. Or if she'd seemed bitter and resentful, I would have known she was brooding about Vera being chosen *Fjallkona*. But if anything she seemed happier, more excited than usual.

"You're not coming?"

"I'm staying home this year. I've got work to do."

And so Birdie holed up in her bedroom churning out her *Word Meadow*. Or so she claimed. Now I know she was doing nothing of the sort. As soon as Mama and Sigga and I left the house on the last day of the *Islendingadagurinn* festival, Birdie began her preparations, packing one suitcase for me and one for her. Checking our airline tickets and passports one last time. Arranging the cab that would take us to the airport. Then setting off to find me, pluck me out of the crowds, out of my Gimli summer, out of my life as I knew it, and as it would never be again.

Islendingadagurinn hadn't been much fun for me without Birdie. The beach was so crowded with visitors you could hardly find a place to lay your blanket, plus it was hot that year, and unusually buggy. I hung around with Mama and Sigga, scratching my mosquito bites while they chatted with every degree of cousin you could possibly imagine. Cousins a thousand times removed. Until you had to wonder if they were even cousins anymore.

It was Monday morning, the last day of the festival, that Birdie finally made her appearance. The sky was dark, heavy with clouds, and I was standing on the curb at the corner of First Avenue and Centre Street waiting for the parade to make its way across town, from Johnson Memorial Hospital to Gimli Park, wondering which would come first, the rain or the parade, when I felt a hand slip into mine. Birdie! She was wearing a coat I'd never seen before, a lightweight salmon pink raincoat belted at the waist (one of several items, I learned later, purchased in her pre-Iceland shopping spree at Eaton's). The color highlighted the pink of her cheeks, and over her perfectly coifed blond curls was a matching head scarf. How fashionable Birdie seemed to me, and beautiful, despite the fact that she was then nearly fifty. I squeezed her hand in excitement. The sounds of the brass band drifted down the street. The crowd murmured and I strained to see the beginning of the parade.

"There's Vera!" I shouted. She looked resplendent in her emerald robe, waving to the crowd from a shiny white car. I jumped up and down, waving my own hands over my head. Birdie seemed not to see. "Where is Anna?" she wanted to know. "And your *amma*?"

"They're at Gimli Park. Sigga needed to sit down. She's eighty-three, you know."

"I know," Birdie said. "Believe me, I know."

"Vera's going to lay the wreath down at the pioneer memorial. And then later she's going to give her speech. I heard her practice it last night. Are you going?"

"Why bother? It's the same every year, those speeches. The glories of the homeland, the glories of the new land. It's bullshit."

"Bull——?"

"Yes, bullshit. A farce. A fraud, a mockery of all we hold truly dear. Oh, once it meant something, I suppose. But now it's just a big hoo-ha. The real culture of New Iceland is dying. The older generation will die off, and soon hardly anyone will be left who speaks the language." She held up the printed festival program. "It's not even written in Icelandic anymore. It's coming to an end, this little world. It's coming to an end. Not that it has to, of course. But it takes more than holding a cheesy festival once a year to keep a culture alive. Skip the *ponnukokur,* people!" She was yelling now, at the backs of the crowd that was breaking up, drifting toward Gimli Park. "Skip the *rullupylsa,* the brown bread! Skip *Islendingadagurinn!*" People turned their heads and stared. Luckily I saw no one we knew. "Teach your children Icelandic! Let them learn it from their grandparents. Our language *is* our culture. Make them read the Sagas. Take them to Iceland, damn it!"

I shrank back in embarrassment, but Birdie grabbed my hand and began leading me away from the parade—in the opposite direction from Gimli Park.

"Hey!" I yanked back with equal force, pulling her toward the crowd she'd been yelling at, toward the park. We stood like that for a moment, in the middle of town, at the corner of Centre and First, tugging each other. Then Birdie put her hands on my shoulders and looked me in the eye. The air smelled like wet metal, and the clouds had turned the purple-green color of bruises.

"*Elskan,*" Birdie began. "Today is a very special day for you. For both of us."

I nodded. For some reason I was trembling.

"I'm taking you somewhere," she continued. "To something much bigger and better than our silly little *Islendingadagurinn.*"

She glanced at her watch, then took my hand again. This time I didn't resist as she began leading me down Second Avenue toward our house. The street was completely deserted; everyone in Gimli was at the festival. What could be better than *Islendingadagurinn*? Better than the tolling of the bell and the laying of the wreath on the pioneer cairn? Or the sight of the Canadian Mounties escorting the *Fjallkona* into Gimli Park? Would I miss Vera's speech she'd been practicing all summer?

"Where are we going?" I finally asked.

"Iceland, Freya *min*. I'm taking you to Iceland."

And then it started, as if she'd orchestrated the whole thing: a flash of lightning, a crack of thunder, then the splatter of plump raindrops. As we ran I caught glimpses of the lake, the wind whipping up whitecaps like dabs of frosting on one of Amma's cakes. The water and the sky drenched the same bruised green. We loved those summer thunderstorms, Birdie and I. Thunder and lightning, thrill and danger. When other people ran in from the rain, we ran out into it. Except on this day. On this day Birdie pulled me through the rain laughing and dripping into the front door of the house.

"Quick, change your clothes. The cab will be here any minute!"

"Cab?" No one in our family ever took cabs.

"We're traveling in style, *elskan*."

"But where are we going?"

"I told you, silly, Iceland!"

"In a cab?"

"We're taking the cab to the Winnipeg airport." Birdie looked at me like I was *vitlaus*, an idiot. But it was all happening so fast. It was hard to keep track. A loud honk made me jump.

"Grab your suitcase, kiddo," Birdie instructed. It was sitting by the door, cherry red and expectant. The next thing I knew Birdie was directing the cabbie to take the long way out of town. To avoid the traffic, she explained. The *Islendingadagurinn* commotion.

To avoid being seen by anyone we knew, I realized later. Much later. And way too late.

And that was how your mother stole me willingly in broad stormy daylight in the middle of the *Islendingadagurinn* parade.

Of course I did, Cousin! It was the first thing I asked, as soon as we got in the cab: Does Mama know?

"Of course she knows!" Birdie answered, a look of shocked offense on her face. "We've been planning this for months, your mama and your *amma* and I."

"But why didn't anyone tell me?"

"We wanted it to be a surprise, that's why, you little fool! Aren't you surprised? Aren't you?"

I nodded. "But why . . ." It was hard to know what to ask first.

"Why what?"

"Why are we leaving in the middle of *Islendingadagurinn*?"

"It's not the middle. It's the last day. Besides, it was the only flight I could get."

"But how can we afford it?"

"Everyone chipped in, that's how. Your mama, your *amma,* me, even your uncle Stefan. They wanted to have a big send-off party for us, but I know how you hate parties. I convinced them you'd like it better this way, the greatest surprise of your life."

"Really?"

"Do you honestly think I would make something like that up?"

"No," I answered. Because that's what Birdie wanted me to answer. The truth was I wasn't sure, but loyalty kept me from expressing any more doubts. If I doubted Birdie's word, I'd be doubting *her.* Doubting her sanity, her suitability, her fitness. I would be thrown into the other camp, of those who betrayed Birdie (there were surprisingly many, by her count), those who scorned her. I believed myself to be Birdie's one true ally in the world, and for that loyalty I was gifted her affection, the heightened magic that was life in her presence. True, Birdie shifted like lake weather, there were times when I fell from her favor, felt the sting of her whip-sharp tongue. But even that was better than the void of dullness that was my life in Connecticut.

Yes, I had one, of course, though looking back over these pages I see I've scarcely mentioned it. There's not much to say. Life with Mama in Connecticut was a limbo I endured between Gimli summers. I kept my promise about being good; I tried my best to be invisible. I never raised my hand in class but answered correctly when called upon. I took care of Mama, kept track of her canes and her sunglasses. It was lonely. At night I dreamt long and wildly, in the morning had no one to tell my dreams. Just Mama, who nodded her head in that vague way that could mean either yes or no. Or nothing.

See me as I was then: thirteen years old and taller than the tallest boy in seventh grade. White-blond hair to my waist, thin and scraggly like the rest of me. It fell in my face a lot and I let it. Kids thought I was strange and I was. In addition to my not-playing, I walked around muttering to myself. Or so it seemed to them. They called it witch-talk. *Freya's witch-talking again!* Actually, I was working on *leggja a minnid*—laying in my mind, memorizing poems Old Gisli had taught me, or ones of my own. And I read. I hid in books, and behind them. I read like an addict, in class with a book sequestered on my lap, during recess leaning against the chain-link fence, bouncing along on the school bus, at the dinner table, by flashlight under the covers after Mama turned my lights out. Reading, reading, and counting the days to the Gimli summer. The only good thing about my life in Connecticut was that no one *knew*. Let them think I was strange, let them think I was a witch. I didn't care. As long as no one knew I'd nearly killed my mother. Turned her dizzy and distracted and old before her time.

Six years had passed since my first Gimli summer. Six years of being good. Six years of being something other than myself. Maybe I actually believed that our surprise trip to Iceland was fully funded and sanctioned by the proper authorities, Mama and Amma. Or maybe I was, simply, ready to go. The storm helped. Sometimes I think that if it hadn't been for that storm, with its scent of danger and thrill of lightning and reckless thunder, I would never have left town with Birdie . . . that on a clear day I would have kept a clearer head.

The storm had subsided by the time we reached the airport, out on the prairie edges of Winnipeg. It reminded me of my first train ride to Canada, how shocked I'd been by the flatness of it all. How Mama and I got out of the train and spied a storm raining down in another corner of the sky. We still took the train every year. Mama was still afraid of flying.

"I've never been on a plane before." We were sitting on plastic chairs in the lounge, waiting to board.

"I know that, *elskan*. You'll be fine."

She held my hand as the plane took off. My heart flapped wildly. Finally, finally, Birdie was taking me flying! Out the window I could see Lake Winnipeg. Gimli I couldn't locate. I wasn't used to seeing our world from on high. "Where's Gimli?" I asked.

"It's a speck," Birdie answered.

"Do you think it rained on Vera's speech?"

"I do, baby," Birdie said with a satisfied smile. "I do."

Poor Vera in her soggy cape, her crowning moment eclipsed by daggers of lightning, her much-practiced speech drowned by thunder. Even though Birdie had said those speeches were bullshit. And that Gimli was nothing but a speck.

The plane banked east, my stomach dipped, and anything I could recognize down below was gone. I stopped thinking Gimli then, began thinking Iceland. Iceland! Birdie had often talked about taking me someday, but my mother always claimed we could never afford it. A trip to Iceland seemed as remote and impossible and enticing as rocketing to Venus.

12

It was a night flight, but it never got dark and I never slept. Birdie never let me. She talked the whole way to Iceland. True night never had a chance to fall, not when our plane was keeping pace with the sun. We raced that sun all the way to Iceland. As we sped through the sky, it was continually setting. Then in some miraculous way, that same sunset became a sunrise in Iceland when we landed.

In the hours between this perpetual sunset-sunrise, while the other passengers turned off their overhead lights and settled under blankets, Birdie got talky, filling my head with visions of an Iceland so marvelous I quivered in my seat. We would take the Ring Road, she began.

"What's the Ring Road?"

"The Ring Road," Birdie explained, "is the crowning achievement of Icelandic engineering. The first highway to circle the entire island, completed with much fanfare several years ago. Now it may not seem like much, *elskan,* this building of a road, but in Iceland even roads face unimaginable odds. Roads take a lot of abuse, they contend with forces of nature you can't even imagine. Glacial floods. Mud slides. Avalanches. Lava. But the Ring Road has been built to survive all that. It's the only way to see Iceland. You can't drive across the island, Freya *min,* it's completely untraversable in a normal car."

Why? I wanted to know.

"The interior, where they exiled criminals in the old days, is nothing but glaciers, my girl, and vast lava deserts, and glacial rivers that change course so quickly that no sooner do you build a bridge than it's washed into rubble. Only huge buses with enormous wheels can cross the interior. Used to be, in your grandfather's time, people rode horses to get from one place to another, or hopped in a boat. But now there is the Ring Road, and on the Ring Road, my girl, we'll traverse the whole island, you and I."

The Ring Road was only the beginning of Birdie's pre-travelogue, the golden thread upon which she strung wonder after wonder, beginning with Iceland's most famous waterfalls, Gullfoss and Dettifoss. Then she waxed eloquent about the greatest glacier of all Iceland, all Europe, Vatnajokull.

"And next to Vatnajokull, Freya *min,* is the glacial lagoon where giant icebergs float. I'll take you there. And right underneath the glacier is a volcano."

I remembered my mother's story about the eruption of Askja, the fall of black snow, the flight of Olafur's family to Canada. "Are we going to see Askja?"

"Of course we'll see Askja, silly! But Askja's only one of them. There's Laki, Hekla, Krafla. . . Volcanoes can erupt at any time. The whole island's alive, I tell you. If you look closely enough, you can see the land breathe."

How long would it take, I wanted to know, to circle the entire island?

"Ten days or so, I've heard. I've never done it. The Ring Road wasn't built when I visited Iceland back in the sixties. It'll be the first time, for both of us."

We would visit Thingvellir, site of the ancient parliament. Sigga, Birdie informed me, especially wanted to make sure I would see that. The original Oddi, too, the farmstead where Snorri Sturluson was raised. And of course we would travel to the East, to visit Olafur's farm, Brekka, the site of the wondrous Olafur story Birdie had told me my first summer in Gimli.

"Brekka is still there?"

Birdie laughed. "Where would it go?"

And multitudes of far distant cousins. Sigga had made a list, Birdie explained, of various people I absolutely had to meet. A lie of course. From time to time, Birdie would toss in little remarks like that—Sigga wanted to

make sure I met so-and-so, Mama wanted me to see such-and-such—
meant to validate the trip in my mind. And it worked.

Traveling to Iceland had seemed about as probable to me as flying. Now I
was doing both. But as night became morning, I began to understand that
there were other reasons for our journey, reasons that went beyond the edi-
fication of Freya.

"I had a very bad winter, Freya *min*. Dark beyond belief. But this trip is
going to redeem everything. I'm going to get the letters back."

"Letters?"

"Olafur's letters. The ones he wrote to his uncle Pall back in Iceland after he emigrated. You see, Pall was one of the ones who stayed behind.
Swore he'd never abandon his homeland. Pall was a famous poet in his own
right, in the farmer-poet tradition, and he mentored Olafur when he was a
boy in Iceland. It broke Olafur's heart to leave Pall behind. And so when
Olafur left for Canada, he wrote to Pall, every week for ten years, until Pall
died. The letters are wondrous, wondrous! Or so I've heard. Remarkable
and detailed descriptions of life in the colony, the tragedies that befell New
Iceland. The smallpox, the flooding, the frightful freezes. Not to mention
the religious disputes that split the colony in two. And of course every letter
contained a verse or two composed by Olafur. These were the very letters
your *amma* Sigga read as a girl when she was growing up in Iceland. She
was a cousin by marriage to one of Pall's sons, and worked for a time on
their farm at Brekka. Pall was dead by then, of course, but his son had kept
Olafur's letters, treasured them, and during the long winter evenings they
took turns reading them out loud. It was those letters that convinced Sigga
to come to New Iceland and meet the poet Olafur himself."

"And marry him?"

"And marry him. But it was the young man who wrote those letters she
fell in love with first. And for the past few years, Sigga and I have been trying to get them back. Me, mainly."

"Why?"

"Why?" Birdie's voice rose. "*Why?* Because Sigga has a right to see the
letters again before she dies. Because they provide invaluable documentation of the early years of the New Iceland colony, through the eyes of a

young poet. Because your uncle Stefan needs access to them for the book
he's writing on the history of New Iceland. And because I've never read
them, that's why!"

"Where are they?" I whispered, hoping to lower the volume of our conversation. Birdie was waking up the other passengers.

"Good question, *elskan*. Good question. Ulfur thinks he can help us find
them. You know who Ulfur is."

I certainly did. I'd never met him, but Birdie talked about him often. Ulfur was a distant cousin of ours, and the great-great-grandson of the farmer-
poet Pall. Ulfur had been Birdie's host when she'd spent an entire summer
in Iceland in 1964 for the hundredth birthday celebration of our grandfather Olafur, *Skald Nyja Islands*. According to Birdie, Ulfur had done more
than anyone else in Iceland to promote Olafur's reputation. Ulfur and
Birdie had worked together, by mail, on a number of translations of Olafur's
work into English. And Ulfur was a very important scholar in Iceland. "Ulfur," Birdie boasted, "was almost single-handedly responsible for arranging
the return of Iceland's precious Sagas from the Danes."

"But why were Iceland's Sagas in Denmark?"

"Because Denmark ruled Iceland for centuries, they tried to own everything about us, they inserted their words, their spellings, into our language.
And they held our ancient manuscripts for *safekeeping*. But once Iceland
was fully independent, they were able to negotiate the return of the manuscripts. The first shipment arrived by boat in 1971. Ulfur sent me a newspaper clipping. Thousands of Icelanders appeared at the harbor in Reykjavik to
welcome our books home again. The Sagas, the Eddas—back in Iceland at
last!"

Ulfur, the way Birdie talked about him, was a near god. Once when
she'd been drinking just enough to get dreamy but not enough to get mean,
Birdie told me she considered Ulfur *myndarlegur*. *Myndarlegur* is a high
compliment in Icelandic, encompassing not one but a cluster of appealing
traits. Handsome, first and foremost, but also stately, hardworking, skillful,
and generous. When I was nine I'd found a photograph of Ulfur in the top
drawer of Birdie's vanity. With his black hair and high cheekbones, he
looked plenty *myndarlegur* to me.

"Do you want to marry Ulfur?" I'd asked her. Without, of course, mentioning that I'd found the photograph. Birdie raged at any perceived invasion of her privacy. Much less an actual one.

"Marry Ulfur? He's already married, baby! He's got a wife and children back in Iceland. He's got a boy around your age, as a matter of fact, named Saemundur."

"If Ulfur weren't already married, would you marry him?" I thought she would scoff at that question too, but she didn't. Nor did she answer.

At some point in Birdie's all-night monologue, our stewardess, Steinunn, brought us trays with baked salmon and parsleyed potatoes, a Coke for me, and for Birdie, the first of several miniature bottles of Brennivin. Birdie chatted with Steinunn while I stared out the window at the green sky and orange sun, barely able to nibble my fish.

"If Ulfur knows where the letters are, why doesn't he just give them to you?"

"Good question. Back in 'sixty-four, he told me he didn't have them, but that he was sure he could locate them in his father's collection. His father, Johann, has an extensive private collection of Icelandic books and manuscripts. But this past winter I got a letter from Ulfur saying he never found them. That he'd looked everywhere there was to look, even put out a call in *Morgunbladid,* but the letters never turned up."

"What's *Morgunbladid?*"

"Iceland's main newspaper. *Morning paper.* Have you forgotten all the Icelandic I ever taught you? Because you're going to have to start speaking it, you know, as soon as we land. *Bara Islensku.* Icelandic only."

"Are you going to look for Olafur's letters while we're in Iceland?"

"Bingo! I doubt Ulfur has even tried very hard. He's got other fish to fry, now that he's been made head of the Arni Magnusson Institute. My theory is that the letters are somewhere in Ulfur's father's library. Or else in a trunk in some old lady's farmhouse in East Iceland." She swallowed all in one gulp her third shot of Brennivin. "We're going to find Olafur's letters, Freya *min.* And we're going to bring them back to Gimli."

13

And then we landed.

And then we landed.

And then we landed.

Three days have passed, Cousin, and I still cannot bring myself beyond that one line. What I fear most is not that I won't be able to remember the trip with Birdie but that I will. It is wedged deep in my memory, lodged in the nether-crevice that separates not-remembering from forgetting.

Spread here on the table in front of me is a map of Iceland. I searched a dozen bookstores over the past few days before finding one; it would have been easier to locate a map of the moon. It was worth the trouble. It's more than a memory aid: this map reminds me that the trip to Iceland was no glorious dream, no brutal nightmare, but an actual physical journey. Still, as I sit here conjuring, I can't help but wonder if I don't look like my mother, with that befuddled, dream-remembering expression crinkling her face.

And then we landed.

The first thing I remember is sideways rain at dawn. Standing outside the Keflavik Airport attacked by ferocious horizontal wind slamming razor-sharp pebbles of water. *Velkomin til Islands!* I clutched my cherry red suit-case, exhausted from lack of sleep, hair wet and whipping against my face. Iceland's rain made Gimli's downpour seem mere drizzle.

Next, Ulfur leaping out of a very small European car and running to-ward us through the rain. His hair was no longer black like in the photo-graph in Birdie's vanity but brilliant silver-white. With a goatee to match. Still *myndarlegur* though. Birdie strode to meet him, looking glamorous in her salmon pink coat and head scarf, but if there was any romance between them, I couldn't detect it in that brief rain-soaked airport hug. For me Ulfur had only a brisk nod and a handshake, his eyes veiled behind misted glasses. Then he tossed our luggage in the trunk of his little car.

From the backseat I rubbed clear a spot in the fogged window. What I saw: black earth. Mile after mile of stark black lava fields. No houses no trees no people. Not even a sheep. This was Iceland? Or had we landed on Venus after all? Pluto perhaps? Whichever was most remote from earth.

During the entire drive to Reykjavik, Ulfur and Birdie talked together in the front seat, ignoring me completely. Mostly it was Ulfur who spoke, in low serious tones I was too exhausted to decipher. I kept hearing the word *hjonaskilnadur*. It was not a word I recognized. *Hjon*, I knew, meant mar-ried couple. Was Ulfur proposing to Birdie? Was that the real purpose of our trip? Then I remembered that Ulfur was married. I studied his face in the rearview mirror. The fog had cleared from his glasses and I could see the color of his eyes, greenish brown, but with dark circles underneath. Not quite as *myndarlegur* as the photograph, I decided. Yet Birdie could not seem to take her eyes off him. Once she even reached over and took his hand. What would Ulfur's wife think?

Out the window to my left was the ocean; the lava seemed to reach to its very shore. I shuddered in my damp clothes, sucked a strand of my hair. *I never said good-bye to Mama*, I kept thinking. *I never said good-bye.* Would Mama have really sent me off to Iceland without saying good-bye? Later, at Ulfur's house, I asked Birdie if we could call Mama.

"Phone Gimli?" Birdie scoffed, in that harsh laugh of hers. "Freya *min*, it would cost a fortune. It would cost practically as much as a plane ticket. Nobody calls Canada from Iceland."

Then she saw I was crying. "You can write postcards," she conceded. "To Anna, and Sigga, and your uncle Stefan. Every day, baby. Think how thrilled they'll be!"

Her face darkened for a moment. Perhaps she was allowing herself to think of those three, not thrilled but frantic, seared with worry. Later I would learn all about those days. How search parties dove Lake Winnipeg, in case we'd drowned in the storm. Or been struck by lightning. At the police station in Winnipeg after our capture, Birdie would insist that she'd left my mother a note saying exactly where we were going and for how long.

"A note?" My mother screamed. "A note? We never found a note. You never wrote a note!"

"Are you accusing me of lying?"

"Oh, I am," my mother said bitterly. "I most certainly am."

Our entire trip rested on lies that shifted beneath us like tectonic plates and eventually collided. Did your mother believe her own lies? I have to doubt that. It was all too calculated. And what about me? How many of Birdie's lies did I believe? All and none. One part of me still wondered if my mother really knew I was in Iceland. It was a fear that rose up in me at least once a day: *Mama!* That one word stood for all my doubts. And then I'd push it down. To believe that Birdie had lied seemed worse to me than to believe her. To believe Birdie had lied to me would mean she was practically . . . evil. And so I chose belief, fragile as a china cup. Once a day for the entire three weeks I wrote Mama a postcard, every inch crammed with my tiny neat script. *Here we are at Thingvellir. Here we are at Gullfoss.* Every postcard ending with *I miss you, Mama,* underlined three times. Birdie gave me beautiful Icelandic stamps to paste into the corners, stamps with horses and puffins and geysers.

Yes, every day I wrote a postcard, and every day instead of mailing it to Canada as she claimed, Birdie stashed the postcard inside the lining of her suitcase. It was Sigga who discovered and delivered them, finally, to Mama. A week after our return. Nineteen cards Mama read all in one sitting, weeping.

Ulfur lived on the edge of a lake in the middle of Reykjavik in a house of books. The house, it turned out, was not Ulfur's but his parents'. He'd moved in with them after his divorce. *Hjonaskilnadur,* that mysterious word I kept hearing on the ride from the airport. I'd made the mistake of asking what it meant.

"It means I am divorced now," Ulfur had explained from the front seat. "Iceland's divorce rate is soaring, you know. One of your American influences, I suppose. And my ex-wife? She is in Spain, discovering herself. Is that not another of your American trends?" He fixed his gaze on me in the rearview mirror. I smiled uncertainly. I had no idea what he was talking about, but I recognized the tone in his voice: sarcasm, ragged as an unhealed scar. Birdie's weapon of choice, her favorite tongue-sword. No wonder she liked Ulfur so much. I knew by then that sarcastic questions were best left unanswered. Instead I nodded my head vaguely, in a way that could have meant either yes or no. Or nothing. I wasn't sure I liked this Ulfur. I turned and stared out at the lava again. After a half an hour or so, the red- and blue-roofed city of Reykjavik came into sight, and we were puttering up cobble-stone streets and over a bridge that crossed a lake to the house of books.

Cousin, that house was the most marvelous thing I had ever seen. Not from the outside. From the outside it was a three-story cement façade painted pastel green. But the inside! Books lined every wall of every room. Books climbed up stairs and rested on landings. Books stretched over the arches of doorways like bridges, stood guard over mantels. Old leather-bound volumes with gilt titles gleamed in glass cabinets. Books in the basement, books in the attic. Four stories of books. How many, I wanted to know.

"Nine thousand, six hundred," Ulfur answered. "Approximately. The largest private book collection in Iceland."

Ulfur's father was the book collector, his mother the cataloger. The elderly couple lived on the main floor. Johann was nearly blind, but Lara was still spry enough to climb the ladders and retrieve books for Birdie. Which is pretty much how we spent our first two days in Reykjavik. It rained and rained and rained, sideways and upside down, with huge gusting winds on the lake. "Not a day for touring," Ulfur would announce each morning with a wry smile. I was restless, eager to get on the Ring Road and start seeing the glaciers and volcanoes and waterfalls. But Birdie didn't seem to mind. In fact, she became terrifically excited. Overexcited, my mother would have said. But of course Mama wasn't there. Birdie was in book heaven, flitting from room to room with Lara's tattered catalog in hand, piling books on every floor of the house. When she wasn't retrieving books she was poring over them, reading lines out loud, exclaiming to herself, making scribbled notes on her worn *Word Meadow* manuscript.

The collection was impressive, even I could see that. And it was pure Icelandica: mythology, history, literature, science, art, folktales, ghost stories, sagas, travelogues, family histories, novels, and poetry. Poetry and more poetry. One whole shelf devoted to our grandfather Olafur, *Skald Nyja Islands;* another to his uncle Pall, who was Ulfur's great-great-grandfather. A copy of the first Icelandic Bible. A nineteenth-century Icelandic translation of *Hamlet.* A seventeenth-century copy of *Saemundur's Edda.* One whole room with four walls of Icelandic Sagas. Ones I knew of, like *Laxdaela Saga, Njal's Saga, Egil's Saga.* And dozens more I'd never heard of. I remember Birdie at midnight, perched in a window seat reading a vellum manuscript by the light of the midnight sun.

Myself, I was drawn to Johann's collection of old and rare maps that hung on the wall of the front entrance to the house. Maps of Iceland through the ages, more lively and colorful than the map now folded open in front of me, with its geologically correct gradations of blue, white, green. My favorite was a sixteenth-century map that showed Mount Hekla with red flames leaping from its cone; underneath, in Latin, the words *Entrance to Hell.* A giant sea monster lurked offshore, men in boats harpooned whales. The maps were displayed in chronological order. If you compared the first with the last, you could see that in the beginning the Icelanders had not yet discerned the shape of their own island, its jagged fjord-addled circumference.

Books and rain, books and rain: those were our first two days in Iceland. And visitors. Nearly as many as the books. They dropped by for morning coffee and for lunch and for afternoon coffee and for dinner and for evening coffee. Always beginning with a discussion of who was related to whom and how. Birdie had brought Sigga's Blue Book with us, and of course Ulfur's parents had genealogy books and charts. Once the establishment of kinship was complete—discussions I quickly abandoned trying to follow—the relatives would turn their attention to me.

"And what do you think of Iceland?" they'd ask, in perfect English.

If I forgot myself and responded in English, Birdie elbowed me. Unlike at home, where Sigga and Birdie were always quick to correct me, these strangers seemed awed that I spoke even a word of their language. My accent, they exclaimed, was flawless. My vocabulary impressive. The grammar, yes, that is difficult. That will come.

At the time I was bewildered by the attention; now I understand how few people in the world attempt to learn Icelandic. It made me something of a star, and I was happy, for once, to let myself shine. A Frey-Star.

14

On the evening of our second day in Reykjavik, Ulfur and his parents held a dinner party in our honor. Yes, the occasion made me nervous, with its echoes of our welcome-to-Gimli disaster party six years earlier. But I was a different person now. The girl who turned the cartwheel was Before Freya. Now I was After Freya, a restrained, contained shadow of my former self. Expect no fateful gymnastics, Cousin. No ambulances, no mothers in comas.

Not to say that nothing happened. Much did. One thing in particular. A thing by the name of Saemundur. Rhymes with *eye-moon-lure*. Saemundur was Ulfur's sixteen-year-old son, who was living with his father while his mother was finding herself in Spain. (At the time it seemed strange to me, this idea of locating your lost self in another country. A place where you'd never been. It no longer seems so odd.) Ulfur's other children were in their twenties, both in graduate school in the States, but Saemundur was like me, a late-in-life child. If he existed at all—something I was beginning to doubt. Two days we'd been at the house of books and still no sign of Saemundur. "Out with his friends," Ulfur would explain apologetically. "Or so he says. He has not adjusted well to this divorce of ours. He blames it on me. He'd rather be in Spain with his mother. He'd rather be anywhere, he says, except here with me."

Saemundur's room was in the basement and had its own entrance. And exit. Only once had I caught a glimpse of him, from a third-floor window as he headed out through the front garden, across the street, and over the bridge in a rainstorm. Saemundur from the back at a distance in the rain: Lanky. Long black hair blowing in the wind. Wearing a blue jeans jacket decorated with brightly colored patches. It gave him a clownish air, as if he were an escapee from the circus. I watched him lope across the bridge like a tightrope walker, long arms swaying for balance against gusts of wind and slanting rain. And then he vanished on the other side, and I hadn't seen him since.

For this special dinner Saemundur was expected, Ulfur announced. And he'd better show up. I was hoping he would. I wanted to see his face.

Two long tables were set with sparkling china and gleaming silver and tall candlesticks. "It's fancy," I said to Birdie. "Are they rich?"

"They are indeed. Not Ulfur but his father. Johann was a Shell executive. Big money."

A shell executive. Maybe in Iceland you could get rich trading precious shells? I didn't have a chance to ask because the guests began arriving, nearly twenty of them. Some were relatives I'd met already, or not; others were people with an interest in Olafur's work: the chair of the Icelandic Literature Department at the university; a number of contemporary poets; the head of the National Library. Ulfur's mother, Lara, and a few other women had control of the kitchen; as usual, Birdie took no interest in that. I remember cream of lobster soup served in large white tureens, a platter with the largest whole salmon I'd ever seen, lamb that tasted like an entirely different breed of meat. Toasts were made, to me and Birdie, to Olafur, to Iceland, to Canada. *Skal!* the guests would cry, then lock eyes before drinking. Only one seat at the table remained empty: Saemundur's. Ulfur would glance over at it and shake his head angrily. I too stared—would I never meet the mysterious Saemundur?

The dinner party conversation was fast-paced and often heated; I followed it only in fragments. What I do remember is Ulfur dominating the discussion.

—*No sooner were we rid of the Danes then along came the Americans.*

—*They've never owned us.*

—*But they've got their army base here.*

—*We're in NATO, what do you expect?*

—*Exactly. And I'm not alone. Remember the anti-NATO riots of 'forty-nine?*

—*Without NATO who would protect us?*

—*An Icelandic army?*

—*We could be neutral . . .*

—*And who do we need to be protected from? We kicked the British out of our waters for good just two years ago. We didn't need the U.S. army for that.*

—*Cod Wars are different from Cold Wars, Ulfur minn.*

And another argument, equally heated, about the Canadian immigrants. One of the guests had flown to Canada to attend the hundredth anniversary celebration of the Icelandic settlement in Gimli.

—*You should see this festival they have—Islendingadagurinn, they call it. Much honor paid to their pioneers.*

—*I don't see what's to honor them for,* Ulfur said.

—*I agree—abandoning our country in its time of need!*

—*They had no choice. They were starving.*

—*And there was the eruption, the terrible ashfall.*

—*And besides, they made more room for everyone else. That region in the East was overpopulated. It couldn't sustain all those people. After the immigrants left, conditions improved.*

—*They didn't know that at the time!*

—*Who knows anything at the time?*

—*It's easy enough to look back and call them traitors.*

—*And I say call them adventurers in the old Viking style. This was not the first time our people voyaged to North America. Remember when the Norse settled Vinland one thousand years ago?*

—*Really, can the emigration have been so terrible, if it produced the great poet Olafur, Skald Nyja Islands?*

—*Canada didn't produce him!* Ulfur had become red in the face. *Iceland produced him. As you well know, he was mentored here in Iceland by his uncle Pall. Olafur is an Icelandic poet through and through.*

—*I disagree. He was only a child when he left.*

—*But he wrote all his poetry in Icelandic. Using Icelandic verse forms. And traditions.*

—*Poetry about the life in* Canada.

—*And his childhood in* Iceland, *don't forget.*

Birdie, who'd been oddly quiet during these discussions, stepped in. "My father was a man of two lands. He saw himself as straddling the ocean, one foot in Iceland, the other in Canada. And speaking of Olafur, Freya would like to recite for you one of his greatest works."

I felt Birdie nudge me with her foot from across the table. Luckily, she had warned me in advance of her plans. I'd tried to object, but Birdie had insisted. "How else are you to repay their hospitality?"

How else indeed? I got up from the table and stood in front of the fireplace with my hands behind my back, as Birdie had instructed me to do. Everyone was watching me: the dinner guests, the gallery of ancestor photos behind me on the mantel. And Saemundur's empty chair. I set my eyes on it and was about to open my mouth when out of the corner of my eye I saw Birdie gesturing wildly with her hair—the signal that I was to push my own long hair off my face. "You hide behind that hair like a veil," Birdie would say. I tucked my hair behind my ears and began. It was Olafur's signature "New Iceland Song," a poem of eighteen stanzas that I'd worked on memorizing all summer. (I wonder now if Birdie had been preparing me for just this occasion. In fact I'm sure of it, as sure as I can be of anything related to that trip.)

Olafur's "New Iceland Song" was the most difficult piece I'd memorized yet, but I'd been grateful for the challenge. In the past year I'd begun to tire of Old Gisli's funny verses and lying rhymes. I did not refer to them as *apamensskubragur* (baboonish nonsense) or *arnaleir* (eagle muck), no. But I was coming to appreciate Olafur's complex phrasing, the subtle musicality of his lines, his command of the Icelandic language, which seemed in his hand a different order of language altogether.

"New Iceland Song" recounted the immigrants' saga, from their beginnings as impoverished but literate peasants on their remote island, then the sun-obliterating fall of ash, Askja's terrible eruption, which as a child Olafur had mistaken for the onslaught of the mythic *Ragnarok,* destruction of the world. How haunting was the fourth stanza, echoing the words of the ancient poem *Voluspa*: *The sun turns black, fumes reek, cast down from heaven are the hot stars . . .* And then the journey, these once-accomplished seafarers no longer at the prow of a Viking ship but stuck deep in the hold, seasick and bereft and clinging frantically to the feeble dream of a new life in a new land. And that first year in Canada—one child after another buried from the smallpox, the entire colony quarantined, struggling to build clumsy log shelters before the first storms of winter—storms more bitter and freezing than any they had known in Iceland. Then in the midst of hardship the settlers scraping together funds for nothing other than a print-ing press! To outsiders perhaps a strange act by a strange people, for words are not food on the table. Unless you're an Icelander—then the words, the stories, the poems in your language are what sustains you. Oh, how beauti-fully phrased was the last line of that stanza, and I paused there, dared to lift my eyes from Saemundur's empty chair and pass them over the tables where the guests were listening, rapt. A few even had tears running down their cheeks. How thrilled I was in that moment. I thought of Mama and Sigga and Stefan, and Olafur, *Skald Nyja Islands,* how proud they'd be to see me here in Iceland, reciting the poet's greatest work! I opened my mouth to begin the next stanza.

And then I saw him. He stood in the doorway that led from the back stairs to the living room, leaning against the threshold in his jeans jacket, arms folded across his chest, head cocked to one side. His hair was so black and his skin so white he seemed nothing more or less than a ghost. From across the room I could see his eyes, the color of moon. The strange green moon of some other planet. Not ours.

Across his wide full lips was something like a smile. A smile with a twist. A smirk? I imagined suddenly that I looked like a fool. A foolish girl-child reciting for the grown-ups. I heard Birdie prompt me with the first words of the next stanza, and somehow I stumbled through the rest of it. My concentration was broken. I let my hair fall across my face. I squinted my eyes and stared at my feet. And when it was over and I finally looked up, the first thing I saw was the empty doorway. And Saemundur's empty chair. No one else had seen him, I realized. Not the guests or Birdie or his father, who certainly would have had something to say. Sly Saemundur and his vanishing act!

Birdie was staring at me quizzically: *What went wrong?* I looked away, hurried back to my seat. I had failed, I had stumbled. My cheeks burned.

But the guests were clapping and murmuring and smiling at me. Luckily my performance was quickly overshadowed by the conversation that followed. A conversation, I understand now, that was no accident but entirely orchestrated by Birdie to bolster her cause with Ulfur. That she chose that particular poem for me to recite—that too was part of her plan. Unless I am becoming as paranoid as Birdie herself. But no, that poem would easily lead the dinner table conversation exactly where she wanted it to go, and it did.

"What a marvelous poem!" someone remarked.

"And the only one he wrote, was it not, about the early life of the colony?"

"Interesting you should say that." It was Birdie speaking. "Actually, there are others. But they seem to be lost."

"Lost? What do you mean lost?"

Birdie had the attention of the entire table now. She paused a moment, looking carefully around the room, then began speaking in an urgent, almost conspiratorial tone. "After Olafur left Iceland as a child, he wrote a series of letters to his uncle Pall, during the first ten years he was in Canada. In the letters he enclosed poems, mostly juvenilia, of course, but some may have been better than that, composed in his early twenties, when his talent was truly flourishing."

"You have seen these letters, these poems?" The man who asked this question I remember clearly. He had a full beard, a loud voice, and he was head of the largest publishing house in Iceland. His name was Sveinn.

"Me? No. But my mother has. She heard them read out loud when she was a child on Pall's farm. Pall had died by then, but his son treasured the letters, and the poems."

"But where are they now?" Sveinn demanded.

"My question exactly!" Birdie paused, dramatically, then looked over at Ulfur. Ulfur pushed his glasses up to the top of his nose.

"I always thought they were here," Ulfur explained. "In my father's collection."

"Are they not listed in Lara's catalog?" Sveinn was growing increasingly alarmed.

"No, they're not published. Not in book form. I was sure I'd seen them, in a homemade binding, somewhere . . ."

Sveinn turned now to Ulfur's elderly father. "Johann, what do you say to this?"

"I say I've never seen them. Anyone claiming these were in my possession, that is nonsense."

A silence fell over the table. "I have come to Iceland," Birdie began, "to find these lost letters and early poems of my father. Ulfur has kindly promised to help."

"Where will you start?" someone asked.

"In the East. Some of Pall's people still live there."

Ulfur brightened. "Yes, yes, I think there is a good chance the letters will be found in a trunk in an old farmhouse. Mystery solved!"

"And then you will need a publisher," Sveinn suggested, more calmly.

"Oh, absolutely," Birdie said. "And I'll translate them into English myself. A double volume, of letters and poems."

"And what of your own work, Ingibjorg?" Sveinn again.

Birdie hesitated. "It is nearing completion. Whether it is worthy of your attention . . . well, I'll leave that to Ulfur to decide. He has promised to read it." She winked at me, acknowledgment of her false modesty. To me she'd confided her belief that it might be the greatest poem ever written in Icelandic. Perhaps the greatest poem ever!

"Yes," Ulfur said, recovering from his embarrassment over the letters. "We are taking a bit of a vacation, now that the weather is clearing. Tomorrow we leave for the summerhouse at Thingvellir Lake. And from there we will show our young Freya the sights, and I will read Ingibjorg's manuscript—the manuscript of the daughter of Olafur, *Skald Nyja Islands*!"

"And then we'll head east," Birdie added. "To look for the letters."

This was all news to me. I could scarcely take it in. My cheeks were still burning with shame. Worse things had happened to me than forgetting the line of a poem, but at that moment I couldn't remember what they were. How stupid I must have looked standing there with my mouth open in front of all the guests! In front of Saemundur Sly Ghost.

While the guests drank coffee I slipped away from the table, but instead of heading up the stairs to the guest room on the third floor, I took the back stairway down to the basement. There were two doors: one led to the outside, the other to Saemundur's room. I stood for I don't know how long in darkness outside Saemundur's door. I was afraid to switch on the light. I listened. My heart beat. I tried not to breathe. Then I heard a sound in his room, and I bolted out the back door and into the garden.

Ulfur was right: things were clearing up. For the first time since my arrival I could see sky. It was nearly midnight but there was no darkness, only clear sky and dim sun. I stared out at the lake, imagining Saemundur crossing it like a tightrope walker. I thought about his moonish eyes. Searched the sky for moon and saw none. Where did the moon go on these sunstruck nights?

Back in my bedroom it was too bright to sleep, and I lay awake for hours envisioning Saemundur's face in my mind. Like a mime, with his wide expressive mouth, his high cheekbones. A mime, a clown, a tightrope walker. Haunting me like a ghost. *Eye-moon-lure,* I whispered. *Eye-moon-lure.*

15

Nothing, not even Birdie's magical spiel on the airplane, could have prepared me for what lay beyond Reykjavik. Iceland is land alive, the earth split open, forming and re-forming before your eyes. Vast vistas of swirling black and neon green moss-drenched lavascapes. Volcanoes in all directions and at every stage of existence: smoldering, dormant, extinct. Glaciers on the move, their hoary tongues licking the edges of meadows. Water falling everywhere, trickling spilling clamoring rumbling down rocky crevices and canyons. And spitting up boiling hot from holes in the ground. Meandering through this riot of lava and ice and emerald slopes as if it were the most ordinary scenery in the world: wild horses, stout-bellied and thick-maned, peering out from behind fringed bangs. And the ubiquitous sheep, with their spiraling horns and shaggy dreadlocked coats. "We're outnumbered," Birdie would say when we'd round a bend and confront six sheep napping in the roadway. By this she meant the fact that there are more sheep than people in Iceland. Far more. Everywhere you go it's sheep agraze: munching grass on top of turf-roofed ruins, nipping at odd bits of growth in barren lava fields, hoofing it up the rocky bank of a waterfall. "We let them roam free," Ulfur explained. "And this is why they taste so good. The lava moss gives them a particular flavor. So we give our sheep the run of the island."

I wanted the run of the island. I'd never seen nature so wild. I was used to the timid rolling hills of Connecticut, the flat scrubby shore of Lake Winnipeg. Forests. In Iceland there are no trees to speak of.

"Trees get in the way," Ulfur explained. "They block the view."

Trees can't grow in Iceland. That's the truth of it. Little does.

But I could grow there. I felt myself expanding. For the first time since Mama's accident, I had no dutiful routines, no canes to keep track of, no Mama to tend. It freed and it terrified. I began wearing my hair pulled back. The wind made me do it—in Iceland it never stops blowing—and at first I felt bare-faced. Then Birdie touched her fingertips to my cheekbones.

You're a beauty, she told me.

Me a beauty? I shook my head laughing, but during those days at Ulfur's summerhouse, I allowed myself to believe it. Or at least to consider the possibility. The landscape itself emboldened me. I spoke up more, dropped my shield of shyness and silence. I began to speak only Icelandic, then to think and even dream in it.

The Summerhouse Days. That's how I came to think of them later. As much as I tried not to. Some memories refuse oblivion. In the Summerhouse Days, Birdie was in high spirits. Too high. The kind of free-spiraling high from which you can only free-fall crash and burn. I should have recognized the signs: the rapid speech, the frenetic flow of ideas. *Birdie's getting talky,* my mother would have said, if she'd been there. *Birdie's going over.* But Mama wasn't there, Birdie had made sure of that. And to my mind Birdie seemed nothing less than magnificent in the Summerhouse Days. Cheeks apple bright, eyes sparkling like sun on lake. Everything was about to happen for Birdie: she was about to recover her father's long-lost letters. Ulfur was about to read her years-long manuscript and declare it brilliant and pass it along to the loud bearded publisher Sveinn. *Word Meadow,* Birdie confided to me, was on the verge of great acclaim on both sides of the ocean. Even the weather was splendid in the Summerhouse Days. By Icelandic standards, anyway. Which means it rained daily but never all day long. And at least once each day (or night) we glimpsed bare and unclouded sun, sometimes for hours at a time. Weather is Iceland's only true god, and truly fickle in the way of all gods. In the Summerhouse Days the weather god was merciful.

How many days? I can't say exactly. A week or more. Sure, I could figure it out by checking the daily postcards I wrote to Gimli. But they're buried deep in a storage locker in Queens, along with the rest of my mother's belongings, which I packed up after she died and never looked at again.

Yes, I pay a monthly rent to store my dead mother's things. In case I should want.

I don't.

So, we'll estimate here. And really, what does *day* mean when you're talking about an Icelandic summer? Every day was like two in one. More happened to me in those Summerhouse Days than in a whole Gimli summer or an entire humdrum year of school in Connecticut.

I may share your mother's penchant for exaggeration, but I hope you'll believe me when I say those Summerhouse Days were the happiest of my life. Yet the beginning of that trip was inauspicious. The morning of departure, the morning after the dinner party and my faulty recital, Birdie and I rose early. Out our third-floor window I saw for the first time since our arrival in Iceland blue sky. The colored rooftops of Reykjavik were set against white-capped Mount Esja, the lake shimmered in sunlight. Leaving Birdie upstairs to do her makeup, I raced down to breakfast, then came to a halt outside the kitchen door. Ulfur and Saemundur were arguing.

"All summer you've been complaining that we don't go to the summerhouse. And now we are finally going and you don't want to come?"

"Exactly." Saemundur's tone was calm and defiant.

"Explain that!"

"For me you're too busy to go. But now the American Princess arrives, the American Princess and the Canadian Queen, now you have time to go to the summerhouse. Anything for the daughter and granddaughter of the great Olafur, *Skald Nyja Islands*! For me, for Mama you have no time. Only for consorting with the descendants of dead poets. And recovering precious manuscripts. It won't be so easy, will it, recovering your wife? Your son?"

Long silence.

Then Saemundur, again: "You don't trust me to stay here without you?"

"Trust you? How can I trust you after—"

Then a hand on my shoulder: Ulfur's mother, Lara. "Come, *elskan,*" she said, loudly enough to interrupt the argument. Silence fell in the kitchen and we entered the room. Lara led me to the table and to my horror seated me next to Saemundur. The table was laid with sliced brown bread, boiled eggs, cheese, cured lamb. Delicious *skyr,* a bit like yogurt, a bit like sour cream. But I wasn't hungry. *The American Princess:* Saemundur meant me. Was that how he thought of me? As a spoiled goody-goody who recites for company? Ulfur greeted me with a gruff good morning, but Saemundur didn't say a word, didn't even glance at me. I tried not to look directly at him either, though I couldn't help notice his wiry tightrope walker arms reaching rudely past me for bread, meat, cheese, coffee. I stared at my empty white plate, let my hair fall in my face. Even when Birdie came to the table I didn't look up. I allowed her to fill up my plate like I was a child who couldn't choose for herself.

Unlike Stefan's roomy Rambler, Ulfur's car was European and compact. Saemundur and I sat in back leaning against opposite doors, faces pressed out opposite windows. Yet our long legs cramped at odd angles verged perilously close. We'd each adopted a similar strategy: by pretending to sleep, we wouldn't have to talk, not to each other or to Ulfur and Birdie up front. I missed the scenery that morning, for the sake of that huddled silence. Birdie leaned over the front seat and stared at us, then turned back to Ulfur.

"They're sleeping. Both of them." She used the word *krakkanar,* which means something like kids.

"Saemundur's no kid, but he acts like one. Rejects any kind of responsibility or authority."

"How Icelandic of him!"

"What do you mean?" Ulfur sounded defensive.

"I only meant . . . you're a fiercely independent people."

Was she referring to the famous book by Halldor Laxness, *Independent People?* I was supposed to be sleeping so I couldn't ask.

"Independent, yes," Ulfur agreed, "but on the other hand, we are a very responsible society."

"Oh yes, so *duglegur!*" That favorite word for hardworking.

"I'd like to see more of that trait in Saemundur. He is barely passing in school. I tell you, he is a boy who is refusing to grow up. Reckless. Like that incident I told you about last summer."

I sensed Saemundur stiffen beside me. I hoped Ulfur would say more, but he fell silent and Saemundur relaxed again.

"And Freya," Birdie said. "She is too grown up for her age. She doesn't let herself act like a child."

"She does seem awfully serious, for an American girl."

I held my breath. I was afraid Birdie would reveal my whole story. And what did Ulfur mean, *an American girl*? That seemed to sum up precisely what he thought of me. I was a child, a girl, an American. He'd hardly said a word to me directly the entire visit. I could see why Saemundur resented him, but Birdie couldn't seem to get enough of him. I continued listening as their conversation shifted to a discussion of where we would go on our trip to the East to find Olafur's letters. Who to visit, where to search . . . I tried to follow, but Saemundur pulled my attention like a magnet. Even in my blind silence it was impossible to erase his presence. I could smell him, an intoxicating mix of stale cigarette smoke, grimy jeans, boy-sweat. Once, his leg fell against mine. I let it stay. Warming then burning at the point of contact. He was truly sleeping now, and I could take him in surreptitiously through half-closed eyes. The raven-black hair that fell in waves to his shoulders. The high planes of his cheeks. The dark slashes of his brows. His wide mouth, set tight all morning, now loosening, lips full and slightly parted. His moon eyes eclipsed by closed lids. And beyond him the strange swirling land.

Then the car hit a bump and he jolted awake and caught me staring. Flashed me a dirty-moon glare and jerked his leg back.

I must have slept too. When I woke we were driving along a lake, and for a confused moment I thought I was back in Gimli. Except this was a lake of a different order, a lake bordered not by sand and scrub and spruce forests but by bare rocky plains and distant mountains.

"Thingvallavatn," Ulfur announced. "The largest lake in Iceland. It may look calm to you at the moment, but it can turn rough in the blink of an eye."

Lake weather shifts fast.

After following the lakeside for a few miles we turned onto a dirt road which eventually narrowed into a driveway. Saemundur was awake now too, and when Ulfur stopped the car at a wooden gate, Saemundur leapt out and opened it. He turned his face toward the lake as we drove through. Ulfur stopped to let him back in the car, but Saemundur waved him off. Out the rear window I watched Saemundur latch the gate and walk slowly toward the house.

Ulfur's summerhouse was plain blond wood, set on stilts. Tall grasses grew up around it. Out front was a tan mud-clotted jeep. *Jeppi.* We would use it for touring, Ulfur explained. I peered inside. I'd never ridden in a jeep. The keys were dangling in the ignition.

"Couldn't somebody steal it?" I asked. "When you're not here?"

Ulfur laughed. "That, fortunately, is one of your American trends we have yet to adopt!"

Inside, everything was made of the same simple blond wood. A large plate-glass window framed an expanse of lake and mountains. I had the feeling Birdie had been to the house before—she glanced around with a wistful smile, then carried her things into a bedroom. I was still staring out the window. "It's beautiful here," I said, to no one in particular.

"Too bad it's sitting empty all summer," Saemundur answered, without looking at me, but clearly in response to what I'd said. Did that count as speaking to me?

"We're here now," Ulfur replied. "So enjoy it."

First lunch, Ulfur announced. Then Thingvellir. Thingvellir, it turned out, was just a short drive from the summerhouse. *Thing* means parliament, *vellir* means plains; Thingvellir is the site of the ancient parliamentary gathering. "Thingvellir," Ulfur proclaimed, "is the single most important place in Iceland. The history of Thingvellir," he continued, "*is* the history of Iceland."

Thingvellir! Birdie winked at me across the table. All through the years, whenever we came across a reference to Thingvellir in a story or a poem or a conversation, Birdie would say, "I'm going to take you there, *elskan*. Just wait. Someday I'll take you to Thingvellir."

And now we were going. I felt a sudden burst of love for Birdie. If it weren't for her I would never have come here, never had a chance to see

Thingvellir with my own eyes. Mama would certainly never bring me, Mama who was afraid to fly, Mama who was old before her time. With a twinge of guilt I realized I would see something my mother never would. Like when I was four years old, scaling the giant maple and peering down at earthbound Mama far below.

Unlike me, Saemundur seemed not to care about visiting Thingvellir. I watched him devour two sandwiches in large, rushed bites without speaking, without seeming to hear a single thing his father said. Then he tipped his head back and took a long chug of milk that emptied his glass, wiped his mouth with his sleeve, and stated that he had no desire to go to the single most important place in Iceland. He's been a million times. He could stay home and fish for trout on the lake and have dinner ready by the time we returned. Then he smiled, and in that smile I could see it was all a joke to him. Suddenly, I was no longer entranced with Saemundur. I was tired of his sulking and brooding, his surly remarks. This was *my* trip, not his. My only chance to see Iceland. "Then don't come," I wanted to say. "Stay home and fish. Drown, if you like." But of course I said nothing, and at first neither did Ulfur. Then he folded his napkin and stood up from the table. To me and Birdie he said, "Bring warm jackets. It gets windy at Thingvellir." Then he turned to Saemundur. "Start up the jeep. We'll be out in a minute."

When we got outside, Saemundur was sitting behind the wheel of the jeep and Ulfur was next to him up front.

And that was that.

16

I want to take you to Thingvellir once I find you. Birdie would have wanted that for you. In the meantime you'll have to make do with mere words.

Thingvellir, Cousin, is no Parthenon. There are no majestic ruins to behold; there were never any buildings in the first place: no columns, no arches, no roofs to support. Thingvellir is simply a seam of our planet, a raw and jagged spot on a volcanic plain, split by rocky chasms and chunky fault lines, surrounded by distant mountains, veined by river, and bordered by lake. Complete with the requisite waterfall. These were pagans, remember, who held their rudimentary parliament here each summer. In bare nature they worshiped, and so it should not be surprising that in bare nature they convened their government. But first they had to discover a need for one.

In the beginning, as Ulfur explained it to us that day, the settlers were lawless, and proud of it. They had arrived in Iceland at the end of the ninth century seeking freedom from Norway's tyrannical King Harald. Iceland was empty, save for a scattering of Irish monks. The immigrants could do what they liked. And what they liked was to be kingless. The settlers lived together in homesteads consisting of families, servants, and slaves under the power of local chieftains, who provided a localized sort of justice.

But after a while—maybe fifty years or so—the settlers began to feel the need, if not for a king, then for a common law. There were disputes, and no universal method of resolution. Law was necessary, they agreed, and they set about devising not only a set of laws but a government as well.

"In the end," Ulfur continued, "Thingvellir was the spot they selected for the convening of the first parliament, the Althing."

We were standing then, the four of us, at the Law Rock, from which the law-speaker annually recited Iceland's laws from memory. Behind us rose the steep wall of Almannagja (everyman's chasm), below us the remains of the stone booths inhabited by the *godi*—pagan chieftains doubling as parliamentary representatives—during the two weeks of the Althing.

"And you should not imagine," Ulfur went on, raising his voice over the rising wind, "that the annual Althing was an occasion only of solemn courts and heated legal wrangling. There were contests of sport and wit, telling of tales and reciting of poems, matchmaking and courting, drinking, and of course fighting. It must have been a lively scene indeed."

I looked out across the plain. A blue tourist bus had pulled up and was unloading passengers at the Thingvellir church, a nineteenth-century addition to the old pagan site. The dark clouds that had been stuck to the distant mountains like magnets were now being drawn toward us at dizzying speed. I realized we were down to three. "Where's Saemundur?"

Ulfur turned and stared down the Almannagja chasm, first south—no Saemundur—then north. There he was, leaning over a bridge.

"What's he doing?"

"Visiting the Drowning Pool, I imagine. His favorite spot."

I left Birdie and Ulfur at the Law Rock. By the time I reached Saemundur he was climbing along the rocks below the bridge, his black hair whipped by the wind. I peered into the pool of clear water, which seemed scarcely deep enough for drowning, then followed Saemundur down the rocks to the pool's edge, clambering as nimbly, I hoped, as a mountain goat. Proving myself no princess. Not that Saemundur noticed. He glanced up at me only once, then returned to staring into the pool. I squatted next to him.

"I'm looking for bones," he said at last.

"Whose? Who drowned here?"

"Many people. Women, I should say. Men they beheaded, but women they drowned. The pool was deeper back then. They pushed the women and held them underwater with a pole until they drowned."

"Why?"

"Babies out of wedlock. Sorcery. Although most of the supposed witches in Iceland were men."

"That was how the Althing used their laws?"

"Well, by that time the Danes had taken over Iceland, so it was Danish judges who came here and passed the verdicts of drowning."

"What about children?"

"What about them?"

"If men were beheaded and women were drowned, what happened to children who committed crimes?"

"I don't know. I've never heard of such a thing. Children committing crimes!" He looked at me, I said nothing. "Why, have you committed a crime, young Freya? An innocent such as you?"

I blushed. "I'm not innocent," I mumbled, as if to imply I led a secret life of crime—I didn't of course; that came later—but I wanted Saemundur to think so.

He threw a stone into the pool and watched it sink. Around us rose the sound of water burbling from the stream into the pool. Farther off I heard a louder rush. "Is that the waterfall?"

"It's upstream."

We climbed up a steep trail to the top of the Almannagja chasm. Saemundur was wearing his jeans jacket with the colored patches, and as I scrambled to keep up with him I could see that the patches represented different countries.

"Have you been to all those places?" I asked as we climbed.

"What?" he shouted.

The wind had scattered my words far across the plains. It blew even more wildly from the top of the chasm, where the view seemed to sprawl across half the planet. I felt breathless, from the view and the climb and this unexpected proximity to Saemundur. I reached over and touched one of the patches, a windmill.

"Last summer." He smiled at the memory. "Holland, France, Italy, even Portugal."

"You saw all those places in one summer?"

He nodded.

"That's amazing."

"My parents didn't think so."

"Why not?"

"I went by myself."

"You ran away?"

"You could call it that. But I sent them postcards. I was always planning to come back. To tell the truth, I hardly thought they'd miss me. They were too busy fighting and divorcing and all that. I hitchhiked all over Europe by myself."

For a moment I was too awed to speak.

"I don't know what my father was so upset about. I mean, his precious saga character Egil Skallagrimsson took off on Viking expeditions at twelve years of age. But my father hasn't forgiven me. He says he'll never trust me again."

I nodded, thrilled by this sudden intimacy. Yet I couldn't imagine doing such a thing, not telling my mother where I was, even for a few hours. A sudden fear rose up in me: *Mama!* We were walking along the ridge of the chasm, side by side, heading north to the falls. *Mama knows where I am,* I assured myself. *Doesn't she?*

And then we were standing on the edge of the waterfall. Far off I could see Birdie and Ulfur by the Law Rock. Saemundur leaned against a large stone on the very edge of the falls and lit a filterless cigarette, cupping his hand and bending his entire body around it to block out the wind. I wondered if his parents knew he smoked, even let him smoke, but I didn't ask. I didn't want to sound like a princess.

He stood up straight, the tip of the cigarette glowing bright for a moment as he inhaled. "Ever smoke an Icelandic cigarette?"

I shook my head. Mama, of course, had forbidden me to smoke. But Mama was far away, and Saemundur was holding the cigarette out to me. I took it tentatively between my fingers and raised it to my lips.

"Not like that!"

I cringed; Saemundur had that smirk on his face, the same as when he'd been watching me recite Olafur's poem at the dinner party. But he spoke kindly, confidentially. "We hold cigarettes differently here." He came over to the rock where I sat, curving his arm around me and showing me how to pinch the cigarette between finger and thumb. I felt the ropy muscle of his arm graze my back through the worn denim of his jacket. Then he moved away and sat across from me again. I inhaled a tiny puff, then blew it out. Pleased, I offered the cigarette back to Saemundur, but he wouldn't take it.

"Not so fast! We smoke it in a special way here too. Instead of blowing the smoke right out, you hold it inside for a while. For as long as you can."

I tried once, twice, three times, each time coughing, the last time managing to hold in some of the smoke.

"I don't think I like cigarettes," I said, handing it back to him.

"Oh, I think you'll like it. Just wait a few minutes."

I didn't know what he was thinking. I certainly wasn't planning to try it again in a few minutes. Or ever. But it didn't matter. The sun was streaming through a hole in the clouds, lighting up the droplets of waterfall spray in Saemundur's hair. A halo of mist for his dark head. His eyes were closed and his face looked unbelievably beautiful to me. The most beautiful thing I had ever seen. He opened his eyes.

"How are you doing?"

Doing? I had to think about that. I must have thought a long time because Saemundur stood up. "We better get back."

I began following him south along the top edge of the chasm, hypnotized by the sway of his arms and his loping stride. I stumbled on a stone that seemed to appear out of nowhere. As I righted myself, I felt oddly dizzy.

"Be careful!" Saemundur called over his shoulder. "The earth is splitting open under your feet!" He was laughing, teasing me again.

"I mean it," he shouted over the wind. "Right here, right along this very chasm, one tectonic plate meets another." He stopped walking and waited for me to catch up. "You know what the tectonic plates are?"

I nodded vaguely.

"Think of the earth like an egg with its shell cracked. We're standing on one of those cracks. Right here is where the North American Plate meets the Eurasian Plate. Right through the middle of Iceland. And underneath, lava rises up and pushes the two plates apart. That's what causes earthquakes in California. California is on the opposite side of the North American Plate. Iceland is pushing California into the ocean."

I shook my head doubtfully.

"You think I'm teasing you? No, no, this is the truth. According to my brother anyway, and he's a geologist you know, studying at one of the great universities in your country." He peered down the edge of the chasm. "Of course the settlers didn't know that when they chose this spot for the Althing, but they recognized its special energy. Can you feel it?"

I could: a something that surged through the chasm and up my legs and out the top of my head. An almost-dizziness, except instead of spinning, the landscape seemed to be opening up on itself, over and over. The rifts and chasms of Thingvellir folded and unfolded in ribbons of rock. I watched the last of the clouds push past us and suddenly the sun was shining through again, glinting the river, lighting this great crack in the earth. I was trembling. Or was it the ground? *Either the earth is quaking,* I thought, *or I am.* That thought seemed funny, extremely funny, and scary at the same time. I stood fast, laughing and trembling, while Saemundur loped ahead.

"Come on!" he yelled. "They're waiting."

I looked down the chasm and in the distance saw Birdie back at the Law Rock, waving to us, arms crisscrossing in the air above her head. I thought of the day Mama and I first set foot on the platform at Winnipeg Station and Birdie came running through the crowd scissoring her arms through the air in her lilac dress. It struck me then, how big Birdie was, not only in size but in her being. Everything large: her wave, her gestures, her laughter, her ideas, her desires. And me? I felt bigger too suddenly, perched on the tip of a great rift, an edge of the earth itself. *The earth isn't flat,* I thought, *but it does have edges.* It occurred to me then, that I could fling myself off the edge of the earth and into the Drowning Pool. It was not something I thought I *would* do, yet I could imagine it: diving into the Drowning Pool and rescuing the sodden spirits of all the women wrongly drowned. I don't know how long I stood there. A moment now seemed hours long.

"Freya!" Saemundur called again. Suddenly my feet were in motion, I was sprinting toward him, faster, it seemed, than I'd ever run before. "They're here!" I yelled over the rasping wind.

"Who?"

"All of them. The drowned women. I can't see them exactly, but I know they're here." Any moment Saemundur might start laughing at me. Smirking at the very least. Instead he just nodded his head.

"I know," he said. "I know."

And then we both started laughing. Couldn't stop. "Really," he gasped. "Have you really never gotten high before? I thought all American teenagers get high."

"What are you talking about?"

"High. Stoned."

"I don't get high." But as soon as I said it I understood that's what I was. The Icelandic cigarette!

"Don't tell me you've never heard of marijuana!"

It was all a trick, he'd never meant to be nice to me, not for a moment. I turned away.

"Don't be mad," he pleaded. He put a hand on my shoulder, but I shrugged it off. "And whatever you do, don't tell my father. He'll have me put away for sure."

"Put away where?"

"In a home for bad boys. Or a crazy hospital. Who knows?"

"Maybe the Drowning Pool." As I walked off in a stiff-legged stride to where Ulfur and Birdie were waiting at the Law Rock, I could hear Sae-mundur's laughter echoing along the length of the Almannagja chasm. Or was that the wind? Or maybe laughter and wind were now one and the same thing. Another crazy thought. Was it still my thought, I wondered, if I thought it while I was high? I shook my head, as if I could shake all the stoned ideas right out of it, but instead they kept piling up, one on top of the other. Would Birdie be able to tell? As we four walked back to the car, I decided the best thing to do was to say nothing. That, at least, would not seem too out of the ordinary.

On the drive home Birdie sat up front with Saemundur. He was telling her about the geology of Thingvellir, how his brother the geologist had taken him to volcanoes all over Iceland. Even to Askja.

"I would like to go to Askja," Birdie said.

"Not Askja," Ulfur corrected from the backseat. "Nobody goes there but hard-core scientists. Too difficult. There are so many other volcanoes to see. Hekla is a good one. We'll drive you to Hekla."

"I want to see Askja," Birdie repeated. "Askja is the beginning of everything for me. If Askja hadn't erupted, my father's family would never have left Iceland. I never would have been born."

"Just as easily they could have stayed," Ulfur countered. "Many people did. And if they'd remained, your father and mother could have met right there in the East of Iceland, on Pall's farm."

"Still, I'd like to go. Askja's eruption cast a shadow over my father, he told me the story so many times. And if it weren't for Askja, the emigration never would have occurred. There would have been no New Iceland in Canada."

"Well, that's one theory anyway. Blame it all on the volcano. But there were other conditions as well. Freezes. Poverty. Sheep plagues. People were already starting to abandon the homeland, even before Askja erupted."

"What's your point?" I could hear an edge in Birdie's voice.

"My point is that some people stayed anyway. Despite all those terrible conditions. Others decided to leave. That's all."

"And you think the strong ones stayed and the weak ones left?"

"It could be. Or maybe the other way around."

"Well, nothing can change the fact that my father's people left because of that volcano and the incredible havoc it wreaked. And I would like to set eyes on it just once in my life. I consider it," she concluded dramatically, "my point of origin. Practically the place of my birth."

Was that a strange thing to say, I wondered, or was I still high?

"Maybe Saemundur can drive us to Askja," Birdie continued. "While we're in the East."

Was Saemundur coming with us to the East to look for Olafur's letters? I guessed he had to, since Ulfur didn't trust him at home. But the thought made my heart sink. And leap. Sink, leap. *Sinkleap sinkleap sinkleap* ran through my head like a song. I guessed I was still high.

"I don't think that's a good idea, Ingibjorg. You'll have to take my word for it. It's too difficult a trip. Through lava wastes and deserts. No real roads to speak of. Isn't that true, Saemundur?"

"It's true that it's difficult," Saemundur agreed. "You have to have a jeep and know how to drive it, how to cross glacial rivers and ride over humps of lava."

"Exactly!" Ulfur seemed pleased that Saemundur had taken his side.

"But," Saemundur continued, "it can be done. It can certainly be done."

"Well, not by us it won't. Besides, it takes a whole day to drive there, another to drive back. Ingibjorg, you must believe me when I tell you there are better, more important things to do with your time in the East."

Birdie said nothing. It must have been in that moment that she made up her mind. Of course, that's just one more thing I can never know.

After dinner that evening, when Ulfur sat reading Birdie's *Word Meadow* at the kitchen table, Birdie asked Saemundur if he'd take her for a ride in the jeep. Saemundur leapt up and grabbed the keys from the kitchen counter without even waiting for his father's permission. What about me? Was I invited too? It was nearly ten o'clock, my usual bedtime, but it seemed strange to sleep with the sun still high in the sky. So I followed them outside, and nobody said no. The sky was a strange light turquoise color, and I could see a herd of wild horses grazing by the lakeshore. As soon as we'd driven out of sight of the summerhouse, Birdie asked Saemundur to teach her to drive the jeep.

"It's something I've always wanted to learn," she explained. Which struck me as odd. No one drove jeeps in Gimli. Not that I'd ever seen. But Saemundur didn't think it was a strange request, or at least he didn't say so. He just pulled over so he and Birdie could switch places. And that's the way it went, every evening after dinner during the Summerhouse Days. Birdie was an apt pupil, barreling down rutted dirt roads with remarkable aplomb. After a few sessions she wanted to learn to drive across a river.

"Without a bridge?" I asked, incredulous.

"There aren't many bridges in the interior," Saemundur explained. "Bridges just get washed away, or are never built in the first place. It's easy enough to drive through the river instead. You just try to judge the most shallow spot, which is often where the river runs widest."

I held my breath as Birdie sat behind the wheel at the edge of a rushing stream. What if we got stuck? We were over an hour from the summerhouse and nobody was anywhere near. No one but horses and sheep, horses and sheep. But Birdie managed it, she maneuvered the wheels of the jeep along the rocky bottom and across to the other side, where she crowed in triumph.

I should have noticed then the peculiar shine in Birdie's eyes, the mania spurring her along, infusing her with extraordinary acuity and physical strength. But I was too caught up in the moment, and I found myself cheering along with Birdie and Saemundur, the three of us whooping into the sunny night air. We never mentioned the jeep lessons to Ulfur. It was our secret, Birdie said, and we each kept it. Saemundur because it was an act, however small, however meaningless, against his father. Me, because I always kept Birdie's secrets. It was my way of proving my loyalty. And Birdie, well, her reasons would be revealed soon enough.

The morning after our visit to Thingvellir I woke before Birdie. She'd been unable to sleep most of the night—the light she claimed, fooling with her brain—and I'd woken up several times to see her fiddling with the curtains or trying to create a darkened tent out of her bedspread. Now, finally, she'd achieved unconsciousness, tangled in a heap of blankets, and I tiptoed quietly out of the room and into the kitchen. Out the small window above the sink I could see two volcanic craters poking above the surface of Thingvellir Lake. *The earth is splitting open.* Had I liked being high? I couldn't decide. Suddenly I was aware of Saemundur, leaning in the doorway, cupping a mug of coffee in his long-fingered hands. It was our first moment alone since he'd gotten me stoned at Almannagja.

"Would you care for coffee?" he asked. "Special Icelandic coffee?"

I rubbed the sleep from my eyes and scowled at him. "You tricked me."

"Loki's my middle name."

"It is?"

He laughed. "You don't know who Loki is?"

"Of course I do. Loki is the trickster god."

"So there you go." And there I went. He handed me a cup of coffee—my first ever—and smiled his clown-wide smile. I found myself smiling back, half infuriated, half charmed. The coffee tasted horrid-bitter, but I drank it anyway. It didn't matter how much Saemundur teased me in the days that followed, I never stayed mad long and I always went back for more. The teasing, of course, was flirting, but I didn't know that then. I didn't have a name for it; I'd never had a crush before.

In the days that followed we toured the countryside with Ulfur and Saemundur, and wherever we went, wherever we met anyone, we were greeted like minor celebrities: the daughter and granddaughter of Olafur, *Skald Nyja Islands*.

"We have no movie stars," Ulfur explained, the first time a total stranger began reciting my grandfather's poetry from memory for us outside a gas station.

"That's because we don't make any movies." Saemundur grinned.

"True enough," his father conceded. "But I also mean we don't have celebrities, not the way America does. The closest we come is our writers. Our writers are our stars. And by that I mean, those who shine above this nation most brightly."

I was beginning to understand that it was not only my odd little family back in Gimli who revered writing and writers; it was a national trait of the Icelanders. Everywhere you go in Iceland is a plaque or statue dedicated to a writer. "And yet," Ulfur continued. "Writing is not reserved for the elite. Every Icelandic family has a versifier or two, and many people write books of their own. In fact, Iceland publishes more books per capita than any country in the world, and has the highest literacy rate."

"But now we have television," Saemundur countered. "Maybe people will quit reading so much."

"Maybe," Ulfur conceded. I saw no signs of it while I was there. Many people, on learning who we were, recited Olafur's poetry to us, not only scholarly friends of Ulfur's, but ordinary people, like the farmer on the road to the Gullfoss waterfall. We stopped the jeep to help him lift a dead sheep from the road, and in return, he invited us for coffee and recited from memory several of Olafur's most well-known poems. It made me feel special, and Birdie, of course, thrilled at the attention. Oh, she was in high spirits, lively and energetic and full of good feeling toward everyone. Especially me. I was speaking Icelandic all the time, and bit by bit as we rattled through the Icelandic countryside in the jeep I dropped my veneer of shyness and reserve. Birdie approved, and I basked in her approval.

With Birdie and Ulfur and Saemundur as my guides, I was shown marvel upon marvel. I remember running with Saemundur through the spray of the massive Gullfoss waterfall, a rainbow shimmering above our heads.

"*Bifrost*. The bridge to heaven," Saemundur said. "That's what the rainbow was called in the old days."

I decided he wasn't teasing. It made too much sense. Standing on the brink of thundering falls under a rainbow with Saemundur was surely as close to heaven as I'd ever come.

It seemed no place in Iceland—no farm, rock, hill, stream, glacier, or volcano—lacked its own particular legend. I was haunted by our visit to Barnafoss—Children's Falls—where two children, left home on a Sunday morning while the family was at church, disobeyed their mother's orders and played on the stone bridge that crossed the nearby waterfalls. When the family returned home, the children were gone.

"Were they ever found?"

"Not alive," Ulfur answered.

Even the lava had stories to tell. One day we drove past a stretch of moss-covered lava rocks. "The Taking-of-Christianity Lava Field," Ulfur explained. "Nearly a thousand years ago, when the Icelanders were debating whether to adopt Christianity or not, a volcano erupted and the lava destroyed the farm of a practicing Christian. Proof, the pagans declared, that Christianity was a bad bet. But wasn't the pagans' own headquarters, Thingvellir itself, covered in lava? The pagans lost the vote at the Althing."

And of course we visited Reykholt, the estate of the great Snorri Sturluson, who had been raised as a child at Oddi.

"The same Snorri who wrote down the Norse myths?"

"Good memory," Birdie answered. "But he was a politician as well."

"In cahoots with the Norwegian crown!" Saemundur added. "Was it not because of Snorri that Iceland lost its independence for six centuries?"

"Son," Ulfur corrected him. "You know it's much more complicated than that. Snorri alone cannot take the blame. The Icelandic Commonwealth came to an end because the Norwegian crown was more powerful. Snorri, if you remember, was assassinated by order of the king."

"Right here at this very spot," added Birdie. We were standing on the lip of the hot springs where Snorri had been killed. A cool mist drifted down on us from the sky; gentle hot steam rose up from the pool. I sucked the air deep in my lungs and expelled it, imagining it merging with the vapors rising from Snorri's grisly murder scene.

"Me," Saemundur said, "I prefer true outlaws. Like Grettir. Surviving for years outside of civilization, in the wilds of Iceland. Doing battle with monstrous ghosts."

"Were they real?"

"The outlaws were. I don't know about the ghosts."

"How do you know?"

"I've seen evidence. There are some lava caves near here where outlaws used to live. You can see the bones of the sheep they stole from nearby farms littering the cave floor."

"Lava caves?"

"Long tubes of lava. Filled with stalagmites and stalactites. Some are shining with ice."

"You've been inside?"

"Sure I have. I'll take you there."

I thought he was teasing but he wasn't. And he did.

17

Our last evening at the summerhouse Ulfur sat down at the dinner table with a cup of coffee and opened Birdie's *Word Meadow*. "I'm beginning my final review of Ingibjorg's manuscript," he announced. "Tomorrow morning Ingibjorg and I will be discussing the work. Perhaps, Saemundur, you will take Freya out touring for a few hours?"

"In other words, scram," said Birdie, in a burst of nervous laughter. "Beat it, make yourselves scarce!"

Oh, she was in high spirits. You see, Cousin, your mother expected nothing but the best from Ulfur's review of her work. Still, there was a particular edge to her energy that I hadn't seen before. I was practically as nervous as Birdie. *Word Meadow,* her life's work, to meet the eyes of the world at last!

"I'm on the verge of great things," she confided to me on the way out to the jeep. "Greatness, even." Since she couldn't bear to sit in the summerhouse while Ulfur read her manuscript, she'd decided the three of us would venture out for another clandestine jeep driving lesson.

"Lava," Birdie said, the moment she got behind the wheel. "I want to try a lava field."

I was surprised Saemundur agreed to it. But the evening sky had cleared—it was blue, Cousin, bright brilliant blue—and the sun was truly, fully shining. A blue sky at night makes anything seem possible. And Birdie had mastered all the basics, proven herself an agile driver. She could ford a stream, maneuver up and down steep rocky slides that could hardly be called roads. I guess Saemundur felt she was ready.

I don't know where he took us, exactly. There is no scarcity of lava fields in the vicinity of Thingvellir Lake. Wherever it was, I do remember Saemundur explaining that the lava was thousands of years old, worn down and smoothed over. Hardly as sharp and craggy as the sites of more recent eruptions, like Laki or Heimaey. The rock was blackened, humped, and rutted, and driving it was akin to maneuvering an obstacle course on a foreign planet. Saemundur insisted on demonstrating first. "If you crash this jeep, Ingibjorg, I'll have to take the blame, and I don't know what my father might do. Disown me, maybe. Might not be a bad thing, I suppose."

I was nearly as nervous as Saemundur when Birdie took the wheel. I had visions of the jeep tipping over backwards, turning somersaults, spinning off the edge of a lava hillock. But Birdie was focused, surprisingly so, given that Ulfur was reviewing her precious *Word Meadow* at that very moment. She guided the jeep slowly over the first bumps of lava, then eased it along a slanting rut. For me as a passenger it was nerve-racking, but not nearly as nerve-racking as being stuck in the summerhouse with Birdie while Ulfur read her manuscript. In contrast it was nearly fun.

"Am I ready for Askja?" Birdie asked Saemundur after an hour. I thought she was joking, but he took her seriously.

"The drive to Askja is much more difficult than this."

"Are you saying I couldn't do it?"

"Oh, I would never say that. You seem capable of anything."

"Indeed I am." Birdie laughed. And indeed she was. She turned the jeep toward the road that led to the summerhouse, but in the end could not resist one last, sharp crevice.

"I wouldn't try it," Saemundur warned.

Birdie ignored him and eased the jeep over a rubble-strewn slope and down into a deep gulley. I noticed everything seemed darker. Had the sun finally set? I craned my head out the window and saw bulky clouds rapidly filling the sky overhead. A crack of thunder, and then rain was falling in hard sheets that clattered against the jeep's metal armor.

"We better get home," Saemundur urged.

But there was no way forward. Birdie had dumped the jeep into a dead end. Sheer rock wall loomed in front of us, with no room to turn around.

"Disaster," Saemundur said. "Let me take the wheel."

"Let me try," Birdie pleaded. "Please. I have to learn." I was surprised by how desperate she sounded.

"Take it slow then."

Birdie shifted into reverse, then pushed steadily on the accelerator, but the jeep resisted going upslope.

"Harder."

Now the wheels began to spin. The engine made a grinding sound.

"Cut it."

She gunned harder.

"I said cut it now."

The jeep sputtered still and we sat for a moment listening to the rain. There was no way out. I envisioned us abandoning the jeep, tramping through the sodden lava field at midnight, announcing to Ulfur we'd dumped his precious jeep in a lava pit.

"I'll check into things." Saemundur opened his door, but Birdie put a hand on his shoulder and pulled him back in.

"Let Freya do it," Birdie said.

"Freya?" Saemundur was incredulous.

"Yes, Freya," Birdie insisted. "She has to learn how to do these things."

Let me tell you, Cousin, I had no inclination to climb out of the jeep and go poking around the wheels in the pouring rain. That had always been Saemundur's role when the jeep got stuck, and I'd been happy to let him do it. Now, for some reason, Birdie was determined to put me to the test. Afraid of looking like an American princess in front of Saemundur, I complied. Even in the rain it was easy enough to see what had gone wrong. Our drive down the slope had loosened a mini landslide, and rubble had piled up thick behind the wheels. I felt important as I reported this information to Birdie.

"Then clear it," was all she said.

"I'll do it," Saemundur offered.

"Freya," Birdie insisted. She wanted to see what I was capable of, and I was as driven as ever to try to please her. Back in Connecticut I was known as being *strong for a girl*. Why shouldn't I be able to clear some rubble?

It's one of my sharpest memories from the trip: crouched behind the jeep, picking up stones and throwing them to the side, kick-pushing with my foot the heavy ones, soaked through but triumphant when Birdie finally maneuvered the jeep back up to solid ground again. I scrambled up the slope and climbed in.

"That's my girl," Birdie said.

My teeth chattered wildly the whole drive home.

Who slept well that night?

Not Birdie, awaiting Ulfur's morning verdict on her life's work. Not Ulfur, dreading the delivery, as I now know he must have been. And certainly not me, for reasons unrelated to *Word Meadow*. For reasons known as Saemundur. I had not forgotten that in the morning he and I would be on our own. It was Birdie's big moment; she wanted no teenagers, sulking or otherwise, to sully it. So we would make ourselves scarce. We would scram. And then? I had never been alone with a boy before. What exactly I expected I don't remember, if I even knew at the time. Something. I expected Something. And that something made it impossible to sleep. Below me on the bottom bunk Birdie sat, journal propped on her knees, scribbling the interminable night into dawn.

Saemundur seemed unusually *hress* that morning, as Birdie commented, lively and in good spirits.

"I need to be *hress*," Saemundur replied. "Today I am going to be the *leidsogumadur*."

"What's a *leidsogumadur*?" I asked.

"Road-story-man. A tour guide for the American Princess."

He was making fun of me again. Was that how the day would be? I swirled cream into my bowl of *skyr*, slowly and not once looking up.

Birdie laughed. "And where will you take our princess?"

"Yes," Ulfur prompted. "What is your itinerary, Son?"

"Hveragerdi. To see the thermal greenhouses."

I sucked a spoonful of *skyr* into my mouth with a sour burst. I'd forgotten to sugar it. Hveragerdi. I felt vaguely disappointed. Greenhouses, thermal or otherwise, did not appeal to my teenage imagination.

"Be back by noon," Ulfur warned. "One o'clock at the latest. We need to pack up."

It was our last Summerhouse Day. We would spend a day or so back in Reykjavik, then head east with Ulfur to try to track down Olafur's lost letters.

We left them sitting at the table, Ulfur and Birdie, facing each other, the breakfast dishes cleared, the manuscript between them.

Good luck, Word Meadow. My last thought before heading out the door.

Saemundur and me up front together in the jeep. That was a first. In the backseat a cloth knapsack with our lunches. At the gate Saemundur stopped and I jumped out, swinging the gate open, then tying it shut again. See? I'm no princess. I half-skipped to the jeep, but just as I reached for the door to climb back in, the jeep jerked forward, then sputtered to a stop. I raced to catch up, reached for the door again—and the jeep lurched forward again. This time it didn't stop. I stood in disbelief as Saemundur disappeared down the dirt road in a cloud of dust. He was leaving me! He had no intention of taking me anywhere! I was ditched. Dust and tears stung my eyes. Where could I go? Not back to the summerhouse. Not while Birdie and Ulfur were holding their all-important discussion. Forget them all. I would walk by myself to Thingvellir Lake. And I wasn't coming back either. Let them come look for me.

By the time I'd crossed the road, the jeep had turned around and was skidding to a stop beside me. Saemundur laughing, his wide mouth clown-mocking. I kept walking.

"Hop in, Freya!

"It was only a joke!"

"You are so serious, you know that? You are the most serious girl I have ever met." He was driving along beside me. I wouldn't look at him. Only at my sneakered feet treading gravel and to the left of my feet the wheels of the jeep.

Whap! Saemundur had stopped the jeep just ahead of me and opened the passenger door. Just in time for me to walk into it.

"I'm sorry, Freya. I didn't mean it. Just a joke. And not a good one. But come on. We have to get going now."

"I don't want to go to Hveragerdi," I said. But I climbed in anyway.

"That's fine," Saemundur said. "Because we're not going there."

"We're not?"

"No. Though I'd better tell you something about the greenhouses, in case my father quizzes us when we return. He doesn't trust me, you know. And why should he?"

That was a lot for me to take in. Not only had Saemundur lied to his father and Birdie but now I would have to lie too? "Where are we going then?"

"You don't remember?"

"Remember what?"

"What I told you."

He was teasing me again. It was too complicated, this being alone with a boy.

"The lava caves, silly. Remember, I told you I would take you there."

"But why did you lie to your father?"

"Because I can. And it's fun. And because he wouldn't let us go. He thinks it's too far a drive."

"Is it?"

"If you take the long way it is. Not if you take the shortcut through the glacier pass. It's called Kaldidalur. Cold Valley. It's the high road between Thingvellir and Husafell. He thinks it's dangerous."

"Why?"

"Snow."

"In August?"

"Oh yes, sometimes they have to close it. But I've driven it many times. It's spectacular. You'll see."

And I did. Saemundur drove fast, twice as fast as when Ulfur was in the car, as fast it seemed as anyone could go on a surface that was nothing like what I knew as road. Once we hit a rock and the jeep bounced off it, careening sideways. In a flash Saemundur guided the wheel straight with his long wiry arms, then grinned.

"You're not scared, are you? I can slow down if you want."

"I'm not scared." It was the truth. I didn't want him to slow down. If anything scared me it was how unscared I was. Dozens of glacial rivers and streamlets scissored back and forth across the road, but I'd become used to fording them. *Mama!* I thought as Saemundur barreled the jeep through a particularly deep stream. *Mama, look me now!*

Recklessness arose in me. *No one knows where I am.* Not Mama, of course, or Sigga. Not Birdie or Ulfur either. For the first time in my life, no one on the entire planet could say where I was. And I liked it. Oh, how I liked it!

I mark that moment as the beginning of my adolescence.

It began to rain. We passed Egilsafangi, the grasslands where travelers can rest their horses. And a cone-shaped tuff mountain called Fanntofell, Home of Giants. The rain turned freezing as we climbed higher toward the glaciers. Only once did we stop on our mad drive to the lava caves, at a cairn where travelers—back when travelers came by foot or on horseback—were expected to compose a verse and leave it inside a sheep's leg bone for the next traveler to find. We climbed out of the jeep. The cairn was twice as tall as Saemundur, the land around it rubble. Stones and nothing growing. As we circled the cairn, sleet turned to snow. I stuck my tongue out to catch some flakes.

"Is that an American thing? Eating snow?"

"Every day," I joked back. "We lick our freezers inside out."

"Then you will be right at home here in Iceland."

Every direction I turned my head was another glacier. I saw more glaciers in one morning than most people see their entire lives. Saemundur knew them all by name, like old friends. The white tops of the glaciers melded into the white underbelly of the freezing sky. And everywhere the ground was just stones. *Nothing could grow here,* I thought. Then I looked down and saw the tiniest flower possible sprouted among the rubble, pink petals tipped with ice. *Land of fire and ice:* if you have heard anything of Iceland, Cousin, it is probably that phrase. Hackneyed but utterly apt. According to Saemundur—and I was never sure when to believe him—volcanoes lurked under many of the glaciers. When such a volcano erupted, well, there was fire-and-ice havoc to be reckoned with.

I left myself an invisible message in the *beinakerling*: *Return to this place.*

Hours.

I don't know.

Maybe three or even five. We had no watches. There was no sun or moon. No stars.

Surtr is the giant who set the world ablaze. *Hellir* means cave. Surts-hellir was the name of our cave.

He took my hand in the cave. Saemundur. *Eye-moon-lure.*

One flashlight between us. We walked we stood we crouched we knelt we crawled on our bellies, we lay on our backs gazing up. We walked more.

"You know where you're going." I tried not to make it a question.

"I've been here a million times."

"You know the way out?"

"Of course!"

"You won't . . . leave me?"

"You don't trust me, do you?"

Trust him? After he duped me into getting stoned? After he lied so art-fully to Ulfur and Birdie? After he left me in the dust outside the summer-house? Of course I trusted him. Or rather, I trusted myself to him. The way metal trusts magnet. Trust in these cases is not something you do. It's some-thing that happens to you. I let him take my hand. I let him lead me through the lightless caverns.

Stalagmites grow up, stalactites hang down. Saemundur showed me a pair that nearly kissed, the down-flung tip of one grazing the up-thrust tip of the other. Only an icicle's breath between them.

Away from his father, Saemundur knew things. How the crater Jokulkrokur had cascaded molten lava between the glaciers Langjokull and Eiriksjokull all the way down to the river Hvita, forming the lava field called Hallmundarhraun, riddled with caves. Outlaws lived here, back in the tenth century. See the stone-built walls. And animal bones.

Sitting side by side on Saemundur's slicker, leaning against rough cave wall. Swirls of lava you could stroke with your hand. Saemundur switched off the flashlight, introducing me for the first time in my life to pure dark. Utter-black-of-the-universe dark. Soul dark, heart dark, mind dark. Left with nothing but your breath. We sat in the dark breathing. Then Saemundur said, "This is real Iceland. The Iceland that existed before we humans arrived and that will be here long after we're gone. My father says if I love the land so much I should go to university, study geology like my brother. But you don't learn earth from books. When I was little I wanted to be an *aevyntyramadur*."

Adventurer.

"But now I think I should be a guide. Take people to these places. Deep into caves, onto glaciers, through hot lava fields."

"You'd be good at that."

"And what are you good at?"

Darkness. "Nothing."

"Nothing?"

"Nothing."

"Well then, what do you like to do?"

More darkness. "Write."

"What?"

"Write."

"No, I heard you the first time. I mean, what do you write? Poems? Stories?"

"Different things." I sounded like an idiot to myself.

"Then you should do it. Be a famous writer like your grandfather Olafur. Freya, *Amerikuskald*!"

He was teasing again. Me, a poet? Like Olafur, like Birdie? "Do you think he liked it?"

Saemundur knew exactly what I was talking about, had followed my invisible train of thought. "I doubt it. I doubt it very much."

A rush of anger, defensiveness. "How can you say that? You've never even read it. Birdie is a brilliant writer!"

"Undoubtedly. But my father is not a brilliant reader. Oh sure, the old stuff, he can read that. He loves that. But anything after World War I? My father's old school. He believes poetry should rhyme, like your grandfather's work. Traditional nineteenth-century stuff. And I don't imagine Birdie's poetry is very traditional, is it?"

"No. It doesn't rhyme, she's told me that much. I've never read any of it though. She keeps her *Word Meadow* very secret. But it's beautiful, I know it is."

"You don't have to convince me. It's my father who will need convincing."

"Why did he offer to read it then, if he doesn't like anything written after World War I?"

"Oh, he won't admit to it. Doesn't want to look old-fashioned, out of step. So he reads modern work, then condemns it."

"That's not very fair."

"I agree. He should just stick with the Dark Ages, where he belongs. The Prime Minister of Sheepskin Manuscripts! And your *vitlaus* modern aunt. Quite a pair!"

Vitlaus. Witless. Meaning: one, stupid; two, wrong; three, crazy. I knew which meaning he meant. I'd heard it said of Birdie before, back in Gimli. Birdie said it herself.

"Don't say that, okay?"

"You shouldn't be so afraid of her."

"I'm not. It's just that . . . you have to stay on Birdie's good side."

"Why? You're always trying to please her. She makes you perform in front of company like a pet poodle."

"She makes a lot of enemies. I don't want to be her enemy."

"But you're just a little girl."

"I'm older than you think."

"Thirteen, right?"

"Yes, but . . . I take care of my mother."

"What's wrong with her? Is she sick?"

"She had an accident."

"A car accident?"

A cartwheel accident. "Sometimes it's more like I'm the mother."

"Why didn't she come to Iceland?"

"She's afraid to fly."

"How sad for her."

"Where's your mother? Do you miss her?"

"She's in Spain. And no. I'm too busy hating her. Leaving me here with *him*." He reached into the pocket of his jeans jacket and pulled out a small bottle. A flask. Took a swig and passed it to me. "Try this."

"What is it?"

"Brennivin. Black Death."

The first sip I spat out. The second I swallowed. "I nearly killed her once." And a third. And a fourth. "I didn't mean to. I did something. Something that . . . scared her. And she fainted and fell and hit her head and went into a . . . What's the word in Icelandic? For someone who is sleeping and can't wake up?"

"*Daudada?*"

Daudi, death. *Da*, trance.

"For six days. It made her . . . different."

"Different how?"

"She gets dizzy, loses her balance. Walks with a cane. Her hair turned white. She looks like a grandmother."

"What did you do?"

"At first I felt terrible. But I learned how to take care of her. I make sure she has her sunglasses and her cane—"

"No, I mean, what did you do to make her fall?"

A fifth swallow, a sixth. "I don't know."

"You don't know what you did?"

"I don't know it in Icelandic."

"Describe it."

"It's stupid. A trick, something little kids do. American kids. Maybe Icelandic kids don't even do it."

"Do what?"

"You put your hands on the ground and spin your legs through the air. Like a wheel."

"You were spinning like a wheel and this scared your mother?"

"Don't laugh. It's not funny."

"I'm sorry."

Seven eight nine. "I crashed into a cabinet made of glass. Mama thought I was hurt. She saw me lying in the glass. And she fainted. Almost never woke up."

My voice had turned hoarse, my throat strangled with sadness. My tears fortunately invisible. I'd told it. I waited for what he might say.

"Take the last sip." Pressing the bottle to my mouth. I felt the cold glass against my lips and shivered. Then the burn of Brennivin. "Here, put this on." His blue jeans jacket with the bright patches. Now I was inside it, smelling his smell.

"I want to show you something."

Ishellir: ice cave. Blue-white ice. Ice-floors ice-walls ice-ceilings. Ice fingers dripping down from the top of the cave, ice candles growing up. A curving ice chamber. A place you could slide into. Brennivin makes you slidey. Luckily Saemundur caught me. I felt something on my lips again. Not bottle.

Lips soft as fox pelt. And then his tongue melting into mine. Nothing like ice.

We kissed so long the tears dried on my cheeks.

I gashed my hand on a stalagmite scrambling out of the cave.

"*Sauddrukkinn!*" Saemundur teased.

"Sheep drinking?"

"Drunk as sheep. Let me see." Shone the flashlight on my wounded palm. Kissed it.

In the jeep on the ride back to the summerhouse, drinking coffee from an Esso station, Saemundur filled me in on everything I'd need to know about the greenhouses at Hveragerdi, the place we hadn't seen that day. In case we got quizzed. "The main thing is to act suitably impressed at the great technological ingenuity of the Icelanders. Harnessing our mighty geothermal power for prosperity. My father loves that stuff." He took a long sip of coffee from the cup, maneuvering the jeep's wheel one-handed. We were speeding through the glaciers again, not even stopping at the bone cairn. The view from the jeep was dreary white: white glaciers, white sky, and nothing but rubble for miles around. Not every girl's idea of the perfect vacation. But I was happy, Cousin. I was in thirteen-year-old heaven.

Who knows what time it was when we finally circled the top of Thingvellir Lake and parked the rattling jeep in front of the summerhouse? We were late, but how late I couldn't guess. It was still light, but that's not saying much. We sat in the jeep a few more minutes, avoiding the inevitable. The house looked so tiny, perched in its island of tall grasses. I was hoping for one last kiss, but Saemundur seemed nervous.

"I wonder how it went," I ventured.

"Good or bad, they're waiting for us."

"I guess they are."

"We could have left sooner."

"We could have."

"They'll be mad."

I nodded. "In English it's both *angry* and *crazy*."

"What is?"

"The word *mad*. The way *vitlaus* means stupid or crazy. *Mad* means either angry or crazy. Or both."

We walked from the jeep to the summerhouse with our secrets thick between us. I could see Ulfur through the window, still sitting at the table. His head was in his hands. Then Birdie opened the door to greet us, mad in every meaning of the word.

18

Must I continue? Can't we please linger in the ice cave? In my delicious first kiss soft as fox pelt, in the swoon of pure velvet cave-black darkness? Me, I've been attempting to return there ever since. Yes, my darkroom job. It soothes me. It's how I stop the world when the mere spin of this planet makes me dizzy. I switch off the red safelight and there is nothing but that utter-black-of-the-universe cave-dark night. Remember the mythical *Ginnungagap*: no sand no sea no surging waves, no earth no heaven, nothing but the yawning gap? I've got it, anytime.

I find myself wanting to protect you, Cousin, from what comes next. Prepare you, at the very least. And so I ask: What do you know of manic depression? Nothing, I hope, if that's not too much to ask. Mood disorders are wickedly heritable. Suicide too runs in families. But let's assume for the moment and against the odds that you're untouched. These days the doctors call Birdie's malady *bipolar disorder*. But why settle for psychiatry's static nomenclature of an illness that is itself a shape-shifter, manifest in multiple and torturous forms? In the spirit of our ancestor poets, I could easily spin a thousand kennings for this disease: *word bubbler, speech rocket, gabber, charmer, pun spawner, brain champagne, ecstasy's consort, giddy fix, midnight sun, sleep thief, marvelous party, big spender, synapse leaper, delusion peddler, rager, grudge holder, thrower of fits, ringleader, god maker, eternal flame.* And:

brain glacier, tongue freezer, hope snuffer, sob story, shut in, doom spell, stun gun, death wish, wrist slasher, pocket of stones.

Melter of wings.

Okay, I'll quit stalling. Here we go:

Birdie opened the summerhouse door screaming mad. True, we were a pair of lying teenagers drunk as sheep returning hours late from a reckless jaunt. Enough to make any normal adult angry. And maybe Saemundur caught hell for it later. I'll never know. But Birdie? She didn't care if I'd seen the ingenious thermal-powered greenhouses of Hveragerdi. There was no time for that. The Wolf was on the loose.

Yes, you heard me. *The Wolf is on the loose!* That's what your mother screamed when she met us at the door, maddened and looming large. *Berserk,* I thought. She's gone *berserk.* It was a word Birdie herself had taught me, from the Old Norse *berserkr,* a pagan warrior who fought with maniacal, inhuman frenzy. I froze in terror. Saemundur gave me a horrified glance, then fled into the house. Birdie swooped, caught me by the shoulders, and hiss-whispered in my ear: *Ulfur has betrayed us!*

And so unfolded the most god-awful of Birdie's god-awful scenes. We were leaving, Birdie informed me, blocking my entrance into the summerhouse. Our suitcases were packed and in the trunk of Ulfur's car.

"Where are we going?"

"Back to Gimli."

"Gimli? What about our trip to the East, what about Olafur's letters?"

"What about you shut up and get in the car?"

Birdie's words could slap your face and leave it stinging sure as any hand. In the backseat of Ulfur's car, I sat next to Birdie silently crying. *Help me, Saemundur.* But all I could see was the back of his head. Ulfur drove.

"Leave us at Thingvellir," Birdie commanded. "We'll take the bus back to Reykjavik."

"That's unnecessary, Ingibjorg. I'll drive you to Keflavik."

The airport in the black lava field.

"Thingvellir, I'm warning you," Birdie snarled. "Or we'll get out of this car right now!"

You would have thought Ulfur was threatening us. And I guess in Birdie's mind he was. *The Wolf is on the loose!*

The Wolf looked at his watch, said something about our catching the six o'clock bus, the last one of the day. How grim he looked, not in the least wolfish. No longer brimming with self-importance but depleted and exhausted. For all I knew Birdie had been railing at him for hours, the entire time Saemundur and I were gallivanting across glacial passes and crawling through lava caves. With words alone Birdie could grind a person into mute surrender. I'd seen her do it many times, to Mama and Stefan, even Sigga. Me. And now Ulfur, all the way across the ocean. Why had I expected Birdie to behave in Iceland, when she never could back in Gimli? What was my mother thinking, letting Birdie take me to a foreign country? *Mama!* And even more than my mother I wanted Sigga to appear and take charge. To say, *Enough of this nonsense, Ingibjorg! Shape up or ship out.* But we were far beyond Sigga's reach, far beyond anything. I felt only dread as I saw Thingvellir's rocky plains swing into sight. How desolate it seemed to me. *Godforsaken,* my mother would have said. And suddenly it was over. I was standing alone with Birdie in the Thingvellir parking lot watching Ulfur's tiny car putter off. Holding my cherry red suitcase. Shivering in mean wind. A speck of misery on that vast tectonic plain.

How could Ulfur have abandoned us there? you ask. Did he not see how dangerous Birdie had become? I suppose he believed that we were as Birdie said returning immediately to Gimli, and that was the best outcome he could have wished for all concerned.

Just before Ulfur drove away, Saemundur rolled down his window and called my name. I ran to the car and he grabbed my hand, pulled me close, and whispered, "Be careful, Freya *min.*"

Freya mine. True, they all called me that—Mama, Birdie, Sigga, Stefan even. But from Saemundur's lips it sounded altogether different.

"What did he say to you?" Birdie demanded.

"Nothing."

"Liar!" That's when she grabbed me by the shoulders, started shaking me, accused me of being in cahoots with Ulfur and Saemundur. Her hair came loose from her scarf. "Why did he give you his jacket?"

I looked down at myself in surprise. In all the chaos, I'd forgotten I was wearing it, forgotten to return it to Saemundur. The jeans jacket with the European patches. "He said good-bye. That's all, I swear."

She let go of me. I sat down on my suitcase to wait for the bus, staring up at the stony wall of Almannagja, then down to the Law Rock at its base, where a group of tourists stood listening to a tour guide. The wind picked up and I huddled on my suitcase, long skinny arms wrapped around long skinny legs, chin pressed to bony knees. Iceland was wearing me down with its ear-stinging eye-tearing hair-tangling wind, its sideways rains, slushing sleets, August snows. Gloomy glacier-smothered mountains, bleak volcanic deserts. So we were running back to flat little Gimli? Fine with me. I'd be happy to spend the last few weeks of my summer lazing on the hot muggy kid-crowded beach swatting blackflies. The old mundane routines seemed suddenly enticing. The prospect of escorting Mama to Betel, wasting a morning watching old ladies knit and old men play chess seemed fine, just fine. Shelving books for Sigga in the Gimli library? Nothing better. And Birdie? Birdie could go to hell. I imagined Birdie dropping into the fiery mouth of the volcano Hekla as it was painted on the antique map at Ulfur's house.

And then the bus came gliding down the long curving road into Thingvel-lir. I leapt off my suitcase, stood jumping lightly foot to foot in the freezing wind. The tourists made their way from the Law Rock to the parking lot, where they huddled in a group, bracing themselves against the wind. There were ten or twelve of them, and I watched impatiently while they climbed on the bus ahead of us. I wanted to board but I had to wait for Birdie. She had the money. Finally the last tourist climbed on.

"Come on!" I called to Birdie, grabbing my suitcase. "The bus isn't going to wait all day."

"We're not taking the bus," Birdie said.

"What do you mean?"

"Just what I said. We're not taking the bus." And to prove her point Birdie waved to the driver, to indicate he could leave without us.

I considered it. At that moment I definitely considered severing my fate from Birdie's. Climbing on the bus and leaving her behind to carry out alone whatever awful scheme she'd concocted. Why didn't I? I had no money, and more important, I had no concept yet of my own autonomy. I was a child still, dependent on adults to move me from place to place. And Birdie was watching me as I wavered on the edge of betrayal.

"Freya!" she called. It was a warning and a plea. Or so I heard it. I was both afraid of her and afraid for her. The bus pulled away and I stared at Birdie in disbelief.

"Why?" I was angry and I didn't care if Birdie knew it. "Why did we sit here freezing waiting for a bus we're not even going to take?"

"You thought we were waiting for the bus?" Birdie laughed. "Oh no. *We are waiting for the Wolf to clear the area.*"

"But that was the last bus! How will we get to the airport?"

"The airport?"

"Gimli!" I shouted into the wind, and the wind blew it back in my face.

Birdie studied me. An hour earlier she'd been a rage-monster; now she was glacier-cool, mountain-steady. "We're not going back to Gimli, *elskan.*"

I began to cry. Not the hot stunned tears I'd cried back at the summer-house. No, this time I wailed. I howled into the wind. I fell to my knees and sobbed. *Mama!* I cried. My dear befuddled gray-haired plain-Jane gentle loving Mama who was afraid to fly. *I want Mama!* I cried so hard my teeth chattered and I began to hyperventilate.

And suddenly Birdie was back, the old Birdie who comforted me from nightmares was putting an arm around my shoulder, soothing me until my teeth stopped chattering and my shoulders quit heaving and I began to breathe slow and normal breaths again. Then she knelt beside me on the gravelly pavement and took both my hands in hers.

"Dear Freya," she began. Her voice was calm, no hint of agitation. "I should have explained to you sooner. I forget you aren't a child anymore, you're nearly grown up, you can understand things. I'm going to confide in you the truth of our situation. We're in danger."

"We are?"

"The important thing is to act quickly." She took my hand and we began walking with our suitcases, following the road the bus had taken out of the park. I didn't ask where we were going. I was too numb. We crossed the bridge over the river Oxara, passing the cheerful white Thingvellir church and its graveyard of moss-encrusted iron crosses. On the other side of the bridge, Birdie glanced around, as if to make sure no one was watching us— there was no one, Cousin, no one anywhere!—and then clutching my hand she pulled me off the roadside and we began following a trail that circled the lake.

On and on we walked, no longer hand in hand—the trail was too narrow—but single file, me struggling to keep up with Birdie's frenzied strides. Sometimes the ground was nothing more than rock split into chasms brimming with the clearest water I'd ever seen, orange and blue stones gleaming in the depths. White and yellow wildflowers spiked the tall grasses, purple ones grew on the pebbled banks of twisting streams. White puffs of milkweed bloomed like the heads of miniature grazing sheep. In some places the earth was so thick with moss it felt like sponge beneath my feet. The wind picked up, the wind died down. The lake lay like glass, then frothed into whitecaps, then calmed itself again. I noted these things without finding them beautiful. Beyond it all the vast Thingvellir plain surrounded, over-whelmed us. I felt we were nowhere. Thingvellir may be the big Somewhere in Iceland. But there's nothing there. No towns, no houses. Only mountains looming in the distance. A single road, and we weren't on it.

Even if I couldn't see it, even if the sky was still a bright light gray, I could feel night beginning its fall. The twittering and shrilling of birds turned to silence, and still we walked, and while we walked, Birdie got talky again. Explaining, justifying, blaming, scheming. Shouting things at me over her shoulder and above the wind. Establishing the germ of delusion that in the coming days would mutate in countless directions, forming plots and subplots and archplots, holy synchronicities, malevolent coincidences.

"This may come as a shock to you, Freya *min,* but Ulfur has been plot-ting against us this whole time."

"Plotting . . . ?"

"To steal Olafur's letters for himself. He wants to keep them in Iceland. Did you see how eager he was to be rid of us? He never had any intention of helping us find the letters. All ruse. I wouldn't be surprised if he is on his way to the East now, to track down the letters himself. What a coup that will be, another feather in the hat for the great scholar and recoverer of lost manuscripts!"

"But aren't the letters ours?"

"Of course they are! But never forget: Ulfur is sly. He tricked the Danish government into relinquishing Iceland's ancient manuscripts they'd pos-sessed for centuries! Be prepared for slick legal maneuvering, claims that the letters are his because they were originally mailed to Olafur's uncle Pall, and Ulfur is a direct descendant of Pall's. More important, he believes the letters belong in Iceland, to Iceland. He may be able to convince others, build a case for it. Remember what he said at the dinner party back in Reykjavik? That Olafur should be considered an Icelandic poet, not a North American one? And don't forget his remark about the emigrants. Why should we honor them, he asks! He despises us, Freya *min*. He despises everyone who left and their descendants as well. No one should write in Icelandic but an Iceland-born Icelander. That's why he wants to suppress my manuscript."

"He didn't like it?"

"Oh, Freya. You don't understand, do you? It's not about like or dislike, literary merit. He won't admit that of course. *Arnaleir,* he called my manuscript!"

I felt an inkling of outrage at Ulfur, protectiveness toward Birdie. *Word Meadow* was the sum of her life. Who was Ulfur to call it eagle muck?

"Ulfur is terrified of my brilliance," Birdie continued, as if she'd heard my silent question. She was making her own slick case, wooing me to her side, setting me up as her accomplice. "You have to look at things in context, Freya. Who has written any modern poetry of worth in Iceland? No one! The would-be poets of today are weighed down by the old forms, by the long-lost golden age of Icelandic literary prowess. It is only when Icelanders travel across the ocean that they can break free. Like Olafur, *Skald Nyja Islands*. And now me. It's too much for poor Ulfur, to see all this literary achievement taking place among the descendants of the emigrant traitors. And so he will suppress my manuscript, call it eagle shit, drive me back across the ocean, while he steals for himself Olafur's letters and all the lost poems they contain. He'll be the one to arrange and edit them, to write the introduction, and to publish the collection to great fanfare! Oh, certainly, he'll invite us to the celebrations. So he can gloat!"

"He told you all this, this morning?"

Birdie laughed. "A clever schemer like Ulfur reveal his designs? Never. Too sly for that. That is why we have to act quickly, Freya *min*. We have to get to the East before Ulfur does. Not because he thinks we'll be there. No, I've convinced him we are on our way back to Gimli."

"But how will we get to the East without Ulfur to drive us?"

"The jeep, of course!"

"Ulfur said we could use it?"

Birdie laughed again. "So innocent, Freya. But the time for your inno-cence is over. No, dear girl, we do not have Ulfur's permission to take the jeep east."

"You mean we're going to steal it?"

"Borrow, Freya, borrow. We'll return it when we're done. He'll never know it's gone. The next thing Ulfur will hear of us is news from the other side of the ocean, that the letters have been located and are in our posses-sion!"

Unbelievable, you say? It does appear ludicrous now, I admit, Birdie's deluded cloak-and-dagger scenario. And yet at the time it seemed reason-able or at least possible to me. Birdie's thinking was still linear then, if ob-sessive; the extreme thought-jumping was yet to commence. Nothing she'd said to me was beyond the scope of reality. I turned it all over in my mind as we trudged through that strange terrain. I remembered Ulfur saying the things Birdie now quoted, that Olafur should be considered an Icelandic poet, not a Canadian one. That the emigrants had abandoned their nation in its time of need. And it was true, too, that Ulfur was ambitious. So am-bitious that he neglected his wife and children. And Olafur's lost letters were clearly important. I'd seen the reaction among Icelanders whenever Birdie had mentioned them. It all added up, well enough anyway. The fact that I'd never liked Ulfur, the way he dismissed me as a mere *American girl,* made it easier for me to swallow the bad things Birdie said about him. Ulti-mately, Birdie was terrifically persuasive, answering each of my questions, quelling my doubts, then hooking me in by claiming she needed my help. How, exactly, she didn't specify, but I felt a sense of importance I'd never known. She appealed to my child's sense of utter uselessness in the world. Now I had a role to play, a mission to accomplish. It was what my mother and grandmother wanted for me. They'd saved their money so that Birdie and I could take this trip, so that I could see Iceland, so that we could bring Olafur's letters home. Birdie and I would be heroes. My past crimes would be, if not forgotten, perhaps absolved. And so when Birdie asked, finally, *Do you still want to go back to Gimli?* truthfully, I didn't.

And of course I was exhausted, my judgment was impaired. We'd been walking for hours, Birdie carrying my suitcase most of that time. At some point she led us back onto the Thingvellir Lake Road, and the first car that drove by slowed and offered us a ride. How strange we must have appeared, carrying our suitcases on that deserted road, Birdie in her bright salmon pink coat and matching head scarf. Birdie waved the driver off.

"Why can't we take a ride?" I protested. "Saemundur says it's safe to hitchhike anywhere in Iceland."

Birdie shook her head. "Agents of the Wolf are everywhere."

I didn't like how she kept calling Ulfur "the Wolf." True, it was his name; *Ulfur* does mean wolf in Icelandic. Animals are not uncommon first names, a pagan throwback, I imagine. Hrafn (raven) is a common name, and so is Bjorn (bear). But to call Ulfur *Ulfurinn—the* wolf—was something different altogether. It sounded crazy. Sure, Ulfur was a bit arrogant and pompous, but a wolf? And would Ulfur really send agents to follow us? Especially if he believed we were on our way back to Gimli?

I said nothing, kept walking; I hadn't forgotten the shoulder-shaking Birdie had given me back at Thingvellir. Soon I began to stumble, then tripped on a pothole and skinned my palms when I fell. When the next car offered us a lift, Birdie accepted. The driver, a gruff farmer, made no attempt at conversation. If he was an agent of the Wolf, he did a good job of disguising it, and left us at the summerhouse gate in under five minutes. As it turned out, Birdie and I had covered nearly the entire distance from Thingvellir to the summerhouse on foot, at least twelve, maybe fifteen miles I'd guess, looking at the map of Iceland spread in front of me. Nothing to a mania-fueled adult, but for a thirteen-year-old girl who'd spent a long mid-summer's day delving into the forbidden—caving, drinking, kissing—then enduring Birdie's god-awfulest scene, it had been a bone-tiring expedition. My feet felt tender and blistered, my legs trembled as we slipped through the metal gate and walked up the driveway to the little wooden cottage, now dark and empty.

And there was the jeep glowing in the twilight, the keys dangling from the ignition as if Ulfur had actually left it for our use. I walked past it up the steps to the summerhouse.

"Where are you going?" Birdie called.

"To bed?"

Bed was not to be. "You have to start *thinking,* Freya *min.* What if Ulfur hasn't returned directly to Reykjavik? What if he is on his way to the East right now, hours ahead of us?"

"With Saemundur?"

"I wouldn't be surprised if he's roped Saemundur into his plot. Saemundur's allegiances remain to be seen."

I had already decided not to tell Birdie about the kiss in the ice cave. It was beginning to seem *vitlaus* to me: not crazy, but stupid, wrong. Why had I squandered my first kiss on a boy I would never see again? A boy, as it turned out, whose father was trying to bring Birdie down? And yet still I delighted in the scent of him that clung to his worn jacket. I traced its patches, Holland's windmill, France's Eiffel Tower. Places Saemundur had been. Birdie kept plenty of secrets from me, I reasoned. Could I not keep this one from her?

I climbed into the front seat of the jeep and waited. After a while Birdie emerged from the summerhouse laden with provisions: jars of pickled herring, rye crackers, a flashlight, an unopened bottle of Brennivin, two sleeping bags, and a brown paperback book, which she handed to me. *Iceland Road Guide.* "You're going to navigate, Freya. That will be your job." I studied the book's front cover. "Be on the safe side," it advised. "Use the *Iceland Road Guide.*"

As it turned out, my navigational skills would not be required for quite some time. Birdie made a beeline for the East. Or as close to a beeline as you can get in Iceland, which meant the Ring Road. Yes, finally, we were taking the Ring Road, just as she'd promised on the plane. The glorious Ring Road, from which one can see all the marvels of Iceland. If one stops. We did not, except for infrequent and rushed breaks at various Esso stations.

"Our sightseeing days are over, Freya *min.* You might as well climb in the back and sleep."

And so I lay curled on my side, hip sunk into the gap between the seats, cheek pressed against the stiff leather seat cover, Saemundur's sleeping bag opened on top of me, while half of Iceland—half of the entire island!—disappeared behind us. The marvelous sights Birdie had promised to show me, all vanished unseen. Disappointment stung my eyes, clenched the back of my throat. I no longer tried to follow on the map, or consult the *Ice-*

land Road Guide. What was the point? There was only one: to get to the
East before the Wolf. Birdie drank hot coffee from a thermos spiced generously with Ulfur's Brennivin and drove like the maniac she was, pushing the
jeep to bone-rattling, heart-jostling speeds along the treacherous Ring
Road, which was in many places unpaved, unmarked, unlit, and even one-
laned. *Einbreid Bru*, the signs warned. As if a one-lane bridge could scare
Birdie, or a *Blind Heid*. Countless blind rises. Who knew what you might
meet over the top? More often than not it was nothing, no one. Iceland is
among the least populous nations on the planet. Even in the height of summer tourist season, we had the road practically to ourselves. Once I woke to
find us traveling through a fog thick as wool.

"Please stop," I pleaded. "It's not safe." I longed to *Be on the safe side, use
the Iceland Road Guide*. But there was no stopping Birdie. She plowed
through the fog until we slammed into something with a terrible thud. It
turned out to be a sheep. I heard its spiral horns crack on the pavement as it
fell. Saw blackish blood seep through its woolly chest. Birdie just backed up
the jeep, circled around it, and kept going.

"But what if it's hurt?"

"Of course it's hurt."

"What if we killed it?"

"Then it's dead."

"Don't you have to pay the farmer if you hit one of his sheep? That's
what Ulfur says."

"What *Ulfur* says?"

I knew I shouldn't have mentioned his name.

"Ulfur," she continued, "would like nothing more than for us to set up
camp by a dead sheep on the side of the road while he gets his wolf-paws on
Olafur's letters! Freya, Freya, Freya, crying over a sheep. Why don't you cry
over my *Word Meadow*? Why don't you cry over Olafur's lost letters?"

And on we drove.

19

The next time I woke it was five a.m. and the sun was streaming brightly across the far horizon of the ocean and into the jeep. The road leaned perilously close to steep ocean cliffs, not a guardrail in sight. Just Birdie chugging Brennivin-laced coffee from her thermos. The steep twists and turns made me woozy. What would keep us from plunging into the sea? Birdie, reckless, yet keen, hugging the jeep around those curves hand in glove.

I slept a few more hours and woke again as we turned from the fjord-jagged coast and began winding inland up a series of narrow switchbacks. Out the jeep's back window swirled stupendous views of cascading canyons. I turned forward again; I was sick of stupendous views. We passed no one: no car, no building, no signs warning *blind heid* or *einbreid bru,* not even a sheep. I must have dozed sitting up. The next thing I knew we'd arrived at Brekka.

Yes, the same Brekka where Ingibjorg the light-mother spied the newborn Olafur's teeth and cried *Skaldagemlur!* The Brekka where Olafur's uncle Pall challenged him to memorize the poem *Voluspa.* The Brekka where Olafur's uncle and father debated the merits of emigration until Askja punctuated their quarrel with a frisky quake, then erupted full-blown three months later, blackening the sun and tricking little Olafur into thinking *Ragnarok* had commenced, the world's end begun.

Yes, that Brekka. Except, of course, it was no longer that Brekka, imprinted by Birdie in my child's mind exactly as Olafur had left it a hundred years earlier, its turf roofs peaked in ashfall, its fields of hay wilted into barren corpse-yards of famished livestock and fume-choked birds. But nothing dies utterly, not even in Iceland. After some years even the ash-wasted East had succumbed to earth's green insistence. If Olafur and his family had stuck around they'd have seen the earth rise again fair and green, just as the *volva* foresaw at the end of *Voluspa*.

The current residents of Brekka, as it turned out, were not even kin, but despite being no relation to either Pall or Olafur, they took seriously their obligation as guardians of the famous farmstead. Hrefna and Eirikur were their names, a pair of retired schoolteachers from nearby Egilsstadir, both well versed in the poets' lore. On that first morning they led us to the two stone monuments (one Olafur's, one Pall's) that rose like cairns at the site of the old homefield. Visitors, they explained, often came to pay homage to the farm that had borne Iceland such splendid literary fruit. While they couldn't allow people inside the original sod-roof farmhouse—it was too ruined, even dangerous in its decrepitude—they invited many travelers into their own cement home, across a stone-stubbled field from the original Brekka, to see their shrine to the poets. Portraits, photographs, books by and about the two poets, even a plate glazed with an image of Pall's face—all were stored in a glassed-in cabinet in their tiny living room, already overstuffed with their own families' artifacts. But Olafur's letters? No, they'd never heard of any, much less set eyes on them.

"I see," Birdie said. And then: "Has Ulfur Johannsson been here?"

Not that they remembered. They even checked their guest book. Assured that the Wolf was nowhere in the immediate vicinity, Birdie explained to them our quest. Prefaced, of course, by my recital of Olafur's "New Iceland Song," which as Birdie had calculated, made their eyes shine with sentiment. They immediately offered—insisted—on putting us up, letting us use their house as our base of operations.

Birdie did not hesitate to take full advantage of their kindness. Relying on the list of likely contacts she'd compiled with Ulfur, we set up appointments by phone, sometimes three or four in a day, then set out in the jeep, Birdie at the wheel, me navigating from the front seat, *Iceland Road Guide* in hand. Some of the contacts were distant relations of Pall's, others local people with an interest in his work. We soon developed a routine, the Freya and Birdie dog-and-pony show: after introductions and a series of suspicious questions from Birdie regarding Ulfur (all answered in the negative), I would recite Olafur's "New Iceland Song," then Birdie would relate the sad tale of the lost letters. It was a moving performance on easy marks, since Olafur and Pall were East Iceland's main claims to fame. All the farmhouses we visited, all the people we imposed upon! People with names like Halldora and Stigur and Skuli, who lived on farms with names like Skeggjastadir and Hallfredarstadir and Arnarstadir, dug through their attics and archives, libraries and storage rooms, closets and cabinets, and made endless phone calls on our behalf.

"What about Sigga's people?" I asked.

"What about them?"

"Aren't we going to visit them?"

"They have nothing to do with the letters!"

"But doesn't Sigga want us to meet them?"

Birdie stumbled, recovered the lie again. "Of course, they're expecting us. But they're a bit farther north. After we find the letters, then we'll go see them. After we find the letters, we'll do anything you want."

"Visit the glacial lagoon?"

"Absolutely."

At the end of each futile day we'd return to Brekka empty-handed, driving along the road that followed the northern bank of the Lagarfljot River. How beautiful that drive was, the low-lying glacial river, pale and blue and calm, far from its icy source, meandering where it pleased, fluted with lush green banks, framed by rounded sheep-grazed hills and distant lavender-hued mountains. Despite its name, Iceland does know true green, its summer brief but showy, a shameless display of emerald brilliant as winter's northern lights, the island's entire circumference a perfect circle of verdancy. But Birdie was immune to weather or beauty or anything but Olafur's letters. Her single-mindedness consumed not only her but me as well. I became nothing but an appendage that recited Olafur's verses on command and navigated routes to remote farms that might lead us to his lost letters. I was tired? I was hungry, thirsty? I missed my mother? Birdie was beyond not caring; my complaints, being non-epistolary in nature, simply failed to regis-

ter. Luckily our various hosts insisted on feeding us; otherwise I doubt
Birdie would have thought to eat or even remembered food existed. With the
strangers we encountered she poured on the charm, but alone with me in
the jeep she became increasingly bitter and dispirited. There was less than a
week left before our flight back to Winnipeg, and as each day passed Birdie's
desperation flared more and more frequently into paranoia. Sometimes she
claimed that Ulfur had set people in the East against us.

"But no one's even met him," I'd protest.

"So they say, *elskan*. So they say."

Other times, she seemed convinced that the reason the letters were
nowhere to be found was that Ulfur had had them in his possession the entire time. New strands of Ulfur's plot continually unfurled in Birdie's
fevered brain. The Arni Magnusson Institute, the foundation Ulfur headed
whose charge was to recover and preserve ancient manuscripts, was probably in on it as well.

What had Saemundur called his father? *The Prime Minister of Sheepskin Manuscripts*. "But the Arni Magnusson Institute only cares about the
really old stuff," I pointed out. "That's what Saemundur told me. Vellum
manuscripts, that kind of thing."

A front, Birdie declared, for more malevolent objectives. Different people we'd met on the trip entered Birdie's set, each with a role to play.
Sveinn, the bearded publisher at Ulfur's dinner party who'd expressed an
interest in publishing Olafur's letters once they were found, became a central figure in the plot. "How well Sveinn played his part that night," Birdie
complained. "Feigning surprise at the existence of Olafur's lost letters! He
probably has them typeset at his office in Reykjavik, ready for publication."
Even Ulfur's father, the elderly near-blind Johann, was incriminated, accused of hiding the letters from the world all those years, secreting them
among his thousands of books.

Birdie's anxiety leaked onto me. I found myself unable to sleep at night
on the little cot in the living room at Brekka, wracked with worries. Not
Birdie's worries, not Ulfur and his various spies and agents, but my own.
What if we returned to Gimli empty-handed? Would Sigga be disappointed
in me? Who was walking Mama to Betel in the morning? Who was keeping
track of her canes? Did Saemundur hate me now for stealing his jacket?

When I finally slept, the sheep we'd struck and left for dead on the Ring Road appeared with bloodied wool and cracked horns, chiding me with plaintive bleats.

A night of ruins and a ruined night.

Our last evening at Brekka, Birdie yanked me from sleep, rushing me into jeans, sneakers, and a wool sweater topped by Saemundur's jacket, then snuck me out the front door and across the rubbled field to the old Brekka farmhouse. The moon was massively full, bursting silver bright, but the sun was a goner, not officially set but obscured by the cliff that towered over Brekka like a menacing giant.

"My father's house," Birdie said, and took my hand.

I thought that was all she wanted: for me to see it. Like the time she dragged me from sleep to my first orange-grinning sunrise on the lake in Gimli. This time we gazed not upon a morning lake but at the five conjoined wood-framed structures built into and dwarfed by the immense cliff. Long grasses fringed the boarded doors and windows, a green hump of earth formed the roof. The stone walls were crumbled, covered with moss and lichen. The wooden face of each structure weathered to the color of bone.

It was a stunning sight by moonlight. I squeezed Birdie's hand. Sight seen. I yawned and turned away.

"Where do you think you're going?" Her salmon coat hideous pink in the moonlight.

"Back to bed?"

In my dreams.

Birdie's plan was for me to find a way inside the ruined farmhouse. I would be small enough to fit through a window. Once inside, I was to find a door and let her in too.

"But why?"

"The letters, little fool." Birdie hiss-whispered though no one could hear, our schoolteacher hosts, Hrefna and Eirikur, asleep in their homely farmhouse across the stone-littered field. Did Birdie really believe we might find Olafur's long-lost letters stored safe and sound in this rotted century-old farmhouse?

She did.

I mustered my courage. "Can't Eirikur open it for us in the daytime?"

Birdie laughed. "You don't get it, do you? Eirikur is being paid off by Ulfur or the Arni Magnusson Institute or the university or the National Library or the government or Sveinn the publisher to guard the letters stashed in the old farmhouse. Once we leave the country, *eureka!* Ulfur 'discovers' the letters; cameras and news teams and reporters and scholars and ordinary Icelanders flock to the scene; the letters get published; and Eirikur's farmhouse is restored and designated a national monument! All thanks to Ulfur, esteemed scholar and national hero, savior of Iceland's oh-so-precious literary heritage. What else is left in life for poor Ulfur? All the ancient manuscripts have been peaceably returned to Iceland by the Danish government and displayed under Ulfur's directorship at the Arni Magnusson Institute. Fanfare subsides, wife deserts, children rebel, nothing remains for poor Ulfur but to siphon our rightful fame—"

I took the flashlight from Birdie's hand and started up the grassy slope that led to the roof of the farmhouse, preferring the unknown horrors of ghostly ruins to her rambling diatribe against Ulfur. When I reached the top, I looked down to see Birdie waving me onward, pink head scarf fluttering wildly in the wind. I knelt down and unlatched the one rooftop window that hadn't been boarded up. It creaked open and I shone my light through to a room down below. What if instead of landing on my feet I crashed right through rotten floorboards into a musty dank hellhole beneath the earth?

Mama!

I landed on my butt in a thud-puff of dust, but the floor held. I surveyed the room with my flashlight. Nothing but raw wooden-plank walls, floorboards, and ceiling beams. Nothing painted, every surface coated with dust. Eirikur had told us the building had been abandoned only thirty years earlier, after the War, but the air I breathed in, then coughed out, tasted centuries old.

After a moment I realized I must be standing in the *badstofa,* the lofted living-sleeping quarters of Olafur's time. This was where Olafur's family had gathered for their evening readings, where Olafur had recited the poem *Voluspa* that fateful Easter night. For a brief moment I felt a thrill—I was standing where Olafur, *Skald Nyja Islands,* had stood, maybe the exact spot!—then remembered my task.

The top edge of a steep staircase appeared under my light. Down below was where the sheep had been kept in the wintertime, to keep the humans warm above. I remembered that from Mama's bedtime story—*sheep in the house?*—and imagined falling asleep to the bleating of sheep. Then my dream-sheep rose woolen-bloody in my mind.

A piercing "FREYA!!!" broke my nervous reverie, a scream that could raise the dead or at least our slumbering hosts across the field. Not *Freya-are-you-okay-in-there?* but a scary Gryla chin-teeth-sharp-and-glistening voice, an *answer me or I'm coming after you* voice.

The stairs creaked but held solid as I crept down by flashlight. "Just a minute, Auntie!" I called out, like this was an ordinary house and I was answering an ordinary door. Except the door once I finally found it wouldn't open. Nailed and boarded shut from the outside, why would it open from the in? Why indeed? Birdie had tricked me, sent me in under false pretenses. The dirty work was mine alone in that creepy stone ruin that was nothing more than a cave minus Saemundur. Instead, Birdie stuck her head through a broken window and directed my search. "Look in that corner, Freya, try lifting those boards."

"There's nothing here!" I kicked angrily at a pile of splintered wood, capsizing a rusted iron pot big enough to bathe in.

"Keep looking. The next room."

"How?"

"Through the passageway. Olafur said the rooms connect through a passageway at the back."

Tunnel more like it. I had to slouch my way through, and the rough stone walls snagged at the patches on Saemundur's jacket. Finally I emerged into another room, barren-dank as the first. What was Birdie thinking, that we'd find the letters safe and dry in a locked metal box labeled "Olafur's Lost Letters"? I called out my weary inventory of naught, not knowing or caring whether Birdie could hear me. "A broken loom. Leg of chair. Pile of bones, dog or fox." Then, "Stones." A wall crumbled into a pile of rocks, blocking the passageway that led to the remaining rooms. Happy day!—or night or whatever it was—there was nowhere left to look.

I made my retreat, back through the passageway and up the rickety stairs to the *badstofa*. But how to hoist myself through the window? I had nothing to stand on. Yet I was tall, wasn't I, *Freya the Tall* Birdie had called me on our first meeting, and my arms were long enough to reach the sill, my legs strong enough to prop myself on a narrow ledge that ran horizontally around the room. From there I wriggled out through the window head-first and stood for a moment on the turf roof, wheeze-breathing fresh air into my dust-irked lungs. Then I glared at Birdie down below and raised both my arms up in a gesture of empty-handedness: See, Birdie? Sweet failure. I saw it clearly: our whole mission, doomed from the start and inane to the core. Surely even Birdie understood that now?

Nothing for it but going home. Gimli home.

The sky was cloud-smudged and heavy the morning we departed Brekka, our spate of sun-sparkled days suddenly rescinded. Justly so, I decided. I felt ashamed as we said our good-byes to our hosts, Hrefna and Eirikur. For sneaking into their boarded-up farmhouse at night without permission. For using their beds and their food and their time and their telephone and giving nothing in return. Yet they seemed pleased by the visit. *Daughter and Granddaughter of Olafur, Skald Nyja Islands, at Brekka!* We signed the guest book, then Eirikur helped us pack up the jeep and we were off, jostling along the gravel road that followed the slinking Lagarfljot River. I was sullen. Our entire trip, as far as I was concerned, was no less ruined than the old Brekka farmhouse. A shambles. Now we faced a two-day drive to the airport in Keflavik. I stared bitterly out the window.

"Cheer up, *elskan*. Why so glum?"

"This isn't fun."

"Fun? You want fun? Then we'll be tourists again, Freya *min*!"

At first I thought she was being cheery-mean, sarcastic, but no, it was just another lightning-quick mood shift. All the places we hadn't seen on our drive east, she assured me, we'd see on the way back. We'd stay overnight in the spectacular harbor of Hofn, take a boat trip on the glacial lagoon, visit the magnificent beach at Vik and even the original Oddi, where great men of letters like Snorri Sturluson and Saemundur the Learned had lived.

"Really?"

"Really!"

Fooled again. Birdie's promises not vows but bribes easily doled. Or maybe she did intend in that moment to take me to those places. Plans, re-alities shifted quickly now. Suddenly she veered off the road and down a driveway.

"What . . . ?"

The Valthjofsstadir Church, Birdie explained impatiently. As if I should have known. Worth checking for Olafur's letters, but the pastor and his wife had been out of town the past week. Returned last evening, according to our Brekka hosts, who'd called ahead and made us an appointment.

Valthjofsstadir was just downstream from Brekka and set against the same massive cliff. It was the very church, Birdie explained, that Olafur and his family had attended, and where Olafur's grandfather had served as pastor. It was not impossible that Olafur's letters could have found their way there.

The pastor, a long-faced man with a dark beard and drooping eyes, was waiting for us at the gate to the churchyard. He took us inside the church and we stood talking in its chill, stale air. As in all the old churches of Ice-land, the walls and ceilings were painted a bright and heavenly blue. I felt my spirits lifting from the defeated departure at Brekka. The pastor let me stand in the pulpit, and I giggle-preached in English, "We are gathered here today . . ."

At that Birdie lost whatever patience she had mustered. She had no time for church tours, much less childish shenanigans; she cut right to the chase, skipping the usual queries about Ulfur, my tired but perfected recital of Olafur's "New Iceland Song."

"We're looking for some family letters," she began.

"Yes, I've heard." The pastor paused, stroked his long beard, seeming to carefully formulate his words before speaking them. "In fact, after I learned you were coming today I put in a call to my old friend Ulfur Johannsson in Reykjavik. We were at university together. He takes quite an interest in Olafur's work. As you well know."

From my perch in the pulpit I saw Birdie stiffen. *The Wolf!*

"As you know," the pastor continued, "Ulfur is quite familiar with your quest. He mentioned that the two of you stayed with him at Thingvellir Lake. But he seemed to think that you had already left for Canada. I as-sured him that was not the case, that you were here at Brekka. He was quite disturbed. Upset, actually."

THE TRICKING OF FREYA

The silence that followed grew so heavy it seemed that heavenly blue ceiling was pressing down upon us. Birdie quickly buttressed it with lies.

"Oh, that Ulfur!" She laughed, high and girlish-squeaky, most un-Birdie. "He can get quite confused. The absentminded professor!" Then she took my hand and pulled me down from the pulpit and out the door with the pastor calling after us.

"Get in the jeep!" She opened the door and shoved me in.

According to Birdie, the pastor was calling Ulfur in Reykjavik that very moment. Telling him we had his jeep. Ulfur in turn would alert the police. The Wolf too would be on his way east in no time. We were being hunted, we were on the run.

The funny thing, Cousin, is that out of all Birdie's cloak-and-dagger scenarios, this one proved true. As I found out later, the pastor did call Ulfur as soon as we left; Ulfur did call the police; the police did alert the entire island by radio and newspaper to keep an eye out for two Canadian fugitives. Not because we stole a car. No, the stolen property was more precious than an old jeep. KIDNAPPED CANADIAN CHILD IN ICELAND, read the headline of *Morgunbladid*. A policeman showed it to me a week later at the airport. You see, Birdie had left out one link in the chain of events she predicted that day: once Ulfur hung up with the Valthjofsstadir pastor, he called Sigga in Gimli. Birdie's house of lies collapsed. Everything blew open. The nearly three-week-long search for me and Birdie that had widened from Gimli to the entire Interlake region and Winnipeg and all of Manitoba now shifted exclusively to Iceland.

In the jeep screeching away from Valthjofsstadir, I neither knew nor could have imagined any of that. Remember, I wasn't aware we were missing in the first place. In my mind our goal was simple: to get to the airport in Keflavik before we were discovered by the police in the stolen jeep. For once I shared Birdie's urgency, urging her faster and faster along the gravel road that followed the Lagarfljot River to the Ring Road. She needed no urging from me, pushing the jeep to demon speeds.

Then out of the blue she slammed on the brakes in front of a run-down farm. We'd passed it many times in the previous days as we'd scurried around the East searching for Olafur's letters. It was a weathered gray cement building shedding scabs of plaster and topped by rusted corrugated tin. A stone slab served as front step. Abandoned-looking but inhabited; an unrusted car sat in the driveway. The truly strange thing about the house was its tree, grown astonishingly large by Icelandic standards, its branches scraping second-story windows. Now I saw there were things hanging from one of its lower limbs. Some kind of small, dead, furred animals hung by the neck with blue string. Tiny heads cocked, paws dangling, long dark bodies swaying in the wind. I watched in astonishment as Birdie stopped to stroke each one, then yanked a couple of them from the tree and tucked them under her arm. She continued around to the side of the house. There stood a drying rack, and like an escaped con stealing laundry from a clothesline, Birdie swiped the things she wanted, nimble-fingered and nimble-footed, racing lightly and silently back to the jeep. I was biting my lip nearly through. What if someone came out of the house? No one stirred. Whoever was inside must be old, I hoped, and sleeping.

Birdie dropped the things on my lap and I screamed. Animal skins with gristly tendrils still clinging to the hides. Birdie took them from my lap and tossed them in back on top of the sleeping bags. Started up the jeep again laughing her loud raucous laugh. "Hush, *elskan!* That's enough fuss. Cat skin is called for, but I imagine seal hides and mink pelts will suffice."

She was shifting again, into a state of what seemed to me pure nonsense, mumbling *Odin the hanging god, sacrificing himself to himself, discerning runes from branches, humans strung from the World Tree, anything for inspiration*—until I thumb-plugged my ears and merged her words into engine-rumble and wheel-spin on gravel. *Birdie's mad.* The old Gimli rumors truer than true. Utterly *vitlaus,* crazy-stupid-wrong. Something broke in me then, a sickening shift of my own. Odd as it may seem to you, Cousin, up until that moment I had revered your mother; yes, she was moody, some-times rageful, but she was also a charm-sparkling genius. I'd been enthralled in both the modern and ancient senses of the word: enchanted, enslaved. Now the spell had broken and I saw her as something sick and terrifying, hands trembling on the wheel, a tic I'd never seen before twitching the cor-ner of her mouth, words rushing from her lips in a wide-ranging deranging torrent. No fanciful word-meadow but a nauseating word-spew. My lip was bleeding by the time we reached the town of Egilsstadir.

Maybe it's grown by now, but Egilsstadir then had nothing but a gas sta-

tion, grocery, post office, and a few stores. Birdie pulled into the Esso station, yanking the pink head scarf nearly over her face before approaching
the attendant, an uninterested teenager who clearly did not know us from
Egil. No one else was around. Tank full up, Birdie maneuvered the jeep
over a sidewalk and behind a closed fish-packing plant, hidden from the
road. She ordered me to lie down in the backseat and covered me with Saemundur's army green sleeping bag. *Don't move.* I did not. I lay panic-
stiffened under Saemundur's cover, inhaling its musk plus a stale stink of
canned fish, worrying our fate. Jail in Reykjavik? Returning not only empty-
handed but handcuffed? Certain disgrace. Or maybe Birdie would lose
control on the way back, wreck the jeep over a sheer cliff and into an icy
fjord below . . .

Birdie was back. Ordering me into the front seat while she loaded the
back with two plastic jugs of water and a bag of groceries. Then she unfolded a map she'd bought in the gas station and studied it a long time before starting the engine. Time we didn't have. I should have understood
then or at least suspected that we weren't headed for the Keflavik Airport.
That trip required no consult with a map: it was a straight shot on the Ring
Road. Soon Birdie was veering off the Ring Road onto a dirt track. A sign
said F88. I reached for the *Iceland Road Guide,* began thumbing its pages
frantically.

"Don't bother," Birdie advised. "It's not listed."

Then I understood the why of the new map. The place we were going
was purposefully excluded from the *Iceland Road Guide*. It was not a place
for tourists; it was not safe to drive.

The next sign we saw read OSKJULEID.

Askja Way.

20

Pause with me, Cousin, if you will, at these crossroads proverbial and literal, the juncture of the Ring Road and Askja Way. Don't worry, I promise not to hold up the story with cowardly tangents. Not for long, anyway. You want me to go on and I will. Though I can't say I don't resent you for it, you who dog me forward into the past. No fair, you protest, you don't even know I exist, may not even exist yourself? Granted. I write as much for me as for you; there's no point pretending otherwise. And I've vowed to keep nothing from you, you whose very birth was a state-sanctioned secret, you who were sent into this world swaddled in lies.

So fear not, Cuz. There's no turning back now. Just reassure me that once you see this last Birdie, this end-of-the-road reckless madwoman, you'll still remember the Birdie of before, a kind of star I had no name for yet fervently revered, the Birdie who enchanted me with kennings, who told me I was named after a goddess, the Birdie who promised to teach me to fly.

Rarely in life are the fateful roads we turn down actual.

"Askja?" My heart pounded.

"Askja, Freya *min*!" Birdie spoke gaily, her eyes shone. The paranoid urgency of the last several hours lifted. Askja, she assured me, guiding Ulfur's jeep down a road better called a dirt track, would shield us. Askja was our light-mother, the volcano that gave birth to us, its steaming crater our own embryonic lagoon. No one on earth would ever look for us there.

Right you were, Birdie mine.

Askja Way, rutted like the corrugated tin roof of a decaying Icelandic farmhouse, made the Ring Road seem a velvet ribbon. Soon we were deep into the terrain known as *grjot,* a black-pebbled wasteland stretching out to the ends of the visible earth. Through the *grjot* charged a muddy river, whose source was the immense Vatnajokull glacier. Askja Way followed the river's twisted path; what else was it to do? That river was the only sign of life; to leave its side would be suicide; even the road knew that much. Birdie never hesitated, steering the jeep with fierce certainty over ruts that bounced us like jackhammers, impervious to fear. I had no such immunity. I would have preferred apprehension by the authorities and a tidy little prison cell with bars to the anxiety I felt riding unfettered through the reeling *grjot,* the menacing taunt of flat black deadland and the glowering clouds pressing down on us from above. *Mama wouldn't like this. Mama wants me out!*

"This place is creepy," I said out loud. No, that sounded too adolescent. I tried to summon adult reason. "I think we should turn back. We won't be in trouble, Birdie. We'll just say it was a misunderstanding about the jeep. That we thought Ulfur loaned it to us. No one will care." I paused. "This is dangerous, Ingibjorg." I'd never called her Ingibjorg before. I was hoping to sound like Stefan, the most steadfastly rational person we knew. It didn't matter. Birdie had counter-reasons all her own.

"We can't turn back. She awaits us at Askja."

"Who?"

"Freyja."

I was quiet for a moment. Then I said, as gently as I could, "I'm right here, Birdie. I'm sitting right here next to you."

Birdie shrieked with laughter, slapped the steering wheel with both palms. "Of course you are, little fool! Do you think I've lost my mind? I refer, dear girl, to Freyja the goddess."

Worse yet. "Birdie . . . she doesn't exist."

"Slander! Was it not said of Freyja, a full two centuries after the onslaught of Christianity, that *she alone of the gods yet lives*? That entire marvelous pantheon—Freyja's twin brother, Freyr, hung like a wild ox; brawny Thor, an occasional cross-dresser but man enough to challenge Christ the interloper to a duel; Baldur, son of Odin, fair and beautiful and doomed to die by one of Loki's lowliest tricks; Loki himself, who consorted with giants and demons, who bedded a giantess that bore him three monsters—the Fenris Wolf, the Midgard Serpent, and a daughter named Hel—instigator of *Ragnarok* and the end of the world; and finally Odin, the All-Father, the One-Eyed God of inspiration who intoxicated men in battle and infused poets with verse—all vanished. True, gods come and gods go, forcibly retired mostly: banished, outlawed, discredited, disgraced. But this was not the End-Time they'd envisioned for themselves, no pitched Armageddon, no wild doomed battle with cataclysmic demonic forces, but instead a pathetically peaceable usurpation by a lone god and his tragic son. Whoosh! An entire pantheon relegated to the grinning void. *Except Freyja.* She alone of the gods yet lives! Fertility goddesses die hard, my girl. Yes, Freyja awaits us. Mistress of divination, bestow on me your mantic gifts—"

I interrupt her now, Cousin, because I can. At the time I was helpless, it was not possible to slip a word in edge- or any-wise. She was uninterruptible, she was hemorrhaging words. Hour after mile after hour after mile we bounced and jostled at tortoise speed on rutted track through tortured landscape, and hour after mile after hour after mile Birdie talked on on on. Sometimes I listened, sometimes I managed to block her out, sometimes I could scarcely decipher the gush of words bleeding together in a bewildering mix of English and Icelandic. Thought interrupted thought, idea generated idea, her brain a Big Bang of associations impossible to track.

Yet she was not stuck in her head. Or rather, she was, she inhabited her mind, but she inhabited the world too. Her senses grew acutely sharp. She noted every rut, every knife-sharp rock, and deftly steered the jeep to avoid them. When we got stuck in a sand pit, Birdie, without missing a beat, without skipping a word, slipped the jeep into neutral, leapt out, and single-handedly pushed the jeep out of the ditch. I was watching, I saw her. Mania endowed her with physical strength and acuity beyond human. She believed herself godlike and she was. She kept an eye on the sky, on the clouds, the wind, the temperature, the road conditions, talking talking all the while. It is impossible to replicate, Cousin, this state of your mother's. Or at least, I am not up to the task. The fluidity of thought and motion, the concordance and elegance of her speech, the perfect symbiosis of world and mind. A pile of stones on the road could spark a discourse that ranged hundreds of years in mere minutes. Something like this:

"Cairns," Birdie began, pointing to a tower of rocks out the window, "are called *prestar* because like priests they point the way but do not follow it. An old Icelandic joke. Ha! Are you aware of the Icelanders' long history of resistance to religious authority, how even as pagans they were for the most part inconstant and opportunist, switching allegiances on a whim? Don't think for a minute they abandoned the old beliefs wholesale when Christianity was announced as the national religion, and Thor's and Odin's men accepted sprinkling with water right there at the Althing in the river Oxara, though some waited until the horse trek homeward when they could dunk themselves in hot springs instead of cold ones. True they built churches and attended them, baptized their babes, but when it came to matters of real import, old ways readily resurfaced. What fool would pray to the new White God before a fishing trip when Thor was still ready to assist? Remnants of lost beliefs persist to this day in transmuted forms, rural superstitions, the old pagan land spirits, the *vaetir,* transmogrified into folklore's Hidden People. Iceland is a numinous island, is it not? A paradise for pagans, for all who believe that every thing lives and is imbued with spirit. What is the Icelanders' obsessive interest in dreams but a leftover of the Norse practice of *seidur,* shamanic divination by a seeress. Prophecy, Freya *min,* is a woman's gift! Write your dreams down. Pay attention. No one rivals your namesake in the art of augury. Our Mistress of Vatication!" And then glancing out the side window, indicating the entire moonscape before us, she began speculating on the ratio of glaciers to lava deserts. ". . . the primordial nature of Iceland's habitat. What looks like destruction is actually creation. Earth is being thrust up, birthed beneath our feet! Iceland is a baby, Freya, a geological and political infant, the last settled of the European nations, the penultimate holdout against Christianity, dragged a thousand years later kicking and screaming into NATO. Independent people, indeed. Protesters teargassed, nearly blinded. Freyja's eye-rain or eye-hail or eyelid-showers or cheek-storm or eyelash-cascades, all kennings for gold. Gold itself is moving-current sun. Sun-month. So much more poetic, the old names for the twelve months: sun-month, hay-month, harvest-month, slaughter-month, frost-month, ram-month, Thorri, Goi, single-month, cuckoo-month, seed-time, lamb-fold time. Eagles are lamb-enemies. Arm is falcon-perch, ships are surge-horses. Heathens practiced pre-Christian baptismal water rites. Good Lutheran fourteen-year-olds receive confirmation, Freya. You turn fourteen this winter, do you not? I've never seen you on your birthday. Summers only! Your Connecticut winters must pale, my dear. Manitoba boasts colder mean temps than Iceland—*mean* being the operative word, hoary and hoarfrost and hoar. Yes, they called Freyja a whore! Reviled our Mistress as a she-goat in heat, the gods' own slut and a shameless brother-fucker. Ah, the degradation of fertility cults and dominance of all-father sky deities! Of all my enemies is Ulfur not the worst, cloaked in his Arni Magnusson, rescuer-of-manuscripts holiness? Only in this book-sick ancestor-worshiping nation could a man like Ulfur be revered. Don't forget, the Fenris Wolf is the demon bastard of Loki. I am the true poet of the age, Freya *min*! Wisdom cannot be stolen, only divined. Look at Odin, hanging from the World Tree, sacrificing himself to himself, self-revealing the mysteries of the runes. Let Ulfur call it eagle shit, *Word Meadow* is divine divination, I tell you. Odin, I know where your eye is concealed, hidden in the well of Mimir—but where are Olafur's letters concealed? Hidden in the well of Askja! *Askja* means box, caldera, but *aska* means ashes, box of ashes, ash districts. Ash blew as far as St. Petersburg. Fleers of ash. We descend from those who fled, who bid Iceland good-bye and in some cases good riddance. Did you know that some emigrants refused to speak again of *that barren land,* never wrote home, reinvented themselves as Canadians and Americans, passed down no stories, only bitter glimpses, 'life in Iceland was a living hell,' a distinct lack of nostalgia for wasted lives of near-indentured servitude, nineteenth-century Iceland a semifeudal society, while back in Iceland *emigrant* became synonymous with *traitor*? Of course not all newfoundlandlings turned their backs so decisively, many indulged in homeland sickness, misty-eyed longings. Olafur foremost among them. You can only have one mother, one motherland, and so descendants of pioneers invent a New-Iceland-of-the-diaspora, an Iceland-of-the-mind and -memory, a mythic homeland, an oddly old newworld Gimlian golden age—"

It took a river to shut her up. A tributary of the glacial river drew a line in the sand and dared us to cross it. I was sent to scout the shallowest spot. "Like Saemundur taught us!" Birdie yelled. I cursed Saemundur. Was he the one who made her think she could do this? The odd thing—and I swear I remember this though it seems implausibly impossible, hallucinatory even at the time—the river's banks were blanketed with bright pink flowers, lurid as Birdie's salmon coat against the jet-black sand. I blinked my eyes; the pink vision remained. What had Saemundur advised? *You just try to judge the most shallow spot, which is often where the river runs widest.* The widest point was easiest enough to find—about twenty yards downstream from where Birdie waited in the jeep—and it was calmer, too, a flattened pool compared with upstream's muddy torrent. But what if it contained unexpected depths? *The glacial sediment,* Saemundur had said, *makes it hard to judge. Jeeps and trucks being towed from rivers are not uncommon sights in Iceland. They make for good rescue photos!* If our jeep got stuck in this river, there'd be no one to rescue us. So bootless I waded in. Glacial melt instantly flooded my sneakers. Ankle-high, then shin- and knee-deep in ice water. Any deeper than my thigh and we'd be sunk for sure. I glanced upstream and nearly lost my balance and plunged in. Birdie was waving me out of the river. I waved back, motioning her downstream to where I stood. "This is the best place to cross," I announced, climbing into the jeep, hoping it was true. The jeep lurched through wheel-deep, and when we made it to the opposite bank a wild-childish pride surged through me: *If Mama could see me now!*

If Mama could see me now she'd fall into another dead faint, that's what she'd do. On the other side I climbed out of the jeep to shed my water-logged sneakers and jeans, exposed in my underwear for all the world—meaning no one in the world—to see. A blast of wind sent me scurrying back into the jeep barefoot. Why does Birdie get to stay dry? She's the driver, the road-story maniac. I shivered and chattered and all Birdie said as she steered the jeep back onto the track was "It's going to rain" and it did. Fat wet plops blurring the windshield. I closed my eyes and when I finally opened them again the rain had stopped and the jeep had stopped and we were staring at an oasis. A gigantic patch of desert-defying green stuff.

"Rises the earth out of the foam, fair and green," Birdie intoned, quoting *Voluspa,* and for the first time in hours what she said made perfect sense.

Life is persistent, I'll say that for it. Where nothing should grow sprang some of the richest vegetation I'd seen in Iceland, against the backdrop of the magnificent table mountain Herdubreid, shaped like a birthday cake with ice cap icing. We sat awestruck in the jeep, Birdie reciting the last stanzas of *Voluspa* by heart.

"I'm hungry," I said finally, but Birdie of course could not hear me, lost in the currents of her verbal spew. *"I'm starving!"* I shouted.

That she heard. And stared at me as if *I* were insane. "No need to yell, *elskan*. There's food in the back, help yourself."

Food indeed: an entire shopping bag full of licorice. Twenty-some packages of multiple varieties: salty, super salty, and sweet. Why? I didn't have to ask. The answer was clearly printed on each package: *Freyja* brand. With a black cat logo. Was this Birdie's idea of a joke? I was far too old by then—any remnants of my child status were rapidly vanishing—to think candy for dinner either funny or fun. But there was nothing to say, or rather, no one who would listen. So I sat in the jeep sucking salty mouth-puckering licorice while Birdie surveyed the oasis on foot, a tall blond flash of salmon pink weaving through tall green grasses.

Singing woke me from a sitting sleep, a haunting melody, Birdie serenading me outside the jeep window. *Ride, ride and follow over the sand . . . the outlaws of the Odadahraun are herding sheep . . .* "I've found it, Freya *min*, Fjalla-Eyvindur's hideout, his very shelter, one of the greatest outlaws of all time, sheep rustler, Icelandic Robin Hood, folk hero who survived here in this very hut through the horrendous winter of 1774 on angelica root and raw horse meat—"

I would say it was the most miserable night of my life except the next was far worse. To call it cold would not do it justice; assume from here on the meanest of temps. Birdie and I in a cramped stone hut huddled in sleeping bags sucking licorice. The little I slept I dreamt, not unreasonably, that I was back in the ice cave, hearing Saemundur's name as I shouted it echoing off the frozen walls unanswered.

Signs awaited us come morning: antler and sand.

I woke alone, stiff and hungry with a licorice-thick fuzz coating my mouth, my clammy sneakers oozing glacial silt. Outside the hut it was a sunny day bit by razor-sharp wind. I found Birdie kneeling on the black-ened bank of the river, holding something in her hand. A single enormous reindeer antler. Artfully sculpted. *Freyja left us this sign, elskan. See the shape of Fehu, rune of Freyja and Freyr, Fehu the first letter of the Runic alphabet, now we learn our ABC's, good pagans knew their futhark: Fehu, Uruz, Thurisaz, Ansuz, Raido, Kenaz. She is near, elskan. She is near.*

I left Birdie scratching rune shapes with the antler tip in the riverbank's black sand. I knew we had to get out, turn back, and it was up to me to make this happen. I squatted in the grass to pee, filled the plastic water jug from a spring, rolled up our sleeping bags, and tossed them into the jeep. By this time the wind had picked up and as I took Birdie by the hand and led her to the jeep, still clutching the antler, we got slammed by a wall of sand. It swirled so thick we couldn't see, could only run toward the dark shape of the jeep, arms covering our faces. The jeep was a haven but a stationary one. There was no going anywhere, even Birdie could see that. Curtains of sand blew over us, spattering the windows, a weird desert blizzard that trapped us for an hour or more. For once Birdie wasn't talky. She fell into a deep, almost catatonic, silence, head slumped on the steering wheel. Wouldn't answer when I spoke, wouldn't move when I shook her. What if she was slipping into a coma? When she finally spoke her words came slowly, heavy as stones.

"We're doomed, Freya *min*. Doomed."

"Then let's turn back."

"Impossible," she declared, after another long silence. You see, the doom she referred to was not our own, hers and mine, but the world's. Slowly, as if she were only just learning to speak, she explained it to me. Ulfur was a sign. The second coming of the Wolf who will swallow the sun as the *volva* foresaw. Only Birdie had the power to forestall the end. But she needed in-struction. Freyja would tell us what to do. *She alone of the gods yet lives.* And Freyja was at Askja. We were stuck in the jeep while the doom of the world was unfolding! Excitement crept into Birdie's voice again, she brushed a tan-gle of hair from her eyes, the sand died down, and she was steering us back onto that rutted wretch of a road, Askja Way. As we drove, the river turned rougher, foaming and surging through banks of dark lava. We were nearing its source, the Vatnajokull glacier. Then the road veered sharply west and we left the river behind us. Now there was nothing between us and Askja, nothing but the Odadahraun: Burnt Land of Evil Deeds, in the old days a desolate refuge for criminals outlawed to the interior of Iceland, the most expansive lava flow on the island, training ground for astronauts.

"Astronauts?" I interrupted, and for once she heard me, spared a moment to explain.

"It's true, Freya *min*! I kid you not. NASA stationed them here in the Odadahraun to train for the moonwalk in 'sixty-eight. It's the most moonlike spot on the planet."

For a time she was silent, navigating the jeep over the treacherous mounds of lava just as Saemundur had trained her.

The road to Askja ended in snowdrifts. Not a problem, Birdie declared. We would ascend the crater on foot. She turned off the jeep calmly, then began preparing herself. First she belted the salmon pink coat tightly around her waist, then reached in the back of the jeep and pulled out the animal skins she'd stolen from the farm. One mink she wrapped around her neck; the other she slung from her belt. The large one, a sealskin, she draped over her shoulders like a cloak. Cat fur would be best, she explained. But Freyja will understand. Everyone has to improvise. We trudged up a long rocky slope. I carried the water jug and Birdie carried the antler high in the air like a torch, though we had no need of one: the sun sparkled and the sky was mocking blue. A fierce cheer. Wind knifed us in the back as we climbed, I stumbled again and again in my slushy sneakers over the loose rubble. And still Birdie talked. Her delusions gradually took on a clarity for me. Your mother, Cousin, believed she was the next *volva,* a prophet, a seeress, chosen by Freyja herself to deliver to Iceland, to the world, the next fateful prophecy.

As we reached the rim of the caldera she took my hand. Far below us down a sheer slope of scree lay a milky green pool. Saemundur had told us about it: Viti—an Icelandic word for hell—was the crater formed when the volcano collapsed in on itself a hundred years earlier. Olafur's eruption.

"Greetings, light-mother!" Birdie called out. I shivered with shame though there was no one to hear or see. And then to my horror she began making her way down the slope, half-scrambling, half-sliding. The mink fur fastened to her belt swung wildly. She was halfway down before I could bring myself to follow. This will be it, I told myself. This is why we have come. Birdie would dunk herself in the steaming waters of Viti and emerge reborn. And then we could climb back up the scree and down the other side and if we were lucky and there was enough gas left we'd make our way back through the treacherous Odadahraun to Egilsstadir. Then Reykjavik. Then home to Gimli.

At the bottom of the slope Birdie disrobed. Animal pelts first, then salmon pink coat. Then wrinkled blouse and pants, bra and underwear, socks and boots. "Naked as the day I was born," she yelled gleefully, then plunged in, laughing and splashing. "And they say there's no going back to the womb!" Around us towered the ugly scraped raw rock of the caldera. Birdie swam out toward the middle, a pale spot of flesh in milkish water.

She emerged skin steaming and began to dress. No clothes this time, only the stolen sealskin draped over her shoulders. She was a *volva* now, sitting on a rock that jutted over the pool of water, the antler gripped in one hand. She began chanting herself into trance. A poem of some sort, the words seemed to rhyme. Her voice was melodious with an undercurrent of urgency. I sat mute at the water's edge, sucking salty licorice. The words went on and on. Was she chanting the poem *Voluspa*? Her own *Word Meadow*?

I listened for as long as I could, until my entire body shook with cold and my feet turned numb in the snow. *We could die out here.* It was the end of August. The roads to the interior would close soon, that much I knew. Saemundur had said so. Askja might not see visitors again until next summer. And what would they find? A pile of bones wrapped in mink stoles and sealskin.

I stood up. Stared Birdie in the eye. She didn't blink, continued chanting. I braced myself against the wind and began scrambling up the scree.

21

I was found the next day inside Saemundur's sleeping bag in the middle of Askja Way, lying between the twin ruts of jeep tracks. Not by tourists or scientists but by a search and rescue crew. In the midst of the Odadahraun. Twelve miles from Askja, they say. I must have walked it, but I don't remember. Honestly. For once, I truly don't.

For my life, I have Saemundur to thank. Askja was his idea. The last sighting of us had been at the gas station in Egilsstadir. After that, nothing. We should not have been hard to miss in Ulfur's tan jeep, a blond woman in a pink coat and a teenage girl in a patched jeans jacket whose photos were plastered on TV and in newspapers across the country. But there were no sightings, anywhere. Vanished into thin air, the headlines claimed.

That's when Askja crossed Saemundur's mind. At first Ulfur thought it preposterous that Birdie and I could travel to Askja by ourselves . . . until Saemundur confessed to the secret driving lessons. Ulfur called the police. A search crew left from Akureyri, the only other place in Iceland aside from Reykjavik that could reasonably be called a city. Two sets of two men in Land Rovers. After waking me, questioning me, feeding me a hard-boiled egg and a piece of bread, they laid me in the back of one of the vehicles covered in blankets and drove me to Akureyri. I was in shock. The other group continued on to Askja in search of Birdie. You have to find her, I insisted. Over and over. *Please.* I felt I'd betrayed her. Abandoned her. If she didn't survive it would be my fault. And if she did?

At the hospital in Akureyri I was treated for exposure. Many people came to visit me. Eirikur and Hrefna, our schoolteacher hosts from Brekka. A woman named Thorunn, who said she was Sigga's niece. Even a television crew. Plus Ulfur and Saemundur. Everyone so sorry for what had happened to me. Especially the Wolf. But I didn't feel like a victim, I felt like a criminal again. I pretended to sleep whenever someone entered the room. Once I opened my eyes and Saemundur was standing above me with his dark waving hair. *Eye-moon-lure.* He smiled with his wide mime grin and I forgot myself and smiled back. I told him I had his jacket. He said I could keep it. I talked to my mother and Sigga by phone once a day.

Birdie's mania reached its peak in the hospital in Akureyri. She was revved so high she nearly expired, her heart beating so fast it almost burst. I heard two nurses discussing her in the hallway outside my room. Shortly after, the mania collapsed into severe depression and Birdie was transferred to Klepp, the mental hospital in Reykjavik.

A few days later I was flown from Akureyri to Reykjavik in a tiny plane— I think we flew directly over Askja but I couldn't be sure—and then from Reykjavik to Winnipeg on the last charter flight of the summer.

Everyone met me at the airport, Mama and Sigga and Stefan. Birdie was still in Reykjavik. Ulfur was not pressing charges. They were keeping Birdie at Klepp until she had stabilized enough to travel. Then they would fly her back to Canada and admit her to the Selkirk Asylum. After that, we didn't know what would happen to her. At least, no one was telling me. We got into Stefan's Rambler. I sat in back with Mama. She held my hand and wept. Everything seemed flat: Winnipeg, the prairie, my life. I don't remember speaking at all. I couldn't look my mother in the eye. I just stared out the window. I was surprised when Stefan pulled into the train station.

"Aren't we going to Gimli?"

We were not. School was starting in less than a week back in

Connecticut, Mama explained. And besides, she added, holding back a sob, you are never going back to Gimli as long as Birdie is alive.

"That's enough of that, Anna," said Sigga. "Time will tell."

"Time will not tell," my mother answered. "I will tell. I will decide. If you want to see us, you can come to Connecticut."

At first I was relieved to be back home in Connecticut with Mama. She was no Birdie, and suddenly I loved her for that. Her moods did not turn on a dime or shift like lake weather. She did not hate me one moment, then profess to adore me the next. Her love was constant and, now that I had been returned to her, even more intense. She never blamed me for going off with Birdie, and for that I was grateful. But she never let me mention Birdie's name again. As if she could erase her sister completely.

I worried about Birdie constantly. In our monthly phone calls, Sigga assured me Birdie was "recovering nicely" at Selkirk. I couldn't imagine it being very nice. But what could I do? My mother was true to her word. We never went back to Gimli while Birdie was alive, which wasn't long. She killed herself six months after I was flown back from Iceland. On my fourteenth birthday.

Cousin, I'll tell you what I know about your mother's death, which isn't much. When Birdie was finally able to talk, to feed and dress herself, the Selkirk Asylum released her to Sigga's care. Two days later she was found dead of an overdose in her bedroom at Oddi. That was all my mother would tell me. It was my fourteenth birthday. My mother insisted that was coincidence, that Birdie no longer knew one day from another. I knew better, I knew how her mind worked. When I left her side at Viti, when I turned my back on her world-saving prophecy, when I sent the men to capture her— she put me in the enemy camp. I was no better than the Wolf. Maybe worse.

If Birdie had lived, would we all have reconciled eventually? I like to imagine so. That each sister would have forgiven the other. That Birdie would be cured and understand that I was only trying to save us both. And our strange little Gimli summers would have resumed again. But I doubt that. I think the rift would have been permanent. Vague, befuddled Mama became suddenly sharp and clear on one thing: she would never forgive

Birdie for kidnapping me and endangering my life. Even after Birdie died, I don't believe she ever did.

I had trouble wrapping my mind around death. I dreamt of Birdie constantly, woke weeping. By day I hid behind my veil of long hair and somehow sleepwalked through my first year of high school. Mama never trusted me again. I tried hard, but it didn't matter. My fateful cartwheel she would never remember, but my Iceland escapade she could never forget. Suspicion clouded her eyes. She looked at me like I might disappear at any moment. And so I lived up to her expectations. I became a sneaky teenager, an escape artist. I started hanging around with bad kids. Smoked cigarettes, then pot. Drank beer under the train trestle. Had sex with a boy while supposedly bowling. Made friends with a small circle of girls. Listened to their secrets, kept my own.

How did I feel? you ask. As little as possible. Whipped off my homework in half an hour after dinner and got straight A's. I figured as long as I kept up my grades and didn't get caught, no one could really complain. And no one did. I was just one more girl with long straight hair parted in the middle wearing a patched jeans jacket and rolling joints through the late 1970s. I didn't stick out. I was invisible, Hidden Folk. I studied French, pushed Icelandic out of my head. Airy-singing words replaced lilting-throaty ones. I was mistress of the double life; I continued keeping track of my mother's canes and habitually lied about my whereabouts.

The summer after eleventh grade my mother suggested we go back to Gimli. Just for a week? Sigga was very old, didn't I want to see her again? I wouldn't go. It was a way of punishing my mother for not letting me see Birdie again. And I couldn't bear to show my face in Gimli. All those good people searching Lake Winnipeg for me while I was cavorting at Thingvellir. My mother, rightly, did not trust me enough to leave me alone, so neither of us went.

I drifted through high school, then on to college in Massachusetts. Yes, I'm rushing, Cousin. I realize that. But I'm trying to get back to your story, or rather, my story as it relates to you. And Birdie. And those years in between relate to nothing. I was a shell. So I'll be brief. I couldn't wait to go away to college, but once I arrived I was aimless. I studied some (psychology, history, more French), drank my way through semesters, found a new crowd of bad kids who were good to me.

I missed my mother. Who was keeping track of her canes? I imagined her sitting alone knitting Icelandic sweaters in our darkened house, haunted by ancestor photos. Sometimes I talked about leaving school and coming home again, but Mama wouldn't hear of it.

"College is your time, Freya," she'd say. "I'm fine here. You put me right out of your mind."

If only.

Iceland and Gimli were easier to forget. The immigrant Icelanders are so obscure you could easily go your entire life in this country and never hear a word about them. The English, the French, the Italians, the Irish, the Eastern Europeans, the Japanese and Chinese, the Mexicans, the Norwegians and the Swedes, even the histories of the African slaves and Native Americans were touched upon in my college history classes. Not fully, not truthfully, but at the very least mentioned. Of the Icelanders who settled in Manitoba, Ontario, British Columbia, the Dakotas, Minnesota, Wisconsin, even Utah, not a word. And why is that? you ask. For you yourself, I imagine, have never heard of us either. New York, New Jersey, New England, New London, New Brunswick—all the old world places made new—but New Iceland? Nobody's heard of New Iceland. Was it because we were so wretchedly oppressed? Hardly. If anything, the opposite was true. We assimilated more quickly than most, with our fair features and devotion to literacy, our ability to persist through hardship etched in our genes. No, the answer is simple enough, it seems to me: there were too few of us to matter. All said, only fifteen thousand Icelanders emigrated at the tail end of the nineteenth century—a droplet lost among the million-size waves of immigrants who flooded North America's shores. It's no wonder we never made it into my college history books.

And that was fine with me. Gimli and the house called Oddi; Sigga and her Blue Book; the old ladies at Betel recounting their dreams; the old men at Betel peering at chess pieces through wire-rimmed glasses; the annual *Fjallkona* spectacle; Gisli and his lying rhymes; Stefan and his historical expeditions; Birdie and her *Word Meadow*—especially Birdie—gone, gone, gone.

Icelandic? I never spoke a word. When people asked about the origin of my name, as they inevitably did, I answered, *Scandinavian*. So pleasingly generic. Or sometimes, *A Norse goddess*. Guys liked that. Guys liked me. I was tall and blond and thin. And if I bordered on being too blond with my wispy white-blond hair, and too gangly thin, and so pale I verged on ghostly—no matter. My near-albino looks were considered exotic; my reserve was mistaken for confidence, my shame for mystery. No one knew me, of course; I let no one in, distanced myself most especially from myself. Alcohol is good for that. I skidded along on the desperate surface of things. Only at night did my old life emerge, dream images flashing like a drowning swimmer bursting to the surface: the ice cave, Brekka, Askja. Kaleidoscope dreams splintered with fragments of lava and glacier and ash and the brightest greenest grass on the planet.

It was at the end of my junior year, on a hungover May morning, that my mother dropped dead in the A & P supermarket. Yes, just like that. No comma this time. Just a full and sudden stop. Aneurysm. Related to the original fall, the coma, the brain damage? The doctors couldn't say. They weren't sure. She didn't suffer, they assured me. But I did.

How could Mama up and die like that? Before I'd ever had a chance to confess, to tell her *It was me*. Before I ever had a chance to apologize for vanishing to Iceland. Granted, I'd had years and years to say those things. But I was young, I believed I had years and years more. It never occurred to me that my mother could die. My father had died, my aunt had died, but my mother? After her first lucky resurrection, I guess I'd come to believe her immortal, or at least . . . enduring.

I left school and returned home to Connecticut. Stefan and my mother's dear friend Vera flew in from Winnipeg. It was a shock to see them after so many years. But everything was a shock. Vera arranged the funeral, she was good at that kind of thing. She'd run the Ladies Aid, she'd been the *Fjall-kona*. Stefan came as Sigga's emissary. Sigga was ninety, too frail to travel. He was to discuss with me my plans for the future. He was to convince me to come back with them to Gimli. If only for a visit. It'll do you good. It'll do your *amma* good. Maybe in August, for *Islendingadagurinn*? Maybe, I finally agreed. I was nothing if not a good liar. Not brilliant like your mother,

Cousin, but competent, convincing. I would return to school, I promised, as soon as the house sold. Above all, I insisted, I would be fine.

As soon as Vera and Stefan returned to Gimli I began to cry. Weeks on end. It was not the only thing I did. I also watched television, lying on the living room rug with my chin propped in my hands, my feet crossed in the air behind me. Talk shows, mainly. A lot of incredible things were going on in people's lives. Twins separated at birth, living with a longing and never knowing what it was . . . reunited at last. Fathers who had never said "I love you" to their sons . . . choking out the words for the first time. When the guests cried, I cried. But where was my second chance?

After three weeks of crying I turned off the television. I would contact the real estate agent Vera had found and start the process of selling the house. I would pack up Mama's things and . . . do what with them? I walked through the house. My bones felt oddly light, like the wings of origami birds. And my vision seemed strangely keen. Certain objects belonging to Mama seemed to . . . glow. *Glow* is too strong a word. To emanate. As if something of my mother remained inside. Like a cut flower in a vase, dead but with some life still coursing through the stem. This was how I saw my mother's hairbrush sitting on top of the television set, the reading glasses attached to a woven red cord hanging from the kitchen doorknob, a pair of brown leather loafers, molded exactly to the shape of my mother's small wide feet. The essence of Mama's life still clinging to her belongings. But how long, I worried, until that essence would begin to evaporate?

I found my mother's camera, which itself did not have the glow—the camera had not been much used—then drove Mama's car to the drugstore and bought a roll of black-and-white film. Why black and white? It seemed more . . . objective. Scientific. By the time I got home the sun was setting. I had no flash. I had to work fast. I brought each object into the den, where a narrow beam of setting sunlight streamed onto the carpet. First I laid one of Mama's lace cloths on the floor. Then each object by turn—hairbrush, loafers, sunglasses—I photographed, from different angles. Even through the lens I could distinguish the glow of my mother rising out of the objects from the ordinary late afternoon sun falling onto them.

A week later the photographs were back from the drugstore. I sat behind the wheel of Mama's car and opened the package. The hairbrush was a hairbrush. The shoes shoes. The glasses glasses. All nearly lost against the white lace background. It was something about the exposure, I decided. That was why you couldn't see the glow. So I took the train into Manhattan, to a professional photography lab on the far West Side. Klaus Steinman's Photographic Ltd. "Specializing in black & white," the ad in the yellow pages claimed. I took a screeching old freight elevator two floors down, then rang a bell on the counter and waited. A small man with age spots on his forehead and only a lick of white hair down the middle of his skull like a skunk appeared from a back room. Klaus Steinman himself, the hot-tempered ex-Prussian army officer who would become my first employer, although of course I didn't know that yet.

I handed the package of photographs to him. "They didn't come out very well," I explained. My voice sounded thick; I hadn't spoken to another person since the funeral. "I was wondering if you could fix them. Reprint them."

"Let's take a look-see." His voice was gruff, with a heavy accent I couldn't place. He opened the envelope and spread the prints on the counter. Then he smiled oddly, and I saw for an instant the photographs through his eyes: hairbrush, shoes, sunglasses on a white cloth on top of a green shag rug. Except it wasn't green but a medium shade of gray. He was shaking his head, still smirking.

"Not sure what you are wanting such pictures for," he said finally. Quizzically.

There was no reason to tell him, but I did. "They were my mother's."

"Ah." Nodded his speckled head. Then he opened up the envelope again and held the negatives against a board that was lit up. He clipped each strip to the board and studied it.

"There was a light," I started to explain.

"Not enough light, that's the problem, missy." He didn't understand. "But I can work on these for you. Get them a bit sharper. Bit of dodging do the trick."

When I came in the next week to pick them up, the photos were sharper, clearer. But still no glow. He sensed my disappointment. "Best we could do, I'm afraid. Of course, there's always more tricks we could try, if you're willing to pay for it."

I nodded; he took me by the arm. "Come on back, I'll show you some things we can try. Ever been in a darkroom?"

I shook my head and followed him through a curtain down a hallway. "This door here," he said, "is called a light trap. Does just what it says. Go through it like a revolving door. Keeps the light from leaking in."

In the darkroom there was only one red light on. Everything seemed to glow. The air was close and stank like vinegar, and worse. Klaus made me pick one of the prints for him to work on. I chose the one of the shoes. The shoes had glowed the most. I watched while he fitted the negative in the machine, set a timer, flicked a switch, and in the brief seconds of exposure fluttered a piece of paper over the negative with the delicacy of a butterfly in flight. *Ding*. The light went out; the exposed paper he dropped into a tray. And there while I watched emerged my mother's shoe. It didn't matter, then, that the glow was gone. It was enough to see Mama's shoe come out of the darkness like that. I wanted to do it. To give some image its watery birth.

"Can I try?" I asked, surprising myself.

"Don't see why not. No business now anyway. Lemme just put up the CLOSED sign."

He left me alone in the darkroom. I stared at the print of my mother's shoe, which now hung by metal clips to dry. I walked across the room to the red light. It had the kind of switch that's set into the cord, a small nubby wheel you slide with your thumb. I pushed it and it clicked and for a moment I stood alone in the darkness. Absolute. I took a deep whiff of vinegar-air into my lungs and held it there. Not breathing. Still.

I never tried to explain to Klaus about the glow, even after he took me on as an unpaid intern, then a lowly apprentice, then after three years a full-fledged printer. Certain things can't be photographed as seen. You get as close as you can.

I sold Mama's house, but there wasn't much money left over—she'd mortgaged it to pay for my college—and I used up the proceeds subsidizing my apprenticeship. A few blocks of day are all I see on either side of my subway ride, East Side to West Side on the L train. Then I drop down two floors on a rickety freight elevator to the Sub. Such is my life, if you'll grant me that. A sub-life. All of it I considered temporary. When I was good and ready I'd emerge from my lair, hungry for world again. I was just calling time out, getting my bearings.

Meanwhile, the earth circled the sun. Then again. Years passed. Eight, to be exact. I continue taking my own photographs, seeking to animate objects. A bit of the pagan, I suppose. I have boyfriends here and there, most less than a year, one for nearly three. All make the same complaint: Ice Queen. A conspiracy of exes. For friendship I rely mostly on my darkroom compatriot, Frank, who is gay and nearly as reclusive as I am. Each in our own light-sealed cell, we listen to the same talk radio shows, chat on the intercom, and ally ourselves against Klaus and his rages.

Before my mother died, before I dropped out of college, I'd imagined that forging an adult life involved setting goals, making decisions, taking actions. Not so! My underground existence simply formed itself, untethered to any grand plan.

And that, Cousin, is how I got from there to here. Abbreviated, yes. But this is not supposed to be my story, exactly. Or only partly. This is the story of how I knew your mother, and then, how I came to find out about your existence. I have to stay focused. I may find you soon, and I want this letter to be finished when I do.

22

This past August a thick cream-colored envelope arrived in my mailbox, an invitation to the one hundredth birthday celebration of my one and only grandmother Sigga. And what did I do with it? Nothing. I took no action, I let it pend.

Living without light, the fish of caves became not only blind but eyeless. A month later, I lay sprawled on my futon on the floor watching a nature special about evolution. Pale lumpy fish swam across the screen. It took a few millennia of living in caves, the voice-over explained, for the fish to lose their eyeballs completely. The narrator had a crisp, almost British clip to his voice. *Their eyes outlived their usefulness. Now all that remain are vestigial bumps.*

Then the phone rang, and the proper male voice on the other end sounded so strangely like the narrator's I became confused.

"Stefan *who*?" I demanded.

"Your uncle Stefan, that's who!"

Can you blame me? I hadn't spoken to him since Mama's funeral eight years earlier. Since then our only contact had been cards exchanged at Christmas. I knew he disapproved of me, of my refusal to visit Sigga in Gimli. And now here he was on the phone, with his old-fashioned Icelandic Canadian accent. It sounded foreign to me, it had been so long since I'd heard those faintly rolling r's. He wanted to know if I had received the invitation to Sigga's birthday celebration.

I had.

And would I be attending?

A long international silence. I could hear the coins clicking in my head. Then Stefan cleared his throat, the sound traveling across the phone line as a pillowy *harumph*.

"I can't get away from work. It's impossibly busy."

"Then just come for the weekend. The party is on a Saturday night."

He had me there.

"Freya, Sigga's not going to live much longer."

"Is she ill?"

"Quite healthy actually. Physically, anyway. But not many live beyond a hundred. Though there was Runa Black, she made it to a hundred and eight." He paused, and I heard the spark of a match, then the thin draw he took from his pipe. He used to let me climb on his lap and hold the flame over the bowl, then blow it out. "The point is, Freya, you never know what can happen."

"Believe me," I said. I took out a cigarette, lit a match of my own. "It's not that I don't want to see her. It's just that . . . well, honestly, I can't afford it. The airfare and all."

Liar. I wanted him to say it. But he was silent. Sucking his pipe. "All right then, Freya. I thought that might be it." He didn't sound angry, or even disappointed. Just relieved. As if he hadn't really wanted me to come but promised Sigga he'd try. He hung up. *Happy birthday, Amma,* I whispered into the dial tone.

And that was the end of it—until a round-trip ticket to Winnipeg arrived in my mailbox a week later. The fish dreams began that same night. Even awake, in the darkroom with the safelight turned off, they swam through my mind, blind and eyeless.

What, you ask, did I so fear? A host of ghosts awaiting me in Gimli: Birdie, Mama, and my long-lost phantom self, worst of all. How could I face that girl who had devoted her childhood summers to the writing, reading, memorizing of poetry? Who had promised her auntie she would be the next poet in a line that skated all the way back to Iceland, to the Viking poet Egil Skallagrimsson? How could I tell that girl I'd turned my back on words?

And there would be the living to contend with: Sigga, Stefan, Vera. Even if they'd managed to forgive me the crimes of my past (sending my mother into a coma and ruining her for light, and life; absconding to Iceland with Birdie and allowing her to climb, then plummet from the brink of madness; dropping out of college after my mother's sudden death, and never returning; and finally, and still, turning my back on my grandmother, my only living relative)—what would they think of my life now? My grimy, chemical-infused existence seemed hardly worthy of the granddaughter of the Great Olafur, *Skald Nyja Islands*.

But my worst fear of returning to Gimli was of coming unglued. My bones could turn to origami wings again.

The plane ticket Stefan sent rendered all my excuses moot. If I didn't go now, I could never look myself in the mirror again. I would go. I steeled myself, icier than ever. And then one morning—the day before departure—it occurred to me as I rode the lurching, screeching subway to work, gripping the pole for balance though it would have been impossible to fall, wedged as I was on all sides by the anonymous press of strangers, that maybe it was the not-going back that was holding me back. The darkroom job, the basement apartment: those were supposed to have been temporary measures, a way to step off the spinning globe after my mother died and regain my footing. Instead the temporary holding pattern had gradually shifted into permanent status, a rock-solid inertia.

Maybe I needed to be shaken up, loosen my grip on that underground pole. Maybe the visit to Gimli would not so much derail my life as re-rail it in a new direction.

Of course, I didn't know about you yet, Cousin, you who have become my confidant, inquisitor, and holy grail. My conceit.

But I had an inkling of something, an obsolete eye.

23

And so Freya returned to Gimli.

The goddess Freyja? Lusty mistress of fertility and birth, sage adviser to the lovelorn, deity of crops and wombs? She who cruised the heavens in her cat-drawn chariot, flew to other worlds wrapped in a cloak of enchanted feathers? Freyja the mother of all seers who instructed Odin himself in the divine art of divination? Back in Gimli? The same Gimli the gods built as their new home after the coming of *Ragnarok,* when the Fenris Wolf swallowed the sun, and the serpent Garmr that circles the earth, tail in mouth, rose up from the ocean in a tidal wave of terror? And the earth sank in the sea, and cast down from heaven were the hot stars, and the sky itself was scorched with fire? And then the earth rose up from the waters, fair and green, and the gods built a new home brighter than sunlight, thatched with pure gold, and named this shining palace Gimli? That Gimli?

No, not that Gimli, and not that Freyja either. Merely me, a lowly mortal in a rental car slinking into town under cover of night after a sixteen-year, self-imposed exile. Stefan had called before I left and offered to pick me up at the airport, sounded miffed when I'd refused. I couldn't bear to trouble him, I explained, and for once I spoke the truth. I felt undeserving of that Gimli-sweet kindness. Underneath it, I believed that Stefan, like Sigga, like my mother, like Vera and anyone else who held an opinion on the matter, blamed me for Birdie's suicide.

No, no one had ever said as much. They didn't have to. It was obvious. True, the Iceland escapade had been Birdie's idea, her master plan, but I'd gone along every step of the way. If I had been a different kind of child—more timid, more responsible, less impulsive—I might have dug my heels in when Birdie intercepted me in the midst of that *Islendingadagurinn* parade, insisted on a proper send-off by my mother. But Birdie knew me, knew that I was prone to fancy and enthusiasm, that I would fly without thinking at the first invitation.

I also declined Stefan's offer of a place to stay for the weekend. "You've already been far too generous," I told him. I meant not only the plane ticket but the care he'd given Sigga over the years. Care I should have given her myself.

Instead I reserved a cheap car, booked a room at the Viking Lakeside Motel. A hideout and a getaway vehicle, should I need to escape on short notice. The rental office at the airport was out of economy cars when I arrived and "upgraded" me to a luxury van, a ten-seater, same price. Black no less, a rented hearse, plenty of room for all my ghosts if they could manage to sit upright. I headed north on Highway 9 at dusk, hands trembling. Smoked five cigarettes. Hands trembling still. It was the prairie, unnervingly flat. In the city I'm propped up, secure in my thicket of buildings and bodies. Out there, there was nothing vertical to hold me. Just the black stripe of the road ahead. Flattened fields to the left, shimmery glimpses of Lake Winnipeg to the right. My old lake!

The sun dropped and it became truly dark. Not the muted city darkness I've become accustomed to—dim subway tunnels, basement apartment—but the deep black of a starless country night on a road without streetlights and only the rare brief shine of an oncoming car. As I neared the turnoff for Gimli, twin strands of longing and dread wound inside me: speed on, turn back. On. Back. Or maybe . . . out, into the lake. No one would ever know. I hadn't told my darkroom pal, Frank, about the trip, or our boss, Klaus. I'd left on a Friday afternoon, would be back to work on Monday morning. That way I could erase, if I needed to, the entire trip. Like the rest of my life, before I'd reinvented myself in New York, it might simply never have happened.

It was the sunrise that woke me my first day back in Gimli. Not the early, gentling light I remembered from Birdie's lakeside sunrise but the balled yellow fist of the thing itself. Smack in the eye. I'd forgotten to pull the shades the night before, or change out of my plane-rumpled clothes. I'd just checked directly into the Viking Lakeside Motel, plunked on the bed without turning back the skimpy covers, and crashed into a sleep black and flat as the night I'd driven through. And then I was suddenly, brutally, wide awake, blinking and squinting, burrowing under the covers and yanking the musty motel pillow over my face, defending myself like any subterranean creature from rude solar assault. Of course, it was only our ordinary star, making its daily rounds. I'd forgotten how bright the sun can get: even after I squeezed my eyes shut its brassy imprint remained, a penny-size hole persisting in my mind as I dozed back to sleep. A pretty sight I must have made, all six feet of me sprawled diagonally across the single bed, arms flopped off one side, feet dangling off the other, torso tangled in the dingy top sheet. A hard knot crunched between my brows.

I did not want to go back there; I had a long day ahead of me. We'll let me sleep.

And while I sleep, will you allow me to tell you, dear Cousin, about *The Tricking of Gylfi*? It's one of the old Norse myths documented by our esteemed ancestor Snorri Sturluson and recounted to me as a bedtime story by our very own Birdie.

King Gylfi was the ruler of what is now called Sweden. During Gylfi's rule, a new race of people came wandering into the northern lands. The Norse called them the Aesir, believing them to be of Asian origin, and they were awed by the Aesir's gifts and prowess. But after being badly tricked by one of the Aesir—likely the goddess Freyja in disguise—Gylfi decided to travel to Asgard, the Aesir's legendary headquarters, to discover for himself the source of their great powers.

Before departing on his quest Gylfi prepared himself a disguise, because a people as clever as the Aesir would never reveal their most prized secrets to a king as powerful as Gylfi. So Gylfi shed his royal robes and donned the cloak of a vagrant, calling himself Gangleri, which is just another name for wanderer.

Were the Aesir fooled by Gylfi's disguise, even for a moment? They were not. Well skilled in the art of prophecy, they saw Gylfi coming a long way off. When "Gangleri" arrived in Asgard, the Aesir were ready for him. In place of their ordinary dwellings they conjured out of thin air a vast hall, brilliantly shingled with the shields of warriors. The hall was higher than any Gylfi had ever seen, so high he could scarcely see the top of it.

Awaiting Gylfi inside was none other than Odin himself, disguised as not one but three rulers seated in a three-tiered throne, calling themselves High, Just-as-High, and Third. High wasted no time. He told Gylfi he was welcome to food and drink, like anyone else in the great hall. But had he further business there?

Gylfi did: he wished to find out if there was anyone learned in the hall.

The three kings stared at him a moment in shocked silence. Learned, indeed! Gylfi knew full well that any ruler would take such a request as a challenge to his honor, and these three proved no exception. High was especially offended by Gylfi's comment and warned him that he would not escape the hall alive unless he could prove himself the more learned. "Stand out in front while you ask: he who tells shall sit."

And so began their famous contest of wits. Through it Gylfi hoped to learn all the secrets of the Aesir—and as long as he won in the end, he would be able to return home a more powerful man himself. If not, well then, he would die. Such were the rules of the game.

Gylfi took his place standing in front of the throne and started with an easy enough question. If the Aesir did not know the answer to this then surely they knew nothing at all.

"Who is the highest and most ancient of all gods?"

"All-Father," answered Third, not missing a beat.

Gylfi decided to try a harder line of questioning. "But what was the beginning? How did things start? And what was there before?"

High spoke down to Gylfi from the highest throne, recounting the beginning of the world, the great nothing of *Ginnungagap,* the cluelessness of sun and moon, the homeless stars.

All three kings nodded in satisfaction, then stared down in royal condescension to await Gylfi's next question. Oh, they were a pack of know-it-alls, this royal trinity. Whatever question Gylfi asked, they had an answer, however bizarre and improbable. The questioning went on for hours, and Gylfi began to fear for his life. He could not stump them. They knew how Bor's sons killed the frost giant Ymir and out of Ymir's carcass made the earth, from his blood the sea, rocks from his bones, trees from his hair, from his skull the sky, and out of his brains nothing less than the cruelest clouds.

Of course the three kings knew all about the End-Time, too, how the wolf would swallow the sun, the earth sink in the sea, brothers slay brothers, and gods fight giants in *Ragnarok,* the greatest battle of all.

"And then?" Gylfi asked. He was sweating now, fearing his own end-time drawing near. It seemed there was not a single question he could ask that they could not answer.

"And then," proclaimed High, "the earth rises again fair and green, and the gods who survive build their new gold-roofed palace called Gimli!"

And with that the three kings crossed their arms across their chests and glared down at Gylfi in triumph. Clearly they considered themselves the winners. But Gylfi had nothing to lose, nothing but his life. "And then?" he asked softly.

Ahem. And a royal silence. Finally High spoke. "Beyond that we do not know," he conceded. "But who does? I've never heard anyone tell further into the future of the world than that." The other two nodded in agreement.

Be that as it may, Gylfi had stumped them, and spared his own life in the process. As soon as High conceded his lack of knowledge, poof! With a big bang the whole thing vanished: the triple kings on their triple throne, the shield-shingled hall. Gylfi found himself standing alone, on open ground, having won the contest, perhaps—was he not still standing?—but tricked yet again by the magic of those clever Aesir!

And so this tale has come to be known as *Gylfaginning,* which means *The Tricking of Gylfi,* though despite having been tricked Gylfi made out just fine in the end. He returned home, as all good heroes eventually do, and presented to his own people everything he had learned from the three kings, who were none other than Odin himself in disguise. And these same stories were then passed along, generation to generation, and became in time that marvelously overwrought cosmology known these days—though it is hardly known at all—as Norse mythology (of which I've provided only a mere and cursory summary, for if I stopped to tell every tale those three kings told—the strange characteristics of each of the nine worlds, not to mention the name of practically every last dwarf and giant—we'd never get on with our own story).

And what of our story, yours and mine? What does Gylfi have to do with us? I drove into Gimli in my rental hearse not with a pack of questions but with a bundle of fears. Yet I would have questions soon enough, and plenty. Face trickery and deceit. Still, maybe in the end, Cousin, you'll decide Gylfi has nothing to do with us. Or that there is no "us," and you want nothing to do with me. So be it.

The next time I woke it was high noon. As I crossed the motel room to the window I felt something coarse underfoot: sand tracked by the room's previous occupants, gritting the bare soles of my feet. But I was lakeside, that's what mattered. I'd arrived too late the night before to discern anything more than the lake's dark presence, though walking from my car to the motel I'd heard its soft lap, inhaled the familiar lake-water smell. Now in the daylight I gazed at it out the window, lazing large and blue to the horizon. There it was. There I was. I'd expected to feel something, something big, but instead . . . a watery nothing. Nothing I could put a name to. The far shore wasn't visible and never was, I remembered, even on the clearest days. Lakes in this part of the continent get big as small seas. But on this morning it seemed most unsea-like, dull and pond-still.

I sat on the sagging edge of the bed and smoked a cigarette. If the lake was disappointing, the motel room was outright depressing. The lingering stink of wet swimsuits, the sand on the floor. The Viking, I realized, was a dive. As if I'd rented a bed at the bottom of a grimy, empty aquarium tank. I took a last deep drag on the cigarette, then tossed the butt in the toilet. Gloom be gone. It was time to begin my first day back in Gimli. I left the hearse parked in front of my room at the Viking and set off along Gimli's sandy beach toward town.

My plan had been to spend the morning getting acclimated, then the afternoon visiting with Sigga. But now the morning was spent, and I found myself not lingering as I'd intended but striding down the beach, which was utterly empty. The early morning sun had disappeared—lake weather shifts fast—replaced by dense banks of cloud. Everything seemed diffuse: the gray expanse of cloud cover, the gray expanse of lake. Against this backdrop like a film played my beach memories: there I was in my blue checkered swimsuit, burning lobster bright. There was Birdie lounging majestically and tossing me mandarin orange bits. I blinked my eyes, the visions vanished.

I walked on. In the distance to the south I could see Willow Point, where the Icelanders had first landed. Stefan and Birdie had taken me there, recounted that well-told story of our origins. How hard Birdie had worked to edify me, imbue me with a vanishing culture. I took off my shoes, waded the shore like I used to. What had she called me then? An egret, with my fringe of white-blond hair, my long gawky legs. An egret and a poet. What would she call me now? If she made a ghostly appearance— and I wouldn't have put it past her to suddenly surface in the water, shaking her head like a wet dog and laughing raucously as a seal—she would see that all her effort on me had been wasted. My life a deliberate erasure of all that history, lore, and myth. I lived by what could be seen and pho- tographed, in black and white, here and now.

Each step I took produced an icy, satisfying splash. Too bad, dear dead Birdie. People emigrate, they assimilate. The Vikings weren't the only roamers. The earth's people are always moving on, swarming the planet in endless migratory trails, losing great chunks of their histories in the pro- cess. Who stays put anymore? Who can lay claim to anywhere? Not me, certainly, and not to Gimli. My grandfather may have been one of the orig- inal settlers and a great poet to boot, my grandmother a fixture of the com- munity, cataloging its books and family lines, but I myself had never been more than a summer visitor. And the bland Connecticut suburb where I'd spent the balance of my childhood—I have no ties to that anymore either. I haven't been back since my mother died and I fled to Manhattan. And the city? I'm a transient among transients, my roots phantom. In a year, I could be anywhere. Unlikely, but possible.

I turned from the waterline and headed across the beach toward town. At the curb I sat down to brush the sand off my feet and re-shoe. Whatever membership I'd had in Gimli was long expired. I expected no great welcome, prayed, in fact, not to run into anyone I knew. Not yet, anyway. I gave the lake one last glance before heading up Centre Street into town. Yes, Centre Street. Compared with all the Icelandic place names that abound in the re- gion, names like Arborg and Hnausa and Geysir and Hecla, the street names

of Gimli seem almost comically plain. Centre Street runs through . . . the
center of town. Where it meets . . . Main Street. The rest is a grid, numbered avenues running north-south, numbered streets east-west. In New
York City it makes sense, but there in Gimli it struck me as ludicrous, to
bother numbering such a simple grid. As if it were possible to get lost in a
town with only five streets running in any one direction.

I stood for a few minutes at the juncture of Centre and Main, citing the
old landmarks that still remained: Golko's Hardware, Tergesen's General
Store, the Esso station, the Gimli Theatre. A few new establishments, but
not many. It was the same little Gimli, and yet I began to sense that things
were entirely different. An eeriness begging capture. I took out my camera
and began wandering around snapping photographs: the tiny cement shack
still bearing the chipper OLSON FISH sign with its smiling fish mascot and a
chalkboard announcing PICKEREL. The cluttered windows of Tergesen's,
est. 1899, with the staid blue VELKOMIN sign. And then it dawned on me,
the source of the strangeness: I was the only pedestrian in sight.

In the old days, *my* old days anyway, the streets were mobbed with visitors, licking ice cream cones, buying postcards and fishing lures. Maybe
Gimli had become a ghost town after all? Then the breeze picked up and I
remembered it was late September, the high season long past. I'd never visited Gimli in the fall, though it was not quite autumn yet. The elms were
still green, a toughened dusky end-of-summer shade. A few maples were
starting to tip yellow. The sun was shining again, the clouds had scattered.
I began to feel as if I were dream walking. I had spoken a word to no one.
There was a curtain, a barrier between me and Gimli, as real and invisible
as the air itself. I might have been looking at a postcard, strolling a movie
set. I couldn't make it feel real. And I wanted to. I'd come all this way, traveled miles and decades, and I wanted to feel something. Of course, I had to
consider the possibility that I had nothing left to feel, that I'd rendered myself incapable of true feeling.

Or maybe I just hadn't had my morning coffee yet.

The bakery had moved itself across the street sometime in the last sixteen years, but it was the same establishment with the same Icelandic
breads and pastries, thick with doughy-cinnamon smells. I stood in line behind a silver-haired woman who was having trouble making up her mind.

"What do you call this?" she would ask the teenage girl behind the counter. "And this?" Each answer produced a short chuckle. Then she turned to point to something in the glass display case to our right and her face revealed itself in profile. My heart leapt—Sigga!

Not Sigga. My first ghost. There was a resemblance though: this woman could have been Sigga thirty or forty years ago, in her sixties perhaps. And she spoke English with an accent similar to Sigga's. The woman was an Icelander, and what she was doing in Gimli in late September I couldn't imagine. When Icelanders came it was usually in the summer, especially in early August, so they could attend the Icelandic festival and consort with distant cousins.

"This you call *vinarterta*?" the old woman asked the girl.

"It's an Icelandic pastry," the girl explained, tucking her lank brown hair behind her ear impatiently. I was beginning to feel a bit impatient myself.

"An Icelandic pastry indeed!" The woman laughed. "In Iceland I think we don't have so many layers as this one! How many layers is that?"

The girl leaned over and counted. "Seven," she reported, in her flat Manitoba accent.

"Seven! No wonder I do not recognize this. In Iceland, it is made only with three. Maybe four."

"My grandmother always makes it with seven," I said, surprised at myself for jumping in. Doubting if at one hundred Sigga baked much of anything anymore. Could she still read? Walk? Had she finished the Blue Book, traced us all the way back to Egil Skallagrimsson?

"Lucky for you." The woman was facing me now, smiling, and I couldn't help but feel she looked familiar, aside from her resemblance to Sigga. Yet she wasn't from Gimli, I was sure of that. She turned back to the lank-haired girl. "I'll take one piece of the *vinarterta*, please."

Then she was gone. And although I hadn't planned to I ordered two pieces of *vinarterta* myself, along with a large black coffee. As I walked back down Centre Street, sipping the dark stuff from my cup and nibbling the *vinarterta*, I thought of Sigga teaching me to make *ponnukokur* my first morning at Oddi. *What's ponnukokur?* I'd so innocently asked, provoking Birdie's horror that Mama had taught me nothing of Our People. Did it matter, Birdie, was it worth it, in the end, to rake Mama over the coals like that? To force Icelandic grammar into a seven-year-old's lazy summer brain? True enough, I was willing. I savored my time with Birdie, adored her, mostly. And there was no harm in it, not in the Icelandic lessons or the telling of Olafur's stories, the obscure Norse myths. The harm was something else. The way Birdie had flown me to distant lands, real and imagined, her wing tips grazing heaven, then dragged me graveward when she plunged back down.

The *vinarterta* took a too-sweet turn in my stomach and I dropped the last bite into the gutter for a lucky gull. The second piece I was saving for Sigga, whom I was on my way to see. Even though I hadn't called ahead to arrange anything, had in fact had no contact with Sigga at all either prior to or since my arrival, I had my heart set on a private visit before the birthday party that night. No public reunions, please. I was nervous enough without subjecting myself to the inevitable small-town scrutiny. I found myself wondering who would be at the party, who would remember me and, worse, remember my part in that final summer with Birdie. Who would shake their heads disapprovingly behind my back, as if they understood something, when I myself never had and I was at the tangled center of the thing?

To hell with all of it! Betel was gone. I was standing on the corner exactly where Betel once stood, and *there was no Betel*. I turned around in bewilderment; across the street rose a new, L-shaped building. I crossed over and was staring at the building hesitantly when an old woman nearly knocked me over. A thin, tiny person, but not frail, no. Despite her cane she was making good time, nearly brisked me right off the path.

"Excuse me," I called after her. "Can you tell me where Betel is?"

The old woman turned and gave me a perplexed and toothy smile. "Why, this is Betel. You're standing in front of it."

The new Betel. Of course. I remembered now, Stefan telling me about it in his Christmas card last year.

"Are you here for a visit then? We do love visitors."

"To see Sigga Petursson. Do you know her?"

"Know Sigga? Of course I know Sigga! I just happen to be one of her very dearest friends, Mrs. Halldora Bjarnason. And who might you be?"

"I'm Freya. Her granddaughter." We'd reached the entrance by this time and I held the glass door open for the old woman, though I had no doubt she was strong enough to do it herself. But Halldora didn't move, just stood on the front step staring at me through thick-lensed glasses that magnified her eyes into wobbling brown marbles.

"Sigga's been waiting for you," she said finally. Crossly?

"Well, my flight got in late last night, and then I overslept a bit this morning—"

"Years!" Halldora interrupted. Then marched into Betel with a loud rap of her cane.

Living in New York these past eight years, I'd come to think of myself as brave. Hadn't I arrived as an orphan in a city of strangers, then reinvented myself as a skilled black-and-white printer and aspiring photographer? Each day I braved the crowded subways, lecherous men on street corners, my bossy boss, toxic darkroom chemicals, and on top of it all spent hours taking and developing my own photographs in my spare time. True, I rarely showed them to anyone, not, I told myself, because I was afraid to but because I was waiting until I was good enough.

But there is a difference between being tough and being brave. I see that now. Standing in the doorway to Betel was far more terrifying than a nerve-racking wait at a deserted three a.m. subway station. If I were truly brave, I would have returned to Gimli long before. No, I was nothing but a tough-skinned chicken two chicken steps from fleeing town in a disgrace of feathers and fear.

Once, twice I circled the block, rebuilding my confidence with cigarettes and desperate attempts at reason. If Sigga hated me, she would not have invited me to her party. Simple as that. If other people despised me, well, that was their business. If the old ladies of Betel wanted to think of me as an ungrateful, coldhearted, kin-denying, selfish American of a grand-daughter, let them. They were probably right.

24

Hesitantly I opened Betel's front door and entered the foyer.

Dr. Brandur Gudmundsson was the first Icelander to obtain a medical degree in North America, a revered leader among the Winnipeg Icelanders, and the founder of the Betel retirement home. So read the plaque under his oil portrait hanging prominently in Betel's entryway. It was the same painting that had hung in the entrance to the old Betel. *Bless that man for his good works,* Mama used to say each time she passed it. Good old Dr. Gudmundsson, father of Mama's dear friend Vera. Would Vera be at the party? Of course she would. In the portrait Dr. G had a sweeping handlebar mustache. Birdie liked to call him a pompous patriarch, claimed it was actually the hardworking women of the Ladies Aid who were the driving force behind Betel. She herself would never end up in Betel, Birdie claimed. Betel was for good Lutherans, and she was nothing of the sort. Right she was.

The entry area over which Dr. G presided smelled faintly of Lysol with an undercurrent of the sickly-sweetish odor emitted by the extremely aged. The room itself was empty, but around the corner I found an administrator sitting behind a desk.

"Can we help you?" The woman was alone, the plural institutional. She wore a pantsuit, and her hair was cut neatly at the shoulders.

"I'm here to see Sigga Petursson."

"Are you a relative?"

"Yes." I took a breath, then forged ahead with the awful truth. "I'm her granddaughter."

"Ah yes. We've heard you were coming." She seemed genuinely pleased, unlike cranky Halldora. She took my hand. "I'm Sylvia Johnson, Director of Care. The party starts this evening. Downstairs here in the reception room, six o'clock."

"I'll be there," I promised. "But I was hoping for a visit beforehand."

"I'm sorry, dear. But no visitors for Sigga today. Big day ahead. Needs her rest. I'm afraid you'll have to wait to see her at the party, along with everyone else."

That would not do. But I knew better than to attempt to sway the forces of bureaucracy. "Of course," I responded. "I understand." I even managed a smile. "I used to come here," I added. "Not here, but to the old Betel. When I was child. My mother and I came every morning to sit with the old ladies and knit socks."

"Is that so? How good of you. Is this your first time to the new Betel then?"

I nodded, and the next thing I knew I was getting the grand tour. The new building had cost $4.7 million to construct, boasted state-of-the-art medical equipment, offered recreational and social services. Everything was shiny spanking new: the dining room, the reception room where Sigga's party would be held, the chapel, the library (a gift from the government of Iceland), the lounge, the residents' floor. "How wonderful," I exclaimed. And then, just as I was turning to go, "Is there a bathroom I could use?"

Three minutes later I was sneaking down the residents' hall on the second floor, scanning nameplates outside each door. Mostly Icelandic, a few Ukrainian and Anglo. Through partly open doors I glimpsed white-haired heads on pillows. A pair of bare, blue-veined feet sticking out from under a sheet. A children's cartoon show on a television in an empty room. A cart stuffed with dirty linens standing outside a washroom door, unattended.

I found Sigga's room at the far end of the hall and knocked on the door, lightly. Again. Then loudly. Then gave up and opened it. The room, like everything else at the new Betel, was new. New dresser, new visitors' chairs, new bookcase. Fresh paint. And there on the bed was the one thing not-new, an old woman thin and wrinkled as a wet sheet frozen on the line to dry. Could that be Sigga?

"Amma?" I whispered. "Amma?" Then, *"Amma!"* But there was no an-swer, and after a moment I understood there never would be. Sigga's body was completely still. Eyes closed, mouth set, arms folded neatly on her chest, which did not rise or fall. Dead and obviously so.

My first response was to laugh, a choked, harsh snort of disdain for the universe. Tricked! I bit my lower lip at the stupidity of it, hard enough to taste blood. All this way for nothing! And for Sigga to choose this, the morn-ing of her hundredth birthday, to make her exit. I had no doubt that death is a choice. Birdie was my first lesson in that, and though my own mother's death was no suicide, I was certain it was just another means of giving up. And now here was Sigga, a no-show at her own party, leaving the long-lost Freya only a corpse's greeting: Sorry, *elskan,* you waited too long.

And what was I supposed to do now? Call for help? I found a red emer-gency buzzer hanging from a cord tied to the rail of Sigga's hospital bed and almost rang it. But what was the rush? The dead have plenty of time. I'd take a moment alone with her first, then let some efficient nurse come wheel Sigga away to wherever dead people went.

I lit a cigarette and stood at the edge of the bed smoking, no doubt breaking yet another one of Betel's rules. I imagined Dr. G glaring down at me from heaven, in which as a devout Lutheran he surely believed. I myself am a devout nothing. The only thing I am certain of is that death in no way prevents the dead from interfering with the living. They're haunters, my dead, hangers-on. And now Sigga would be joining the pack, before I'd even had a chance to make some kind of peace with her.

I pulled an orange plastic chair to the edge of Sigga's bed. Except it wasn't Sigga. Sigga was tall and commanding, a master librarian, round-faced and spectacled, queen of the *vinarterta.* Not this stark assemblage of spindly limbs and sparse wiry hair, a frozen sheet of a human being, the discarded wrapping of a life. I lit a new cigarette from the tip of the last, leaned back in the chair, closed my eyes—I couldn't bear to look at Sigga's body for more than a second at a time—and let the tears fly. Head in hands I wept and wept, raw gulps of sadness and chest-shaking hiccups of grief, years of pent up *stuff*, humiliating streams of tears and snot. Soon I was sobbing, sobs rasping and hollow as the yelping of an abandoned mutt—

—and Sigga was finally woken from her midmorning nap. She peered at me through watery gray eyes, mere slits among the folds of skin.

"*Elskan!*" she cried out, her voice surprisingly clear. I'd wondered if Sigga would recognize me, but she showed not even a flicker of doubt about my identity. Only a tremulous, grandmotherly concern. "Whatever is the matter?"

I stared, brain reeling to accommodate the hard, physical evidence: Sigga was alive. "I thought, I thought, I thought you were—"

"Now, now, child. You'll have to wait a minute. Can't hear a thing." Sigga reached for two putty-colored hearing aids on her bedside table, then fumbled them into her ears with swole-knuckled fingers. Tricked again! Sigga was never dead, just dead asleep. Dead to the world. The coma-like respite of the near-deaf at the end of a century of life. I laughed—I couldn't help myself—and this time, Sigga heard me. She tilted her head in bewilderment.

"What's so funny?"

I hesitated only a moment before blurting out the truth. "I didn't know you were sleeping. I thought you were dead. That's why I was crying."

"Oh my," Sigga said, her wrinkled brow wrinkling even deeper. She handed me a box of tissues from the bedside table. "I gave you a fright. Is that what you're riled up about?"

I nodded, then wiped my salt-streaked cheeks, blew my nose. "I'm so sorry," I began.

"Sorry about what?"

"That I haven't been to visit."

"Now, *elskan*, I'll have no more of that. With your life the way it is. You're here now, that's what matters." She reached out and took my hand in hers. Her skin was papery and dry against my tear-sticky palm. I wondered what exactly Sigga knew about my life. What had Stefan told her? But it didn't matter. When Sigga took my hand, a helium lightness swelled inside me. So this is it. This is what it's like to feel forgiven! It's what I'd come for, I realized, that moment of blessed absolution, one that seemed to free me not only of the sin of not visiting but of everything wretched I had ever done, or not done. The light blue walls of the room seemed to glow like the inside of one of those old Icelandic churches.

"Happy birthday." The words floated like balloons from my newly lightened being.

"Oh yes," Sigga said matter-of-factly. "I suppose it is."

"I came for the party," I reminded her.

"Oh, that. Stefan's behind it, isn't he? Silly, really, a party for an old woman like me." She paused. "When is this party?"

"It's tonight."

"Of course it is. You'll have to excuse me, I've gotten a bit forgetful. It's terrible, really. No one should be allowed to get this old."

"I brought some *vinarterta* for you." I put the bag on the bedside table.

"You always made lovely *vinarterta*," Sigga said. "But I'm not hungry just now. We'll have some later."

I was certain I'd never made my own *vinarterta*, but I easily pardoned Sigga's lapse. If she wanted to believe I made a lovely *vinarterta*, it was fine with me. We sat in silence for a moment, still holding hands, and then Sigga asked a strange question.

"Where is the baby now?"

"Baby?"

"Oh, I suppose she's not a baby anymore, is she? I lose track of time. But the little one—are you bringing her to the party? Everybody will want to see her."

Sigga was looking directly at me, seeing someone else. "I don't know—" I answered, dropping Sigga's hand. "I don't think you know who—"

"Just for a short time then." Sigga sighed, exasperated, as if we'd had this conversation many times before. "You ask too little of that child. She's perfectly capable of behaving at a family occasion. It's your sister I'm worried about."

"My sister?"

"Just keep an eye on her, that's all I ask! Make sure she doesn't drink too much. Will you do that?"

"I don't think—"

"Please!" Sigga's voice became agitated, high and fluttery. "You know how wild Birdie gets when she starts drinking."

A chill came over me. The hairs on my arms actually stood on end. Sigga hadn't forgiven me. She wasn't even talking to me. She was talking to my mother. Tricked again!

"But, Amma," I began. "I think maybe you're a bit confused, I think—"

"I think Sigga needs her rest, that's what I think."

Standing in the doorway was tiny Halldora, leaning on her cane. "How did you get in here, anyway? I left strict orders that Sigga was not to have visitors today." She sniffed the air with her beaked nose. "Have you been smoking in here? Against the rules, against common sense!" In a brisk moment she'd opened the window, and the scent of harbor wafted in.

What could I say? That I'd only smoked because I believed Sigga to be dead? I said nothing, just watched Halldora as she leaned over Sigga, who had a startled expression on her face. Halldora clicked a button, and the top half of the bed began to rise. "It'll be time for your bath soon. You rest until then."

She motioned for me to follow her out into the hall, then shut the door behind us, staring at me with her wobbling eyes, waiting for an apology, or at least an explanation.

"Sigga's senile," I snapped, too angry to feign polite. "Why didn't you tell me? When we met outside?"

"She's nothing of the sort," Halldora answered, leaning calmly on her cane. "You just got her riled is all. Exactly what I've been trying to avoid."

"She thinks I'm my mother!"

"Well, she gets confused now and then," Halldora admitted. Her voice had softened. "I'll set her straight on that point later. But she needs to rest. I think you should go now."

Oh, I'd go all right! I pounded down the back stairs of Betel and out a side exit propelled by a rage that would have done Birdie proud. Half an hour later I'd checked out of my gritty motel room and was heading out of town in the black van, speeding through the quiet side streets of Gimli, past the quaint little cottages and neatly trimmed lawns. I was done with all of it, this depressing little remnant of Icelandica, the grandmother who didn't know me from a skunk, my crazy aunt, my long-suffering mother. I would brook no more interference from the dead. It was time to close this chapter of my life, shut the door on the past, any metaphor would do, the point was that I was on the verge of something truly new: that great black hole called my future. Bring it on!

It was my sole and fierce intention to speed directly out of town. Luckily, we are not ruled by our intentions, not conscious ones anyway. Instead, I just happened to drive down the old block, and I couldn't exactly pass by Oddi without stopping to look, could I? I had to see it, the old white farmhouse with the song-yellow trim on the corner of Second Street and Second Avenue. Stefan had mentioned in his last Christmas card that Sigga was thinking of putting the house up for sale, but whether it had sold or not I wasn't sure. It looked shabbier than I remembered, not neglected exactly, but in need of what Sigga would have called *sprucing up*. It had a sleepy, musty look. The rosebushes had grown huge and rangy, the grass shaggy. All the shades were drawn. If anyone new owned it, they weren't here at the moment, though I knocked just in case. Not surprisingly, no answer. And then, because we must always try doors we know to be locked, I turned the handle. The door opened.

What I saw inside that house alarmed me. Not how much it had changed but the simple fact that it hadn't. Even in the dim light of the parlor I could make out the familiar moss-green velvet couch curved like a crescent moon, the china cabinet against the wall, the brass-plated clock on the mantel. Beyond the parlor the white gleam of the kitchen. I stepped inside—

—and the lights flashed on and everyone jumped out from behind the couch yelling *Surprise!* The two dead sisters, Birdie and Anna, arm in arm, raising tiny glasses of cognac to celebrate my return. Sigga in her pearls and gold-rimmed glasses clasping her hands in delight, and even the long-gone Olafur, *Skald Nyja Islands,* lighting his fragrant pipe and chuckling at the great joke of it. In a merry dance we reunited, living and dead alike, all wrongs forgotten, chattering in a rush of Icelandic that fell over my ears clear and sensible as water.

No, of course no merry ghosts came to greet me. I sat on the couch listening to the sound of dust falling. Then I wound the clock on the mantel with its large brass key and the room filled with its gentle ticking. I ran my finger along the gilded frame of the painting that hung over the mantel, a nearly abstract landscape of Iceland, swirls of black lava and green hill-sides. Birdie's purchase, appreciated by no one but herself.

Over the arm of Sigga's rocking chair lay a gray-and-white striped shawl my mother had knitted the summer I was ten. I remembered one evening Birdie expounding on the special properties of Icelandic wool, how it natu-rally repels water, insulates the sheep against snow. Burly sheep with curl-ing horns, nibbling moss from the lava-crusted hillsides. Without those sheep, Birdie claimed, the Icelanders would never have survived to see the twentieth century, we'd have perished like the Greenland colony, vanished without a trace. Did we know that to this day there are more sheep than people in Iceland? We owe our lives to those sheep! Bless the sheep! Baaaaaaaaah! Birdie trilled in perfect imitation. Baaaaaaaaah!

I screamed. I was not expecting a man's footstep on the stairs to startle me from my sheepish reverie. But this time, I recognized his voice instantly.

"Terribly sorry, Freya. Terribly. To frighten you like that!"

It was Uncle Stefan, more slender even than I remembered, a lanky gi-ant who ducked his head as he came down the stairs. He looked as profes-sorial as ever in his cream-colored cardigan with knobby buttons, his camel brown corduroy slacks, his black-framed glasses and well-trimmed white beard. A square, Birdie had called him, behind his back. But he, at least, knew who I was, and I found myself relieved to see him. He switched on the standing lamp with its fringed shade, another one of Birdie's acquisi-tions. "Lovely to see you, Freya!"

I was still too spooked for words. He motioned for me to take a seat on the couch. He was packing things up, he explained. Sigga was finally ready to sell.

"I just saw Sigga. At Betel."

"I figured she sent you over here, to see if there's anything you want. You can have any of it, of course. Except Olafur's things. Those are all being do-nated, the books to the University of Manitoba, and his personal effects, his writing desk, his pen and inkstand—all of that I'm reconstructing for the museum."

"Museum?"

"The New Iceland Heritage Museum. It's opening next summer. A whole room is to be dedicated to Olafur, his life and work. It takes up most of my time, now that I'm retired. In any case, we'd be honored to have you back for that momentous occasion."

I started to laugh, then realized it *was* momentous, at least to Stefan. He'd devoted his life to this little niche of history.

"And your grandmother—she must have been so happy to see you!" He said this warmly, with not a twinge of the you're-a-disgrace-of-a-granddaughter treatment I'd received from Halldora. Though I hadn't forgotten that Stefan's emotions tend to be tucked well below the surface. I wanted to answer him in kind, but my tone came out sulky as a six-year-old's.

"She was happy to see me, all right. But that's only because she doesn't know who I am. She thought I was my mother."

Stefan seemed genuinely surprised. "A natural enough mistake, I suppose, at first glance."

"It wasn't first glance. It was the whole visit. She's lost her mind. She even thought that . . . Birdie is still alive." This last piece of information was difficult to speak, hard too, I saw, for Stefan to hear.

"Sigga's been more forgetful lately, Freya, but I wouldn't say she's lost her mind." He rubbed his beard thoughtfully. "Though I can see why you might find such an incident disturbing. However, I'm fairly certain she'll snap out of it. Perhaps the stress of tonight's event. It's not every day a person turns one hundred. And speaking of"—he pulled an old-fashioned watch chain from his pocket—"there are preparations still. I'll leave you here to poke around. The party starts at six."

That was the moment to tell him I was heading out. I owed him that much at least. "Actually, I'm not sure I'm—"

"Everyone will be glad to see you, Freya. Including Sigga. I'll make sure she knows who you are this time." He smiled wryly. "Did you know that one of your Icelandic relatives will be there?"

I shook my head

"Thorunn Bjornsdottir, Sigga's niece. She's the daughter of Sigga's sister, Stefania. I don't think you've ever met her."

I cringed: the silver-haired woman from the bakery! That must have been Thorunn. I *had* met her before, and I don't mean at the bakery in Gimli that afternoon. She was one of Sigga's People who had visited me at the hospital in Akureyri after Birdie and I had been rescued from Askja. Not a memory I cared to revisit. Wasn't Gimli enough?

"Thorunn," I repeated. "She came all the way from Iceland for Sigga's birthday?"

"Marvelous, isn't it? You'll like her. She's been here a week already, visiting with Sigga every afternoon, catching her up on all the relatives. No wonder Sigga got confused when you showed up today!"

I smiled gamely at Stefan's attempt to reassure me, but inside I felt defeated. My mad dash from Gimli, foiled. Thorunn had come all the way from Iceland. Stefan was packing up my grandmother's house, a duty more clearly mine than his. There could be no slinking away now, even for a skunk like me.

After Stefan left I ventured upstairs, sliding my hand along the dark wood of the banister as the stairs creaked underfoot. My palm came up covered in a film of dust that made me sneeze. At the top of the stairs were our two bedrooms, mine and Birdie's. I entered mine first. It was tinier even than I remembered it, a closet practically. The lace curtains that had shimmered in the summer breezes hung gray and still. I sneezed again, and my eyes started to burn from the dust. I began yawning, repeatedly, each yawn triggering a deeper one. The mere thought of picking through Sigga's possessions depleted me. I stretched out on the little bed, still covered with its puckered white spread, but my legs hung off at the knees. In the years since my last visit I'd grown, changed, but into what I couldn't say. How could I blame Sigga for not recognizing me? Most days I hardly knew myself. I rolled onto my side in a fetal curl and slept.

25

Are you ready for Sigga's one hundredth birthday party?

I wasn't. I overslept, back in my little room at Oddi, and the party was in full swing by the time I arrived. I stood a moment in the doorway of the reception room, the pride of the new Betel with its floor-to-ceiling arched windows and gleaming piano, matching tables and chairs set off against the spiffy shine of the floor. Nothing grand, as my mother would have said, but very very pleasant. And lively. Maybe fifty guests. I'd expected a circle of old ladies singing "Happy Birthday," like at the parties my mother and I had attended during our Betel days. But that was the old Betel, and this was Sigga. It was a swanky event, by Gimli standards. Buffet and drinks, even live music—various old folks taking turns at the piano. And people of all ages milling about. Strangers, or simply older versions of people I once knew? Oldsters and youngsters, women with babies, a couple of teenagers lurking by a back table. They reminded me of Vera's boys, from that long ago coffee party. I could have gone to the beach with them; instead I'd stayed behind and turned the fateful cartwheel.

Where was Sigga? At the center of it all, installed on a couch near the piano, receiving her guests one by one. In her blue silk dress, her silver hair neatly coiffed, her favorite double strand of pearls around her neck, our grandmother was as composed and elegant as any person could hope to be upon entering a second century of life. I wish you could have seen her, Cousin. Chatting and smiling, kissing cheeks and clasping hands, she seemed an utterly thawed and transformed version of the frozen sheet I'd stumbled across that morning.

Next to Sigga on the couch was Halldora Bjarnason, tiny and still. Her cane leaned against her neatly crossed legs, her hands were folded diminutively in her lap, but her large brown eyes bobbed back and forth across the room like worried chaperones. Despite Halldora's keen watch, it was Stefan who spotted me first. He was beaming in his neatly pressed gray suit, and kindly made no mention of my lateness.

"Freya, you look lovely."

I did not. Or rather, not a Gimli kind of lovely. Prepare for my ghoulish entrance: everything remotely nice I own is black. It works in Manhattan, but in Gimli—well, I looked like I was dressed for a funeral in my long black skirt and black boots. Mama always said black didn't become me, not with my pale skin. But the dead only get so much say in this world.

The next thing I knew, Stefan was leading me by the hand across the room to Sigga. The guests that surrounded her parted, the piano music faded to a tinkle. Was it because I was late, or I looked like a ghoul, or did everyone know I was the long-lost disgraced granddaughter? In any case, people stared. Suddenly I was the center of attention, in the very moment I'd most dreaded. Sigga's failure to recognize me earlier had chilled me, especially since both Halldora and Stefan had seemed surprised by her lapse. Maybe it was less senility than some awful kind of repression. Maybe she despised me so much she'd managed to actually erase me? If she failed to recognize me again . . .

"*Elskan!*" Sigga reached up with both hands to clasp mine, then motioned for me to sit beside her on the couch. Out of the corner of my eye I noticed Halldora on the other side, pointedly tapping her watch. Was she intimating that it was late, that I was late, that Sigga didn't have much time? I decided not to care. Sigga was sparkling, her eyes bright, cheeks flushed.

"Freya *min*," she said.

It had been so long, Cousin, since I'd heard those words. *Freya mine*. In New York I am nobody's Freya. My eyes teared up; she knew me.

"I'm so happy to see you! Just look at you!" Clutching my hands in her papery thin ones. Then, in a quavering voice, "I'm afraid I was a bit muddled this morning."

"It was my fault, Amma. I should have called first."

"Preposterous is what it is. How could I not recognize you?" She cupped my cheeks in her hands, fingers tremulous against my skin. "It's just, you've changed so much. . . . But Stefan and my dear Halldora have set me straight now. Tell me, dear, are you all right? I worry about you, alone in that city, with no family . . ."

"I'm fine, Amma."

Sigga nodded, doubtfully. In her view, it was not possible for a person to live far from family and be happy. "Tomorrow we'll have a good long visit, just the two of us." She leaned forward. "I have things I want to talk to you about. *Family things*."

"Well . . . my flight leaves tomorrow."

"Tomorrow? But didn't you just arrive? Or am I confused again . . . ?"

"I have to be back at work on Monday." I hated to say it, partly because it was hardly true, I had weeks and weeks of unused vacation time, and partly because of Sigga's disappointment, which drained the pink flush from her cheeks. Even her pearls seemed to loose their shine.

"I see."

"But I can come to Betel first thing in the morning."

"That will be fine." Though I could see it was not. "Now, tell me, have you spoken with Vera yet? She is so looking forward to seeing you."

And there was Vera. How long she'd been standing there I wasn't sure. I don't think I would have recognized her, an old woman in her mid-seventies. The same age my mother would have been. But Mama had grown old before her time, so I guess it makes sense that she died before her time. Vera appeared vigorous as ever, pulling me to her in a no-nonsense hug. Like Stefan and Sigga, Vera sends me Christmas cards every year, and most years I manage to send her one as well. Hers always contain an invitation to visit; mine never mention the possibility. Still we send the cards, back and forth, year after year, images of Christmas trees and angels and wreaths, best wishes for the season! No, I'd never been fond of Vera, Birdie had succeeded in turning me against her, and so I was surprised to find how happy I was to see her again. *Dear Vera.* A piece of my mother. She led me off to the side and cornered me with questions: how was I managing, was there anyone special in my life, was I really leaving the next day, would I consider staying longer, she would so love to have me stay with her in Winnipeg, and her boys too, who hadn't seen me in years, they were there, at the party, had I met them yet? She led me over. Men they were now, Vera's boys, both balding and in their forties, with teenage sons of their own. There, at the back of the room—the boys I'd seen on my way in. Vera's boys had boys of their own. And what did I have?

I began to lie. I had to. It wasn't just Vera, it was everybody she and Stefan introduced me to. *Here is Sigga's granddaughter. Meet Anna's daughter.* I cringed, and I spun myself. Not in the old way, red-sneakered feet planted in the middle of our green postage-stamp lawn, twirling with propeller-blade arms. A different kind of spin. I spun the life I'd like to have, or think I should have. A life where I show my photographs in galleries, am busy preparing for a one-woman show, live with a boyfriend who I'll probably marry sometime, when we get around to it. Kids, someday soon. Don't wait too long! Oh, I won't. Stefan overheard one of these conversations, arched his brow. *A one-woman show?* he seemed to inquire. *I hadn't heard.* No, you wouldn't have, I answered back silently. And then moved on. I was introduced to the director of the Icelandic Collection at the university library in Winnipeg and various members of the Icelandic Department. All who knew and admired my grandfather's work. Olafur, *Skald Nyja Islands*! It had been so long since I'd heard that name. There were people who knew about me and people who didn't. The people who didn't would make innocent remarks, like *I never knew Sigga had grandchildren.* Or *Do you get to Gimli often?* The people who knew about my kidnapping and Birdie's suicide and my long neglect of Sigga, they were easier to pick out. Asked me fewer questions. Studied me more keenly. Or so I imagined.

From the buffet I piled my plate with smoked lamb imported from Iceland, creamed potatoes, pickled beets, but the food I hardly touched. It was the beer that sustained me, loosened my tongue. One, then another. After my third I was ready for a cigarette. I found myself circling the outside of Betel for the second time that day. This time the air felt unmistakably autumnal, the sky black, the stars crisp. I took comfort in that: the day was nearly done. The party nearly over. Then I'd visit with Sigga in the morning, drive the rental hearse back to Winnipeg, and be airborne. It would all be over with. That wasn't so hard now, was it? I leaned against the building and lit a second cigarette. Out the window came the sounds of the party: the chatter of voices, the clatter of dishes and glasses, someone at the piano again, tinkering at a tune not quite remembered. And then I heard it. Unmistakable, Cousin, clear as ice. Two women, in lowered voices.

"*Ingibjorg's child,*" said one.

"*Oskilgetid,*" said the other. A word I didn't know.

I edged closer to the window frame, but not directly in front of it. I didn't want to be seen. I wanted to hear more, and I did.

"*Birdie's, I tell you.*"

"*Don't speak of it.*"

And that was it. A scrap of conversation. Then the piano rose over their voices and they were gone altogether. *Ingibjorg's child. Birdie's, I tell you.* What could they have meant, *Birdie's child*? I dropped my cigarette, picked it up, took one last drag, snubbed it out with my foot. Birdie never had a child. Someone else's child? But there was no other Birdie than Birdie. A child? I rushed back inside, to see who had been standing by the window, but by the time I entered no one was near the windows; everyone had gathered in the center of the room, around the birthday cake. A hundred candles lighting up Sigga's ancient face. "A hundred wishes for everyone," she announced. "Please, you all must help me." And so we did, as a group, blew out the candles on the three-tiered cake, in a single collective gust of goodwill. Stefan began a speech about Sigga, her long life, her many contributions to the community, her devotion to the library, not only to preserving the Icelandic literary tradition but to fostering the love of literature in new generations. "A librarian is the true heart of any community of Icelanders," Stefan concluded. "And the heart of Sigga Petursson is the richest, biggest, warmest heart—" He paused for a moment, and I wondered if he too had been drinking. "It is Sigga's heart that sustains us all!"

"Hear, hear!" Applause. Someone began playing the piano, the same tune tinkered with moments earlier. But this time I recognized it: the Gimli Waltz. Sigga, I saw, was crying. With happiness, at the love that had risen up in the room for her? Or grief, that she had outlived the majority of her friends, her beloved husband, and worst of all, her two daughters? The party began breaking up. Vera helped Sigga back to her room, guests started collecting coats, saying good-byes. I wanted to say good night to Sigga, but I couldn't move. *Birdie's child?*

"And you are Freya?" It was the elderly woman from the bakery, who indeed turned out to be Thorunn, Sigga's niece visiting from Iceland. "It is too bad we are only just meeting, Freya. I hear you are leaving tomorrow. I am leaving then too."

"I'm sorry," I said. Had I done anything except apologize since I'd arrived in Gimli?

"We met once before, Freya. I don't think you remember. In Akureyri, when you were in hospital, with Birdie."

"I'm sorry," I lied. "I don't remember you. It was a difficult time."

"Of course. We are hoping, you know, that you will come to Iceland again. To visit us. Sigga has many relatives there, we would love to have you, Freya."

Iceland! At that point in my life, you could not have paid me to return to Iceland. Gimli was enough, more than enough. I nearly laughed. "That would be nice," I answered. "Thank you."

"My mother always missed her sister so. She could never believe that Sigga would just leave like that, just pack up and move to another country! All her life she missed Sigga!"

"Didn't Sigga visit?"

"Only twice, in all those years. The expense, you know."

I nodded. And then, maybe because I was a little drunk, I said, "My mother and her sister were never close. There was so much trouble between them."

"It's like that sometimes, in families. *Fraendur eru fraendum verstir.*"

Kin are worst to kin. I smiled. "Sigga used to say that. About the two of them."

"We were so sorry to learn . . . Both of them, imagine! And you without family. I do hope you will think again about this invitation to Iceland. We are quite serious, you know."

Stefan offered me a ride back to my motel. That's when I remembered that I'd already checked out. My suitcase was in the rental car, parked in front

of Oddi, so I told Stefan I'd decided to sleep at Oddi instead. And then declined his offer of a ride, graciously, I hoped. I felt unworthy of his company, certain that he was probably glad to see me go, sick of my lies and
excuses. The truth was I needed to think. Clear Canadian air is good for
that. A brisk Manitoba night, stiff breeze off the lake, a full moon to boot.
It shone on me as I walked, it shone on me as I lay in my child-bed at Oddi.
A shiny dime-silvery light blasting through the frail lace curtains. My head
lay on one of Mama's pillowcases. I fingered the embroidery, the green
vines and pink flowers. *Mama!* The moonlight did nothing to clear my head.
Mama and her spruce green eyes and gentle touch, gone. Birdie with her
pupils black and shiny as a vinyl jazz record, gone. As I child I'd found myself too often standing between the two sisters, the subject of yet another
argument. Back then, it seemed only natural that they would fight about
me. I was trouble, wasn't I?

Or not. Maybe the trouble wasn't me, not who I was, but the fact of me.
The fact that Mama had a baby and Birdie did not—anymore. Birdie had
had a child. That's what the woman had said. *Ingibjorg's child. Birdie's, I tell
you.* A vanished child. Stillborn? Given up for adoption? In any case, illegitimate, if a child can be such a thing. *Oskilgetid,* that word that had floated
out Betel's window and into my ear: I'd looked it up in the Icelandic-English
dictionary in Olafur's study when I returned from Sigga's party. Birdie never
married. Mama married, Birdie had affairs. I'd always sensed that Mama
was forced by some sisterly logic to share me with Birdie, because Birdie
was childless. Sisters share. And if Birdie had had a child, and lost it,
then . . . it could explain things. Why Birdie took to me so, took over me so.

I lay awake for hours in my child-bed at Gimli, twisting and shifting, dis-
placing pillow and covers, trying to force-fit my long-limbed body into a
space it had outgrown. That miraculous feat of shape-shifting known as
growing up. I curled on my side, legs bent at the knees, my thighs, back,
neck, and head curved into a half circle. The very line of my body resolved
into the shape of a question mark.

26

Sigga's kitchen the next morning. Plates, cups, saucers stacked neatly in the glassed cabinets with the bronze latches that went *clickety-click, clickety-click*. The yellow Formica table with the bowed chrome legs. A row of tin canisters labeled in white cursive SUGAR, FLOUR, SALT. A glass Cadillac of a blender with a black rubber top. The kinds of things people in New York buy for a lot of money and call retro. I felt retro, sitting there with Stefan eating chocolate donuts and coffee he'd brought from the Gimli bakery. Retrograde to the old days, when Stefan would often drop by unannounced. Hoping for a visit with Birdie, happily settling for me or Mama or Sigga. On this morning he'd knocked loudly, then let himself in. "Sorry to disturb you," he'd called up the stairs. I was awake but far from up. "I'm hoping to get an early start on packing this place up."

What a good man, old Stefan of the stiff upper lip, in his rust-colored sweater-vest and corduroy slacks. A man with no family of his own who devoted himself to minding other people's families. Teaching pimply high school students, researching obscure genealogies of common people, assisting old women who have outlived their relations. Or been neglected by them.

"I appreciate you doing all this," I said, taking a sip of weak coffee.

"It's nothing, just a couple of donuts."

"No, I mean what you're doing for Sigga. Packing up the house. I wish

I could stay and help." A lie. I wanted my buildings back, brick protection from gaping skies, streets thick with strangers, nights that are never truly dark, city lights burning brighter than mere and distant stars.

"I wish you could stay longer too. It would do Sigga good. We worry about you, you know. We never hear from you."

"Don't worry about me. I'm fine. Just busy, is all." Another lie, feebler than the last. But I would be busy, soon, I thought, remembering yesterday's resolve to emerge from hibernation, get on with my life. As soon as I returned to New York I'd start anew, will my life into its robust future. Abandon my basement sublet, for starters, maybe find an airy loft. Quit my miserable job. But for now I had questions. *Ingibjorg's child.* I figured I might as well ask him, this keeper of family trees, not to mention Birdie's lifelong friend. I took another sip of coffee, tepid now as well as weak.

"Stefan?" I began breaking off little bubbles of Styrofoam from the lip of the cup. Just ask. If anybody knew it would be him. "Did Birdie ever . . . have a child?"

Stefan froze midbite. Then swallowed, brushed crumbs from his beard, and stared at me like I was mad. "What do you mean?"

"I mean . . ." I couldn't think of another way to say it. "Did Birdie ever have a child?"

"You know she didn't, Freya."

"I know," I admitted. "I mean, I thought I knew. But I heard something, last night. Some people at the party, talking. I overheard someone say something about *Ingibjorg's child.*"

"Who?"

"I don't know, I was outside having a cigarette. I heard through the window."

"Surely whoever it was didn't mean Birdie. Ingibjorg is a common enough name."

"In Iceland, maybe. But how many do you know around here?"

"Well, none, offhand. None still living. It's no longer so common around here. But in Iceland it's still very common. So maybe it was Thorunn. In fact, I think Thorunn's sister has a daughter named Ingibjorg, who has a child of her own. *Ingibjorg's child.* Mystery solved."

"But I heard them say Birdie's name, too."

"Be that as it may, Freya—and it would not be surprising to hear Birdie's name mentioned at her mother's one hundredth birthday party—Birdie never had a child. It's nonsense. I would know. I knew her all her life. A pregnancy takes nine months. Don't you think I would have seen? It's not the kind of thing you can hide."

We sat in silence for a minute. Then Stefan spoke again. "Really, Freya, I wish you would focus on present concerns. Consider extending your visit. It would mean so much to Sigga."

"I can't. I told you that before." Guilt and resentment fused together, indistinguishable, my voice as indignant as if I believed my own lie. "I have to be at work tomorrow."

"Freya, I hope you won't take this the wrong way. God knows you've been through a lot, losing both your parents, and your aunt so . . . horribly. But surely you must see . . . Sigga needs you."

"She didn't even know who I was."

"I was hoping that you might take more responsibility for your grandmother. You have a chance to make things right with Sigga before she dies."

"It's too late for that."

"I'm sorry you feel this way. Well, I suppose there's nothing more to be said on the subject." He stood up, carefully pushing the vinyl yellow chair back under the table. "I'll be working on packing Olafur's study today. Take what you want from the rest of the house."

I could hear him as I went upstairs to get my things, packing Olafur's books into boxes, to be carted off to the University of Manitoba. I knew Stefan despised me, but I was certain I despised myself more. I took nothing from that house, because nothing was what I believed I deserved.

Outside it was cool and crisp. Heavy dark clouds. What Mama used to call *brisk.* As a child I'd imagined wind as the whisk of invisible brooms, whipping white froth on the lake, white froth in the sky. Whitecaps and white clouds, dabbling the bright blue surfaces of lake and sky. I stood outside Betel, looking out on the harbor, composing myself after the argument with Stefan. *Discussion,* as Mama would say. I never asked him to buy my plane ticket. Anything he chose to do for Sigga was of his own free will. And had nothing to do with me. Visiting Sigga that morning was my last remaining obligation, and then I would be gone from there, done with that.

Fortunately, Sigga knew me again. I found her in the Betel library, new as everything else there, though when I looked closely I saw that most of the books on the shelves were old ones with Icelandic titles. Stefan collected them, Sigga explained, from people's attics. When the old folks die. Hardly anybody left in Gimli reads Icelandic anymore. So there sat our great sagas spine to spine with large-print mysteries and *Reader's Digests*.

"How does it feel to be a centenarian, Amma?"

"Exactly the same. My joints are no more creaky today than yesterday. But no less so either."

"Amma, can I ask you a question?"

"Of course."

We were sitting in two adjoining chairs, which meant I wasn't facing her. That made it easier to ask. But not easy. "Did . . . Birdie ever have a child of her own?"

Silence. Then, "Whatever gave you that idea?"

"I overheard some women talking last night. At the party. They said something about *Ingibjorg's child*."

"Oh my." Sigga closed her eyes for a long moment, and when she opened them again it was with a faraway gaze. "She was a lovely child. So lively and bright. A handful!"

So Birdie did have a child! "Tell me more about her, Amma."

"We just adored her. We did everything we could for her."

"But . . . what happened to her?"

"I don't know, really. I suppose they were there all along, those parts of her nature. That made her so wild, and so . . . depressed. But when she was a child those aspects were bearable. Charming even. Oh, how Olafur loved that child! She was his favorite. Sometimes I think that's what went wrong, that if he hadn't doted on her so, given in to her—"

"Amma, who are you talking about?"

"Birdie. Aren't we?"

"I thought we were talking about Birdie's *child*."

"Birdie's *child*?"

"Amma, I need to know this." I spoke slowly, clearly, loudly, right into her hearing aid. "Did. Birdie. Ever. Have. A. Baby."

Sigga's mouth was open, as if she was about to say something, but no sound came out. Her eyes had shifted, she was staring at something past my shoulder. I turned in my seat to see Halldora standing in the doorway, watching us through her thick-lensed glasses.

"Here is my darling Halldora!"

"I didn't mean to interrupt your visit."

"Interrupt? It's no interruption. You're to come and join us. Have you met my Freya?"

"Oh certainly, I have. A lovely girl she is."

Halldora and I exchanged tight little smiles, then she sat down on a small love seat opposite Sigga and me.

"I was just about to tell Freya something," Sigga announced. "But for the life of me I can't remember what. My mind is going, I'm afraid."

"Nonsense," Halldora assured her. "But didn't you have a big day yesterday! How did you sleep?"

"Oh, fine, I suppose. But I had one of my dreams. Freya, I'm afraid Halldora doesn't think much of my dreams."

"But dreams are so important," I said pointedly, pleased to contradict Halldora in that, or anything.

"I think so too. Would you like to know what I dreamt?"

I nodded. It didn't matter now. We couldn't talk about anything important with Halldora there.

"It took place back in Iceland, on the farm where I grew up. It was summertime and it was my job to mind the lambs in the pen. Usually my eldest brother did that chore, but in the dream, it was my turn. I sat on a little rock and read from a book late into the night. It must have been June, the sun was that bright. Every once in a while I threw a little something on the fire, pieces of wool or dung or moss, anything to keep it smoking. The smoke kept the eagles away, and the foxes. They'd come to steal the baby lambs.

"In the dream I was watching over two lambs and two ewes resting in the pen. And the grass was so green, greener than I'd ever seen it, and their wool was very white against the green. I can't remember what I was reading, but I must have been very involved in the book. I wasn't paying proper attention to my duty. And then suddenly I heard a terrible screaming and I looked up to see a large eagle making off with one of the lambs. I'd let the fire go out while I was reading. It was an awful sight, the poor thing squealing and struggling under those huge dark wings, and I could see blood in its wool, where the talons pinched. I stood watching until the eagle and the lamb were a speck in the sky."

"What a horrid dream," Halldora said.

"Oh, that wasn't the end of it," Sigga continued. "There's plenty more. My father was in the dream, and he was very gloomy. It was no small thing to lose a lamb. And meanwhile, the other ewe, the one that hadn't lost its young one, stopped giving milk. So we'd lost one lamb, and my father was fearing we'd lose another because its mother had no milk. But then a strange thing happened. One of the dogs came trotting up with the dead lamb hanging from its mouth. The eagle had dropped it. So my father took the dead lamb and he skinned it. And then he took the skin of the dead lamb and sewed it onto the live one, the one whose mother wouldn't give milk. He presented the fake-skinned lamb to the mother who had lost her own little lamb, hoping that she would recognize its smell, I suppose, and mistake it for her own. This was done, you know, by the farmers back then. You could also try to get a ewe to adopt another ewe's lamb by introducing them to each other in the dark. But in the dream my father did it this way, by sewing on the skin of the dead lamb."

"Did it work?" I asked. "Did the mother accept it?"

"Oh, she accepted it all right. But the funny thing was, the second skin, we just left it on the lamb. Never took it off. So the lamb had a funny, lop-sided look. A queer shagginess. And then my father sold it, in the end, to a family in the next valley. It left me with a terrible feeling, when I woke up. I don't know what it all means."

"Too much excitement last night is all it means," Halldora declared. "Whenever you have too much activity, then you have one of your dreams. Nothing mysterious about it."

"I suppose not."

"Amma." I stood up. "I have to go now."

"Didn't you just get here?"

This same conversation, again. Sigga's memory a sieve. "I got here Friday," I explained, but patiently. "And now it's Sunday, and I have to be at work in New York tomorrow."

"I wish you could stay a little longer."

"I do too." Even a few minutes longer, a few minutes without Halldora there. So Sigga could answer my question. Did Birdie ever have a child? Sigga had been just about to answer me when Halldora had interrupted. Meddlesome Halldora!

Sigga's thin cracked lips brushed my cheek like the wings of a trapped moth, her clouded eyes shining with tears. I was unable to say anything.

"Bless, elskan," Sigga called after me. "Bless bless!"

Bless means good-bye in Icelandic.

It began to rain as soon as I turned the rental hearse south onto Highway 9. *The heavens are weeping,* Mama used to say when it rained. Let them weep. I drove past field after sodden field. Good-bye to Gimli, to Amma and *vinarterta,* to ghostly surprise parties, to the house thicker with memory than with dust, to shifty lake weather, to distant relations I'd never see again, to the brand-new Betel and cranky Halldora, to Stefan and his precious genealogies. Let him spend his life in the muck of the past. I was done with it, I was moving on. The only thing hard to leave behind was Sigga.

By the time I reached the outskirts of Winnipeg, the rain had stopped and the sun was breaking through, glinting on the brick of crumbling buildings. I nearly pulled over to take a photograph—brick is a favorite of mine—but there wasn't time. And plenty of brick awaited me in the city, which I found myself thinking of, maybe for the first time, as home. Good-bye to my basement apartment, hello to the sunlit loft. My mind hopped from one eager plan to the next as I pulled into the car rental lot, returned the van, checked in at the Air Canada counter.

And then I was sitting in a hard plastic chair in the waiting area with an hour to spare, suddenly exhausted. I'd hardly slept that night. I closed my eyes, but instead of entering my own dreams I found myself in Sigga's. The eagle swooping up the lamb. The dog appearing with the dead lamb in its teeth. The dead lamb's coat sewn onto another lamb that had been taken from its true mother because she couldn't give milk. A queer shaggy disguise, to fool the new mother. A farmer's trick.

And then I got it, the real trick: the bird's lamb = Birdie's lamb = Birdie's child. Sigga had been about to answer my question when Halldora appeared. So she answered it instead with the dream. Maybe Sigga hadn't understood the dream, but I did. Birdie had a child she couldn't raise, so she gave it up for adoption. A new mother took it as her own. Plain as day.

I stood up, no longer sleepy, and began pacing the waiting area. There *was* a child, I was sure of it. No matter what Stefan said, or didn't say. Sigga had as much as told me so, in the language of dreams, which does not lie. Birdie's child! What would such a person be like? Fragments of Birdie. And an unknown father. Growing up in a Birdie-less world. Ignorant of kennings or Gimli summers.

Maybe I could even find Birdie's child, now grown. There might be records I could locate. Wouldn't Birdie have wanted that? Didn't I owe that much to Birdie? But first I had to find out if it was true. And the only one who knew was Sigga. Any answers would die with her.

And that is how I came to the decision not to board the plane but to return to Gimli, for a few more days, a week at the most. To see what I could find out. About-face! There were no buses to Gimli late on a Sunday, but Stefan was delighted to retrieve me. I did not tell him my true motivations. Of course not. I said simply that I'd decided to stay and help him pack up the house, visit more with Sigga. Then I left a message on my boss's answering machine that my grandmother was suddenly ill. I was in Canada, I'd check back later in the week.

It began raining again, and through the window I could see my plane arrive, watch the other passengers board. I left myself behind.

27

And so I re-returned to Gimli. Because of you, Cousin. Remember, I knew nothing about you at that point, nothing concrete, not when or even if you'd actually been born. But you became my excuse, my quest. Like King Gylfi, I arrived back in Gimli bearing questions. One question, actually, and not even one of the Big Ones. As I walked along the beach the next morning— a bright blue day of wavelets plashing the shore and a few cloud-puffs jaunting across the sky—I cared not how the world began or how it would end. No, I intended to learn the answer to one simple question: Did Birdie ever have a child? Surely that was not too much to ask, not after everything I had been through, for even if I was not, technically, an orphan (too old), still, the death of my father (true, I don't remember him, but isn't that itself a loss?), the suicide of my aunt, the sudden death of my mother, didn't these count for something?

No. I was lapsing into self-pity. I ordered a coffee and two slices of *vinarterta* at the bakery from the lank-haired girl, then made my way over to Betel. Still, if the answer was yes, there was a child—and I felt convinced as I walked along First Street sipping weak Styrofoam-cup coffee that it must be so—then the child would be . . . what? Not a lost key, no, or a missing piece of a jigsaw puzzle, or even the long-sought solution to a mys-tifying riddle. Those things were too precise, too simple. No, the child would be more like the knot whose untangling might begin to unravel the monster snarl where my life and my mother's life and Birdie's life fatally meshed. Ensnared in these thoughts, I walked with my head bent ground-ward, as if the child might be found right there on the sidewalk, or there, on the doorstep of Betel, still red-faced and squalling after all these years—yes, the child would explain—

And then my thoughts were jolted right out of my head. I'd nearly knocked over a little old lady entering Betel's front door. Luckily the woman caught her balance, as did I. The only one to take a fall was the cup of cof-fee. "Oh, I'm so so sorry, I didn't see you at all," I stammered. And no won-der. Peering down—the woman was so short and humped over she barely reached my ribs—I recognized Halldora.

"I'm easy enough to miss, I suppose." Fixing me with her impossibly huge eyes. "But I thought you left us yesterday." Sounding not the least bit happy to see me.

"I did. I mean I was supposed to. But I decided to stay for the rest of the week . . . so I could spend more time with Sigga. And help Stefan get the house ready." This last sentence especially had such a virtuous ring, surely even Halldora could not help but be impressed.

"Well, isn't that something."

"It's nothing, really."

"Nothing is it? That house will sell for more than nothing."

"I didn't mean—"

"Children move off to the city, can't be bothered to visit, then come sniffing around when it's time to collect. Believe me, I know all about it! Now, please, dear, be sure to clean up this mess, because it doesn't take much for an old person like myself with brittle bones to slip and fall and break a hip and end up in hospital catching pneumonia and never coming out again. Happened to Mary Stevenson just two months ago, rest her soul."

And then she was gone, with a smart rap of her cane, leaving me down on my knees sopping up the spilled coffee with a paper napkin.

An aide was helping Sigga dress when I arrived on the second floor. I stood in the hall leaning against the pale green wall waiting for them to finish, gathering my spilled thoughts. A door opened at the far end of the hall, but no, luckily, it wasn't Halldora, only an ancient man in a wheelchair, pushed by an attendant who guided him briskly, expertly through the doorway and around a linen cart. That's the way, I decided. It was just a matter of finding the right route. Sigga had been on the verge of answering my question yesterday, when Halldora had interrupted. All I had to do now was gently maneuver Sigga's wandering mind back to that same point in the conversation.

Just then Sigga's voice rose sharply and escaped into the hallway. "I can do it myself, Hannah, thank you." Sounding, to my surprise, not in the least decrepit, but instead exactly like the old Sigga, or rather, a less old Sigga, the Sigga of my childhood: gracious but commanding, the Sigga one dares not cross. Sigga the Queen.

Hannah gave up whatever it was she was trying to do, passing me outside the door with a wan, just-doing-my-job smile. I took a breath and entered. Sigga was seated by the window at a small table draped with an oddly oversize linen tablecloth that nearly reached the floor. I recognized it from our old dining table at Oddi. Sigga seemed not to notice my entrance. She was wearing a dark green dress, her head was bent toward her lap, her hands fiddling with something behind her head.

"Let me help you, Amma."

Startled, Sigga dropped the necklace she had been trying to clasp. I picked it up off the floor, ran the smooth pearls over my palm. It was the same double strand she'd worn for her birthday, smooth and polished against the sagging skin of her neck. I reached around her to fasten it, but she pushed my hands away. "Just put it on the dresser." As if I were Hannah, or some other aide, and I wondered for a moment if Sigga knew me that morning.

"I remember that dress. It looks lovely on you."

"Nonsense," Sigga said crossly. "It hardly fits anymore."

The soft wool fell in empty folds over her chest, the shoulders drooped. And yet somehow it did look lovely, still. "I can come back later."

"But you just got here."

"If this isn't a good time . . ."

"No, this will do. Just take a seat at the table here and we can visit. Stefan called last night to tell me you could stay. I was terribly surprised. How can you do this, Freya? What about your job?"

"I told my boss you'd suddenly taken ill."

"Oh my." Sigga shook her head. "I don't think that was a good idea. Nothing good ever comes of a lie."

"It was the only way, Amma."

"I suppose so. And surely Stefan could use your help. It's a big job, I'm afraid, packing up that house. I should have gotten rid of more things over the years. Honestly, I feel terrible about it."

"It won't be too bad. With the two of us working, we can have the whole thing packed up in a week." A bit of false optimism. Sigga didn't fall for it.

"A week!" She shook her head. "Oh, I doubt it. All that . . . stuff."

She seemed shaken by my last-minute change of plans, and nothing I said reassured her. She kept smoothing the linen tablecloth, flattening it against the table. Out the window, the puffy clouds continued their jaunt over Gimli harbor.

"Elskan," she began at last, "as I mentioned to you at the party, I have things I need to discuss with you. Things about our family." Sigga's voice seemed clear suddenly. Her mind too. A wave of dread washed over me. I knew, instantly, what was coming: my day of reckoning. Sigga would finally confront me about the trip to Iceland with Birdie, the events leading up to Birdie's suicide. Over the years I'd imagined the interrogation over and over again. *Why did you go with her? Why didn't you let us know where you were? Why didn't you get help?* But no one had ever asked. Not the police or the doctors or my mother or grandmother or Stefan or anyone. Except me. I became an expert in the art of self-interrogation. Defending myself against imaginary accusations. Deposing myself to no avail. That was all rehearsal. This would be the real thing. If I wanted absolution, I would have to take the stand; for how could Sigga forgive me without understanding what, exactly, I had done, and not done? The dread was mixed with relief. Finally, someone would extract the story from me, piece by piece, even if only to confirm my guilt. I stared at the floor, waiting.

"There are things you didn't learn when you were younger," Sigga said finally. "But you're certainly old enough now."

I got it then. Sigga wasn't planning to *ask* me anything. She was going to *tell.* Everything that happened. About Birdie. About Birdie's child. I wouldn't have to ask a thing. Or answer. I needed only to sit back and listen. All would be revealed. I relaxed into my chair. "I'd like that, Amma," I said calmly. "I think I'm ready now. Old enough. I have questions about it all."

"Of course you do. How old did you say you are?"

"Nearly thirty."

"Oh, that's old enough, I suppose. Though a youngster compared with me! Anyway, you were too young before."

I nodded.

"The question is where to begin."

Of course, I thought. That was always so, in anything to do with Birdie. Nothing was simple. Though Sigga seemed not in the least bit troubled by the prospect. For the first time all morning she was smiling. Odd, considering the topic we were about to embark upon. But not nearly as odd as what came next.

"Are you aware, *elskan,* that on my side of the family we go straight back to Aud?"

"*Aud?*" I sat up straight again. I'd never heard this name before. "Aud who?"

"Aud *who?*" Sigga stared at me in disbelief. "Aud-the-Deep-Minded, that's who."

I smiled uncertainly. Was Sigga teasing me? "I don't remember hearing about Aud. When was she born?"

"I don't know exactly," Sigga answered. "Mid-eight hundreds, I suppose."

"The mid-*eighteen* hundreds, you mean?"

"No, I didn't mean that. Really, Freya." Sigga's stern librarian tone was back. "You're going to have to listen more carefully. Are you sure you're really interested?"

Aud-the-Deep-Minded. Of course. Daughter of the Norwegian chieftain Ketil Flat-Nose, wife of Olaf the White, mother of Thorsteinn the Red, sister of Jorunn Wisdom-Slope. According to Sigga, Aud was not only deep-minded but formidable. One of the original settlers of Iceland, she arrived without the protection of husband, father, or son but lost no time consolidating power and claiming land. I'll spare you the details, Cousin, as Sigga told them to me that day. You can read them yourself in *Laxdaela Saga.*

Finally, just when I felt I could stand no more—I had not returned to Gimli, had I, to learn about Aud-the-Deep-Minded!—Aud came to the end of her life. Never, Cousin, was I so happy to see someone die. But it was not a speedy death, no. Not the way Sigga told it. Aud invited her kin and all families of note from all over Iceland to the wedding feast she was holding for her favorite grandson, to whom she planned to leave her vast wealth. Regal still, though ancient, Aud was tall and stately, striding through the great hall, past the long tables of guests eating and drinking and toasting, and then without anyone noticing she exited the hall and entered her own sleeping closet, where she lay down with great dignity to die.

"Remarkable," I commented.

"Not really," Sigga replied. "Those Viking women, they were no frail flowers. Aud did what she had to do in her life."

"Did Birdie?" (Not subtle, I agree. But I was desperate; I had been sitting with Sigga for over an hour and we were still in the ninth century.)

"Birdie?" Sigga queried.

"Yes, Birdie. Did Birdie do what she had to do?" I was referring to Birdie giving up her child. But perhaps Sigga thought I was referring to Birdie's suicide?

"Birdie?" Sigga repeated, and I could see then the leap had been too much for her.

"Ingibjorg," I said gently. "Your daughter."

"I know perfectly well who Birdie is," Sigga snapped. "Why—"

I'll never know what she might have said, or not said, next, because right at that moment someone knocked on the door. Yes, it was Halldora. The door had been open, so the knock was mere formality. I glowered at her in greeting, but Sigga's face lit up.

"Why look who's here!" She clapped her hands lightly together. "It's my darling Halldora."

Darling indeed. Uncanny, the woman's timing. She entered the room pushing a little wooden cart. Off the side of it hung her cane, on top of it a lace cloth, three cups on saucers, a plate of cookies. I had the distinct impression that Halldora had been standing outside the door for some time. Halldora-the-Snooping-Minded.

"Isn't Halldora a dear? Every morning she brings coffee and we have ourselves a little visit. She's a spry one, my Halldora is. Of course, she's barely eighty—that's young in my book! After lunch she pushes the reading cart around to all the residents who can't make it down to the library. She was a nurse, you know, for forty years. Oh yes, she makes herself useful, Halldora does."

"*Sveltur sitjandi krakum, fljugandi faer,*" Halldora said, and Sigga chuckled.

"What does that mean?" I asked, not wanting to rely on my rusty Icelandic.

"*Sitting crows starve. Flying ones catch.*" Halldora looked smug.

That was Halldora, I decided, a crow. Flapping about in everybody's business. "Well, I'm sure even the busiest crows need a vacation now and then. How about for this week, I'll bring Sigga her coffee in the morning, and Halldora can have a little break?"

"That's a fine idea, Freya," Sigga said. "She does go to a great deal of trouble for me, my Halldora does."

"Oh, it's no trouble. I wouldn't miss our morning coffee for the world. Unless you don't want me . . . ?" Her huge brown eyes wobbled pathetically.

"Not want you?" Sigga looked truly shocked. "Of course you're welcome here, dear." She reached out and laid her hand on top of Halldora's. "She's practically family, Freya. That's how good she is to me. And speaking of family— Well, I'm happy to tell you, Halldora, that Freya has finally developed an interest in the family history!"

"And with relations such as yours, it would be a wonder if she didn't." Halldora fixed her wobbling eyes on me. "Imagine, being the granddaughter of the poet Olafur, *Skald Nyja Islands,* himself. Of course, I never knew him. I didn't meet your grandmother until after Olafur was gone from this world. And on to the next."

"Actually," Sigga continued, "I was planning to tell Freya about *my* side of the family. I've already documented Olafur's side fairly well, but of my branch, well, I'm afraid she knows nothing. Although I didn't get off to a very good start. Really, I didn't mean to go on about Aud-the-Deep-Minded."

"It's all right, Amma. But . . . maybe we could talk about more recent events in the family. Like Birdie."

"Birdie?" That same puzzled, tremulous question.

I had no chance to explain. Halldora interrupted, and not surreptitiously this time. "There's no good in mentioning that subject," she scolded. "Too upsetting. Now, Sigga, how about some coffee?"

"I brought *vinarterta*," I said, offering up the paper bag with a feeling of defeat. "Only two, though."

"How lovely, Freya. Halldora and I can share a piece. At our age one's appetite dwindles, you know. You take half my piece, darling. Isn't it fine?"

Halldora took a small bite. "Fine enough," she agreed. "For store-bought."

As if Halldora's stale little cookies and bitter coffee were any better. I waited impatiently through their chitchat, the sipping and the nibbling, for the moment when Halldora would leave and I could be alone with Sigga again. But that was not to be.

"Nap time," Halldora announced, tidying up the coffee cart. "Sigga always has a late morning nap."

Sigga smiled weakly. "I suppose I've worn myself out, with all that talking. I hope it wasn't too boring for you, dear."

"Of course not," I insisted. "I'll be back tomorrow."

"That's good. We have a lot to cover. You mustn't let me wander so!"

Back at Oddi I let myself wander so.

Stefan was planning to arrive in the late afternoon with a station wagon load of empty cardboard boxes. Until then I drifted room to room, memory to memory. Examining the evidence, which all pointed to one thing: it happened. Everything I'd so conveniently forgotten. But *forgotten* is the wrong word. I've never forgotten anything; I simply choose not to remember. Memories sink deep if you let them. It's easy enough, the prerogative of only-child orphans. No witnesses, no corroborators.

True enough, my way has costs of its own. Amnesia, estrangement: expensive practices requiring constant vigilance, relentless attention to the gritty present. Photography helps. Each click is now, now, now. And moving to New York was a good choice. There is nothing there to remind me of Gimli or Iceland or even small-town Connecticut. Because New York is like nowhere else, it's mercilessly reminder-free. I suppose that's why so many flee there.

And no, I'm not always successful. My dead don't allow it. They have not moved on, my dead, to heaven or wherever. They're hangers-on. They talk. Not *whooooo-whooooo* ghostly taunts but eerily precise voices: authentic accents, real-life cadences. Little things, usually. Fragments. *Indeed, elskan,* Birdie will comment. *Oh dear,* remarks Mama. These are not things I can vanquish, or even guard against. And in dreams my dead run wild. Even my no-man's-land father makes a cameo now and then in his rectangular black glasses. Birdie and Mama are regulars. I'm always losing track of Mama, spending the entire night desperately searching for her like a misplaced cane. Birdie, on the other hand (and she was always on the other hand, wasn't she?) is the pursuer. Birdie comes after me in her salmon pink coat, fomenting one of her god-awful scenes, and all I can say about those dreams is thank heaven for morning.

But dreams are the very definition of ephemeral. Oddi provided me concrete proof, a veritable museum of memory-soaked artifacts. If I sat on the green couch, next to me lay the child Frey stroking Foxy. The parlor chair held Mama knitting and hymn-humming. At the dining table Sigga with the Blue Book spread before her. Upstairs Birdie's bedroom and the raining type, *splick splack* through the night. But I wasn't venturing into Birdie's room yet. Maybe never. I studied the china cabinet: the three lower shelves were crowded with blue-and-white willow china from Eaton's—replacements. On the top shelf, the Lucky Dozen, spared by a seven-year-old's gaudy taste. The survivors seemed to me now overly precious, full-bellied cups perched on tiny legs like fat ladies in high-heeled shoes. The lime green one with pale pink buds on the saucer. Blacky, with stars and a gold-lipped rim. *Lord, Frey!* And Mama's down.

I was packing up the Lucky Dozen one by one in Bubble Wrap when Stefan arrived, boxes in hand.

"Where should we start?" he asked.

"How about the kitchen?"

"Don't you think we should do that last? I mean, how will you eat?"

"With my fingers."

"Really, Freya, there's no need—"

"That was a joke."

"Yes, of course it was."

"We'll just save out a few plates and cups, some silverware I can use this week. But the rest of it . . ." I knew Stefan was right, the kitchen was the least logical choice, but it seemed safest to me, the least Birdie-laden room in the house. The kitchen had been Sigga's realm. I opened a drawer and began pulling out implements, wrapping them in newspaper. The wire whisk for whipping egg whites into frosty peaks. The sturdy tines of the potato masher. Aluminum measuring spoons on a silver ring. As a child I'd liked to nest them one inside the other. The mixing bowls too came nested in a set of four, white with bright blue bands circling the rims. Three sizes of measuring cups. Each object radiant with history, but somehow not sad to the touch. Maybe because Sigga wasn't dead, yet. And when she did die, she'd have lived a long life, not interrupted, like her one daughter, or discarded, like the other. I closed up the box and sealed it with tape.

"Are you sure you don't want to take any of this back with you, Freya? What about this *ponnukokur* pan?"

"I'm not much of a cook."

"Perhaps you'll want it when you get married, set up a house."

"Who says I'm getting married?"

"I just—" Stefan blushed beneath his gray beard.

"Anyone I'd marry would have even less of an idea than I do about how to make *ponnukokur*. Besides, maybe I'm like you. Not the marrying type."

I looked up at him and he looked away, then hefted my box off the table and into the pantry. "I think we can store all the boxes here, until we're done."

I followed him into the narrow pantry. "What about Birdie?"

"What about her?"

"Why didn't she ever marry?"

"Not for a lack of suitors, I can tell you. I suppose she was too . . . volatile."

A *lack of suitors*. "She did have boyfriends?"

"So I heard. She never told me so directly."

I could see why; Stefan appeared embarrassed by the entire topic. I pressed on. "Then she could have gotten pregnant."

"Ah," Stefan said. "Back on that again." He took a step toward the kitchen. I did not move out of his way. I was sitting on the pantry counter, legs bridging over to the opposite counter, casually but effectively blocking his passage.

"I can't get it out of my mind," I continued.

"Freya." He paused. "Don't you think I would have noticed, if Birdie was, if she . . . carried a child to term?" He seemed satisfied with that phrase. "Such things can't be hidden easily."

"But didn't Birdie disappear sometimes? She'd go off without telling anyone, for long periods of time?"

"Depends what you mean by long. It seemed long enough when we were frantically wondering where she was and if she was all right. Every day is long when someone is missing. But we're talking a few weeks at a time. She was never gone long enough to bear a child."

The air in the pantry was still, musty. I knew I should let him out of there, but I figured it was precisely there, in that narrow closet, that I was more likely to extract the truth from him. "What about one of the times she was hospitalized at Selkirk Asylum? Could she have borne the baby then?"

"She was only committed a few months at a time. Rarely longer."

"Ever?"

"Several times, yes," he conceded. "It always seemed to be after spending a summer in Iceland. Those trips unhinged her."

I knew all about how Birdie could be unhinged by a visit to Iceland. But I had to stay focused. If Birdie had given birth after one of her Iceland trips, that would be a way to narrow down the date. "When did she go?"

"Her first trip was sometime in the mid-fifties. She stayed mainly in the East, with Sigga's niece Thorunn. Then again in 1961, I believe. And of course in 1964, for the centennial celebration of Olafur's birthday. Sigga couldn't make the trip, so Birdie represented the family."

"I know, she told me about that trip, the fanfare and the speeches, the dedication of Olafur's monument. But she never mentioned being hospitalized after."

"An understandable omission. She was committed for nearly a year. Refused visitors the entire time. I thought she might never come out again."

Long enough to have a baby. But I said nothing. It was clear to me then that if Stefan knew anything about Birdie's child, he wasn't about to divulge it to me. And he looked so pained, so pale and aged. I climbed down from the counter and let him pass. We talked little after that. I knelt on the kitchen floor, rummaging into the backs of cabinets, sorting through baking dishes, cake pans, Jell-O molds. Stefan reached into the upper cabinets, pulling down old silver vases and cracked butter dishes.

A dear man, I heard Mama say. *Indeed,* Birdie added. And for once I don't think she was being sarcastic.

When dusk fell, Stefan switched on the fluorescent light and surveyed the room. "Mostly done here, I'd say. Guess I'll head off. Are you sure you're all right? With staying here?"

"It's fine."

"Because if it's . . . uncomfortable for you, you're welcome at my house. I have plenty of room."

"I like it here," I lied. "Besides, I'm used to living alone."

"Okay then. And you're set for dinner?"

"I picked up some things at the market."

"Then how about tomorrow night, I'll make you a real meal. Out at my house at Willow Point."

I stood at the door smiling after him. Mama was right, Stefan *was* a dear man, practically family, and God knows I have little enough of that in this world. But the moment I reentered the house I felt desolate. The kitchen bleak in its bareness. I tried to heat a frozen lasagna in the oven, but soon a putrid odor wafted out. As if some small creature had perished deep in the stove's bowels, and now its stench was resurrected, burned back to life.

28

Sigga was not in her room the next morning when I arrived at Betel. The bed was empty, loosely made, an old afghan my mother had knitted folded at the foot of it. Out the window the harbor was empty as well. No boats. Just water, still and blue.

"She's in the library. That's where we'll have our visit this morning."

My visit. I didn't need to turn around to know that it was Halldora.

"I'll take you down." Halldora was dressed in a dark brown pantsuit that made her look smaller than ever. A tiny mushroom stalk with a poofy gray mushroom head.

"That's all right," I said, as politely as I could muster. "I know where it is."

Halldora frowned. "That, child, is not the point. The point is that I've been waiting for you to arrive so you can help me bring the book down. I can push it all right, on my cart here. I just need you to lift it on for me."

"A library book?"

"No, my dear, your grandmother has requested that we bring downstairs the Blue Book, it's that one on the third shelf up—"

Unlike most things not seen since childhood, the Blue Book seemed just as huge and heavy as it had to me back then. Of course, it might have grown in the meantime; the chronicling of a family history is by its nature an ever-expanding endeavor. I couldn't resist flipping its pages before placing it on Halldora's cart. Genealogies of all types were crammed between

the blue leather covers, some in English, some in Icelandic, some handwritten, some typed, some photocopied from books. I remembered as a child being dulled into near-oblivion by the lists of names and dates. They seemed
no less wearisome now. Even so, I handled the book tenderly. It was Sigga's
lifework, this exhaustive exhausting tome of ancestry.

Sigga was waiting for us in the library, seated at the table. I kissed her on
the cheek, lightly, her skin so fragile I was afraid even my lips might bruise
her. Then I placed the Blue Book in front of her and took the seat opposite.
Halldora sat next to Sigga, hands neatly folded in her lap.

"I want you to have this, Freya," Sigga announced.

I reached across the table, but she stopped me with her hand. "Not now.
Now I'm just going to show it to you. Get you oriented. But after I'm gone.
I'm leaving it to you. Soon you'll be the only one of my people left on this side
of the ocean. You'll become the keeper of the family history. Of course I'd
always planned to leave it to your mother. Birdie never had the patience for
this type of work. Anna was the one for details. A very smart person, your
mother, not flashy like Birdie, but keen. To think that she . . . and leaving
you alone in the world . . . Are you sure you're managing all right, Freya?"

"I'm fine, Amma. Really I am."

Sigga said nothing, and I wondered if she saw through me. She was
never easily fooled. But no, she was drifting.

"Oh dear, where was I?"

"Freya is to take on the responsibility," Halldora prompted. "That's
where you were."

Sigga nodded.

"But, Amma . . . what will I do with it?"

"Do with it? You'll save it of course. Keep it up to date. All these pages
with paper clips, you'll see, I've written the changes in pencil but they need
to be typed up. Can't type anymore because of the arthritis. I've heard you
can put it all into a computer. Do you know how to use one? Stefan won't
have anything to do with that, he's so old-fashioned. But one of our relatives
in Reykjavik is doing a lot of this work on the computer. You can get information from him. And then, eventually, you'll pass it on to your children."

"What if I don't have children?"

"Not have children?"

"Some people don't. Birdie didn't." I scanned Sigga's face for a reaction, but there was none. "Anyway, I don't know if I will. I'm almost thirty, I'm not even married."

"Women are waiting much too long these days," Halldora commented.

"Well, Freya still has plenty of time." Sigga looked at me reassuringly. "Now, let's begin. You'll need to listen very carefully. And I've made Halldora promise to stop me if I ramble. Imagine spending all that time yesterday on Aud-the-Deep-Minded, when you don't even know the names of my own sister's children back in Iceland! And they're related to you on both sides, you know, through your grandfather and me. In fact, that will give us a good place to start, since you'll be meeting them this summer."

"They're coming for the festival?" Halldora asked.

"No, Freya is going to Iceland! Thorunn invited her!"

"Did she now?" Halldora looked skeptical, with good reason. I wondered if I should bother telling Sigga I wouldn't be making the trip to Iceland in the summer. It didn't seem worth upsetting her. Let an old woman believe. Who knew if she would even be around by then, or have enough of a memory left to remember who I was, much less where I'd promised to go? It seemed impossible and impossibly sad to me that a mind like Sigga's could ever lose its way. But I'd already seen it starting to happen, mistaking me for my mother . . . Sigga-the-Deep-Minded was as good as gone.

"Sigga," Halldora prodded. "I think it's time we get started."

"Started?"

Halldora reached in front of Sigga and opened the Blue Book. "You were going to show Freya how you and Olafur are related."

"I was? Yes, yes, of course. And we're going to begin with this." She pulled out a folded piece of paper lying loose in the front of the book, opened it, and spread it flat on the table. "My niece Thorunn from Iceland had this prepared for me by a genealogist, brought it to me last week as a birthday gift."

In front of us lay a handmade drawing that I mistook at first for a map of the solar system. It was a particular type of Icelandic genealogical chart, Sigga explained. She pointed to her own name handwritten in a small circle at the exact center. Surrounding her name expanded a series of concentric rings, the closest one sectioned in half, the next into quarters, the next into eighths, etc. Ten circles in all filled the page. Ten generations. The ring closest to Sigga's name, bisected horizontally, contained her parents' names, her father in the top section, her mother in the bottom. The next ring contained in its top two sections her father's parents, and in the bottom two sections, her mother's parents. And so on. As if you dropped yourself like a stone in the middle of time's lake and all your ancestors rippled out around you in perfect concentric symmetry. It was quite beautiful, actually, like some ancient alchemical diagram, all the names handwritten in neat foreign script. The chart went back to the early seventeenth century, Sigga explained. "It could go even further, but the genealogist ran out of room."

"But there are only first names . . . ?" I puzzled.

"The first name is what matters. You can figure out the last names easily enough. Just look to the next ring to see who the father is, and add *son* or *dottir*. Easy as pie. But there are no siblings in this kind of chart. Just parents and grandparents and great-great-greats."

The lack of siblings gave the chart its symmetry. Instead of forking wildly in all directions like the branches of a traditional family tree, it unfolded like the rings inside an old-growth trunk, circling backwards generation by generation over time. I swirled my finger through the names like a labyrinth, the Thorunns and Ingibjorgs, the Palls and Jons and Gunnars.

Next Sigga turned to another genealogy chart in the Blue Book, this one working forward in time with neat boxes and lines, documenting parents and children, grandparents and greats, aunts, uncles, nieces, nephews, cousins. This was the genealogy Sigga had worked on so painstakingly during my Gimli summers, tracing Olafur's side of the family; it ran about forty pages.

"Did you ever reach the Viking poet Egil Skallagrimsson?" I asked.

"That's a separate chart, in the back. We'll get to that later." Sigga was hitting her stride, focused and intent. "Right now I'm going to show you exactly how your grandfather and I are related. Actually, we're related in several completely different ways—can you imagine that?"

I could. Not specifically, of course, but it seemed entirely possible and indeed probable to me that every Icelander is related to every other Icelander somehow, if you're willing to look back far enough. The real question was, Did I *want* to imagine, much less understand, such ancestral connections in all their exhausting intricacies? I did not. I could not. The truth is that even with the aid of three cups of Halldora's coffee and a couple of stale

butter cookies I barely managed to keep my eyes open as I attempted to follow Sigga's crosscuttings between the circles and squares. Olafur's third
cousin had married Sigga's mother's first cousin. And so on.

"Amma," I pleaded. "I don't think I'm cut out for this."

"Nonsense, *elskan.*" She patted my hand reassuringly. "You'll catch on
soon enough."

After my tedious lesson in Blue Bookology, I took Sigga back to her
room and settled her in bed.

"I do hope you'll see Vera, Freya. She called yesterday, I forgot to mention it, and when I told her you'd extended your stay, well, she practically
insisted you go to Winnipeg and pay her a visit."

"I don't know, Amma, I—"

"Your mother's dearest friend in all the world," Sigga reminded me.

Dear Vera, Mama sighed. *Indeed,* Birdie smirked inside my head.

That afternoon Stefan and I packed up the parlor. The old brass clock that
had been a wedding present for Sigga and Olafur, *Winnipeg* etched in tiny
lacy script on the clock face. Had Sigga's sister come from Iceland for the
wedding, and bought the clock in Winnipeg? Maybe at Eaton's? I detached
the pendulum and wrapped it separately in tissue paper.

"Why don't you take it, Freya? I can ship anything you want to New York."

"Thanks. I'll . . . I need to think it over. Figure out what I have room for."
My basement apartment flashed through my mind. It was not large, but there
was plenty of room. In the eight years I'd been there I'd never furnished it; it
was only temporary, after all. If I took the furniture from Oddi, I could have
a real bed instead of a futon on the floor, a desk instead of a door balanced on
two file cabinets, a dining table, a couch. Wooden bookshelves instead of
milk crates. A dresser or two. I could rent a U-Haul, drive it all back to Manhattan. But did I really want an apartment furnished by my dead?

In a box labeled "Family Photos" I wrapped in tissue paper the framed
portraits from the mantel. Surely, Stefan commented, I would want these. I
nodded vaguely, like my mother, in a way that could mean either yes or no, or
nothing. I emptied out the rest of the china cabinet while Stefan collected
lace doilies and knickknacks from the coffee tables.

"What about this?" I pointed to the fringed lamp Birdie had brought back from one of her shopping sprees. "Why don't you take it, Stefan? Just your style."

For once Stefan actually laughed at my humor. "Birdie surely had extravagant tastes," he admitted.

"Remember when she came back with those awful presents for us? The rooster for Sigga, and the scarf with acrobats for me, and . . . what did she get for you?"

"The dog statue. 'For our ever-loyal Stefan.'"

"Birdie could be cruel."

"She certainly could."

Indeed.

"Well, I guess we better get to it," I suggested.

"Get to what?"

"Birdie's room." I still hadn't gone in there. But maybe with Stefan it would be easier.

"Freya," he began, then paused. "I thought you knew. Birdie's room is . . . empty. I packed it up a long time ago. After . . . it happened."

Of course. I'd just assumed that since the rest of Oddi was a perfect time capsule, Birdie's room would be too. "What did you do with everything?"

"Actually, it's all in my attic. Sigga asked me to store it until she could bring herself to sort through it."

"And she never has?"

"Not yet. She blamed herself for Birdie's suicide. Felt she should have kept a better eye on her after she was released from the Selkirk Asylum. But Birdie always did what she wanted. There was no stopping her in anything. Anyway, you can take a look at Birdie's things when you come for dinner tonight. I'll take you up to the attic, pick anything you want. Or all of it."

Or none of it. Then again, I could just have Stefan ship it all to my storage locker in Queens. Then the two dead sisters' belongings could keep company, getting along more peaceably than their owners ever had.

Stefan's house was a large and rambling affair, with many rooms, way too big for one person—yet none of the rooms was empty—each was stuffed to the brim with Icelandica. It seemed less a house than an archive with a bedroom and a kitchen.

"Why start a museum?" I joked. "Just have people come here."

Stefan laughed. "Actually, I'll be loaning many of these pieces to the museum." On the tour of his house I saw countless old trunks, a handcrafted bed frame, display cases with carved figurines, and a bedroom furnished in the style of a nineteenth-century Icelandic farmhouse. One large upstairs room was completely filled with file cabinets.

"Where does it all come from?"

"I'm a collector. A scavenger. And people know that. When the old-timers die the relatives call me in to help sort through things. See if there's anything of historic value. The children never know what to do with it all. Often they're grateful to simply unload it onto me. Boxes filled with letters from people they've never heard of, unlabeled photographs, books in a language they can't read a word of. They know I'll take good care of these things. And then the detective work begins. Tracking down the names behind the faces in old photographs. Identifying images of buildings that have long since crumbled. Reading through tattered letters."

"People must trust you a lot."

"I suppose."

"You probably know more about families around here than all the old gossips at Betel combined." He laughed. I was warming him up, and it was working.

"My head's full of family secrets. But most of those people are gone now. There's no one left to tell."

Tell *me*, I wanted to say. About Birdie's child. For suddenly I was certain again that he knew, something.

Dinner was roast chicken, rosemary potatoes, a salad with the last of the tomatoes from Stefan's garden. "You're quite the cook," I said. "For a bachelor."

Stefan blushed. "One learns to take care of oneself, I suppose."

"Some learn better than others." I was referring to myself, but he didn't know that.

"I hear you may be going to Iceland next summer, Freya."

"Well, Thorunn invited me. But I can't say I'm exactly anxious to return. Not after my last trip. What a disaster. I made quite a bad name for myself,

you know. We were all over the newspapers. Half the island was out searching for us. A couple of outlaws."

"All the more reason to go back."

"To exploit my notoriety?"

"That was Birdie's notoriety, Freya, not yours. Go see Iceland with your
own eyes."

"Maybe." I felt a glimmer of temptation. Then again, I was on my fourth
glass of wine. Stefan had had quite a few himself. Maybe I could loosen
that stiff upper lip of his yet. "How did you and Birdie meet?"

"In high school, in Winnipeg. She and your mother and grandmother
moved there after Olafur died."

"That's when they stayed with Vera Gudmundsson's family."

"Exactly. Birdie was a vision, even then, in bobby socks and saddle
shoes."

"Were you in love with her?"

For a moment I thought he wasn't going to answer. "I suppose. At least
for the first few years. Completely unrequited. I sent her love poems and
she returned them to me marked up in red. 'How cliché!' she wrote. But I
stuck with her. She was the most exciting thing around. A rare bit of Manitoba glamour."

"Did you want to marry her?"

"For a time. But eventually even a loyal dog like me gets kicked once too
often. We were more like siblings than anything. Your mother had Vera, and
Birdie had me. And then I went off to the war, and when I got back three
years later, Birdie was wilder than ever. Having affairs with married men.
Drinking and spending and shocking the entire West End. I didn't want her
anymore after that. Not as a wife. But I stuck by her through the years.
Doggedly."

"And you never met anyone else?"

"I never did."

"Birdie used to say you were like those old bachelor farmers."

"Except without the farm." He stood up and began clearing the table.

After dinner Stefan took me to his study to show me his work in progress.
"The nearly completed *New Iceland Saga,* all eight hundred-some pages of

it. A comprehensive history of the original New Iceland settlement, family by family. It's actually based on the structure of *Landnamabok,* the Icelandic book of settlements written in the twelfth century that accounts for all the original settlers of Iceland. The important ones, anyway."

"Slaves didn't count?"

"Exactly. But mine's more democratic. Everyone's included here. If they took a plot of land in the 1870s, they're in the book. There's also a couple of hundred pages of background material, life in Iceland—history, economics, climate, folklore, living conditions—followed by a complete history of the New Iceland colony. I'm trying to include as much original source material as possible. I'm hoping to have the book ready for next year's *Islendingadagurinn* and the opening of the new museum." He started flipping through the typewritten pages, the photographs and charts taped in place.

"You know, Stefan, it's practically as long as Birdie's *Word Meadow.* I think that was nearly a thousand pages. Has it ever turned up?"

He shook his head. "She must have burned it, before she . . . Or dumped it in the lake. Who knows what? All her writing, her letters and journals, her poems, everything. Gone. A damnable waste, if you ask me. Anyway, I've got a photograph of Birdie here that I thought you might like to see."

The photograph was of Birdie and a man standing in front of a statue. "The unveiling of Olafur's monument in Reykjavik," Stefan explained. "There's Birdie. That must have been 1964, the centennial celebration of Olafur's birth."

"Who's the man?"

"Ulfur Johansson. He's—"

"I know who he is," I interrupted. I studied the photo closely. Strange to see this younger Ulfur, with his shock of dark hair. So *myndarlegur,* Birdie had said. Before he turned into a Wolf and came after her. In this photo there was no sign of discord. In fact, she seemed to be looking into Ulfur's eyes. Gazing? "What if Birdie fell in love on that trip, and got pregnant?"

"With Ulfur? He was married already, I believe."

"Did that ever stop Birdie before?"

"No. But really, Freya, I hardly think Birdie would have had time to fall in love. The Icelanders kept her very busy, giving lectures about her father, touring her around the island. It was a lot of pressure on her, too much.

After she got back she just . . . collapsed. Into a deep depression. She was convinced she'd failed her father somehow. That's when she tried to kill herself. Nearly succeeded."

"What do you mean?"

"Just what I said. She swallowed a whole bottle of pills, who knows what. Then lay down in the bathtub. I think she thought she would drown. But Sigga came home unexpectedly and found her. A close call. She was committed at Selkirk the entire next year."

"I never heard about that."

"No, I don't suppose you would have."

"But . . . why didn't anyone tell me?" I was angry suddenly.

"You weren't even born yet."

"I know that. I mean later."

"When? When you were a child, you should have been told such a thing?" Stefan too was sounding angry, his voice still quiet, but harsh.

"No, I don't mean that!" I didn't know what I meant. "I mean . . . after Birdie died. Someone could have told me then."

"Why on earth—?"

"So I wouldn't have blamed myself. That's why on earth!" I was nearly shouting. The louder I got the quieter Stefan became. It must have driven Birdie crazy.

"Blamed yourself?" He was whispering. "But it wasn't your fault. Surely you knew that."

"I knew she killed herself on my birthday. My fourteenth birthday. How about that? Don't tell me that was coincidence, or that she didn't know what day it was. She knew. She was punishing me."

"For what?"

"For turning her in, at Askja."

"You mean for rescuing her, saving her life?"

"Birdie didn't see it that way. She called me *svikari*. Traitor. It was the last thing she ever said to me." I was crying. "She died hating me."

"No, Freya *min*." It was the first time Stefan had used that endearment with me. It just made me cry harder. "Never think that. Birdie loved you, you were a great joy to her. You did the right thing."

Oh no I didn't, I wanted to say. If I'd done the right thing I never would have stepped on that plane with Birdie in the first place. Stefan put an arm around me, awkwardly, but I let him, even leaned my head against his shoulder. I remembered the time so many years earlier, when Mama was in the hospital and Stefan had comforted me on the couch at Oddi.

"Freya, I'm not sure it's helping, this idea you have that Birdie had a child. Nothing can bring her back to us. Not even a long-lost child. Besides, I just don't think it's true."

Maybe he was right. Maybe this child was simply a figment of my pathetic imagination. Maybe whoever said *Ingibjorg's child* was talking about some other Ingibjorg. Maybe Sigga's dream was about exactly what it appeared to be about: lambs and eagles.

"Why don't I drive you home?"

"I want to see Birdie's things."

"Maybe another night would be better. When you're more . . . composed."

"I'll compose myself." And I did. I went into the bathroom and blew my nose and washed my face. Then I followed Stefan up a steep narrow staircase and into the attic.

High noon and a very low tide exposes more beach than seems decent, littered with flotsam, glinting tangles of shell-encrusted seaweed wrapped like a second skin around knobby chunks of driftwood. I poke a soggy, half-decayed gull wing with my sneaker. Then I spot it, bobbing close to shore. Something red. I wade out to my knees, then thighs, but the closer I wade the farther away from me the thing floats. When the water reaches my waist there's nothing to do but start swimming after it: my old cherry red suitcase, merrily bobbing just out of reach, a cartoon version of itself, wily and slick, darting below the surface so I have no choice but to follow it down into the cold dark depth of the lake, where I skim along the slimy bottom like an eyeless fish. Then I run out of air and shoot to the surface, gasping and treading and longing for everything I've ever lost.

Sweat-slick I kicked off the covers, waking up zombie-rigid in my childhood bed at Oddi. I wasn't having it. I was not giving up. That had been a moment of weakness at Stefan's, deciding that Birdie's child was nothing but a pathetic figment. True, my investigation so far had been a wash. Posing the question to Sigga had proven impossible, with Halldora flapping around every moment of the day. And even if I could manage to get Sigga alone, and get her to understand and then answer the question, could her information be trusted? Could I consider her a reliable source, she who had mistaken me for my dead mother? Stefan was useless too. No, not useless. Stefan is one of the most useful people on the planet—*a dear man,* yes, I know, Mama—helping old ladies and teaching high school students and setting up the new museum. But he was not useful in this matter. In this matter he knew nothing, or claimed to. Nor had anything turned up among Birdie's things in the attic. Like Stefan had said, all her writing was gone. Mostly clothes and jewelry, things I wasn't interested in. And her old Underwood on a typewriter stand, along with three books. "That's how Sigga found things," Stefan explained, "when Birdie . . . died. The books and the typewriter. So I put them back together up here."

A reconstructed suicide altar. I stayed only a minute before climbing back down the narrow stairs. It was time to turn elsewhere. If Birdie had had a child, her sister would have known. And if her sister knew, in all likelihood her sister's best friend would have known as well.

As much as I dreaded it, it was time to visit dear Vera in Winnipeg.

29

The next afternoon I borrowed Stefan's station wagon—an updated version of his old Rambler—and drove Highway 9 to Winnipeg to visit Vera in her house of knickknacks on Victor Street. It was just as I remembered it: outside, the formidable brick façade with the wrought-iron gate; inside, the figurines and china and silver all dusted and polished and gleaming in their display cases.

Vera wanted to talk about my mother. Vera loved my mother like a sister, Vera missed my mother terribly after she married and left for the States, and then when she passed away, well, tragic was the only word. Tragic! Of course, Anna was never the same after that terrible fall. She became an old woman overnight. Her hair turned gray and she had to walk with the cane just to keep her balance. How forgetful she became, a shadow of herself.

As if I didn't know!

And on Vera went about my mother, and on and on. I let her, although her every word pained me. I could not cut to the chase and ask the question I had come there to ask. I had to be subtle, not risk offending Vera's sense of propriety. The last thing Vera would want to discuss was Birdie. And so I saved her for last.

Painful as it was, the truth is that I loved hearing about my mother. In my life in New York no one knows my mother; they know only that I no longer have a mother. And if there is anyone left in this world who really knows my mother, it is Vera.

"I remember so well when your mother's family came to live with us here in Winnipeg, right after Olafur died. And oh, when they first arrived! What a pair, fresh off one of those New Iceland farms. Birdie a wild thing, Anna so shy she barely spoke. Despite the fact they'd been born in Canada those two girls spoke English with thick Icelandic accents. Raised to speak only Icelandic in the home! Can you imagine? My own father Dr. G. would not allow such a thing. Not that we Gudmundssons were ashamed of being Icelanders! What's to be ashamed of? But he wanted us to do well in this new world. No child of his would suffer with the taint of an immigrant accent.

"Birdie was only twelve when they came to Winnipeg, life here was easy enough for her, she loved the excitement of the West End. But your mother was sixteen, she had to fit in at high school, it took her longer to adjust. She was awkward and awfully shy. Other kids teased her. I was the one who protected her, tucked her under my wing, took her shopping at Eaton's, taught her proper Canadian ways. But don't think our friendship was one-sided. Oh no. Your mother was the dearest, sweetest friend I could have asked for."

Here Vera opened the album she'd set out on the coffee table and began showing me photographs. Anna and Vera in Winnipeg, standing outside the old brick school. Vera and Anna singing in the choir at the First Icelandic Lutheran Church, two doors down on Victor Street.

"Your mother had the voice of an angel, but she never showed off. That was the difference between your mother and her sister. Birdie was a show-off as soon as she arrived in town. Had to be the cleverest, prettiest, wildest girl in the West End. Anna was expected to look after her, but there was no keeping up with Birdie. Soon after she arrived, she threw her farm shoes into the sewer because she wanted a new pair—this during the Depression, mind you. City shoes, she insisted. Next thing we knew she was cutting school and meeting boys and smoking cigarettes. So Sigga took a job teaching school in Gimli, and that's when she and Birdie moved into Oddi. Sigga wanted to remove Birdie from what she called the *city influences*. Anna stayed here with us. We both attended secretarial school—that's what bright young women did in those days—but a few years out of high school your mother met your father. He was in town for an accountants' convention. He proposed, they got engaged, and six months later, Anna was gone. Oh how I cried! I missed her like a sister, I tell you. Of course I wanted only happiness for her. But I don't know how happy she ever was in Connecticut. The homesickness was terrible. And being unable to have a child all those years. And then, finally, you came along. What a joy for your mother! A miracle. I still have the letter—all her letters—when she wrote to tell me the news. She was just over forty by then. It was a difficult pregnancy and birth, so Sigga took the train to Connecticut and stayed with your mother the first couple of months after you were born. But Anna never complained to me in her letters, about the pregnancy or the birth. She believed you were the best thing that ever happened to her."

Vera paused, finally, and looked at me. As if she did not entirely agree.

"Can I see her letters?"

"They're in the attic, somewhere. I'll have to have one of my boys dig them out. Now that Joey's gone I depend so on my boys. You can see the letters next time you come. You must visit again, Freya, maybe for the Icelandic festival next summer? Please don't stay away so long again. It does me so much good to see you. I believe your mother is looking down on us right now from heaven, watching Vera and Freya drinking tea!"

She showed me more photographs. The one I remember most clearly is of Mama and Birdie, dressed identically in saddle shoes, bobby socks, and pleated skirts. Mama had a vague look to her even then, pleasant but blurry around the edges. Birdie was all angles, staring directly into the camera and at anyone who came along to gaze at her in the future.

"Your mother may have been no beauty like her sister," Vera commented, "but she had a kindness that did not go unnoticed. Your mother was pure goodness, Freya. She watched out for that horrid sister of hers all her life. And then for Birdie to do such a terrible thing! I thought Anna was going to have a heart attack when you disappeared, I truly did. Day after day passed and we had no word of you. Just vanished into thin air! We were all in Gimli for *Islendingadagurinn* when it happened, I was the *Fjallkona*, you know, and I stayed with Anna the next few weeks while we searched and searched for the two of you. Did you have any idea of the worry you caused us?"

I shook my head, maybe yes, maybe no. Vera went on.

"So many times Anna forgave Birdie. But kidnapping—there's no other word for it, really—she could not forgive. She informed Birdie that she was never to come near you again. It was a perfectly reasonable action, in my book. Birdie could simply not be trusted. Too unstable, dangerous really. Oh, there were some terrible phone calls! Birdie begging and pleading, demanding and threatening. It wasn't really about you. Though I suppose she loved you as much as she was capable of loving anyone. No, she just hated the idea of Anna having any power over her. But she got her revenge, in the end, Birdie did."

"What do you mean?"

"By killing herself. What a selfish disgusting act. Your mother could hardly live with herself after that. That's what she told me in a letter. She blamed herself completely. Which is I'm sure exactly what Birdie intended. Anna always made excuses for Birdie, blamed her behavior on mental illness. Honestly, Freya, Birdie was simply a case of bad character. I think your grandfather spoiled her terribly. She was Olafur's favorite and could do no wrong in the old man's eyes. And so she turned into an ill-mannered, overly excitable, self-absorbed, moody woman who took whatever she could from others and gave nothing in return. She was a deeply flawed human being. I hate to say this to you, Freya dear, but your aunt Birdie was a bad person, through and through."

"Yes," I agreed. "Birdie was a terrible person."

Vera looked stunned. She had not expected me to agree with her. But defending Birdie would get me nowhere, not with Vera. So I forced myself to say what I needed to get the information I wanted. I said that Birdie was horrible, that she'd ruined our lives, and that recently I'd heard even more terrible things about her, things I'd never known before.

"Like what?" Vera's interest was piqued.

"That Birdie had a child out of wedlock."

"Really? Well, I never heard such a thing. It wouldn't surprise me though. Birdie had lovers, stole other women's boyfriends and husbands right out from under them."

"But you never heard about her getting pregnant?"

"No. What makes you think she did?"

"I overheard some people talking. At Sigga's birthday party."

"Who on earth—"

"I don't know. I never saw them. But it led me to believe Birdie may have had a child that was given up for adoption. My mother never said anything to you?"

"Your mother told me everything, she would have told me something like that. Never said a word. And really, Freya, I can't see why that should concern you now. Though it doesn't surprise me, not one bit, that Birdie continues to incite gossip even from the grave. I say let the poor woman rest in peace. Her reputation was ruined enough in this life. Besides, I'm the last person to ask about Birdie. After Anna left for the States, I made it a point to see Birdie as little as possible. Birdie felt the same way about me—she was terribly jealous of me, you know, and went to no effort to spare my feelings. There are other people who know much more about Birdie than I do."

"I've already asked Stefan. He said he'd never heard of a child. And Sigga . . ."

"You're right not to trouble Sigga with such a matter. I don't mean Sigga, or Stefan either. I'm referring to your grandmother's friend Halldora."

"Halldora? But—she won't even let me mention Birdie's name in a conversation!"

"That may be true. But she was Birdie's nurse, after all."

"Her . . . nurse?"

"All those times Birdie was at the Selkirk Asylum. Not her private nurse, certainly. But Halldora was a nurse at Selkirk for many years. That's how your grandmother and Halldora first met, long before they ended up together at the Betel retirement home. Halldora took an interest in Birdie as soon as she arrived at Selkirk, because Halldora is a great fan of your grandfather Olafur's poetry. Reveres the man. So she kept a special eye on Birdie. Sigga was very grateful to Halldora for that. And then imagine, years later, the two of them neighbors at Betel. I'm sure Halldora is keeping a very special eye on your grandmother there."

"Oh, she surely is," I replied. "A very special eye indeed."

"But I don't think you'll find anything out from Halldora either. I feel certain Birdie never had a child. In fact, I've always believed that's why Anna let her spend so much time with you, even though she was clearly a bad influence. Anna had a big heart. I'm sure she felt that since her sister had no child, it was only right for her to share you with Birdie during the summers. Of course, I told her again and again it wasn't a good idea, but she wouldn't listen. A lot of tragedy could have been avoided if your mother had listened to me."

I didn't point out that if Birdie *had* had a child, and given it up for adoption, that was all the more reason for my mother to feel the need to share me. After all, my mother knew what it meant to be childless—for a woman who wanted children very badly, that is. But had Birdie ever wanted children? One more question I might never find an answer to.

No, I was terribly sorry, but I couldn't stay for dinner. I had to drive back to Gimli and return Stefan's car.

She hadn't upset me, had she, with all that talk about Birdie and my mother?

Oh no, not at all. Whatever would make her think a thing like that?

The next morning, Halldora was waiting like a sentinel outside Sigga's door. An attendant was giving Sigga her bath, Halldora explained. And while she did, Halldora wanted to have a word with me.

And there it was, an opening I had not expected. That was fine, I replied, because I wanted to have a word with her as well.

I did?

Yes I did.

Fine then.

Yes, fine.

I took the Blue Book from Sigga's shelf, and Halldora and I went down to the library together. Sigga would meet us there after her bath and Halldora would bring us coffee and we'd have another lovely visit, wouldn't we?

I nodded.

A peaceful visit, Halldora suggested. A calming visit. Because there's no sense getting old people riled about the past, is there?

I nodded again.

Specifically, Halldora went on, fixing me with her huge brown eyes, it would be best if I did not mention Birdie's name again. The subject of Birdie was simply too upsetting for an old woman like Sigga.

"You're right about that, Halldora. Absolutely."

Halldora looked startled, then recovered. "Of course I'm right. I'm glad we're finally seeing eye to eye."

I looked her in the eye. I said there was something I needed to ask her. "Yes?"

"About Birdie."

"Don't start on that subject again!" She clutched at her chest, but I didn't fall for it. I pressed on.

"Why didn't you tell me you were Birdie's nurse at Selkirk?"

"Who told you that?"

"Vera Gudmundsson."

"Oh that Vera. Such a busybody."

"Why didn't you tell me?"

"You never asked, dear."

I couldn't let her get away with that. "How would I have known to ask?"

"It's not something you needed to know. But yes, I was Birdie's nurse at the Selkirk Asylum, as it was called in those days." She stopped and folded her arms across her chest, and I was certain that would be the end of it. I would get nothing else out of her. But no, she was just getting started. "Many times Birdie was committed there. In fact, it was Vera's father, Dr. Gudmundsson, who had Birdie committed the first time. She never forgave him for that. I took the best possible care of Birdie whenever she stayed at Selkirk—not because I liked her, no, not at all—but because she was the daughter of our most accomplished poet. How that man's verses have taken me through life's hard times! Imagine, the daughter of Olafur, *Skald Nyja Islands,* committed to an insane asylum. That's how I met your grandmother. A saint she was, when it came to Birdie. Some families just abandoned their relatives at Selkirk, but not Sigga. Bringing Birdie books, her typewriter, paper, whatever she asked for. Always took her back home again too, despite all the trouble Birdie caused. She stood by Birdie, your grandmother did. I have a great admiration for your grandmother. And then imagine, Sigga and I meeting up again at Betel, years later! God was at work there, I'm certain of that. But that Birdie was a terrible trial, wild in her moods. She could turn on you in an instant. Paranoid, the doctors called it. Everyone out to get her, including your dear grandmother! Imagine."

I could imagine all right.

"Manic depression, it was, terrible disease. Many ended up the way Birdie did, killing themselves. There was no real treatment for it, not until lithium was introduced in the early 1970s. That was a great advance. Many of our patients did very well on it, the ones that took it regularly, that is."

"Was Birdie one of those?"

"Hardly! Getting Birdie to stay on medication was nearly impossible. She claimed it made her a zombie, that lithium was a vampire poison that sucked the life out of life itself. And robbed her creative powers. She thought she was some kind of genius, your aunt did."

"She was a very talented poet—"

"Oh, I'm not denying that. But it's part of the disease, to have what's called delusions of grandeur. Some patients thought they were kings, or presidents. Things like that."

"What did Birdie think she was?"

"Who knew? One time she was admitted to the hospital raving about a wolf that was persecuting her! And she spoke so fast in her mania, mixing the English and Icelandic—they always called me in when she got like that. No one else could understand her. We worried she'd have a heart attack, simply die from overexcitement. Some of them do, you know. Perish from sheer exhaustion. Of course, others kill themselves outright. The way Birdie did. Hung herself right in her own bedroom in your grandmother's house, leaving poor Sigga to find her. What a shock."

"But Birdie died in her sleep. From an overdose. My mother told me."

"She was trying to protect you, I suppose. From the horror. No harm in that. But it was hanging, all right, and I can tell you I've found a few like that myself, and it is not a pretty sight."

The awful truth seemed to tighten itself around my neck. Hanging seemed so . . . barbaric. So self-punishing. Like a sentence Birdie had handed down upon herself: *Death by hanging.* "Did she leave a note, or anything?"

"No, I never heard that. Sigga blamed herself, felt she should have kept a closer eye on Birdie after she was released from Selkirk. But believe me, it's nearly impossible to stop someone who's determined. The suicidal mind is always hard at work, scheming and plotting. They see a window and think *leap*. They see glass and think *cut*. No one's to blame. Everyone has their crosses to bear, life's disappointments, but we don't all up and kill ourselves now, do we? I was afraid Sigga might not recover from the shock, but she's a strong woman. Except now she's turned frail. You can see that, can't you? Any mention of Birdie, and Sigga's mind just seems to . . . go on the blink. So please, Freya. Now that I've told you all of this, promise me you won't mention Birdie in front of your grandmother again."

So that was why she was telling me so much. It was not out of the goodness of her heart. No, she wanted something in return. "I can promise that," I said. "If you can tell me one more thing."

Halldora stared at me.

"Did Birdie ever have a child?"

"A child? Now what in heaven's name gave you that idea?"

"I heard someone say something. And Sigga's dream, about the lambs—"

"Dreams!" Halldora scoffed. "You're as bad as your grandmother."

"Well, did she?"

Halldora didn't answer. I stood up. "I just need to find out, for certain. But I guess you know nothing about it. And the only person left alive who might know is Sigga." I stopped and let that sink in.

"All right," Halldora conceded. "If you must know. Yes, Birdie had a child. While she was in Selkirk. Are you happy now?"

Oh I was. But I kept my cool. I needed to find out as much as possible before Halldora closed her mouth for good.

"What year was that?" I asked, casually.

"Oh, I don't know that I remember exactly."

"Was it after one of her trips to Iceland?"

"Yes, actually. I believe it was."

"She went three times. Once in the mid-fifties, then in 1961, and again in 1964 for the centennial of the birth of Olafur, *Skald Nyja Islands*." I knew Halldora loved to hear the sound of the poet's name. "Maybe it was then," I prompted. "After the 1964 visit. That would make Birdie's child about the same age as me." The thought was startling: Anna and Birdie, who had so little in common, giving birth in the same year. One sister keeping her child, the other giving hers away. But Halldora was shaking her head.

"No," she said. "Definitely not. I retired from Selkirk in 1963. And it wasn't in the 1950s either, because I worked on a different ward then. The incurables, we called them. No, it must have been that other year you mentioned."

"1961?"

"Yes. Not that it matters now."

"Why? What happened to the baby?"

"It was given away to a good home. That's all Sigga would say about it. I never saw the infant. The plan had been to transport Birdie to the hospital when she went into labor. But she delivered so fast in the end, there was no time. Or so I was told. I wasn't on shift when it happened."

"Was it a boy or a girl?"

"I told you, I don't know anything else. Sigga didn't want to talk about it. And of course I would never pry."

I had a hard time imagining Halldora not prying. "But who adopted the baby?"

"I don't know. It was a blind adoption, that's what they call it. The birth mother doesn't know where the baby goes and the adoptive mother doesn't know where the baby came from. It's easier for everyone that way. Or so it's said."

"I want to find Birdie's child."

"I wouldn't count on that. Adoption records are sealed by the government. Now, I hope this information has satisfied you. And that you won't be bothering Sigga about it anymore."

"I won't. I promise. Just one more thing."

Halldora raised her eyebrows skeptically, but I wasn't daunted. "I'd like to visit alone with Sigga today. It's my last day. I promise I won't even mention Birdie's name."

And I kept my word.

Stefan insisted on driving me to the airport at five a.m. that Friday morning. He picked me up at Oddi. It was still dark when I climbed into the front seat of his station wagon.

"I had an interesting talk with Halldora yesterday."

"Did you now? I had the impression you don't care for Halldora much."

"I don't. Did you know that she was Birdie's nurse at Selkirk?"

"Well, yes, I did know that."

"Why didn't anybody tell me?"

"Why *would* anybody tell you, Freya? That was a long time ago. It's not like anyone is hiding anything from you."

"It feels that way." I stared out the window, caught a glimpse of the sun rising over the lake. I remembered Birdie holding my hand at the water's edge for my first sunrise. "She hung herself, you know."

"Yes." Stefan was on his guard now.

"My mother told me she took an overdose of pills. Died peacefully in her sleep. For years I imagined her that way. Now Halldora tells me Birdie hung herself. Right at Oddi. In her own bedroom, from the rafters. And Sigga found her there."

"That's right."

"And you say no one's hiding anything?" He didn't answer, but I didn't let that stop me. "Why would she do that, Stefan? Make Sigga find her like that? She was so . . . selfish. Why didn't she just drown herself in the lake or something?"

"She was a sick woman, Freya. That's all I can say. Who knows what went through her mind that day? But I don't think it was a selfish act. I think it was the opposite. That she thought by ending her life she would ease the pain she caused others, stop being a burden to Sigga. I think Birdie believed she was far more trouble than she was worth."

"Maybe she was right." The sun was up now, spreading light over the lake. "She never left a note?"

"Believe me, Freya. I looked everywhere. Sigga asked me to take care of things. After the body was taken away. There was no note. Just the typewriter with three books next to it on the desk. The window was open. It was February."

"February eighteenth. My birthday."

But Stefan was on his own train of memory. "She'd left the window open, there'd been a snowstorm, and all around her on the floor were little sticks and twigs, blown in from the tree, I guess. And snow piled up on the windowsill."

"How long before she was found?"

"Just the one night. She'd taken her desk and pushed it all the way over to the window, and then she stepped off of it. So she was hanging in front of the open window, swinging in front of her desk, above the typewriter and the three books. Very deliberate. There were even . . . little tiny piles of snow on the typewriter keys. Her hair was frozen."

"You saw her?"

"No. I . . . I heard Sigga telling the police. I'm sorry if this is upsetting you, but you seem to want to know everything."

"I do. And I should have guessed that Birdie would never do anything simple like pills. Not when she could set up a dramatic scene like that." Stefan winced. "I'm sorry, to bring this all up again. I know how you cared for her."

"Oh, I understand. Believe me, Freya. I was angry too, for years. Bitter. Wondered if I should have seen the signs. She seemed to be doing so well, after she was released from Selkirk. Now I realize it was all an act, to get herself released so she could kill herself. All that talent, all the life that was in her, vanished from this earth."

"Maybe not. Not completely."

"What do you mean?"

"Birdie's child."

"Freya—!"

"No, Stefan. I know for a fact now. Halldora told me. It was after Birdie got back from her trip to Iceland in the summer of 1961. She had the baby in the winter of 1962, while she was committed at Selkirk. It was given up for adoption."

Stefan gripped the wheel. We were driving now through an old industrial section of Winnipeg, gloomy in the gray morning light.

"Halldora says the adoption records are sealed, that there's no way to find out who took the baby. But you could find out, couldn't you? You know how to dig things up, documents and birth certificates, things like that."

"But why?"

"Because I want to find Birdie's child, that's why!"

"And then what? The child was given up for adoption, Freya. Presumably to a couple who wanted children but couldn't have any. A couple who were, presumably again, screened carefully, prequalified as being able to provide for the child's physical and emotional needs. These are the only parents the child knows. The child grows up, and then . . . what? You write a letter? Phone out of the blue? Show up at the door and say, 'By the way, did you know that the woman who gave birth to you was a manic-depressive who conceived you out of wedlock and eventually killed herself, nice to meet you?'"

I'd never heard this kind of sarcasm from Stefan before. I'd pushed him too far. I knew that. But I didn't stop. I was angry too. "There was a lot more to Birdie than her illness and her death—you of all people know that. And maybe I'm not the most socially graceful person on the planet, but I think I could manage a bit more tact than you give me credit for."

We were sitting in the airport parking lot. Neither of us got out of the car.

"Of course you would," Stefan replied, though he didn't sound convinced. "But my point is, that child, who is now an adult, can never know Birdie. It's too late for that. So what's to be gained here, other than satisfying your curiosity?"

"*My* curiosity? Honestly, Stefan, I can't believe that you, of all people, don't see it. Here you are a professional genealogist, spending all your free time researching people's lineages back to their great-great-grandparents to the umpteenth power. Don't you think this child might, just possibly, have more than an ounce of curiosity about who his or her biological *parents* are? I don't know about Canada, but back in the States there are legions of adoptees searching for their birth parents. It's all over TV, the searches and reunions. And I have to say, it's pretty heart wrenching. Even for a man of reason like yourself."

Stefan smiled wryly.

"And *presumably* there was a father as well. He could still be alive. They could meet."

"Not all adoptees are even told they're adopted, Freya. How would you feel, if you suddenly found out your mother wasn't your mother?"

"She'd still be my mother. Nothing could change that. Really, Stefan, I think people should know the truth. People want to know the truth about their origins. It's instinctual."

"Some people do, granted. Listen, I give you my assurance that if a stranger ever drives into town claiming to be Birdie's long-lost child, I'll phone you straight up."

"Thanks."

"I just don't think it's ethical, Freya. Besides, it's all speculation. We don't even know if there is such a child."

"But we do! Halldora told me herself."

Stefan nodded wearily.

"Are you saying Halldora is lying?" The thought had never occurred to me.

"I know how insistent you've become about this subject, that's all. Halldora may have resorted to telling you exactly what you wanted to hear. Just to get you to let up on Sigga. Halldora is a fierce protector."

"You're saying she invented the entire story to shut me up?"

"I just think it's strange, that no one else has ever heard a word about this so-called child of Birdie's. I've never seen a shred of evidence that such a child was ever born."

"But you yourself said there would be no access to records."

"True."

"You know, Birdie was right about you."

"How so?"

"You're trapped in a closed little world of the past, where only facts matter, details and documents, birth dates and death dates, and anything that can't be proven doesn't exist and never happened. She said you're the most literal-minded person she'd ever known." I knew I'd gone too far, probably wounded him deeply, but I no longer cared.

"Is that what she said about me?"

Strangely, his tone didn't sound hurt. Almost . . . pleased? Flattered? Maybe because these are, after all, the values he openly adheres to in life, truth and documentation, fact and logic. Or maybe it was being reminded that Birdie used to talk about him, know him. Even if she teased him. He'd spent years of his life in love with her, after all. He was probably trying, in his way, to protect Birdie. And that allegiance was far stronger than any inclination he might have to help me get at the truth. A truth which might, in his mind, further tarnish Birdie's already tarnished memory. As if an innocent baby could ever be a tarnish.

"You won't help me."

"Freya, even if I wanted to—even if I believed that is what Birdie would have wanted, and somehow I doubt that very much—I wouldn't be of any use to you. I've tried a few adoption searches myself, you know. In the past it was nearly impossible, but recently they've begun to liberalize the laws.

Here in Manitoba, they've set up a mutual consent registry, so that all parties to an adoption can get information on request. But both parties have to register in order for a search to be initiated. Obviously, Birdie can't register, since she died before the registry was initiated."

"I could register."

"You're not a close family member."

"Not a close—"

"What I mean is, not a party to the adoption. If you were a child searching for a parent, or a parent searching for a child, or even a brother trying to track down a sister . . . but a cousin?"

Stefan was polite enough to wait with me at the gate. Neither of us could find much of anything to say. A stiff hug, a wave good-bye, and we parted. The plane rose up, the flat expanse of Manitoba drifted farther and farther outside my window. The rest of the flight was all cloud.

30

And so poof! it goes, obliterated as if by the wink of a clever god. Tiny Gimli, mere speck on the lip of a vast sparkling lake, gone. The Betel Home for elderly descendants of Icelandic immigrants, vanished. Marvelous Tergesen's Store with its tin-stamped ceiling and neatly stacked balls of woolly Icelandic yarn. The bakery offering its seven-layered *vinarterta*. The house on Second Street, former residence of the great *Skald Nyja Islands,* and of my Gimli summers, and of Birdie's wintry demise: emptied room by room. And Sigga, Stefan, Halldora: my holy triumvirate, my three inquisitees. Poof! Poof! Poof! Lost under the dense blanket of cloud.

Funny how a place can change on you while you're not looking. My first thought on opening the door to my apartment after my return from Gimli was that I'd been robbed, emptied out. The only things the burglars left were a few pieces of ratty furniture. The brown vinyl-topped card table I'd found on Avenue D. The futon on the floor left by the previous tenant that doubles as couch and bed. The small black-and-white TV sitting on a blue plastic milk crate. Was this all I had? Was this really my home?

Of King Gylfi's homecoming little is told, but doubtless he received a hero's welcome. Fanfare and feasts, speeches and toasts. And then the evenings one after another in the king's great hall, where he told and retold what he'd learned from the three High Ones, and how he'd outsmarted them in the end. And so in the way of all heroes returning from quests Gylfi shared his newfound knowledge with his spellbound tribe, knowledge that circulated up and out and down through the generations until it became the very cosmology of the Old Norse world. Important stuff, indeed.

And with what returned our questing Freya? The answer to one question: yes, Birdie had a child. What became of it nobody knows, is probably impossible to find out, and no one but me seems to care. A partial answer, an unusable answer. And then, too, I'd obtained answers to questions I'd never intended to ask. Birdie swaying in front of her bedroom window, each typewriter key buried in its own neat piling of snow. Her life's work vanished. How everyone secretly took credit: Mama, Stefan, Sigga, me, each of us simultaneously and solely shouldering the same and entire hunk of blame. It was the most startling thing I'd discovered—next to you, Cousin. It made a mockery of the burden I'd believed was mine alone, the sense I've had ever since Birdie's death that at the heart of me there is something bad, something *criminal,* a belief that has fused to my sense of self like a barnacle, tenacious and cementlike in its grip.

So, yes, like Gylfi I returned home with newfound knowledge, but at first there was nothing to do with it. No one to tell. No fanfare, no feasts. No elixir to share with the tribe. Until I began writing you this letter.

After I got started, I wrote to Stefan and asked him to ship me Birdie's old Underwood typewriter. It seemed only fitting.

Oh, Clever Cousin, vanishing without a trace. No birth announcement, no birth certificate. No evidence you were ever born. I returned home from Gimli in late September, hired the detective in early October. Now it's December and I've received conclusively inconclusive news: The detective has found nothing. I got a letter from him today, along with a bill for his services. Not that I regret hiring him. You're worth it. Even the idea of you is worth it.

Don't worry, I'm not giving up. I'll develop new theories, avenues of investigation. A plan even. In the meantime there's nothing to do but keep writing.

I've been reading up. When I can't write or sleep, I read through the night. *In Iceland in winter words take the place of light.* I'm conducting evening-wakes of my own, with the three books that lay on Birdie's suicide altar. Stefan was kind enough to include them when he shipped her type-writer. I like to think she left them there for me, or maybe you. We'll never know. Stefan says she wrote no note: at the end of her life Birdie was at a loss for words.

I've just finished reading the first of the three. If you haven't read *Egil's Saga*, Cousin, I recommend that you do. Not only because some believe it to be the greatest saga ever written, precursor to the modern novel, a crowning achievement of medieval literature. And not only because Birdie was one of those believers. It's a question of influence. Birdie loved *Egil's Saga*. She loved Egil himself, that cruel, charming, cunning, brilliant, impulsive, trollish brute of a Viking warrior-poet. She claimed, in fact, to be directly descended from him, and if personality is any indication, I wouldn't be surprised if this were true.

What strikes me most is Egil's poetry, woven throughout the saga: Odin-sent, bloodstained, tear-riddled, mead-laden, heartless and heartbroken, magical, mundane. And life-saving—Egil nearly committed suicide once, after the death of his sons, but composed himself back into life with his famous poem, "Lament for Lost Sons." *My tongue is sluggish/for me to move,* begins Egil's lament. *My poem's scales/ponderous to raise.* Word by word, line by line, Egil wrote his grief, his rage, his loss, and his ultimate resurrection. (Of course, I shouldn't use the word *write* to describe Egil's process, since he did not write. He did not know how. Christianity brought writing to Europe, and the Icelanders came late to Christianity. Alone on their rugged island, our stubborn heathen ancestors held out against God and pen. Viking exploits, deeds of the gods, law, history—all were preserved in memory like amber and passed through the generations as precious verbal jewels.)

Shall we write it together, Cousin, when we meet? Our own "Lament for Lost Mothers"? Or have I already begun? It has not escaped me that I may be attempting Egil's strategy myself, seeking to resurrect myself with words.

Today my darkroom buddy, Frank, informed me that Klaus is considering firing me.

I have to admit, Cousin, the thought of being fired fills me with terror. There aren't many places left in New York for a black-and-white printer to work, and what else can I do? I never finished college; I don't know computers; even my typing skills are limited to hunt and peck. I have nothing to put on a résumé but *burns and dodges; maneuvers accurately in dark places; discerns the finest shades of gray.*

I should stop comparing myself with King Gylfi. Not because he's a king and I'm a lowly worker bee. Actually, it's Gylfi who's the pawn. The scholar Snorri Sturluson's pawn, to be exact. Yes, the same Snorri who was assassinated in his hot pool. For Snorri, Gylfi is nothing more than a literary device, the king's quest a clumsy platform upon which Snorri can expound to his readers the whole of Norse cosmology, lest it fall into oblivion. As Birdie had explained to me so long ago, when I was far too young to understand, Snorri was worried that the young Christian writers of his time were forgetting the pagan myths from which the baroque kennings of skaldic poetry arose, and without which the poetry is rendered meaningless. And so Snorri—a Christian himself—penned *The Prose Edda,* a treatise on the art of skaldic poetry that preserves the pagan myths for posterity. *The Prose Edda* is the second of the three books on Birdie's altar. In it reside the tales of gods and goddesses, dwarves and giants, that Birdie regaled me with as a child. Freya and Freyr, Odin, Thor, Loki—they're all here. The Tricking of Gylfi too. Along with the hundred kennings for *sword,* plus kennings for *sun* and *stars* and *rivers* and anything else to which a poet might want to refer.

And so King Gylfi's quest and trial were nothing more than a vehicle for Snorri, a convenient format for explicating the old mythology. In the context of Snorri's master vision, Gylfi is a cipher, a mere literary trick. And what about you, you ask? Are you nothing more than a vehicle for my pent-up musings? Good question, Cousin. In the world of the Old Norse, questioning acted as a form of ritual, and as Gylfi learned, posing the right questions can save your life. I intend to keep asking them until I find you.

Do you remember, Cousin, the story Birdie told of how Olafur, *Skald Nyja Islands,* was born in the East of Iceland with teeth cutting through his gums? *Skaldagemlur!* his grandmother Ingibjorg the light-mother had cried out. Destined to become a poet. And you? Were you born with teeth? Are you a scribbler, a versifier? Do tell.

Ah, but you are silent as ever. I'm no closer to finding you than when

I returned from Gimli at the end of September. It's February now, the day after my birthday, Birdie's deathday. Excuse the morbidity. I am thirty years old. Yes, I celebrated, or tried to. In other words, got drunk with my buddy, Frank, from the darkroom. February is not a good month for me.

Saemundur appears in my dreams sometimes, with his black hair, his eyes the odd green of a glacial river. *Eye-moon-lure.*

Did you know that the great god Odin hung himself in a ritual act of self-sacrifice, from the World Tree, no less? I remember Birdie ranting about it on our fateful drive to Askja. You can read about it yourself in the ancient poem "The Words of the High One," which is in the third of Birdie's books, *The Elder Edda,* a compilation of the oldest pagan verses. Here speaks Odin himself:

> *Wounded I hung on a wind-swept gallows*
> *For nine long nights,*
> *Pierced by a spear, pledged to Odin,*
> *Offered, myself to myself.*
> *The wisest know not from whence spring*
> *The roots of that ancient rood.*
>
> *They gave me no bread, they gave me no mead:*
> *I looked down; with a loud cry*
> *I took up runes; from that tree I fell.*

Odin saved himself by interpreting the runes. But nothing saved Birdie. She ran out of words and meaning. Sacrificed herself to herself.

You disgust me sometimes. Yes, you. Don't look so injured. You escaped, whoever you are. I imagine you living a perfect life somewhere and a jealous rage comes over me. It should have been you, not me, that Birdie took to Iceland. Your birthday for her to desecrate.

And now I'm about to lose my job. All because of you. I know, I know. You didn't ask me to embark on this dredging expedition. But if it weren't for you,

I would never have begun. I feel responsible for you. For finding you. And I will.

Maybe getting fired wouldn't be such a bad thing after all.

Sorry about that. I hit a low point there. But things are looking up now. In fact, I'm entertaining a new theory about you. If Birdie conceived you during her 1961 visit to Iceland, then Sigga might have arranged for you to be raised by your father in Iceland. Or relatives of his. Or ours. Kin is my point. No matter what Halldora says, I simply can't imagine Sigga consigning you to a blind adoption, sent off to live with strangers in Ontario or British Columbia. She would want her granddaughter raised by kin.

Why don't I quit speculating and hop on a plane to Iceland and look for you? That's what you're wondering? Good question. With a simple answer: I can't afford it. I wasted my meager savings on that private detective I hired. Who turned up zip. So I'm saving again. Besides, it's winter in Iceland now, a daunting prospect. Who could find anyone in all that darkness? Days so dark they pass for night.

Aefingar 30: Venus loved Adonis. I must buy some stamps and en-
velopes. I hope they will remember to bring my bicycle. They rubbed
their hands for joy when I had finished the story. You need not always be
reproaching me with that; it is now many years since it happened. Is
your wound healed? No, it heals slowly. Turn your gloves inside out.

Do you remember Snaebjorn Jonsson's *Primer of Modern Icelandic*, the book Birdie used to tutor me back in Gimli? I am making use of it again. Your mother would be pleased. In the subway, on the street, in the darkroom, I murmur Snaebjorn's absurd paragraphs out loud. Yes, I'm brushing up. *Ja, Ja* (rhymes with *wow wow*), I'm Iceland-bound.

Don't worry, I am building a more serious vocabulary list as well: *birth born death died mother sister aunt cousin adoption unknown; to look for; to find.*

Klaus has been oddly kind since I gave notice. He lent me and Frank his van so we could empty out my apartment. Most of the so-called furniture— the futon, the card table, the boards and concrete blocks and milk crates, the old door masquerading as a desktop—we piled on the sidewalk outside my apartment building with a FREE sign. The rest we took to my storage locker in Queens. I made Frank unlock the padlock and raise the metal door. I couldn't bring myself to look inside. The plan was for me to hand him stuff from the van; he could put it wherever he saw fit. I guess I forgot to warn him that the locker was nearly full already.

"What is all this stuff, Frey? Are you a fence or something?"

"It's my house. My mother's house. I didn't know what to do with it so I just stuck it all here."

Frank peered at me hunched in the back of the van. "Don't you think you should go through it sometime, keep what matters, sell the rest?"

"If I'd known you were going to be so nosy, I would have hired a professional." I began passing him boxes. By the time we got back to my apartment, all the furniture we'd left at the curb was gone.

It makes perfect sense to me, Cousin. Like one of Old Gisli's rigmaroles I memorized as a child:

> *A dream dreamt I a short while ago*
> *Of that dream there are many things to tell*
> *A whale appeared to me on the heaths bellowing*
> *Over that whale men sat watching*
> *Off those men blood was running*
> *Of that blood drank the ravens*
> *Through those ravens creaked the wind*
> *From that wind turmoil in the clouds*
> *Off those clouds shone a moon*
> *From that moon a very bright sky*
> *In that sky, stars*
> *On those stars grew leeks*
> *And with those leeks maidens played*
> *Over all the lands and islands*

You can't tell me one thing does not lead to another. Birdie went to Iceland. With a man had sex. From that sex conceived. From that conception gave birth. From that birth gave up the baby. Back that baby went, to the man in Iceland.

Of course there are other possible scenarios, but this is the one I've decided to pursue. Even if you didn't end up in Iceland, someone there will probably know where you are. They keep track of us, you know, their far-flung kin.

31

I am writing you now from a four-windowed turret in the house of books overlooking the lake in the middle of Reykjavik. It is five o'clock on a bright June afternoon; I have been in Iceland nearly twelve hours. My intention is to write you every day, to pretend to myself that I am keeping you abreast of my progress, although I know full well you won't read a word of this until it's all over. I am writing by hand, in a red-and-blue spiral notebook I bought in a stationery store in downtown Reykjavik today. The pages are of a different dimension than ours, longer and narrower. It's odd to write by hand again. I got used to rattling out my thoughts on the dark green keys of your mother's typewriter, a one-to-one *tippity-tap* correspondence between fingertips and letters. Birdie's Underwood is now sitting in the storage locker in Queens. And I am here, on the lower lip of the Arctic Circle, pen in hand.

And you?

The Wolf was waiting for me at the Keflavik Airport.

Perhaps that surprises you. Let me explain myself. To begin with, I did not ask Ulfur to host me. Sigga and Stefan put him up to it. I'd planned to contact him, but before I had a chance, a letter arrived: he'd heard from Sigga that I was traveling to Iceland, he would be honored to host me during my time in Reykjavik. My first instinct was to reject his offer. My memories of him from my last visit are not particularly fond. For the most part I remember him ignoring me. I remember his high forehead tilted skyward, his long straight nose in the air. What had Saemundur called his father? The Prime Minister of Sheepskin Manuscripts. I'd secretly called him Mr. Myndarlegur, handsome and ambitious, but also brusque and intimidating. An arrogant man, who for some reason Birdie found appealing.

And there you have it. *I* don't have to like him. Birdie did—until he dismissed her manuscript—and that's what matters. Is not Ulfur my prime suspect? Who else is a more likely candidate to be the father of Birdie's illegitimate child? True, Ulfur was married, but considering Birdie's track record—according to Vera, anyway—that would only make him a more attractive prospect. He even has a child the right age to be you: yes, Saemundur. Impossible, you say? I say maybe not. True, the black-haired Saemundur looks nothing like Birdie. But all that might mean is that Ulfur's genes overwhelmed Birdie's. And Ulfur is certainly a dominating type, after all.

Of course this theory assumes that Ulfur and his wife adopted the child he conceived with Birdie. Unlikely, but possible. Perhaps Ulfur couldn't stand the idea of a child of his being raised by strangers in Canada—non-Icelanders, no less!—and his wife acquiesced. While it might seem unlikely that Ulfur's wife would have agreed to adopting the child of her husband's mistress, maybe she (I have to admit, I don't even remember her name, have never met her; she still lives in Spain) was not the jealous type, had affairs of her own, or simply liked the idea of raising a grandchild of the great Olafur, *Skald Nyja Islands,* whose fame was already established in Iceland at the time.

So tell me now, Cousin: Are you Saemundur?

If not, there is still the possibility that Ulfur is the father of a child by Birdie and arranged for the child to be raised by relatives of his in Iceland. The Icelanders have a long tradition of fostering, dating back to Saga times. Back then, a child might be raised by relatives or close friends of the parents, sometimes out of financial necessity, sometimes as a way of strengthening family or political bonds. This was not adoption in the sense we know it; in a fostering situation, children know full well who their natural parents are, and maintain their original family ties throughout their lives. The tradition has continued up to the present; as far as I've been able to find out, blind adoptions are nearly unknown in Iceland.

And, even if Ulfur proves not to be the father at all—and what kind of proof can he offer me?—he is in the best position to help me track your father down. As part of his duties as host, Ulfur drove Birdie around, introducing her to people all over Iceland. He will know the men she met, and possibly, hopefully, the one with whom she consorted.

Such is the state of my speculations to date, and the main reason I decided to accept Ulfur's offer. Money, I have to admit, is another factor. I purchased an open-ended plane ticket—extremely expensive, but how can I possibly pick a return date? I have no idea how long this search might take. A week, a month, more? Originally I'd planned to stay in a cheap bed-and-breakfast in Reykjavik, but cheap is relative in Iceland, where according to the guidebook I bought in New York, a single glass of beer costs ten American dollars, and you can't rent a car for less than a hundred dollars a day. I had to face the facts: accept Ulfur's offer of a place to stay in Reykjavik, or limit my trip to a measly week.

Still, I feel like a traitor, a guest in the lair of the Wolf, the man who conspired to suppress Birdie's great opus. Except I'm not sure I believe that. I know as well as anyone what it's like to become the object of Birdie's paranoia. Remember how she used to call me my mother's little spy? We've all taken our turns: Sigga, Stefan, my mother, me. And those are only the traitors in Birdie's immediate circle. Birdie could pull enemies out of a hat. True, Ulfur denounced Birdie's *Word Meadow*, called it eagle muck. But who am I to judge even that? I've never read a word of it, Birdie never let me. And readers are entitled to their opinions, are they not?

Yes, yes, I'm rationalizing. And believe me, I was plenty nervous about my decision. I stole the man's jeep, after all, dragged his name into scandal. Yet Ulfur is a known entity, which counts for something when arriving solo in an essentially foreign country. Indeed, when I stepped out of the airport at six o'clock this morning I recognized absolutely nothing. This was because I could see nothing. Fog obscured everything. The air outside the airport was nothing more than an oozing white sponge that turned my skin clammy-damp. I shivered, and was bending to pull a jacket out of my suitcase when I heard someone say my name. I stood up, saw no one. Then a large bald head emerged from the mist like a glowing planet. "Ulfur?"

I imagined I heard Birdie sigh. Gone was her handsome *myndarlegur* scholar; in his place stood an old man, shorter and stouter. His glasses looked impossibly thick, and magnified the bags and wrinkles under his eyes. Not frail, but depleted somehow. He took my hand, then pulled me to him in a hug. I found myself staring down at the barren planet of his head.

"You've grown." He laughed, pulling away and studying me at arm's length. "Or else I've shrunk. Another indignity of aging." He drove slowly through the fog, which lasted nearly the entire distance to Reykjavik. No matter how hard I stared out the window there was nothing but white. The black lava fields were out there, somewhere. I could sense their enormous blankness. But I could see nothing.

"I haven't seen fog this thick since . . . the last time I was in Iceland." The image of the spiral-horned sheep rose in my mind—the one Birdie had hit and run on our madcap race to the East—and I regretted having mentioned the fateful trip so soon in our meeting. Ulfur didn't seem to mind.

"We're good at fog, here in Iceland. It's part of our . . . mystique."

We spoke in English, which I felt slightly ashamed about. *Icelandic only*, Birdie had ordered. But I suppose Ulfur was used to speaking English with American visitors, and I was too exhausted and nervous to attempt anything else. Mostly I listened while Ulfur caught me up on his family news, and I was relieved to find him friendlier, less remote than I'd remembered. He was still living in his parents' house on the lake, he explained; they'd both died in recent years and left the house—and the book collection—to him. Ulfur occupied the first floor, while his daughter, Johanna, her husband, Gunnar, and their children lived on the second and third floors. I would be staying on the fourth floor, in the guest room across from the library.

The house was empty when we arrived. Johanna and Gunnar were both at work; their daughters were visiting Gunnar's parents in the countryside, and Ulfur would be spending the day at the Arni Magnusson Institute, where he was retired in name only. Ulfur assumed I'd want to rest, and I did, but it was not to be. By the time we'd arrived in Reykjavik the morning skies were clear, and the wisps of curtain on the four windows of this turret do little to deter the light. The views are spectacular, distractingly so: the lake in one direction, Mount Esja in the other. My mind was abuzz with memories and plans, and by nine a.m. I gave up on sleep and went out walking. I didn't take a map, I wasn't planning to go far. I stood for a time on the bridge that crosses the lake, the bridge where I first caught sight of the black-haired loping Saemundur. Ulfur had said Saemundur might or might not come to the family dinner tonight. "I left a message on his answering machine. We'll see if he shows up or not. It's impossible to know his schedule these days. He's often out of town."

"For work?"

Ulfur laughed. "I suppose you could call it that. He leads tours into the interior. For hard-core nature lovers. Masochists, I call them. Who would want to spend their summer vacation wandering around a barren lava field? Apparently, people do. 'Deep Nature' he calls this outfit of his. 'Experience the last wild place in Europe.' At least he is employed and not living off the government anymore."

Ulfur's view of Saemundur has clearly not improved much over the last seventeen years. We'll see what I think. If he shows.

But back to the bridge. I stood a long time, letting my thoughts drift along the surface of the sun-glittered lake. Everything I saw seemed extraordinarily vivid to me. The colors of the buildings on the opposite bank appeared bright and saturated, with red-, cream-, and rust-colored bricks topped by red and blue roofs. White birds circled, then alit on a small island in the middle of the lake. Mottled clouds swarmed the distant white-peaked Mount Esja. I felt the shock of it, standing there. I am not in New York anymore. I have no job, no home. There is no more Sub, no more subterranean apartment. Only me here now on the island where I went missing seventeen years ago. I began to walk.

I found myself on Odinsgata. Odin's Street. Then Thorsgata, Baldursgata, Lokastigur: Thor's, Baldur's, Loki's streets. And finally: Freyjugata. Freyja's street. It was quite ordinary, Freyja's Street, trim houses with tiny gardens bursting with red poppies and purple pansies. I remembered the bags of black-cat Freyja licorice Birdie had purchased as our sole source of sustenance for the trek to Askja. Birdie's revered goddess, reduced to branding licorice. And streets. *She alone of the gods yet lives.*

I continued walking, past churches and graveyards and school yards, away from quaint god-charmed streets onto busy urban thoroughfares lined with tall gray apartment buildings, the type you'd expect to see in some stark Eastern European city, but not here. In a place where the weather, the land itself, is so harsh, it's hard to believe people would build such bleak constructions. Compared with New York the sidewalks seemed empty, a few pedestrians here and there.

In a small market I asked the clerk if he sold licorice, in Icelandic. The Freyja kind, I explained. With the black cat. He chuckled—some comic error of my grammar I supposed. And a postcard, I added. I have decided to write Sigga a postcard every day of my trip. To make up for the ones that Birdie never mailed. And this red-and-blue notebook I bought there too. At the corner of a busy street called Sudurgata I found a flower stand, and for three times what I would spend in Manhattan bought a bouquet of freesia for Ulfur's daughter, Johanna, who is hosting me for dinner tonight.

I crossed the bridge sucking salty licorice, inhaling freesia, thinking of you, and your mother, and wondering whether you are Saemundur, and if not, how will I ever track you down? I'll have to speak to Ulfur, as soon as possible. See what he knows of the matter, or rather, what he might be willing to reveal. It's late afternoon now, time to shower and change, ready myself for dinner and for re-meeting Saemundur, bestower of my first kiss, who may or may not show up, who may or may not be you.

Dinnertime. How do I look?

It is nearly midnight now, I am back in my turret room, looking out over the city that seems not to know the meaning of the word *night*. I have so much to tell you by way of my clumsy hand, my fingers straggling light-years behind my mind.

At first, our dinner party consisted of me, Ulfur, Johanna, and Gunnar. Johanna seemed nothing like Saemundur, a serious and sensible brown-haired woman in her late thirties, a linguistics professor at the University of

Iceland. She thanked me politely for the flowers, but I found her hard to read. Her husband seemed even more inscrutable. We sat at the same table where Ulfur and his parents had hosted the welcome dinner for Birdie and me seventeen years ago. The same table with the one empty plate. "Is Saemundur coming?" I ventured.

"Oh, we set a place for him," Ulfur said drily. "Like a ghost." He began carving the roast lamb.

"He's completely unreliable," Gunnar said. "I don't know how he manages that business of his."

"Saemundur," Johanna added, "is feckless. I believe that is the right word. Careless and irresponsible. What you Americans would call the black sheep of our family."

"Baaah!"

A loud and perfect imitation of a bleating lamb, nasal and gravelly, so real I thought for a moment there was an animal in the room with us. It was only Saemundur, standing in the kitchen doorway. He wore a scuffed leather jacket. His long black hair was gone, cut short now, but not neat. Curly and askew. Yet he had that same wide mouth like a mime's, the same high cheekbones. He seemed impossibly handsome to me in that first moment, and at the same time, I wondered if he might in fact be homely and odd-looking, and I was simply under his strange spell again.

He slung the jacket over the back of the empty chair. "I see you have been discussing my bad habits again. Don't worry. I approve. It gives you something to bond about." He spoke in Icelandic, but I understood most of it. Then he caught my eye. His eyes that same strange green, that glacial river color. "Freya," he said, solemnly, still speaking in Icelandic. "Welcome back to Iceland." He came over to my seat, I stood up, and he took my shoulders in his hands and pulled me to him in a brief hug. Then he stepped back and studied me, reconciling the me of now with the me of then? "It's good to see you again, Freya, after all these years. Good of you to give Iceland a second chance."

I nodded, but couldn't speak. My heart quivered like one of those skinny whippet dogs you see shivering on the streets of Manhattan.

"Don't be rude," Johanna scolded Saemundur, in Icelandic. She'd mistaken my silence for incomprehension. "Won't you speak English with our guest?"

"Why? She speaks Icelandic, don't you, Freya?" Saemundur took his seat now, across from me at the table.

I composed a sentence in my mind, then offered it up: "Not very well, anymore. I've forgotten so much. And it's so easy to make mistakes."

Saemundur clapped his hands. "Not bad! And it'll come back to you. If you force yourself to speak it, that is, and don't worry about mistakes. We Icelanders are easily impressed when anyone makes the least attempt with our arcane and ridiculously complicated language, we forgive all mistakes. Except my sister, perhaps. She is, as you may know, the captain of the Icelandic language police."

"Language . . . *police*?" I repeated in English, to make sure I'd understood.

"What my brother refers to," Johanna responded, in English, "is my position on the committee that regulates the Icelandic language."

"The top language cop, that's what our Johanna is," Saemundur countered, in Icelandic again. He poured himself a generous glass of red wine. "She makes sure we keep our tongues utterly pure and uncorrupted."

I thought Johanna might flinch, but she seemed indifferent to Saemundur's teasing. "The committee makes sure that no horrid foreign words infiltrate our precious ancient language," Saemundur continued. "Like viruses. You'd be amazed, Freya, at how many of these words try to cross our borders. Words like *television* and *computer* and *telephone*. Why, if we didn't have Johanna and her word cops, we'd all be speaking English by now. American, no less. No insult intended." He winked at me. "So Johanna and her committee sit around coming up with Icelandic versions of these same words. Hence our word for telephone: *simi,* the ancient word for thread. The word for computer is particularly clever, I think: *tolva,* consisting of the word *tala,* which of course means number, and *volva,* meaning seer or prophet. So a computer is a number-prophet. And a computer monitor, this is my favorite one, is taken from our old word for window, back before we had glass, nothing other than the embryonic sack of a lamb! Quite modern, quite efficient, really, don't you think, this recycling of obsolete words?" He was looking straight at me, but did not wait for an answer. "And the committee protects us from various diseases of the language. The dreaded *dative sickness,* for example, a horrible illness that causes increasing numbers of Icelanders to substitute the dative form of the verb for the accusative. Something that in other countries, mind you, is considered simply the normal progression of language, changing over time. Evolving even. Language is alive, don't you agree? An organism. But here in Iceland, we demand that the language must be spoken exactly as the ancestors spoke it. God forbid any television or radio broadcaster makes a grammatical mistake—why, he could be fired on the spot!" He paused for a moment to take a long deep sip from his wine. "And then on the other side of the table, we have my esteemed father, still toiling away on the ancient manuscripts."

If I thought Saemundur's family would be offended by his tirade, I was wrong. They'd heard it all before. Only Ulfur seemed miffed. "Johanna has made a great and valuable contribution to our society. She does work we can all be proud of."

"And if you'd shut up long enough, Saemundur," interjected Gunnar, speaking his first words since Saemundur's arrival, "then maybe we can hear a little from our guest, who surely did not travel across the ocean to hear you rant and rave."

"Yes, Freya," Ulfur urged. "Tell us about your life in New York."

I did the best I could to make it sound worthy. From a distance, the very act of residing in New York City takes on a certain glamour, and photography can be made to seem a respectable career. Next they wanted to know my travel plans. I told them I planned to visit Sigga's relatives in the East, but beyond that had no itinerary. Immediately I received a torrent of suggestions: Ulfur would show me around the Arni Magnusson Institute, Johanna would take me on a tour of the university and the National Library. And we must take Freya to the Blue Lagoon, Gunnar added. Of course, he continued, there were many things to do outside of Reykjavik as well. I would have to spend a weekend at the summerhouse at Thingvellir Lake. And see Thingvellir itself.

"She's already seen that," Saemundur commented. "On her last trip." A silence fell over the table.

"Or you can let Saemundur drag you onto a glacier," Ulfur suggested, and I realized his old sarcasm had not disappeared entirely. "He is, after all, an official tour guide now. A professional."

"A glacier," I repeated. I felt rattled. I hadn't come to Iceland to play tourist, I'd come to find you, Cousin, and you alone. As I ate the *pon-nukokur* Johanna served for dessert, I thought about Saemundur. Or to be more precise, about whether Saemundur is you. Aside from his dark looks, he seemed to me not so dissimilar to Birdie, with his dramatic entrance, his teasing monologue, his black-sheepishness.

Before Saemundur departed, he invited me out for a night on the town over the weekend.

"I must apologize for my obnoxious little brother," Johanna remarked while we were washing up. "Don't feel obliged to go out with him on the weekend. If that's not your kind of thing."

"Oh, I won't," I assured her. I did not say that I prefer my sheep black, and feckless.

Damn light. It's five in the morning now, and no, thanks for inquiring, I have not slept. Warning: do not expect any leniency from the Icelandic sun. Yes, the *Icelandic* sun. I refuse to believe it's the same star as New York's. The Icelandic sun requires no sleep—it dips under the horizon a bare hour, hardly long enough to rest its head on night's black pillow, and then it's rising again, infusing everything—the sky, the lake, the buildings of Reykjavik, my turret room, my brain—with its sly yellow-gray light. Or maybe it's the light generated by my racing thoughts that's keeping me awake. I feel lit from the inside.

Close the curtains, you say? You think I haven't tried? Flimsy and ill-fitting. I'm tempted to rip them off the windows. No, what I need is to spin myself through a darkroom light trap. Or return in winter, when the Icelandic sun jaunts off to Spain like a wayward wife and abandons her people to nearly unremitting darkness.

Yes, I'm in a foul mood. I've ruined everything, Cousin. I've pulled a Birdie. I've offended Ulfur, irreparably. I might as well start packing.

We two insomniacs met by chance in the library an hour ago. It was exactly as I remembered it: four walls of floor-to-ceiling books, the built-in bookcases making it seem the walls are themselves constructed of books. The same pair of chairs still by the window, where Birdie had sat reading under the midnight sun. Except that now one was occupied by Ulfur, a lamp illuminating his bald head like a glowing globe.

I startled him; he startled me. Ulfur blamed his insomnia on old age; I attributed mine to jet lag. I wished him luck getting back to sleep and headed out the door, but he gestured for me to sit in the chair opposite him.

Mistake. We were both exhausted, strained. And yet I felt wide awake and alert. The conversation began easily enough—we chatted about Sigga's health, and I told him about the new museum opening in Gimli, and Stefan's efforts to complete what would soon become a permanent exhibit on Olafur, *Skald Nyja Islands*.

"I'm sure it will be charming," he said.

I think it was that word, *charming*. It rubbed me the wrong way, and so did the next words out of his mouth. "So, you've come to complete your tour of Iceland?"

An innocent question, you think? I thought not. Beneath it I heard insult: that Ulfur does not take me seriously, that I am a failure, that unlike Birdie or Olafur I could have no serious reason for visiting Iceland. Just another American making the well-worn trek to the homeland, entertaining romantic notions of ancestral connection. Roots for whites, the whitest of whites. "I'm not here as a tourist," I said.

"Really?" His voice had that arrogant tone I'd so hated on my last visit.

"Yes, really. I'm here on family business."

"Not looking for those lost letters of Olafur's, I hope."

"Of course not."

"A futile effort, I'm afraid."

"That's not why I'm here."

Why did I decide that four in the morning was a good time to introduce the subject of Birdie's child? All I can say is that I'm sorry, Cousin. Poor judgment. I got riled. Tactless. "It's about Birdie," I began.

"Oh," he said. "Yes. Terrible. Such remarkable talent, wasted."

"Remarkable talent? I thought you didn't approve of Birdie's work."

"Did she say that?" He shook his head. "Perhaps I was more harsh than was warranted. Birdie's work was very . . . experimental. I'm a bit of a traditionalist, you see. I believe I told her Iceland wasn't ready for her book. I should have admitted it was myself who wasn't ready."

Yes, you should have. But arrogant men don't admit to such things. "She told me you called her manuscript eagle muck."

"Eagle muck? That's hardly— I'm sure I never—"

"Are you saying she was lying?"

"Lying? Clearly, she was delusional. Did you know that she believed I was some kind of wolf, pursuing her?"

"Not just any wolf. The Fenris Wolf. The one that swallows the sun."

We both smiled at that, awkwardly. "She had quite an imagination, your aunt. I misinterpreted everything. I thought she was simply a high-spirited, temperamental writer. Prone to flights of fancy. Still, I should have seen the signs. Realized she was mentally ill."

Mentally ill? Of course Birdie was mentally ill. I know that for a fact. But to hear those words come from Ulfur's mouth incensed me. "That wasn't *all* she was, you know. She wasn't like that all the time. And many people considered her to be tremendously talented."

"Of course she was," Ulfur said. He was placating me. "I only wish there was something I could have done. To prevent things from taking such a terrible turn. It was Saemundur, you know, whom you can thank for your rescue. He knew somehow that she was on her way to Askja. At first I didn't take him seriously, but he was absolutely adamant about it. It never would have crossed my mind—stealing our jeep and fleeing to Askja!"

"I'm sorry about your jeep." Only I didn't sound sorry.

"That doesn't matter. And it wasn't your fault. You were a child. If anyone should be sorry it's me."

And he did sound sorry, and sincere. I took advantage of it. "Actually, Ulfur, there is something you can do now." I studied his face as I explained, and as far as I could tell, his surprise seemed genuine.

"A child? No, I never heard that. But I don't see why I would."

I had to be careful here. "Actually, I thought you might be . . . of help to me. In tracking down Birdie's child. I think the father may have been Icelandic, someone Birdie met on one of her trips here."

Ulfur shifted in his seat. "I suppose that's possible. Do you have any evidence?"

"No, but I know she was hospitalized after her trip to Iceland in 1961, and that during her commitment she gave birth to a child that was given up for adoption. Which would make that child around . . . Saemundur's age now."

No, Cousin, I was not subtle. I admit it. Ulfur didn't think so either.

"Saemundur? What does Saemundur have to do with this? Surely you don't think—that Birdie and I—that Saemundur is—?"

"Is he?"

"Are you out of your mind?" He began to laugh, a dry, hard laugh. Shaking his huge bald head. "Birdie and I were never . . . involved. I swear to you, Freya."

"No, I'm not out of my mind. It's a perfectly logical possibility. Perhaps it's not true, and I've offended you by asking, and if so, I'm sorry. But I have to find out. I have to find Birdie's child."

"Why?"

"Why? Because . . ." But I couldn't get the words out. I'm embarrassed to admit this, Cousin, but I started crying. "Because . . ." I struggled for an explanation that would make sense to Ulfur. "Because Sigga is one hundred years old. After she dies, I'll have no one. Not a single living relative."

"No relatives?" His eyes softened then, and his tone of voice. It's a difficult concept for an Icelander to grasp. So I guess it was the right thing to say—if I prefer to have him pity rather than hate me.

"None." I wiped my eyes with my sleeve, took a deep breath. "Obviously, I've made a terrible mistake. Please accept my apology."

I left the room before he had a chance to reply.

So there. I've wrecked everything, in a scant twenty-four hours.

It's a clear morning in Reykjavik. Out the window the morning sun slants across the lake. A type of white-and-black bird I've never seen before is perched on my windowsill. I feel foreign, even to myself. I've hit bottom, Cousin, up here in this turret. I've given up everything, my life in New York, pitiful as it was, for—nothing. It's clear to me now. You are not Saemundur, and I'm never going to find you. You could be anyone, anywhere on the planet.

What becomes of me now? Your guess is as good as mine.

Pardon my melodrama. It seems I overreacted. That, or Ulfur has a bigger heart than I imagined. He was waiting for me at breakfast with a list of names. "Various men Birdie spent time with while she was in Iceland. I've included only people she met with more than once, or that I remember her particularly liking. Which is not to say—and I must emphasize this—that I have any knowledge of whether or not Birdie engaged in sexual relations with any of these people, or anyone else in Iceland. You must find a way to be more tactful, Freya. Tell them you're writing an article about your aunt's life, trying to learn as much as possible about her visits to Iceland. I don't want to hear about you accusing anybody of anything, is that understood?"

Understood.

The list has twelve names. A dozen prospective fathers for you, Cuz! I'm wriggling like a bloodhound. I'm on your trail. I'm going to find you. Even if you don't consider yourself lost.

32

And that is that. So ends my letter to Birdie's child. Three years have passed from when I wrote that last entry, in the turret room of Ulfur's house of books on the lake.

But don't worry, I won't leave you hanging, despite the fact that you aren't you anymore. I wouldn't skip the ending. Everything needs to end, if only to begin again. The serpent circles the globe, tail in mouth. The blackened earth rises from the sea, fair and green. Or so the *volva* would have us believe.

When I say *you* now, I'm not referring to Birdie's child. That is no longer necessary, or possible. But old habits die hard. I've grown accustomed to my imaginary audience. For *you,* now substitute yourself. Yes you, the reader-you, the plurality of strangers presumably reading this book. You see, certain people have convinced me to publish this pile of pages. It's no big deal, here in Iceland. Everyone writes books, especially biographies, memoirs, family histories. I throw mine in with the lot. And if you've stuck with me this far, you deserve to know how things turned out, how the mystery of Birdie's child got solved, the unanswerable question answered.

The tricking of Freya.

Or maybe you've already figured it out? Maybe you're smarter than I, or maybe I didn't want to see what was right in front of my face, so to speak?

In any case, read on. Or not.

Cousin indeed!

I lied. My letter to Birdie's child did not end with that last entry in early June. Quite the opposite, in fact. In the weeks that followed I wrote like a maniac. The proof sits here in front of me, a stack of red-and-blue spiral-bound notebooks. But it makes no sense for me to transcribe the notebooks verbatim. First of all, some pages, especially toward the end of my journey, are utterly indecipherable. Second, what is legible is not necessarily useful. The details of all my dead ends are of no interest to me anymore, although the friendships I developed with several of the old men on Ulfur's list I maintain to this day. And when I say details, I mean details: in those notebooks I documented every conversation, every interview, every thought that entered my brain, and there were many.

Can I spare you and resort to summary? Consider it an act of kindness.

By nine a.m. that morning I was on the phone; at noon I was sitting down to lunch with my first interview, Snaebjorn Gunnarsson, former professor of Icelandic literature at the University of Iceland. I've always loved the name Snaebjorn, which means Snow Bear. The same name as our old friend Snaebjorn Jonsson, Sometime Translator to the Government of Iceland, who authored the infamous *Primer of Modern Icelandic*. It could only be fitting, I reasoned, for Birdie's child to have a father named Snow Bear. But I cautioned myself not to jump to conclusions, to remain objective, to gather facts, to conduct a proper investigation.

Snaebjorn knocked on Ulfur's door at precisely 1:00 that afternoon, wearing a black suit shiny at the knees and collar, a square-faced man no younger than seventy with thin wisps of gray hair plastered to his head. I invited him in; he declined with what seemed a whiff of disdain.

Snaebjorn turned out to be a man of strong opinions. Over lunch at the university cafeteria, he informed me that Ulfur's family's massive private book collection more properly belonged in a place of public access, such as the Icelandic National Library. Thus the whiff of disdain. *Book hoarder* was, I believe, the term he used to describe Ulfur, though my Icelandic was quite rusty at the time, and the phrase was muttered under Snaebjorn's breath like a curse. Mainly our conversation was conducted in English. Snaebjorn's English was perfect but his accent odd, different from that of other Icelanders, yet somehow familiar to me. I soon came to understand why—in the early 1950s he had spent a number of years teaching Icelandic at the University of Manitoba in Winnipeg. "I helped to establish the Department of Icelandic Language and Literature, the first such department in North America," he recalled proudly.

"Are there others now?"

"I've never heard of any," he admitted.

No wonder his accent seemed familiar—he had become fluent in English through speaking with the Icelandic Canadians of Winnipeg and the Interlake region. Not only did he know Birdie but he had met Sigga, Stefan, even my mother. Snaebjorn had worked on a number of translations of Olafur, *Skald Nyja Islands,* he explained, which is how he first came in contact with my family there. He told me he'd attended the *Islendingadagurinn* festival in Gimli each summer, and his greatest disappointment was that he'd arrived a decade too late to meet the great Olafur, *Skald Nyja Islands.*

Birdie would have been in her early twenties then, Snaebjorn a decade older, but from what I could see he hardly seemed her type: fastidious, orderly, proper. But what did I know of Birdie's type, or types? Keep an open mind, I reminded myself. I told Snaebjorn I was writing an article about Birdie's life for *The Icelandic Canadian,* a publication he not only was familiar with but had edited during his stay in Canada. He nodded thoughtfully. "I don't know what I could tell you about your aunt that you don't already know. Our visits and conversations focused mainly on literary matters, especially pertaining to your grandfather's work."

"Then you never had a . . . romantic interest in Birdie?"

"Me . . . and Ingibjorg?" He made a short, harsh sound, something between a cough and a laugh. "A beauty like Ingibjorg would hardly have wasted a moment on a homely man like me." He sounded wistful, and I had no reason not to believe him.

Yet Snaebjorn still proved useful to my investigation. After lunch he took me on a tour of the newly constructed National Library, a modern-looking building adorned by large red shields. A Japanese influence, Snaebjorn explained, as if to make some sense of it. Inside, he set me up with a microfiche machine and a young library assistant, and I spent the rest of the afternoon flipping through films of Iceland's daily paper, *Morgunbladid,* looking for references to Birdie's visits. I made it through her one visit in the 1950s and the two visits in the 1960s, and left the library with photocopies of several articles and an interview, which I planned to translate with Ulfur's help. (I admit I was tempted, but no, I did not scan the microfiche for the headlines from our 1978 vanishing act. I wasn't prepared to revisit that yet.)

Despite having to cross Snaebjorn off the list, I was far from discouraged. In fact, I considered the day a promising start. There were still eleven names on Ulfur's list, and I remember the feeling of certainty that grew in me that evening. For the second night in a row I was unable to sleep, and I cycled Johanna's bike around the lake at one o'clock in the morning. *Birdie's child is here in Iceland.* The sun hadn't set but the light was muted, an early morning dusk that cast a green glow on the water.

What happened to the blind-adoption-in-Canada theory? you ask. I let it slip from my consciousness. Over the following days and weeks in Reykjavik I became increasingly convinced that I was closer than ever to finding Birdie's child. Propelled by my own blind faith, I pursued the investigation with a nearly religious fervor. *Birdie's child is here in Iceland.*

And I was right.

Friday night Saemundur arrived on his motorcycle to take me out on the town. His pale cheeks were flushed red from the wind. "To sample some of our famous nightlife." He handed me a helmet and I climbed behind him on the bike.

"Is it famous?"

"Quite the scene."

I fastened my hands tight on his hips and we were off. Soon we were bumping along the cobblestone streets of Old Reykjavik, choked with throngs of drunken youth, on foot and in cars, yelling, laughing, singing, fighting, embracing. Dancing to music that pulsed from cars and club windows. "This is *runtur,*" Saemundur yelled, above the roar of the bike and the thrum of the street. "It means circle, or maybe *circuit* is a better word."

Inside a club called Berlin he bought me a beer that cost ten American dollars. The air was thick with smoke and sweat. Saemundur smiled at me, that same wide smile that had made me melt as a teenager. "How do you like it?"

I paused. I wanted to say I loved it, and why don't we dance, and slug my beer like a true drunken fun-loving Icelandic chick. Instead I blurted out, "I don't. I hate crowds. I can't breathe."

I waited for a teasing retort, but Saemundur only shrugged. "Then we'll go."

He didn't say where. He just climbed back on the bike and I climbed on behind him. I felt like a disappointment as we breezed through the night. (It seemed like night somehow, though it wasn't dark.) But I hadn't come to Iceland to sample its nightlife, I reminded myself, or to impress Saemundur. We sped through residential streets, passing young boys kicking soccer balls at midnight, until I had no idea where we were. Then I smelled salt and fish and we came to a stop along a strip of rocky coast.

"If it weren't so cloudy tonight you could see all the way to Snaefellsnes Peninsula from here. That's where I'll be spending the next few days. Leading people across the Snaefellsjokull Glacier. That's the real Iceland. Not Reykjavik's drunken fools."

"Sheep-drunk, you call it?" I remembered the expression from our ice cave escapade.

He laughed. "Yes, *sauddrukkinn*. Drunk as sheep. And why are we speaking in English, when you are supposed to be practicing your Icelandic?"

"I am? I never said that. Really, Saemundur. I can't remember much. Just simple things."

"Then let's talk about simple things," he said in Icelandic. "Did my father tell you I lead tours to the interior? He doesn't approve. But what should he care? He has two successful children, a geologist and a linguist. Two out of three isn't bad." (I'm guessing here at exactly what he might have said. Approximating. At the time I understood only one out of three words at most.)

I struggled to remember the word for tour guide. "You're a *leidsogumadur*," I ventured in Icelandic. *Road-story-man*.

"Yes. But I try not to talk too much on the tours. I let the island speak for itself. And what about you? Have you become your family's next great poet?"

"Hardly. I've become nothing."

"Nothing? You're too hard on yourself."

We were walking now, along a pebbled beach. Small waves nipped the shore. Whatever lay in the distance was obliterated by fog.

"Maybe you should come on the tour to Snaefellsnes, Freya. You've never seen anything like it."

"I can't. I have . . . things to do in Reykjavik."

"Reykjavik!" He sounded disgusted. "The whole point is to get out of Reykjavik. Reykjavik is nothing. The real Iceland is out there."

Same old arrogant Saemundur. "I'm not trying to find the real Iceland."

"Then why are you here?"

"To find Birdie's child."

No, I hadn't intended to tell him. But I did. I talked all the way through the early morning sunset. Sometimes we walked, sometimes we sat on the rocks. The wind blew cold and hard. At one point Saemundur offered me his leather jacket.

"Are you sure you want to do that?"

"You look freezing."

"The last jacket you lent me, you never got back. Do you remember?"

He did.

When I was done talking—and it seemed to me I had never talked so much at one stretch in my life—the first thing Saemundur asked was, "What about my father? Do you suspect him?"

"Yes, as a matter of fact I do. Though he denied it when I asked."

"Do you believe him?"

"Should I?"

"I don't know. I always wondered about him and Birdie, if there was something between them."

"If that's true . . ." I wasn't sure how to phrase it. "Saemundur. *You* could be Birdie's child."

"Me?" He laughed derisively, just like his father had. "I can tell you one thing, Freya. I am no child of your crazy aunt Birdie."

I hated anyone calling Birdie crazy. "How can you know for certain? You're the right age, exactly. And Birdie was here in Iceland with your father in the summer of 1961, nine months before you were born."

"And there were no other men in Iceland the summer Birdie visited? My father, the only man in Iceland!"

He stood, arms folded across his chest, glaring at me. The sound of waves hitting the shore welled up between us. I couldn't blame him. Who wants to hear that the woman he believed all his life to be his mother is not, after all, his mother? At least not in the biological sense. And that his real mother was his father's mistress? Maybe Ulfur was right, I had to learn to be more tactful. But would tact lead me to Birdie's child?

"Saemundur . . ." I tried speaking more gently. "I'm sure you're right. But I have to rule you out. Is there any proof you can offer me?"

"Now I have to prove my identity to you? Really, Freya." I thought he was done then, but he continued. "First of all, if you think my mother would have raised the child of my father's mistress in her own house, as her own—well, you've obviously never met my mother. Inconceivable. Besides that, I have my mother's nose, exactly. And has it ever occurred to you that I look nothing like Birdie? Quite the opposite, in fact? And finally, do you really think that if I were the grandson of the great Olafur, *Skald Nyja Islands,* that my father would be able to keep quiet about it?"

I smiled at that. "You're right. I'm sorry, Saemundur. Like I said, I just had to rule you out." I wasn't sure that I *had* ruled him out, not conclusively, but there was clearly no point in pressing him further. We stood quietly on the beach, listening to the waves. It must have been three in the morning by then because the sun was nowhere to be seen. It was Saemundur who broke the silence.

"Do you have any other . . . suspects?"

"Actually, I do. Your father gave me a list of names, various men Birdie befriended on her visits to Iceland. He cautioned me that he had no reason to believe Birdie had had an affair with any of them. Still, it's worth meeting them. I've got to start somewhere. There are twelve names on Ulfur's list. Eleven, since I already crossed one off today. I don't think old Snaebjorn Jonsson was any match for Birdie."

Saemundur laughed. "Enough to keep you busy in Reykjavik then."

"For a while, yes."

"When you want to escape, when you get tired of questioning old men and decide to see Iceland, let me know, okay?"

"Okay," I agreed, making a different promise to myself: resist *eye-moon-lure*. At all costs. Already I could feel a tug when I met his strange green eyes. I needed to focus, to accomplish this one thing. To redeem myself, if such a thing were possible at this late date, in the eyes of my dead.

"How long are you staying in Iceland?"

"Until I find Birdie's child." And then I said it out loud, the mantra that had been pulsing through my brain. "Birdie's child is here in Iceland."

33

Over the next three weeks I met with nine of the men on Ulfur's list and the
widow of the tenth. Ulfur's roster of potential paramours contained an odd
mix—mostly in their sixties, a few in their seventies, one over eighty—and
in addition to Snaebjorn included a genealogist named Arni Hjalmarsson;
three poets (Bjarni Jonsson, Johannes Kjartansson, Hallur Hallsson); the
publisher Sveinn Vigfusson, whom I'd met years ago at Ulfur's dinner party
in Reykjavik; a distant cousin on Sigga's side, Einar Thorlaksson; a wealthy
fish exporter named Halfdan Jakobsson (quite handsome in his day, hence
his appeal to Birdie; I found him intolerably boorish); plus two university
professors, Bjorn Gislason in Icelandic literature and Eirikur Palmason in
history. I also met with the widow of Tomas Hrolfsson, a Lutheran pastor
descended from the farmer-poet Pall, mentor and uncle to Olafur, *Skald
Nyja Islands*. The eleventh man, Thorgrimur Skulason, was visiting his son's
family in London and would not return until mid-July. Ulfur knew the least
about Thorgrimur, only that he had had some kind of government job, and
that Birdie had met with him on each of her visits to Iceland.

Normally I would have found meeting so many strangers exhausting, if
not impossible. But that June in Iceland I felt an odd change occurring: I
seemed to be shedding my curmudgeonly exterior. After years of near her-
mitude in Manhattan, I began enjoying human company, even craving it.

I couldn't explain it, except to remember that I'd felt a similar opening up the last time I'd come to Iceland. I chalked it up to arriving in a new country, a free agent. It came on gradually, this newborn extroversion, increasing day by day, until I felt as if I could meet every single person in Iceland, if it meant finding Birdie's child. My tongue became the proverbial word-meadow. Introductions and small talk I conducted in Icelandic, which never failed to impress my subjects, and as the interview began in earnest I'd switch to English. I wanted to make sure I understood every word that was said. Anything could be a clue.

My faux-purpose, the writing of an article about Birdie's life for *The Icelandic Canadian* magazine, was only part pretense. I was indeed writing about Birdie, not for a magazine but for her long-lost son or daughter. The stories the men told me I planned to add to my own. After all, I'd known Birdie only when I was a child, and there weren't many people left in Gimli who were able or willing to remember her. These accounts would help round out the portrait.

Unlike my recent experience in Gimli, where Birdie had burned so many bridges, the Icelanders I met with were more than happy to recall their encounters with her. Manics in small doses can be quite appealing, even exhilarating. *Yndisleg* (charming), *falleg* (beautiful), *malgefin* (loquacious), *fyndin* (witty), *skemmtileg* (entertaining), *snjal* (brilliant); also *slysaleg* (unlucky) and *skritin* (peculiar). All adjectives I jotted in my notebook during the interviews. I decided early on to record everything that seemed important, then sort it out later.

Each of the men I met with remembered Birdie fondly and quite clearly, considering the amount of time that had passed, and many went to great trouble to answer my questions, often searching through boxes of old photographs and journals for details about her visits. At some point in the interview, I would discreetly slip in a question related to a lover Birdie may have had in Iceland. I wanted to contact him, I'd explain, to see if he had saved any letters from Birdie. If he had been married at the time of the affair, or if there was any other reason he wanted his identity kept secret, I would ensure his name did not appear in print. I was convinced it was an excellent ruse. It gave the man I was interviewing all the assurance he needed to come forth and admit the affair. As a final touch, I would write my name and Ulfur's phone number on a card, and let him know he could call me if anything else came to mind.

Unfortunately not a single one took the bait. Yet even repeated failure did not deter me. I went on to the next interview equally confident that this one, surely, would reveal himself as the true father of Birdie's child. It was simply a matter of time, a process of elimination.

It took three weeks to schedule and conduct all the interviews. Icelanders are always jaunting off to their summerhouses in the summer—who can blame them, considering what winter brings? Several of the men on Ulfur's list I had to meet with twice, because when I arrived at their homes for what I'd expected to be a one-on-one interview I found instead a large gathering of my subject's family and friends awaiting me. It is not every day that the granddaughter of the great Olafur, *Skald Nyja Islands,* comes to town.

Sveinn Vigfusson, the publisher, I met with several times for another reason: I became convinced he was hiding something from me. His thick beard had turned white since I'd first met him, but he still spoke in a loud and commanding voice. Oh yes, he remembered me quite well from Ulfur's dinner party, when at thirteen I'd shyly recited Olafur's "New Iceland Song" in front of the guests, stumbling through the last verse. He took me on a tour of Iceland's largest publishing house, where he'd reigned for many years and still, he confided, exerted much influence. He began to grow on me, despite his overbearing manner. But whenever we spoke of Birdie, his mood would darken and he'd become uncharacteristically silent. "Such a tragedy, your aunt's death. Such a remarkable and talented woman." No, he had never read her *Word Meadow,* but he'd read some of her earlier poetry and thought she showed great promise. And that was all he could bring himself to say on the subject of Birdie. When I mentioned the possibility of an Icelandic lover, he just shook his head blankly. He'd never heard of anyone, had no further leads for me. He seemed deeply troubled at the mere thought of Birdie, tugging on his beard, changing the subject or lapsing into silence.

I, of course, recorded his every word and gesture in my notebook, and for the entire second week of my investigation became convinced that Sveinn was *the one.* When I finally confronted him directly, he looked sheepish, but the secret he revealed was not the one I'd been hoping for. It seems he'd made a pass at Birdie once, when she was in Reykjavik for Olafur's centennial celebration—and been rejected. "Swatted off like a fly" was the phrase he used. "I can assure you, Freya, to my deep regret, that nothing of that nature ever occurred between Ingibjorg and myself."

Cross another off the list.

What did I do in those three weeks, when I wasn't interviewing old men, insomniacally cycling the lake, or poring over microfiche in the National Library? Even with the sheets of black plastic Johanna had taped to my windows, I slept only a few hours each night. I didn't need more than that. I seemed to have bountiful energy, more than usual in fact. And I found plenty to do. Yes, in Reykjavik, despite Saemundur's claim that *Reykjavik is nothing*. True, it's no Manhattan, no grand European capital, no Paris, no Madrid, not even a Copenhagen. Compared with New York, Reykjavik seems a mere village, and as European cities go it's an infant. Discovered in 874 by the Norwegian Viking Ingolfur Arnason, who named it Smoky Bay for its geothermal steam, Reykjavik has been continuously inhabited ever since. Yet it didn't become anything remotely resembling a town until the end of the eighteenth century, when it transformed itself into a certified trading post, population 300. By 1901 there were 5,000 inhabitants, today just over 100,000. Since World War II, when Iceland gained its independence, it's been nothing but expansion, buildings springing up erratically around the core of the old city, some elegant, some clunky, others frankly odd. Take Hallgrimskirkja, a modern church with a jutting basalt steeple meant to resemble an erupting volcano. Or the Pearl, a glass-domed restaurant that revolves on top of gleaming hot water tanks. These sights I saw and more, by foot, by bike, by bus, sometimes taken in a car by one of the men on Ulfur's list, who rapidly transformed themselves from suspects into gallant elderly hosts. I bathed with Johanna and her husband, Gunnar, and their two little girls in the healing waters of the Blue Lagoon, the silica-rich runoff from the Svartsengi geothermal energy plant, purported to cure all manner of skin diseases and other ailments. Imagine bathing in neon blue waters with silver smokestacks towering above.

Icelanders love to bathe, soak, and swim. Early on, the publisher Sveinn took me to one of Reykjavik's many geothermally heated municipal swimming pools. "This water we are soaking in," he explained, "first came down on our ancestors as rain, one thousand years ago. Scientists have proven this." After that I brought a listing of the city's pools with me wherever I went, and managed to avail myself every day, swimming in the pools, soaking in the hot tubs, imagining the waters as rain on Egil Skallagrimsson's head.

I also spent many an hour at Ulfur's workplace, the Arni Magnusson Institute, located in a nondescript gray building at the University of Iceland. Here I could gaze at the original ancient manuscripts, with their illuminated drawings of Birdie's feared Fenris Wolf, the Midgard Serpent (tail in mouth, circling the earth), one-eyed Odin and his eight-legged horse, Sleipnir, as well as historical characters such as the troll-faced Egil. I visited cafés and sipped espresso while scribbling endlessly in my red-and-blue notebooks. Nor did I let the weather deter me; it was variable, to put it kindly.

Icelander to tourist: "Do you have all four seasons where you come from?"

"Yes," the tourist replies, "but not all before lunch!"

And I took photographs. Of what? Everyone I met. The men on Ulfur's list, of course, each got a portrait. And anything else I saw that caught my eye: violets in the old Reykjavik cemetery, the light reflected on the wing of a tern. Hundreds of photographs I took, maybe a thousand. I even bought a new camera one day, on a whim, a Nikon that cost practically as much as my plane ticket.

Oh, I kept myself busy all right. The fact is, dear reader, I was having a fabulous time.

And there was Saemundur. Yes, I know. I'd promised not to let myself get distracted, but really, I reasoned, what harm could it do? There were more than enough hours in an Icelandic summer day—I could spare a few for Saemundur when he zipped across the lake to Ulfur's house of books. Mostly he was out of the city, leading tours of glaciers, ice caves, volcanoes, and other remote badlands, but it seemed that whenever he was back in town he found an excuse to come by his father's place. When Johanna remarked sarcastically that she'd seen her little brother more in the month of June than in the entire preceding year, I began to wonder if I might have something to do with Saemundur's unannounced visits. Perhaps he had begun to wonder if he was, in fact, Birdie's child? If so, he never mentioned it again, and I didn't press the subject. Time would tell, I hoped. Or maybe he thought nothing of the sort. Maybe instead he felt some obligation toward me, implicated as he was in my last disastrous visit? Not that I blamed him, of course. In fact, I wondered if part of his mystique for me was that he had, quite literally, saved my life.

"I have to thank you," I told him one night. We were sitting in the kitchen after everyone else had gone to bed.

"For what?"

"Saving my life, back then. Alerting the police that we were at Askja. I don't think anyone would have found us in time, if it weren't for you."

"Nice of you to say. But when you look at it another way, it's all my fault. I should never have given Birdie those jeep driving lessons. It was obvious she was up to no good."

"Did you know what she was planning?"

"Not exactly, no. But I felt guilty all the same. And then when I heard she'd committed suicide—"

"Just a minute," I interrupted. "Don't go taking credit for that. You'll have to get in line. As it turns out, everyone I knew and loved felt responsible for Birdie's suicide: my mother, Stefan, Sigga. Even your father. And me."

"You?"

"Especially me. She killed herself on my fourteenth birthday, you know."

"I didn't."

We sat in silence, staring into our empty coffee cups. It occurred to me then that they all felt sorry for me, Ulfur and Johanna, Saemundur. That's why they were being nice to me, indulging me and my investigation. It was nothing but pity. And I was nothing if not pitiable, or so I thought. The tide of enthusiasm I'd been riding crashed in that moment. I was crying, damn it, in front of Saemundur. He reached for my hand, but I jerked it back, pushed my chair from the table.

"Enough sob stories for tonight."

"Freya—"

After that night we didn't mention Birdie anymore, but Saemundur kept coming around, and I couldn't keep myself from looking forward to his visits. One evening when Saemundur had joined us for dinner, Johanna asked after his girlfriend. I flinched. A girlfriend? Of course Saemundur would have a girlfriend. What had I expected?

But he shrugged it off. "Halla? Oh, it's nothing serious with her."

"It never is, is it?"

"I did try marriage, you know. It was a resounding failure."

"You were married?" I blurted out.

"In my twenties. For three years. It seems I'm too selfish, erratic, and arrogant to make a proper husband."

"No surprise there," Johanna remarked.

Saemundur knew better than to take me to more clubs. Usually he'd spirit me off to some odd spot or another. The river Ellidaar, where you can fish for salmon in the middle of Reykjavik. The graveyard on the other side of the lake, where violets and pansies gleamed at the foot of moss-encrusted gravestones. One day near the end of my third week in Reykjavik we visited the town of Hafnarfjordur, nestled in the Burfell lava field. After parking Saemundur's motorcycle, we walked along a street where brightly painted houses seemed to sprout from clumps of black lava.

"Hafnarfjordur is a key fishing center, but more important, it is home to a large population of elves. The residents are making quite a business off that these days. Giving elf tours and selling trinkets."

"People are so gullible. What a bunch of nonsense."

"Nonsense? You don't need to go that far, Freya. What happened to that idealistic little girl I once met?"

"Turned into a cynical New Yorker. Don't tell me you believe in elves, Saemundur."

"I won't say I don't. And you'll find that's the case with most Icelanders. Supposedly over 90 percent of us believe in elves. Or rather, don't *disbelieve* in them. Anyway, that's why there are so many odd twists to the streets here in Hafnarfjordur." We were walking up a hillside where the road abruptly circled a large boulder. "That rock there is an elf home. Construction crews build around such spots, or face the consequences."

"Consequences?"

"All sorts of bad luck. Accidents to the crew, that sort of thing. It's standard practice all over Iceland. There are just more elves here in Hafnarfjordur. So more crooked roads."

"And what do these elves look like? Have you ever seen one?"

"Not personally, no. And remember, there are different kinds of elves. Like the *huldufolk*. Hidden People. They live in the rocks, in a parallel world to ours. They're the same size as us too. They look . . . human. And sometimes they steal human babies."

"Maybe that's what happened to Birdie's child, stolen by the Hidden People." It actually seemed plausible to me, at the moment. "That's why my search is so futile."

"Don't tell me you're giving up."

"No, but I'm not getting anywhere in Reykjavik. I've been through everyone on your father's list who's not dead or on vacation. All dead ends. I'm thinking it's time to visit Sigga's niece Thorunn in the East. I met her in Gimli last fall, she lives on a farm near Egilsstadir. Ulfur says I could fly there in a couple of hours."

"Why fly? You won't see anything that way. Let me drive you. I've got a tour starting in Akureyri, in the north, next week. We'll drive up the East Coast, I'll show you the sights, I'll drop you off at Thorunn's."

"That's a generous offer. But I think I'll take the plane."

"You'll never see anything that way," Saemundur repeated. I could see he was offended, but I had good reason for wanting to fly: the way to Thorunn's was the same route Birdie and I had taken in the stolen jeep. I had no desire to retrace that madcap ride.

That night as I lay sleepless in my turret room I remembered the marvelous sights Birdie had promised to show me. Except that once we were on the Ring Road, there was no time for that. Our tourist days were over. The Wolf was on our trail. Damn Birdie. She'd ruined so many things for me. I imagined drifting in a tiny boat amid a pool of glistening icebergs. Why not see the glacial lagoon now?

Why not indeed?

34

I haven't been honest with you. Looking back on these pages, I see I've left some things out. And made myself sound entirely more sensible than I actually was. It's a whitewash. Sure, I dropped plenty of hints. And maybe you figured it out, maybe you're smarter than I was at the time: during those three weeks in Reykjavik, I had no idea that anything was wrong with me. On the contrary, it felt like everything was right. I viewed the changes occurring in me not as symptoms but as transformation. Hadn't I felt a similar blossoming on my first trip to Iceland? And I was free from my job, for the first time in years, I was out of grimy crowded Manhattan and on an island of endless light. I was on the verge of finding Birdie's child. I was reunited, however briefly, with the long-lost love of my youth. Life seemed expansive, full of possibilities. Looking back, I can see I was ascending into mania. At the time, I simply felt happier than I ever had in my life.

Yes, mania. Or, to be more precise, *hypomania*. A milder form of Birdie's curse. Luckily I suffered no religious delusions, although I did briefly consider the possibility that Birdie's child had been abducted by elves. But my behavior met enough of the remaining criteria to garner the hypomanic diagnosis: a distinct period of abnormally and persistently elevated mood. Decreased need for sleep. More talkative than usual. Flights of ideas, racing thoughts. Increase in goal-directed activity. Spending sprees.

That's what I mean about the whitewash. True, I mentioned the expensive camera. What I forgot to mention is how I spent the rest of the $3,450 in Reykjavik. Much of it went to gifts: I was feeling highly magnanimous. I bought gifts for each of the men on Ulfur's list, to thank them for their time; new tires for Johanna's bicycle; lobsters for dinner on more than one occasion; chocolates and toys for Ulfur's grandchildren; boxes of smoked salmon that I shipped back to New York for Frank and Klaus; a large order of *hangikjot* (smoked lamb) for Stefan; *Freyja Djupur,* licorice dipped in chocolate, for Sigga; a coffee-table book of color photographs of Iceland, for Sigga; a woven blanket, for Sigga.

Nor was I any less generous when it came to myself: a supposedly magical, sterling silver rune-charm necklace; a hand-knitted sweater from Icelandic wool just like Mama used to knit, which cost over a hundred dollars; a state-of-the-art raincoat and hat and pants, so I could cycle in Reykjavik in any kind of torrent; a first edition of Olafur's poetry; a set of advanced Icelandic language instruction tapes that I listened to in the wee hours; expensive skin lotions extracted from the Blue Lagoon; a pair of knee-high black boots with fashionably square toes. I shudder to think what they cost. And other things I'm too embarrassed to mention.

You thought I had no money? I didn't, but I had the manic's best pal, a credit card. Thank God Birdie never got her hands on one of those.

And another symptom: hypergraphia. In the height of my mania I filled a notebook a day. Notebook after notebook, page after scribbled page that I can't bring myself to transcribe. It is said that certain geniuses create their most inspired work during manic episodes. I guess we nongeniuses spew a lot of eagle crap.

The doctors have gifted me with the diagnosis of *cyclothymia.* It's considered a milder form of bipolar disorder, which may or may not progress to the real thing. What caused it, you wonder, to spring out of nowhere? First of all, it didn't. Some cyclothymiacs are primarily depressive. Remember my lost years in the Sub? Hypomania is the flip side, and needs only a trigger. A trigger the Icelandic summer eagerly provides: light.

Light is a *zeitgeber,* German for *time-giver. Zeitgebers* are any environmental signals that are capable of resetting the internal brain clocks that are ticking away in our hypothalamuses. They're how we adapt to life on this spinning planet, some of us better than others. People with affective disorders are especially vulnerable to circadian disruption; it's no accident that Birdie suffered her worst manic episodes under Iceland's midnight sun, or that it was under the same sun that I succumbed to my first.

Some people overdose on drugs, I OD'd on light. Which is not to say I never slept, but even with my windows covered in black plastic I managed only three or four hours each night. I didn't go to bed until one or two, then woke at five each morning to the sun burning an orange hole through the plastic. Strangely, after several days of this I felt not exhausted but energized. It seemed logical to me then: with less darkness, you need less sleep. Indeed, sleep seemed a waste of time. I saw a rainbow at ten p.m., kids kicking soccer balls at eleven, drunken teens spilling from after-hours clubs onto sunlit streets. A child's heaven of perpetual summer twilight. If it's not dark, then it can't be night. And if it's not night, why sleep?

I was gleeful, light-giddy. Can elation really be a symptom? Can enthusiasm be pathological? I have yet to find the line that delineates personality from disease. Whether you call it sickness or not, there is no doubt a change overtook me. I became something other, something faster and freer than myself. And I liked it. Oh how I liked it.

On the road.

On the Ring Road with Saemundur.

Three magnificent mania-fueled days.

This is where it gets indecipherable: my notes, my mind. When I think back to it I get that dream-remembering look on my face, but at the time— at the time!—everything was crystal prism sharp refracting infinitely and precisely and exquisitely.

My brain is an octopus, I wrote. *Extruding tentacles of thought.*

My heart is filled with helium.

I've never felt it again.

I want to, I don't want to. Ever.

Our departure from Reykjavik dragged on like one of those excruciating group photos where you're longing for the shutter to click but so-and-so isn't in the frame or isn't smiling or sneezed or forgot to brush her hair.

Saemundur had driven up early that morning in a slick blue van with DEEP NATURE painted on the side. The van seated twelve, with oversize wheels that raised it off the ground like an old-fashioned coach.

"*En flott,*" I said. How fancy.

"Business loan," Saemundur explained. "Debt on wheels." Saemundur was wearing a cable-knit, cream-colored sweater. Cream against black hair, green eyes. Is he deliberately handsome, I asked myself, or accidentally so?

I climbed inside and found myself perched high off the ground. Like the goddess Freyja, I thought, in her cat-drawn chariot. It was raining, of course, but ever so lightly. Misting. Ethereal. I was ready to soar.

But first we had to wave good-bye to Ulfur, who stood on the step and appraised us skeptically through foggy glasses. Then we had to wait for Johanna to come down with the two girls, and then the girls had to climb inside the van and bounce on the seats and ask if they could come, please please, Uncle Saemundur. Girls got shooed out, bags got loaded, waves and more waves.

"Be careful!" Johanna called out.

Too late for that.

"She thinks you're crazy," Saemundur said. "Riding with me when you could just as easily fly."

He used the word *vitlaus*. The same word he'd used for Birdie, long ago, on the ice cave day. A word that can mean either crazy or stupid. I took out my red-and-blue notebook and wrote: *witless is to witfull.*

I can read that entry because Saemundur hadn't started the engine yet. Mostly I wrote with the vehicle in motion. Manic scrambled car sprawl. Of course it was all clear to me at the time. The only problem as I saw it was that my mind was accelerating and my pen couldn't keep up. *Brain is to hand as millisecond is to eon.* I started writing in a slapdash shorthand, a mix of English and Icelandic, abbreviating words that maybe weren't even words to begin with. I figured I'd explicate it all later. Transcribe it for you-know-who. But as I mentioned, that has become unnecessary. And besides, most of it I can't untangle and what I can may not bear untangling. I remember thinking that embedded in each word I wrote were countless branching thoughts and echoing emotions. *Mind faster pen,* I wrote. *Hand dawdler.* For what it's worth, here are some of the more legible entries:

Birdie's child not only one with mysterious origins   why is your hair
black I ask him it's not very Icelandic of you
   I'm the contrary one   the black sheep
   But where does it come from?
   3,000 Barbary pirates raided the East Fjords in 1627
   So you're the black-haired descendant of a Barbary pirate   is it
true
   About my hair or the pirates?
   Either both
   Teasing grin   What about your hair, Freya?
   What about it
   You cut it short
   So did you   cut yours I mean   it's not the 70s anymore
   But it was so beautiful—
   —it's easier this way

I want him to—

Fluency increasing exponentially   word gobbling   S says I'm
brilliant at Icelandic but I'm talking too much   I know   I can't
stop   look he says look instead   I start taking photos out window
casual roadside waterfalls   sheep   massive clouds   rainbow
more waterfalls   the usual odd splendor   again again again
then he says quit it, quit hiding behind the camera look with your eyes
Freya   I'll hide if I want to   but I put the camera away
superfluous gadget   my brain registers images now   I can file
away   retrieve at will

or against my will   Birdie in her salmon pink coat draped in
dead mink and sealskins bearing reindeer antler aloft to Askja's snowy
caldera   I thought I was going to die out there I tell Saemundur
sucking licorice for dear life   Birdie believing she was the volva and
maybe she was a prophet but me she called a traitor   thoughtful
birthday gift keeps on giving   I'm telling him too much can't stop
myself   tell him everything   dump secrets in Iceland return to

New York hollow new   orphans balk at the future   if my parents weren't dead then what what then   falling in love with a black-haired Icelander

—touch me

S shows me view after breathtaking view   S takes me to Vik dark storm clouds brew offshore   tall pointed rocks like witches' hats rise from roiling surf   sand is black volcanic dust   S takes me to the original Oddi   I tell him Sigga's house in Gimli was called Oddi Saemundur's namesake lived here at Oddi in the old days, Saemundur the Learned   a wizard who attend Black Arts school in Paris who had no shadow   who returned to Iceland on the back of the devil disguised as a seal   S took me on a boat on the glacial lagoon weaving among icebergs floating in pure turquoise water so cold you die nearly instantly upon plunging in   up there is the glacier   underneath it a volcano erupted two years ago   strewed chunks of glacier and a torrential muddy icemelt mess that washed out the bridge and sections of the Ring Road   I drove out here to see it Saemundur said of course you did   Saemundur says he can make me fall in love with Iceland   he has a shadow I know   but at the moment I can't see it   molten glacier indeed

He took my hand on the beach at Vik that roiling coven

He says I remind him of her

Can that be good   she had her good days and her bad days her moods turned on a dime   shifted like lake weather   she said I strode the lakeshore like an egret   she made the sun rise from an ember   she called it a day-star   I called her a star I had no name for

White fox on riverbank swiping duck eggs

Am I getting talky

Mama!

Ratio of dead to living? I fear there are more of them than us

　　　Moss here there and everywhere　　　Cetreria icelandica　　　Icelandic moss according to Saemundur up to 70 percent starch and can be eaten as food in emergency situations　　　Saemundur says　　　Saemundur says this Saemundur says that　　　Simon says　　　Simon didn't say

　　　Night one we sleep at his friend's fishing cabin near the harbor town of Hofn
　　　There's only one bed
　　　and fox-pelt soft kisses
　　　ice cave meltdown

　　　After　　　I don't sleep　　　can't　　　blasted light　　　is this all diversion　　　a Saemundur-shaped tangent　　　from you from finding you you think maybe I've forgotten you　　　maybe I have　　　or are you him and I'm consorting with my cousin? the goddess Freyja it was rumored consorted with her brother, Freyr　　　and what if Ulfur's list is nothing but a dozen red ha-ha-herrings　　　I'd rather spin a cartwheel into the glacial lagoon than return to New York knowing nothing more of you than when I left　　　am I returning to New York　　　maybe I'll just circle Iceland on the Ring Road endlessly round and round and round and round

　　　5 a.m. sun hot in sky

　　　Saemundur silent this morning wondering what he's gotten himself into
　　　Nothing
　　　What?
　　　Nothing

　　　Dare I trust him　　　Son of the Wolf　　　or　　　Birdie's Child or both?

Loki said the goddess Freyja was her brother's lover   am I a
cousin-lover?

Saemundur says he used to dream about me after I left Iceland
I said I tried not to dream after I left Iceland

If this is sex I don't think I've ever had it before   if this is sex I can
see what all the fuss is about   if this is sex why does anybody ever get
out of bed   Saemundur is in the shower we're staying at yet another
summerhouse of yet another friend of his somewhere between the port
of Seydisfjordur and Egilsstadir   we're getting close to the end
we'll reach Thorunn's in a couple of hours he says once we leave here
I don't want to leave here please let's never

It's noon now Saemundur came back to bed and we still haven't left
here   his eyes   his long arms   how he lopes

So you think this Thorunn may know something about Birdie's
child?

I shake my head   maybe yes maybe no   it doesn't matter
Birdie's child led me here   took me by the hand and brought me to
this ice land   this green land   this elf and ghost land this molten
lava land   this moss-encrusted   sun-drenched   avalanche-
prone   ancestor-worshiping   rain-drenched   wind-whipped
earthquake-ripped   island
    thank you Birdie's child

35

Saemundur dropped me off at Thorunn's farm and it began to snow. Thorunn and I stood in the doorway waving at the back of Saemundur's van as it bounced along the dirt track back to the Ring Road, when the first flakes fluttered down on us.

It was the longest day of the year when that blizzard struck. Freakish even for Iceland. Happy solstice! In my mania I failed to recognize a bad omen when it snowed me in the face. Foreshadowing of the most obvious kind. Instead I interpreted it as one more sign of magic, snow falling in late June on the farm and the river and even the distant mountains, what you could see of them. Everything rapidly disappearing in white flurry. I ran from the doorway and began spinning like a two-year-old on a lawn with my tongue extended for flakes, laughing. Thorunn stood in the doorway watching me, smiling.

"It's unusual," she agreed, once we were seated in her living room. "In fact, it's the latest snow I can remember."

But she didn't seem fazed by it. After a lifetime of living in the Icelandic countryside, even the weather must cease to amaze.

I was struck by how much Thorunn reminded me of Sigga, just as she had when I'd run into her in the Gimli bakery. She had Sigga's keen gray-blue eyes and small thin lips. A spare woman who lived in a spare manner, occupying only three rooms of the old farmhouse. The rest was blocked off. "Why heat rooms for people who are dead or gone?"

I could think of no reason. I knew about shutting off one's life to the dead and gone, or trying to.

The living room was small with a low ceiling, crowded with books and family photographs. The first thing Thorunn did after serving me coffee was to take out a family tree and show me how she was the oldest child of Sigga's sister, and how she and Sigga were both related to Pall the farmer-poet and, more distantly and circuitously, to Olafur, *Skald Nyja Islands,* by marriage.

"Now that's settled," she said, "we can begin our visit. I'm so glad you're here, Freya! When I met you in Winnipeg last year, it was only a dream to me that you would come. Birdie came here several times, you know. And now you!" She took my hand and squeezed it. I squeezed back. I felt a tremor of excitement at the mention of Birdie's name. Sigga had told me Thorunn was very fond of Birdie, and I couldn't stop a glimmer of hope from rising up in me: maybe Thorunn knows something. I would have to be careful though. I could see that. No jumping the gun. I willed myself to take it slow. I asked her to tell me about her farm.

It was called Gislastadir, and was situated near the edge of the Lagarfljot River. "Not too near, though!" She laughed. Water rises. At the moment, she explained, the river was only filled with snowmelt, but by the end of the summer it would have glacial melt as well. The old bridge had been washed out several times, but this one, she told me, this one seemed solid. I asked how long she had lived there.

"Fifty-one years," she answered, a bit indignantly. I found out she was the oldest of fifteen children, which is why she had only had one child herself, a boy, grown now and living in Reykjavik. "I had two at the breast at once," she said. "My own baby and my youngest brother. My mother's milk had finally given out, after fifteen children." She took out some photographs. An old black-and-white of a scattering of dusty kids in ragged clothes by the fence of a farm. And then a color portrait of those same kids, all fifteen of them, grown up and standing on the deck of a restaurant in Akureyri. Older, well dressed, looking prosperous.

"Iceland's changed a lot," Thorunn said. "It's easier now, that's certain. Everyone's gone to Reykjavik, abandoned the farms. Like my son, Kjartan. They say there's no making a living here. I say it's just hard. You can manage, but it's hard. Who said life wouldn't be hard? Kjartan wants to move me to Reykjavik, into one of those old-age homes made of concrete. I'd rather die here. Even though I have nothing left."

"You've got this farm."

"It's nothing."

"But I saw sheep, driving in."

"I lease the land. I have to keep something coming in. Arni wouldn't have wanted me to sell it." Arni was her husband, who had died over a decade earlier. We sat in silence for a moment, and I looked around the room. Most of the wall space was taken by bookshelves. On top of the bookshelves were photographs of Thorunn and Arni, of their son, Kjartan, and his wife, and other relatives whose names I didn't know and didn't want to know. Over the mantel two more photographs, both of which I recognized: Pall the farmer-poet and Olafur, *Skald Nyja Islands*. It was the one of Olafur smoking his pipe that had been displayed on my own mantel back in Connecticut. Out the window the snow continued its silent descent, a thin layering of white through which blades of green grass poked through.

"Enough of that depressing subject!" Thorunn went into the kitchen and came back with a plate of *ponnukokur*. "Now it's your turn to do the talking."

That was not a problem. I told her about my drive east with Saemundur. I went on about the rocks at Vik like witches' caps poking up from the surf, sand that was black instead of yellow, floating among the icebergs, visiting Oddi and how our house in Gimli was called Oddi, Sigga had named it that. And Saemundur this and Saemundur that. I could hear how fast I was talking but there was nothing I could do to stop it. I forced myself to take a sip of coffee and a bite of *ponnukokur*. It was delicious, stuffed with berries and cream. In that moment Thorunn managed to get a word in edgewise. "You remind me of your mother," she said. She was smiling again.

I thought that was strange, for the briefest second. "You met my mother?" I asked. But I never gave her a chance to answer. "My mother never came to Iceland, you know. She was afraid to fly. Birdie always made fun of her for that. They didn't get along, Birdie and my mother." And I was off on a new subject. I told Thorunn about how my mother never brought me to Gimli until I was seven years old, how Birdie never forgave her for that, how Birdie and my mother were always quarreling over whether I should learn Icelandic or not, but I was certainly glad Birdie had taught me, even though as a child I'd struggled mightily with *malfraedi,* the wicked grammar, but I wouldn't be here talking to Thorunn now in Icelandic if Birdie hadn't—

Suddenly I stopped, aware that Thorunn was staring at me, a shocked look on her lean face. A couple of times she started to speak, then clamped her thin lips tight again. "Your mother?" she asked, finally.

"Yes, my mother. And Birdie. They fought terribly."

Thorunn continued staring at me. I began to feel miffed. Hadn't she ever heard of siblings who didn't get along? Surely she wasn't on perfect terms with every single one of her fourteen brothers and sisters?

"Your mother," she said again. "Birdie. Tell me about this."

I started talking about the rivalry between my mother and my aunt, how my mother was practical and steady and plain, Birdie wild and charming and beautiful. Thorunn studied me while I was talking.

"She was beautiful, yes," Thorunn said. Her voice trembled. "Such a tragedy, what happened to your . . . Birdie."

Then she stood up and left the room. I drank my coffee in silence while I waited for her to come back, though coffee was the last thing I needed. My mind was racing again. Oh, I would have to be careful, careful indeed. The mere mention of Birdie seemed to have shaken Thorunn. Out the window I saw that the snow was now covering the grass completely, and the sky itself was no longer visible. I vowed to myself not to mention Birdie again, at least not on this first day of my visit. As it turned out, I didn't need to.

Thorunn returned with a shoe box, which she placed on the couch between us. On the lid of the box was written "Ingibjorg (Birdie)." Inside were photographs from Birdie's various visits. "She always stayed with us, when she came to Iceland. No matter how busy she was. Like when she came for Olafur's centennial, and they were busy driving her around the country to speak about her father. Still she insisted that they stop here at Gislastadir." She handed me a photo that showed Birdie, Thorunn, Arni, and a dark-haired man who looked very familiar, all standing in front of the Gislastadir farmhouse.

"Is that Ulfur Johansson?" I asked.

"Oh yes, that's Ulfur. He drove Birdie all over Iceland that summer. He's very important, you know. He was head of the Arni Magnusson Institute. He got our manuscripts back from Denmark. Our Sagas!"

"I know Ulfur," I pointed out. "I've been staying with him in Reykjavik."

She looked embarrassed. "Yes, yes, of course. I'm sure you know him much better than I do. I only met him the one time."

I studied the photograph. Birdie stood with her head close to Ulfur's, her blond hair bright against his dark. I still hadn't ruled Ulfur out, and now my suspicions were raised again.

"And here's Birdie at Brekka," Thorunn continued, "the farm where Olafur, *Skald Nyja Islands,* was born. Birdie always stopped at Brekka, whenever she came to the East. It's just down the river from here, you know. I can take you there tomorrow." She glanced out the window. "If the weather permits."

"I've seen Brekka," I said. "Birdie took me there, when she . . . brought me to Iceland."

"That was a terrible mix-up now, wasn't it? I remember being so surprised, when it came out in the papers that you two were missing, and neither Birdie nor Sigga had even told me you were coming, and then the two of you were found at Askja. . . . Birdie never even called me! But I went to see her anyway. At the hospital in Akureyri. I saw you there too. I stayed with my cousin in Akureyri, so for two weeks I could visit Birdie at the hospital every day, until they flew her back to Winnipeg. I never saw her again."

"What was Birdie like, at the hospital?"

"Pretty terrible. Depressed. She didn't speak. They had her drugged, I suppose. I wasn't surprised, I admit, to hear that she . . . killed herself. Not after I'd seen her like that. But so terrible for you, to have your . . . your Birdie . . ."

"It was terrible all right. She killed herself on my fourteenth birthday. She died hating me."

"Hating you? Oh no, certainly not that. Birdie loved you. She loved you with all her heart."

"How would you know, Thorunn? Did she send you a suicide note? Because she certainly never left one for us. She used her suicide as revenge on me, on everyone she believed betrayed her."

I could hear my voice, the sarcasm, the rage rising up, but I couldn't stop it. I was tired of people feeling sorry for Birdie. As if she were the sole vic-tim of her illness.

"And did you know," I continued, "that Birdie had a child? That the child was taken away from her at birth? And that no one seems to know who or where this child is, or even believes that it exists? I came all the way to Iceland to find Birdie's child, who is now an adult, because I owe that much to Birdie." My voice was loud and excited. I was thinking of all the pages I'd written for Birdie's child, pages that I'd have to burn, because there was no one to read them.

I'd gone too far. Thorunn's thin lower lip was trembling and she brushed her eyes with the heels of her hands. Then she composed herself, speaking in a warm cheery voice again, a voice I no longer trusted. "I'm sorry, dear. Surely this is not something we should be discussing! Not when I am sit-ting here having coffee with the very granddaughter of Olafur, *Skald Nyja Islands*! Tell me about your life, Freya dear."

Suddenly I was tired of talking. I was tired, period. "I want to lie down."

Thorunn set me up in her son Kjartan's old bedroom. I lay on my side on the narrow bed, staring out at the gray sky, the snowflakes spinning down. For once it wasn't bright outside when it should have been dark—it was simply winter when it should have been summer. I fell asleep at five in the afternoon and didn't wake up until the following morning.

At some point while I was sleeping Thorunn came in and laid a quilt over me. Then she did something strange. She kissed me on the forehead.

"*Goda nott,*" she whispered. "*Goda nott, elskan.*"

I think now that when Thorunn kissed me good night she had already decided what she was going to do.

The first thing I saw on opening my eyes the next morning was the white world outside. White sky, white fields, and even the river only the palest gray. It had stopped snowing. I opened the window. It was still and not terribly cold. Muted. I splashed my face with icy water, then climbed down the nar-row wooden staircase. In the kitchen the table was perfectly set, with brown bread, cereal, hard-boiled eggs, smoked salmon, *skyr,* and coffee.

"A feast!" I smiled at Thorunn.

"You slept through last night's dinner," she said. "You must be hungry."

And I was. I hardly noticed how silent Thorunn was through our breakfast, but looking back, I can see it. Looking back, I can see a lot of things.
I've grown so tired of looking back! (At the moment it makes me so exhausted I hardly want to continue. But I promised not to skip the ending,
and I won't. I wouldn't trick you like that.)

After breakfast Thorunn led me back to the little parlor with the low
ceiling. We sat side by side on the couch again. The shoe box marked "Ingibjorg (Birdie)" was still sitting on the coffee table. Suddenly I had the urge
to get up, go outside and see the snow. Anything but sit in the cramped little parlor looking at photographs of dead people.

"Maybe we can go for a drive today?" I suggested. "The snow doesn't
seem too deep."

"Oh that'll be fine," Thorunn said. "I'll take you visiting. There are many
people who want to meet you, you know. But not yet. First I want to show
you something." She picked up a piece of paper from the coffee table and
unfolded it. I could see that it was one of the old-fashioned genealogical
charts, like the one she'd brought to Sigga last autumn in Gimli. The kind
where one person's name is in a circle in the middle, and all the ancestors
ripple out in concentric circles back through time.

Except I could see that this was only half a chart. The top half of the
page was filled with names and dates, the bottom half completely empty.
There were circles drawn, but the contents were blank.

"I stayed up late last night," Thorunn said. "Working on this for you."

Then she handed me the chart, and I saw that the name in the center
circle was my own, and underneath it was the date of my birth. And in the
next band, the one that encircled the top half of me, was Birdie's name, and
the date of her birth and her death. On the bottom half, where my father
should have been, there was nothing.

"This is wrong," I said. The page was trembling in my fingers. "Birdie
was not my mother."

Thorunn took my hand, but I jerked it back.

"My mother was my mother," I said. "I have a photograph of her, right after she gave birth to me. Holding me. And Sigga's standing right there! Sigga
came to Connecticut to help my mother take care of me." But what did any
of that prove? How had Mama always described my arrival? *Out of God's*

clear blue heaven she said I came. Not once had she ever said I'd come from her own womb.

"Birdie was not my mother!" I repeated.

Thorunn was silent. Finally she said, "I thought someone would have told you by now." She spoke quietly. "I never understood why they kept it a secret. So harmful. That's what I said to Sigga's friend Halldora, at Sigga's birthday party in Gimli. Halldora pretended not to know, but she knows. And now you do, too. You are Birdie's child, Freya."

Then she opened the shoe box and handed me Birdie's letter. No, it wasn't a suicide note. But it was desperate all the same. She'd written it to Thorunn shortly after giving birth to me. Not in 1962, as Halldora had claimed, but in February 1965.

Reading Birdie's letter made me feel sick, like a waterfall plunging inside out. "I'm going for a walk," I heard myself say. I remember Thorunn rushing to the door behind me.

"Don't try to stop me," I warned.

She didn't. She held a coat in her hand, a big coat. Not her own. A yellow down jacket, so old the feathers poked through in places. It must have belonged to her husband, Arni, or her son, Kjartan. I remember thinking that.

And then I walked out into the snow. It was deeper than it had looked from inside, just below my knees, higher where it had drifted. I was wearing sneakers. Snow packed into my socks as I lifted each foot up through the dense powder and put it down again. I walked like this along Thorunn's driveway covered in snow and across the road covered in snow. I was heading to the river, the only thing not covered in snow, but it was white all the same. Still as glass and reflecting the white sky. I kept slipping on rocks that I couldn't see because they were covered in snow. That was fine with me. It's what I wanted for myself—to be covered in snow. Because I *was* snow. I was mute and I was numb, and I stayed that way for days, weeks, long after the farmer Thorunn sent to find me pulled me up out of the snowbank on the edge of the Lagarfljot River. I remember struggling against him. Not because I wanted to die out there, nothing as clear or simple as that. I only wanted to curl up in a comma and be snow.

36

Most histories of Iceland subscribe to what I call the birth-death-rebirth theory. It's how I learned it from Birdie, and it goes like this:

After Iceland was first settled in the ninth century came its millennial golden age, an explosion of literary, parliamentary, and religious activity, the high point of Icelandic civilization. Then descended its dark ages, civil strife in the twelfth century that lead to six hundred years of domination by foreign rulers, a long period of general decay punctuated by virulent plagues, unrelenting frosts, and volcanic eruptions. At times Iceland teetered on the verge of extinction. Then finally came the great nineteenth century national awakening and cultural renaissance that culminated with Iceland proclaiming its independence in 1944, emerging at long last yet with great vigor into the modern world.

There you have it in a nutshell: origination, degeneration, regeneration.

Enter the revisionists, a new generation of Icelandic historiographers who are chipping away at the veracity of Iceland's trusty national narrative. The golden age was not so golden, they argue, the dark ages not so dark, the foreign rulers not so nasty, the claims of near extinction most probably exaggerated. Some revisionists even go so far as to suggest that the whole paradigm was merely a propaganda ploy, clever packaging by nineteenth-century nationalists attempting to awaken the Icelandic people from their centuries-long torpor with a rousing call to national pride: We were a great people once, we can achieve greatness once again!

I'm not buying it. I've got nothing against revisionism per se. New facts come to light and require consideration, accommodation even. As you can imagine, I've had to engage in quite of bit of revisionism myself, since that day when I flung myself into the void of a freak June blizzard.

And I do see their point—it's all a bit too neat. Yet I find myself oddly loath to discard the handy birth-death-rebirth framework. True, it's ridiculously ubiquitous. Take the poem *Voluspa*, for example, the *volva*'s prophecy. It begins with the miraculous creation of the world in a fusion of fire and ice, followed by a golden age of the gods, who built the glorious Gimli, where they played chess and fashioned treasures from gold. Upon this sunny scene soon rumbled the battle of the gods, the doom of the earth, stars falling from the skies, and the sun turning black. And yet, when all hope seems lost, the *volva* sees the earth rising a second time, fair and green. . . . Christianity, of course, also has plenty to say on the subject of resurrection. And Buddhism: We're born, we live, we die, we live again.

Bud bloom rot germinate.

Once you start looking, the archetype pops up everywhere: it's the cycle that spins history, love, narrative, life itself. Take my own story: the golden age of my Gimli summers, followed by the dark ages of my darkroom years, and now? Now I'm in some sort of rebirth born of dissolution. Or so I would like to believe. Living in Iceland is a way to start over, begin at the beginning again. And what better place than one of the newest landmasses on the planet? When I walk on a lava field, I'm stepping on brand-new earth, the planet is being born beneath my feet. It does great service to my self-mythologizing.

When did I start knowing so much about meta-theories of Icelandic history? When I went back to school. I'm enrolled at the University of Iceland, majoring in Icelandic literature with a minor in history.

I've lived in Iceland three years now; I'm due to graduate this spring. Both my mothers would be very proud.

The Icelanders have an expression, *hvalreki*, which is equivalent to *windfall*. An unexpected gift of good fortune. It means whale wreck, or stranding of whales. In the old days, if a whale washed up on the beach, it was considered nearly unbelievable good luck. Whale blubber to light lanterns with, meat for food, bones for carving utensils and toys . . .

Sometimes I think of Saemundur as my *hvalreki*. Other times not. What did his ex-wife say? That he was selfish, erratic, and arrogant? I second that. We live together in a small flat in downtown Reykjavik. It hasn't been easy with Saemundur, and whether we'll be together forever, who can say? I doubt we'll marry. Marriage has lost its popularity in Iceland. Other than that, I've promised to say little. There are limits to what I can reveal about Saemundur in this book, limits he himself prescribed, and I don't blame him. He's no fictional character. You can look him up in the Reykjavik phone book under S: Saemundur Ulfursson, *leidsogumadur*. Road-story-man. Sign up for one of his tours, if it pleases you.

And it is Saemundur you can thank for this book, if you wish to thank anyone at all. After I'd recovered from my collapse and moved in with him, I took all these pages—the ones I'd typed in New York on Birdie's old Underwood, plus the red-and-blue notebooks—and stuffed them in a box at the back of a closet. I could never bring myself to read over them again, but neither did I burn them. I was determined not to go down Birdie's path of self-destruction.

One day about a year ago Saemundur was cleaning out the closet, came across the box, and discovered inside a jumble of typewritten pages and notebooks. When he asked if he could read them, I said yes. I keep no more secrets.

When Saemundur was done reading he asked, "What are you going to do with this book?"

I know what you're thinking, that on some level I must have known all along. Maybe so. Yet I tell you it was the biggest shock of my life, worse than Birdie's suicide or even my mother's death. It unraveled me. For a time I believed I was dead. When you can't talk or sleep or eat you might as well be. I stayed at Thorunn's for several days after her farmer friend plucked me from the snowbank, until she telephoned Ulfur, who arranged for Saemundur to pick me up and drive me back to Ulfur's house in Reykjavik. It was a time of nothingness. Nothingness felt good to me, compared with knowledge.

Ulfur wasted no time in getting me to a psychiatrist. It was bad enough, in his view, to have the suicide of the daughter of Olafur, *Skald Nyja Islands,* on his conscience. He would not allow a granddaughter to be added to the list. My depression was so severe there was even talk of admitting me to a hospital. Luckily for me, Dr. Bjornsdottir was a keen diagnostician.

It was obvious that I was depressed, curled into a comma, but through interviews with Saemundur and Ulfur, she pieced together my family history of bipolar disorder and my own recent bout of mania, or hypomania, as she eventually determined. It was Dr. Bjornsdottir who gave me the diagnosis of cyclothymia. I call it manic depression lite.

I asked Saemundur once what I'd been like on the Ring Road trip.

"Like yourself," he replied. "But multiplied. Excessively."

Self-multiplied inventor of spin.

In addition to checking up on me every few months to assess my progress and fine-tune my medications, Dr. Bjornsdottir makes me sit in front of a light box every morning during the winter months, and gives strict orders to regulate my intake of sunlight in the summer evenings. Light, she reminds me, is my *zeitgeber,* the force that in my case most easily meddles with the brain clock that regulates mood. At all costs, *prevent circadian rhythm disruption.*

And I do, I have. I'm terrified of ending up like Birdie. A sadglad bird, a madmad bird. I fear ending up like my mother. Will it confuse you if I start calling Birdie my mother? It confuses me, still. It took me a while to sort everything out. Call me gullible, but I'd actually spent my whole life believing I'd emerged from Mama's womb.

The Tricking of Freya.

After my nothingness period—after the medications began kicking in—I started feeling and thinking again. It wasn't pretty. I wandered the streets of Reykjavik in perpetual rage. Everything began making sense. Why Mama didn't take me to Gimli the first seven years of my life. Why Birdie took such an obsessive interest in me. Even why she kidnapped me, why she killed herself on my birthday. For a time, I hated them all—Birdie, Sigga, Mama. Birdie, always complaining about being conspired against, while it was I who was truly the victim of conspiracy, a conspiracy that stole my very identity, then covered it up with lies. Mama, sweet Mama! Who would have thought her capable of such deceit! Sigga, of course, had not traveled to Connecticut to help with my birth—I had already been born, back in the Selkirk Asylum—but rather to hand me over to my new mother. Sigga the peacekeeper, vainly attempting to placate the two sisters, pretending their rift was nothing more than sibling rivalry. Birdie, somehow, I blamed the least. I'd spent years blaming Birdie. I was done blaming Birdie.

Halldora, of course, had lied to me outright, claiming Birdie's child was born in 1962, not 1965, feigning ignorance over the child's gender, all so I wouldn't suspect the truth. How Halldora insisted the infant had been *given away to a good home.* (That last part was true. Mama was my good home, and even at my lowest point I never regretted that she raised me.) Was Halldora protecting me from a truth she thought I might find too awful to bear? I don't think that for a moment. It was Sigga she was protecting; Sigga was all Halldora had left in this world.

And what about Stefan? I still suspected he knew more than he was saying, and I confronted him the first chance I got. By early August I was well enough to leave Iceland. I had nowhere to return to in New York; Gimli seemed my inevitable destination. I arrived in time for the annual *Islendingadagurinn* festival. All the hotel rooms were booked and Sigga's house had been sold by then—I had no choice but to stay with Stefan. He picked me up at the airport, and I badgered him the entire drive from Winnipeg to Gimli, barely noticing the scrubby landscape unfolding out the window, the appearance of the long flat lake of my childhood.

"I was right," I began. "Birdie did have a child."

"Yes."

"It was me, Stefan."

"I know that now."

Of course he knew, I'd written him a letter. But I wanted it said out loud. It was not as satisfying as I'd hoped.

"You knew," I continued. "You knew from the very beginning!"

"I didn't, Freya, I swear to you. It seems unlikely, I know, impossible even, but I honestly had no idea. Your family kept its secrets well."

"I guess they all had strong motivations. Birdie was terrified that if she let the secret slip, she'd never be allowed to see me again. And of course my mother feared nothing worse than being exposed, afraid she would lose me to Birdie if I found out the truth."

I thought about Mama, all those years keeping her big secret from me, while I was keeping my big secret from her. I never had a chance to tell her, before she died so suddenly, that it was I who'd caused her fall, her coma, and all the miseries that followed.

"I'm sorry, Freya. I'm sorry for all of it."

"Sorry is the story of my whole sorry life, isn't it?"

Stefan had nothing to say to that. It was dark when we pulled into Gimli, and I was grateful. I was still adjusting to seeing things in their true light.

I couldn't bring myself to attend the *Islendingadagurinn* festivities—the parade, the crowning of the *Fjallkona,* the silly contests and games and dances—but I did manage to make an appearance at the opening of the New Iceland Heritage Museum. Sigga had been scheduled to speak during a ceremony honoring her donation of items from Olafur's study to the museum. But she was feeling too frail, or so she said, and insisted I take her place. I think she was just preparing me for my new role as spokesperson of the poet's estate, the only living family member of Olafur, *Skald Nyja Islands*. Since then, I've spoken several times at various literary events in Iceland, but that evening was my first venture into public speaking, and to say I was nervous would be an understatement. Sigga and Stefan assured me I'd done a wonderful job.

And I'm sure both my mothers were very proud.

Sigga was still my grandmother at least, and she seemed for the most part cognizant of that fact. I never told her that I had learned about the Tricking of Freya. I was afraid it would trigger some sort of mental decline from which she might never emerge.

One huge piece still remained unsolved. Whose name belonged in the other half circle of the genealogy chart Thorunn had prepared for me? Who was my father? I'd run into nothing but dead ends in Iceland, and certainly didn't expect to find the answer in Gimli. Yet that is exactly where I learned the truth. It happened when I showed Stefan the letter Birdie had written to Thorunn, after they had taken the newborn-me away from her. There were parts of it I'd never been able to understand, no matter how many times I reread it. Either Birdie's handwriting was too erratic or my Icelandic too poor, or both. Stefan was the only one I could possibly consider showing it to. I gave it to him one night after dinner, and the next morning a neatly typed translation was sitting on the kitchen table. It was dated February 20, 1965, two days after my birthday.

My Dearest Thorunn,

Brace yourself for some terrible news. I've been locked up in the Selkirk Asylum ever since I returned from Iceland last summer. I haven't written you because what was the point? They are censoring my mail, I'm certain of that.

They say I'm mad, Thorunn. And I suppose I am.

A terrible thing has been done to me. They're all saying it's for the best, the doctors and nurses, my mother and my sister.

I've given birth to a little girl. And now they've taken her away from me and given her to Anna, to keep and raise forever! I'm supposed to pretend she isn't mine. This is the arrangement they've devised: I'll be pushed aside like some dotty spinsterish aunt, and dull Anna and her dull accountant husband will raise my daughter in their dull American suburb! Anna will bring her to Gimli every summer from Connecticut. On one condition: I'm never to reveal my identity to the child.

To be fair, they gave me two so-called choices: to give my child up to strangers in what is called a Blind Adoption. I would never see her again and she would never be able to learn who I am. Or, I can give her to Anna to raise. Under the condition that she never knows who her real mother is!

And they say I'm the crazy one.

All of this they've decided without even offering me a chance to prove myself as a mother. Unfit!

Poor Anna, they say. She's always wanted a child. Can't you give her this?

And they call this a choice!!!

But I have promised to abide by this arrangement. Because I know what will happen if I don't: Anna will simply stop bringing the child to Gimli. She'll keep me away from her. Besides, even if I tell the little girl, they'll all deny it. Say it's some crazy idea of crazy Birdie's, and who would believe me against upstanding Sigga and respectable Anna the American?

My closest relatives have plotted against me.

She is gone, Thorunn, gone.

She arrived a whole month early. But isn't that like me, always the speedy one, always ahead of the game?

Think of it as the greatest gift one sister can give to another. That's what one of the nurses here actually said to me. A terrible woman named Halldora Bjarnason, a skinny little bitch, but not to be underestimated. She's in thick with Sigga on this, in fact I believe she came up with the idea. Sigga would never have thought of such a thing herself! It's not the way our people do things, is it, Thorunn? You know that. You told me three of your siblings were given away to families in the district who couldn't have children of their own, but they always knew who their parents were, who their brothers and sisters and grandparents were! There was no secrecy involved, no government cover-up.

They say she'll be better off without me, that I'm unfit to raise a child. They've gotten the court to declare this! My mother my sister my doctors and the Canadian government are all in collusion against me.

Skaldagemlur! My baby was born with a tooth cutting through her gums, Thorunn. Like Olafur. I checked before they took her away from me. She'll be a writer I'm certain, if Anna doesn't stifle the living life out of her.

Even my breasts are weeping.

They want to keep me here still, at Selkirk Asylum. They say we must guard against postpartum depression. But it is not giving birth to a beautiful infant that is depressing, no! It is having your child kidnapped by your closest relatives in collusion with agents of the government! How could such an act not crush one's very soul???

At least they let me name her. Anna would have named her Cathy or some other bland American name.

I named her Freya.

I was finishing my third cup of coffee and my tenth reading of the letter when Stefan came into the dining room. He'd been out tending his rose-bushes, before the heat of the day came on full force. I remember the light sweat on his brow, the streak of dirt left on his forehead when he wiped it off with his gardening glove. The way he slouched slightly in the doorway, impossibly tall and yet never imposing. A square, Birdie had called him once. Herself deemed a trapezoid. And me, a little ovoid, ready to hatch.

"You were born prematurely," he said.

I nodded. One more fragment of truth floating up for air.

"If you count back—" He stopped, then tried again. "I've done the calculations. February minus eight equals . . . June."

None of this was making sense to me, despite my three cups of coffee. Eloquent Stefan, suddenly stammering about February minus June? I sat and waited. He came to the table and sat across from me. When he poured himself a cup of coffee, I noticed his hand was shaking. Trembling. Even though it was cool in the house, a new trickle of sweat was accumulating on his forehead, dripping down his brow in a muddy smear.

"Freya, what I'm saying is . . . I don't think the father of Birdie's child was someone she, someone she . . . knew . . . in Iceland. The timing isn't right. She was there in April and May of 1964. But the child, I mean you, you were born in February, so you must have been conceived in June. After she returned to Gimli."

So I'd been wrong about that too. Searching in Iceland for a lover of Birdie's who never existed, or at least was not the father of her child. Of me. Leave it to logical Stefan to do the math.

"Do you know," I ventured, "if she was seeing someone then? When she got back from Iceland?" I remembered my mother referring to various boyfriends of Birdie's, but never by name. Fly-by-nights, she called them. No-goods. Or married men. No one suitable.

There was a long silence. At first I thought Stefan was thinking, trying to remember back thirty years, distinguish one shadowy paramour from another, lining the dates up in his mind. But looking back, I understand that he was simply trying to summon his courage.

37

So, yes, technically speaking, Stefan is my father. You say you figured that out too? I don't believe you. Stefan himself didn't know, he insists on that, and I believe him. I count myself lucky, that I was conceived during Stefan's sole one-night stand with Birdie, when she returned from Iceland manic and charming and filled with love for everything on the planet, even Stefan the square. I'm grateful my father is not some shadowy tryst I could spend years trying to track down, only to be disappointed.

I don't call Stefan "Dad," but he's the closest I've ever come to having a father. Our bond continues to deepen. The last time I saw him was for Sigga's funeral in Gimli last winter. (Sigga went quietly, excusing herself from Christmas dinner at Stefan's house to lie down in the guest room and expire. Just like the Saga heroine she admired so much, Aud-the-Deep-Minded, who slipped away from a family feast to die in regal solitude.) We write frequently, Stefan and I—he's a technophobe and eschews e-mail—and he plans to visit us in Iceland soon.

I've also engaged Stefan to help me with a special project I've embarked on: translating Olafur's letters. Yes, Olafur's letters turned up. It seems they were here all along, in the basement archives at Ulfur's house on the lake, misfiled. Ulfur was horrified at first, then embarrassed, then thrilled. Then he handed them over to me. Birdie would have been disappointed by that. There was no cloak and dagger, no plots, no legal battles over the letters.

My Icelandic isn't quite up to the task, but there are plenty of people to turn to for help. Ulfur, of course. He'll do anything to help the letters see the light of day. And his daughter, Johanna, Saemundur's sister the linguist. And of course Stefan back in Gimli. He helps with background research on the New Iceland colony, names and places mentioned in Olafur's letters.

No, Birdie's lost *Word Meadow* never resurfaced. But Birdie said I had an ear, a tongue. I was born with a tooth cutting through my gum. Maybe I'll write my own *Word Meadow* someday.

Some things I may never get used to. They leave babies out in the snow here. Oh, they're bundled up, of course, in carriages with stiff awnings, but still it is not uncommon when there's a light snowfall to see carriages put on porches for the babies' afternoon naps. To accustom them to the weather, it was explained to me. It makes them *hress,* vigorous and strong.

Care for some *hakarl*? Take a hunk of raw shark meat and bury it in the sand until it putrefies. Make sure a man urinates on it every few days. After several months, dig up, rinse, and serve. That's how they made it in the old days. Of modern *hakarl*-making methods I know nothing, but the *hakarl* I've tried tastes rubbery and smells of rot. Other traditional Icelandic delicacies include singed sheep head—complete with eyes—and pickled ram's testicles. More common are tasty lamb, fresh cod, and endless variations of soured milk products. Plus the odd supermarket vegetables, impossibly long skinny cucumbers sealed in plastic, heads of lettuce sold in the tiny pots they were grown in, roots trailing obscenely. Hothouse produce, an Icelandic specialty. Food can't be grown on this island, not outdoors anyway. These ingenious Icelanders, with their geothermally heated hothouses. I hear they're working on hydrogen-powered cars next.

Icelanders love gadgets. Televisions and computers and cell phones and every other techno-toy that appears on the market. They have expensive tastes. The simple peasant life of my grandfather is for the most part long vanished. Iceland has one of the highest standards of living in the world, and they're in debt up to their ears to pay for it. Still, can you blame them? After six hundred years of mostly abject poverty, middle-class materialism has a singular appeal.

Lutheranism is the state religion of Iceland, yet somehow it doesn't feel all-pervasive. There are even groups of neo-pagans, modern worshipers of Odin and Freyja. Me, I put my faith in words.

The wind never stops.

I suppose I'll always be something of an outsider here. Icelanders are a welcoming yet insular lot. They don't consider me an Icelander, and I don't consider myself one. The older people call me a *Vestur-Islendingur,* Western Icelander, the name given to those who went west to Canada and America. I think of myself as an American, as much as Birdie hated that. Yet I probably fit here better than anywhere.

Do I miss my old life? It was hardly a life, hardly fit to miss.

A couple of months ago I began having earthquake dreams. Icelanders are disposed to believing in prophetic dreams, and I managed to alarm a number of friends with my visions of planets cracking open. What I saw, again and again, was the image of a nearly round object. Fine lines would appear, fracturing its surface; soon the entire sphere would shatter into pieces. I woke in terror. One morning I realized I was dreaming not of planets cracking open but of an egg hatching.

Saemundur wants us to have a child.

Am I fit? Probably not. My illness could worsen. I could erupt into a full-blown Birdie one of these days. Worse yet, our child could bear these same mood-sick genes.

Or she could be born with teeth cutting through her gums. Or both.

In *Havamal,* that slender tome of Viking wisdom, it says, *A man's fate should be firmly hidden to preserve his peace of mind.* My ancestors believed we emerge into this world with a peculiar fate tucked inside like a seed that unfurls itself over the course of our lives. Our deaths are with us from birth. What matters is not our fate but what we make of it. These days, many believe our fate is sealed by our genes, passed down through the generations in endlessly recombining combinations of DNA. Genes unfurling like seeds throughout our lives, diseases blooming in our veins, dooming us sure as any fate bestowed by God or gods.

Leave it to an entrepreneurial Icelander to capitalize on Iceland's obsession with genealogy—he's starting a company that will catalog and then rent out to the world's scientists Iceland's uniquely chronicled gene pool.

The nation is debating the project hotly at the moment, the potential for abuse—ah, the conspiracy theories Birdie would have fabricated!—the potential for discovering the sources of multitudes of diseases. Even identifying the gene for bipolar disorder.

But none of this helps me now. Saemundur could leave me if I won't have a child. Or I could leave him. Fly back to New York. Don't ask me. I'm no *volva*, I've got no gift of prophecy.

I live surrounded by my people, the living and the dead.

I still miss them both, every day, my two mothers. The gentle one with her spruce green eyes, the wild one with her moods shifting like lake weather.

And even though you aren't you anymore, not the you I was hoping to find, I wish you nothing but the best. Do you remember how to say goodbye in Icelandic?

Bless bless.

Acknowledgments

I must first thank my mother, Edith Bjornson, for so generously sharing her memories, books, family papers, and many, many hours of conversation.

I am very grateful to my steadfast supporters and early readers of the manuscript: Madeline Sunley, Elizabeth Pollet, Atsuro Riley, Amy Blackstone, Marjory Nelson, Susan Fleming, Vanessa Barrington, Vicky Funari, and Charles Baldwin. Special thanks to Paula Harris and Celia Sack for loaning me a place to write.

In Canada I wish to thank Nelson Gerrard, the local historian and genealogist whose remarkable book *Icelandic River Saga* put me under the spell of my ancestors. A huge debt is owed to both Nelson and Sigrid Johnson, Head of the Icelandic Collection at the University of Manitoba, for their careful reading and correcting of the manuscript; any remaining errors are my own. Thanks also to Tommi Finnbogason and Stefan Jonsson.

In Iceland I would like to thank Anna Þóra Árnadóttir, Sveinn Þorgrímsson, Finnbogi Guðmundsson, Ingibjörg Þorsteinsdóttir, Ágústa Árnadóttir, Gunnar Kjartansson, Jóhanna Stefánsdóttir, Óttar Kjartansson, Hrefna Róbertsdóttir, Eiríkur Kolbeinn Björnsson, Halldóra Hreggviðsdóttir, Árni Geirsson, Margrét Lóa Jónsdóttir, Stefania Hrafnkelsdóttir, Böðvar Kvaran and his wife, Lilla, and the Institute of Gunnar Gunnarsson and its director, Skúli Björn Gunnarsson.

I am deeply grateful to my agent, Katherine Cowles, for making it happen, and my editor, George Witte, for his insightful guidance. I would also like to thank my copy editor, Susan M.S. Brown, and the staff of St. Martin's Press.

And especially Oliver Kay, for everything.